HALA ALYAN

Salt Houses

HUTCHINSON
LONDON

1 3 5 7 9 10 8 6 4 2

Hutchinson
20 Vauxhall Bridge Road
London SW1V 2SA

Hutchinson is part of the Penguin Random House group of companies whose addresses can be found at global.penguinrandomhouse.com.

Penguin Random House UK

First published in the USA by Houghton Mifflin Harcourt in 2017
First published in the United Kingdom by Hutchinson in 2017

www.penguin.co.uk

A CIP catalogue record for this book is available from the British Library.

ISBN 9781786330413 (hardback)
ISBN 9781786330420 (trade paperback)

Printed and bound in Great Britain by Clays Ltd, St Ives plc

Penguin Random House is committed to a sustainable future for our business, our readers and our planet. This book is made from Forest Stewardship Council® certified paper.

FSC www.fsc.org MIX Paper from responsible sources FSC® C018179

For my family,

who gave me stories to tell

The Yacoub Family

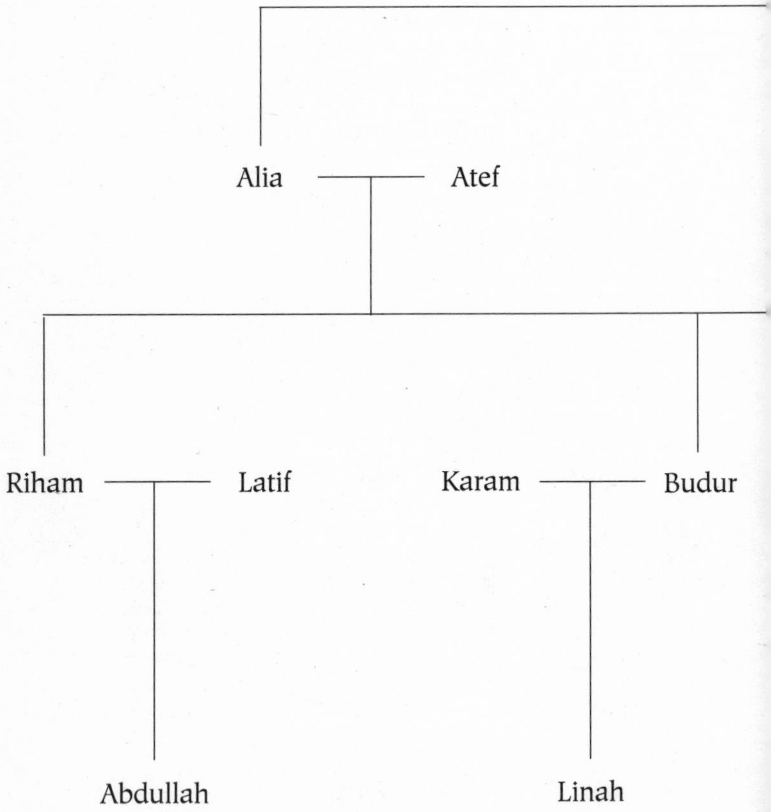

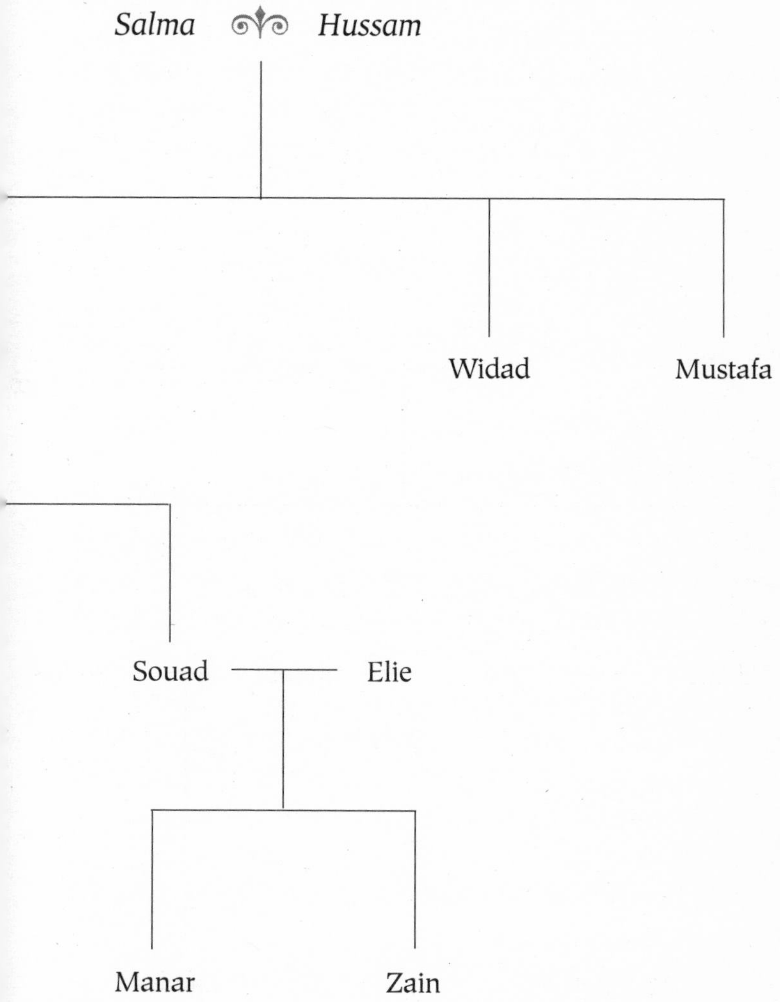
Salma
Hussam
Widad
Mustafa
Souad
Elie
Manar
Zain

SALMA

Nablus
March 1963

When Salma peers into her daughter's coffee cup, she knows instantly she must lie. Alia has left a smudge of coral lipstick on the rim. The cup is ivory, intricate spirals and whorls painted on the exterior in blue, a thin crack snaking down one side. The cup belongs to a newer set, bought here in Nablus when Salma and her husband, Hussam, arrived nearly fifteen years ago. It was the first thing she'd bought, walking through the marketplace in an unfamiliar city.

In a stall draped with camelhair coats and rugs, Salma spotted the coffee set, twelve cups stacked next to an *ibrik* with a slender spout. They rested upon a silver tray. It was the tray that gave Salma pause, the triangular pattern so similar to the one her own mother gave her when she first wed. But it was gone, the old tray and coffee set, along with so many of their belongings, the dresses and walnut furniture and Hussam's books. All left behind in that villa, painted the color of peach flesh, that had been their home.

Salma cried out when she saw the tray, pointed it out to the vendor. He refused to sell it without the coffee set and so she'd taken it all, walking home with the large, newspaper-swathed bundle. It was her first satisfaction in Nablus.

• • •

Over the years she has presented the tray in the same arrangement, the *ibrik* in the center, the cups, petal-like, encircling it. Twice a month the maid takes the tray and other silverware onto the veranda and carefully dabs them with vinegar. It hasn't lost its gleam.

The cups, however, are well worn. Hundreds of times, Salma has placed a saucer over the rim and flipped the cup upside down, waiting for the coffee dregs to dry. She prefers to wait ten minutes but often becomes occupied with her guests, only to remember much later with a hasty "Oh!" And the cup would be righted, the coffee remnants leaving desiccated, grainy streaks that stained the porcelain a faded brunette hue.

This time, Salma is barely able to wait the customary ten minutes. She listens to the women discuss the weather and whether or not the warmth will last until the wedding tomorrow. It will be held in the banquet hall of a nearby hotel, one that has hosted dignitaries and mayors and even a film star, once, in the fifties. Silk bows have already been tied to the backs of the chairs; tea-light candles set in arcs around the plates wait for flames. When lit, they will look like a constellation. Salma has already tested this, she and the concierge circling the tables and kissing the tips of matches to wicks. The concierge dimmed the lights, and the effect, incandescent and lovely, had warmed Salma.

"Throw out the candles. I'll order new ones," she'd told the concierge, aware of his eyes on her, the begrudging awe. *Extravagance*. But it is Alia, Alia to be wed, and no expense is to be spared. No blackened candles with miserable wick-nubs around the table settings.

With Widad, it was different. Ten years earlier, Salma sat silently throughout her eldest's wedding ceremony, a pitiful gathering in the mosque, the scent of incense potent around them. When the imam read the Fatiha, Widad started to cry. Her father had died three months earlier. The dying had taken years. Salma would sit beside him after praying *fajr* and listen to the clatter his chest made as he drew air in and released it. The first light of the day would slowly fill their bedroom. Salma spoke directly to God during those minutes, in a manner that felt shameless to her. She asked for her husband to live. She knew it was selfish, knew his life with its morphine and bloody handkerchiefs wasn't one he wanted to keep.

More than once he cried out into the night, "They took my home, they took my lungs. Kill me, kill me." Hussam fiercely believed his illness was tied to the occupation of Jaffa, the city with the peach-colored house they'd left behind.

"Khalto Salma, has it dried yet?" Around the table, the women watch her with anticipation. Though the captivation, she knows, is mostly among the younger women—her nieces and cousins who'd arrived from Amman for the wedding, Alia's classmates, whom she still thinks of as children. Even Alia, leaning on her elbows—Salma has the desire to tell her to sit up, to tell her that men hate chalky elbows, but then remembers Atef, the man who is accepting her daughter, elbows and all—looks interested.

The elders—Salma's sisters and neighbors and friends—watch the cup reading calmly. They've seen their mothers do this and their mothers' mothers. As far as they are concerned, such happenings are as commonplace as prayer.

"Has it stuck?" one of the nieces asks.

"I wonder what it says."

Salma blinks her thoughts away, rearranges her features. She glances down at the cup, tilts it, frowns. What she has seen is not a mistake.

"It needs more time. I'll turn it around for another few minutes. The dregs must dry."

Poor Widad. Salma feels a familiar ache at the thought of her older daughter. She was a woman, sixteen years old, when they left Jaffa. During those three days of terror before they decided to go, as they waited by the radio for news, it was Widad who cared for Alia, carrying her from room to room, boiling rice with milk and sugar to spoon into her mouth.

She'd made a game of the gunfire and artillery. Widad would raise her eyebrows in mock amazement, feigning delight at the muffled explosions outside. Alia clapped her toddler hands, giggled. *Resourceful*, Salma has often thought about her eldest, though whatever luminosity Widad has seems to materialize only in moments of crisis. Otherwise, she walked around their new house in Nablus wanly, sat through meals without speaking. She never mentioned Jaffa, and when her father, already ailing, told her it was time to marry, she didn't protest. Only with Salma did she cry, tears falling as she sat in the garden, her body hunched over the steam from her teacup.

"He will take me to Kuwait," she said, weeping, and Salma touched her daughter's hair, pulled her to her breast. The tea oversteeped as minutes passed. Ghazi was a good man, had the steadiness and loyalty that would make a fine husband, but her daughter saw only a paunchy, chinless stranger with spectacles, a man who wished to take her to a drab villa compound in the desert. Salma's heart hurt at the thought of her daughter becoming someone's young, unhappy wife in a foreign country, but she knew it was for the best.

She never told Widad the truth, how Hussam had consulted her on the matter of Widad's suitors, which he'd narrowed down to two men. The other was an academic, a professor of philosophy at the local university. Salma knew his sister from the mosque; he came from a well-mannered, educated family. But he was mired in Nablus, in Palestine—he would live and die here. When Hussam asked the boy where he intended to settle down, he answered, "In my homeland, sir. Nothing under this sky will budge me."

Salma, to Hussam's surprise, chose Ghazi. At the time, the logic of her verdict was nebulous to her, half formed. It was only when she sat in the mosque and felt relief that she understood her own actions. Widad would be kept safe in Kuwait, far from this blazing country split in two. Her unhappiness, if it came, was worth the price of her life.

Alia was at the ceremony, of course. Eight years old, in a taffeta dress that made a crunching sound when she sat. She twirled outside the mosque, swung her hips like a bell as Widad and Ghazi emerged wed. When Hussam died, Salma had expected Alia to bawl, demand an explanation. But the girl was the calmest of her three children.

"Baba is not hurt anymore?" she'd asked solemnly. And they all wept and embraced the girl—Widad and Salma and her son, Mustafa.

Alia was distinct as a child, unlike Widad with her gentle dolor or Mustafa who went from a colicky baby to a prickly child, throwing tantrums whenever he was refused anything. There were years between each child, years during which Salma was pregnant and miscarried six times. This betrayal of her body hobbled her; she felt shame at her belly, which stretched only to flatten again. In this way she failed, and, though Hussam was kind, bringing her tea each time she lay defeated in their bed, she knew his disappointment. She'd given him a daughter as firstborn—the first woman in five generations to do so—and was able to carry only one son in the basket of her womb.

It isn't that Alia is her favorite child. All her children are prized; they are the glow of her. It is more that Salma has always felt drawn to her, a magnetism delicate and stubborn as cobweb thread. Alia is a child of war. She was barely three when the Israeli army rolled through Jaffa's streets, the tanks smashing the marketplace, the soldiers dragging half-sleeping men from their homes. There would be the birth of a new nation, they declared. Salma and Hussam's villa sat atop a small hill that overlooked the sea, with orange groves banded beneath it in strips.

Within days the groves were mangled, soil impaled with wooden stakes, oranges scattered, pulp leaking from battered flesh. Alia had cried not at the sound of gunfire but at the smell of the mashed oranges, demanding slices of the fruit. By then, the men who worked for their groves were gone, most having fled, some with bullets nested in their skulls. Hussam refused to leave at first, shaking his fist at the sea and land outside their windows, the view that beckoned them like another room.

"You go," he told her, "go to your uncles in Nablus. Take the children." She begged and begged, but he wouldn't budge. Only when burning rags were hurled into their groves did he tell her, dully, to pack for all of them. They stood on the veranda while the children slept, watching the fire streak across their land, listening to the muffled shouts. The smell of burned oranges rose to them, scorched and sweet.

Only Alia mentioned Jaffa after they arrived at Nablus, with the tactlessness of the very young. She asked for the licorice sticks the grocer used to give her, for the dolls in her old bedroom. She cried at the thunderous sound of automobiles snaking through the Nablus marketplace. Widad and Mustafa looked pained when Alia spoke of these things, glancing at Hussam to see if he'd heard. Their father in Nablus was a transformed creature, cheerless and short-tempered. He no longer made growling sounds when he was hungry, mimicking a lion or bear until they giggled. He no longer asked them to stand straight in front of him and recite Hafiz Ibrahim's poetry, adopting a mock sternness when they faltered. When he spoke with Widad or Mustafa, he seemed to be unfocused. Every evening he listened to the radio raptly.

But Salma was cheered when her daughter mentioned Jaffa. She felt grateful. Salma missed her home with a tenacity that never quite abated. She spent the first years in Nablus daydreaming of returning. The early days of summer, the vision of the house rising as the road coiled around the cliff. Inside, a miracle: everything as she'd left it, even the damp laundry she'd never gotten to hang up. She understood the flaw of these fantasies. The villa was gone, razed to the soil. The groves had been replanted and new workers picked the browned leaves, new owners baked bread with the orange rinds. Still, her heart stirred when Alia, even at six, seven years old, spoke with the reverence of a mythologist about the enormous Jaffa pomegranates, the seeds that could be spooned out and sprinkled with either salt or sugar, depending on their ripeness.

"They were as big as the moon," little Alia would say, holding her starfish hands out, her voice confident.

It would become the girl's most endearing and exasperating quality, how she could become enamored of things already gone.

IT IS WIDAD that Salma thinks of as she waits for the dregs, remembering how the girl begged for a cup reading before her wedding, weeping when Salma refused. She is glad Widad isn't here to witness her disloyalty, shamefully glad that Ghazi's gout had flared up and that Widad—dutiful wife—insisted on staying with him.

Salma hadn't meant to be unkind. She had felt distraught by Widad's tears but could not agree to such a thing. Reading the cup of someone with whom you shared blood was unwise, Salma's mother always cautioned her. The fortune you wished for them would color the fortune you saw, or, worse, you'd be granted clarity and then be bound to reveal what you'd glimpsed. To keep something to yourself when reading cups was treachery. What was seen had to be shared. Many times Salma had read the broken hearts and tragedies of her neighbors, friends, even Hussam's sisters.

Once, here in Nablus, she read in her neighbor's cup the death of a male member of her family. Less than a month later she sat in the neighbor's living room, holding the keening woman as she pulled out tufts of her hair. Her eldest son had spat on a soldier, and a bullet ripped open his neck. When the neighbor was finally put to bed with a sedative, Salma collected the strands of hair from the sofa and rug. The neighbor avoided Salma after that, shuffling away when they met, her averted eyes reproachful. But the others kept coming.

"We are blessed to have this gift of seeing. Allah willed it and we must not misuse it," her mother would tell Salma. And Salma felt that duty profoundly, the connection that it carved ancestrally with her mother and a great-aunt and others who'd died before Salma lived. She felt, whenever handed a hollow, still-warm cup, that she was being entrusted with something profound. Cosmic.

And she has never transgressed. Until now. Widad would've wanted to know if she was marrying the right man. Alia asks no such thing. She is not much younger than Widad was when she wed, is in fact three years older than Salma had been. But Salma worries about Alia, about the way the girl doesn't worry about herself. It is hastiness, Alia's love of Atef, which she has proclaimed to Salma, to her friends, in the most cavalier manner.

"I adore him," Salma once overheard her tell a cousin, as though adoration was a casual, unfussy thing. There is something indecent to Salma about how transparently Alia flourishes her emotions.

Still, Alia looks nervous as she waits for the dregs, unusually somber. Salma had expected some mocking about superstition. Alia is like this, brazen, indelicate with her words. She'd protested the dowry ceremony, insisting that Atef give her only a lira coin as a token and nothing else. Even the sugaring ritual was a battle. She preferred shaving, she announced, sending a cousin for one of the pink plastic razors that had been materializing in recent months on pharmacy shelves. But when the aunts insisted Turkish coffee be brewed for Alia, that the girl drink it slowly so Salma could read her fortune, Alia obeyed. She drank the coffee in silence, her lashes lowered, occasionally blowing on the surface.

"*Ya* Salma," one of the neighbors calls out. "It's been eight minutes. Isn't it time?"

Salma inhales, touches her hair. Since it is only women at the gathering, her veil and those of the aunts are draped along the windowsill.

"Yes, yes." With unsteady fingers Salma flips the cup over.

She revolves the cup between her fingers, using only one hand. Her tendons and muscles have memorized these cups, the curving planes, know even to stop instinctively at the jag of the crack. Monumental little things, heavy and hollow at once, with the contradictory weight of eggs. She leans in once more and brings the cup close to her face. The lingering scent of coffee has already turned stale.

There it is. She had not been mistaken. The porcelain surface of the teacup is white as salt; the landscape of dregs, violent.

Lines curve wildly, clusters streaking the sides. Two arches, a wedding and a journey. The hilt of a knife crossed, ominously, with another. Arguments coming. On one side of the teacup, the white porcelain peeks through the dregs, forming a rectangular structure with a roof, drooping, an edifice mid-crumble. Houses that will be lost. And in the center, a smudged crown on its head, a zebra. Blurry but unmistakable, a zebra form, stripes across the flank. Salma wills her face expressionless, though fear rises in her, hot and barbed. A zebra is an exterior life, an unsettled life.

"Umm Mustafa, what do you see?" one of the girls pipes up. Salma lifts her head to the women gazing at her, their eyes questioning.

"Mama?" Alia asks, her voice sounding small. She is so young, Salma suddenly sees.

Salma's voice is gravelly to her own ears. "She will be pregnant soon. There is a man waiting to take her through a door, a man who'll love her very much." All this is true—the fetus shape near the cup's mouth, the tiny porpoise below the crack.

"Oh, wonderful!"

"Thank Allah."

"At least now we know he loves her." Laughing, the cousins tease Alia, who is smiling and flushed, relief plainly—surprisingly—on her face.

"Open the heart," Salma tells her daughter, holding out the cup. The girl obliges, presses the pad of her thumb to the bottom of the cup, twists it in a half-arc. She returns the cup to Salma, then licks her coffee-smudged thumb.

Alia's print is blurred, the edges speckled with dregs. She made a smear as she removed her thumb, a figure like a wing. Salma sees her daughter's fear, the disquiet the girl cannot say. In the center of the thumbprint is a whirling form. Flight. She looks at Alia's diamond-shaped face.

"It will come true. Your wish," Salma says, this time speaking only to her. Alia blinks, nods slowly. At this, the women cheer and laugh, crowd around Alia with kisses and teasing tones. Salma sinks back into the chair, exhausted. She has given the truth. But amputated.

It is several hours before the men join them for supper. Lanterns are lit throughout the garden behind Salma's house, casting everyone in a spongy, pale light. The elders, aunts and uncles, are all seated. The younger people mill around the radio, swaying to the music. Atef and Alia talk to their friends and cousins but glance at each other every few moments. Mustafa remains by Atef's side, the two men smoking cigarettes and occasionally bursting into laughter. Children run about playing games. The house stands monolithically in the setting sun.

In Salma's mind this remains the *new* house, the Nablus house. She has come to love it, in a resigned way. It is larger than their Jaffa home, the rooms cavernous, high-ceilinged. The previous owners—who'd fled to Jordan—had left their furniture; kitchen cabinets were still littered with biscuit packets and jars of sugar. In the room she was to share with Hussam, she found nightgowns and a stack of the thick, disposable cloths used for menstruation. Widad found notebooks filled with mathematical equations. For weeks, they played a warped game of unsheathing the house's possessions. Salma had thrown it all away. But the house remained ghosted with its former life, the dinners and celebrations and quarrels it had witnessed. For this reason, Salma never changed the color of the walls or turned the room overlooking the veranda into a library instead of a sitting room.

Shame, she admonishes herself. She soundlessly delivers a prayer. Lucky. They are lucky. Lucky to have these walls and lucky—it feels tawdry to speak of this to Allah but unavoidable—to have money.

Money carried them to Nablus, over the threshold of this house. Money kept them fed and warm, kept their windows draped in curtains and their bodies clothed. Salma had been born poor, lived on bread and lentils until Hussam's mother chose her for marriage. Again—luck, Salma possessing a docile beauty that caught the older woman's eye. Widad and Alia and Mustafa, they might have known gunfire and war, but they were protected from it with the armor of wealth. It is what separates them from the refugees in the camps dotting the outskirts of Nablus. Salma still holds her breath, her childhood defense against bad luck, when she has to drive past them.

Many families from Jaffa wound up in the Balata camp, each tent barely two or three steps away from another. Inside, impossible numbers of people shared the space. Salma has never been in one, only seen the white tents blur by from her car window. But she knew of them from an old housekeeper, Raja, who would speak of the mangled ropes that kept tent sheets stamped into the soil, the smell of camel dung and urine. Raja had seven children, and they, she, her husband, and her mother-in-law shared one tent. They slept by taking turns, several of the children often remaining awake at night so the adults could sleep before rising at dawn for work.

Salma is ashamed of her queasiness about the camps, her irrational fear that they are somehow contagious. It was a relief to her when Raja resigned due to flaring arthritis. Salma felt a persistent desire to apologize to her, a feeling that was absent with other housekeepers and nannies she employed, usually native Nabulsi girls. Only Raja hummed the haunting, throaty ballads Salma's own mother used to sing, unknowingly hinting at a kinship that made Salma feel guilty. That this woman should spend days sweeping floors and then go home to a tent. Parallel lives, she sometimes thinks. It was a matter of parallel lives, one person having lamb for supper, the other cucumbers. With fate deciding, at random, which was which.

"I love this song."

"The weather is perfect."

"Do you think it'll hold?"

"It has to."

A group of Alia's friends speak with wistful, slightly envious tones, as unmarried girls will at the wedding of a friend. They wear bright dresses, their legs bare beneath.

Salma touches the young maid's arm as she walks by. "Lulwa, please bring more rose water."

Lulwa nods. "Yes, madame."

The garden is beautiful. If the house remains haunted, an old ownership hanging over it, the garden is completely hers. The former occupants had tiled over the land, turning it into a marbled courtyard.

"I need it out," Salma told Hussam when they moved in. "I need to see the soil." It was the only time she'd ever spoken to her husband like that. Hussam seemed taken aback but obliged her, hiring men to remove every tile.

Beneath it was grayish soil, sickly from lack of sun and strewn with pieces of marble. It is odd to think now, watching people walk around, laughing and listening to music, that below their feet had been nothing but the palest worms, not even a blade of grass.

She worked on the soil for months. Nothing happened. Fertilizer, tilling, pruning. She was on the verge of giving up in despair, accepting that she'd never grow a garden, nothing would bloom.

What astonishment, then, to walk outside one morning with her tea, surveying the wasteland, only to see a sliver of sprouting; a weed, but still Salma fell to her knees and stroked it. She had the urge to run into the house, call for the children and Hussam, to show them something, at last, to lift their spirits.

Instead she remained still, touching the sprout, recognizing in that moment that there were some things we are meant to keep for ourselves, too precious to share with others. She shut her eyes and recited the Fatiha.

The garden has done her proud. After that first blade, lush greenery followed, flowers and shrubs and trees pushing through the soil, all the seeds Salma bartered for in the market, the seeds people bought for her—her love for the garden became famous in the neighborhood—blossoming in the courtyard.

She was greedy back then, Salma recognizes, planting contradictory creatures, roots vying for water, especially in the Nabulsi summer. The roses and the gardenia bush, the tomato stalk and the mint shrub; even the perfume overwhelming in those days, a cacophony of scents clamoring to overpower one another.

She has become more discreet over the years, the trick being to include plants that are restrained in their need. Now the garden is simpler, rows of shrubs extending from the house, an awning vined with grape leaves above the courtyard table. The scent of jasmine laces the air. All throughout this night, she has heard people murmuring and is unable to quell her pride.

"How beautiful."

"Oh, see the gardenia!"

"Those tomatoes are the plumpest I've seen."

Alia and Mustafa had loved to help with the garden, keeping it clear of certain insects and creatures. After Widad wed and Hussam died, it was just the three of them and they spent long afternoons picking bugs. Salma remembers how gleefully they'd untangle long worms from the soil.

Salma considers her children now, standing beneath the awning. The long table is covered with damask. The men have brought *kanafeh* and are slicing the cellophane packaging open with knives. Steam rises from the dessert, orange pastry topped with sprinkles of crushed pistachios. Mustafa is handing a plate to Alia, Atef at her side. All three are laughing at something Mustafa has said.

Salma can hear snatches from across the garden. "Thieves . . . crossing the water . . . ever!" More laughter. A joke.

Both Mustafa and Alia are tall and brunette, similarly complexioned as their father. For all their talk of revolution and oppression, Salma's two youngest are not plagued with thoughts of camps and the people inside them. In many ways, they are careless children, both spoiled, given to mercurial moods. Indulged. As children they were allies, and they remain so.

Alia is speaking now with her head ducked, whispering to the two men. One hand holds her plate, the other gestures. Throughout the courtyard, people watch her, men and women. Alia has never been straightforwardly pretty. Her jaw is narrow, her cheekbones too pronounced, giving the impression of an avid cat. She has the same crooked nose as her father, and Hussam lurks in the wide forehead and broad shoulders as well. But her face arrests, has the arched eyebrows and long eyelashes that made Salma's own mother such a beauty. Unlike many tall women, Alia carries herself well, her spine perfectly straight, the skinny, imperious shoulders squared. When Alia was fourteen and her growth spurt began, Salma had tortured nightmares of her daughter becoming unrecognizable, beastly, her bones shooting out into dreadfully long limbs.

"You should bind her bones," the aunts used to say. "Let her sleep with cardamom sprinkled on her pillow, it stunts growth."

But Salma did neither. By then, Widad had been gone for years and Hussam too, and Salma had begun to recognize that the world was no longer made for certain types of women. There was a need for spine and even anger. Widad had Salma's shape, petite, ample-hipped—all the female cousins were similarly built. Only Alia stood inches above the women, able to look most men square in the eye.

"*Mashallah*, *ya* Salma," Umm Bashar, a neighbor, says. Her veil is damp at the side from perspiration. On her plate a slice of *kanafeh* is soaked in rose water. "She is like the moon."

Salma smiles the muted, modest smile perfected by women and tilts her head. "Thank you, Umm Bashar. We are blessed. Allah is great." She keeps her voice slightly tight, for she knows the power of the evil eye, of even unintentionally drawing envy.

"Although an unusual choice," Umm Bashar says, glancing over at Mustafa. Salma knows what is coming. It is what the guests have been discussing. "For you to marry the younger one first." She sighs. "Although I suppose it's different with men."

"Alia's fate was to be married first. Mustafa still has school to finish and is perhaps going to travel to Ramallah for work." Salma hears her own lie, the weight of it.

"Yes, yes." A slight pause. "Mustafa is how many years older?"

"Five." Five, five. Salma recites the number in her sleep because, although she would never admit it to this woman, it is an old worry.

"Ah, five. Well. Everyone is to do what she must. Although mine will be married off in order. Bashar is getting married in the fall and he is two—no, no, three years younger than Mustafa."

Salma thinks unkindly of Bashar, with his large nose and tiny chin. She has always sensed from Umm Bashar a competitiveness about their sons, because Mustafa is so handsome.

"It is how her father would've wanted it." Salma shuts her voice to signal the end of the discussion. Umm Bashar nods and smiles, overly sweet.

"Well," she says, glancing at Alia, "she certainly looks lovely. Those streaks of henna in her hair, they suit her complexion." Salma feels some relief as Umm Bashar walks off, the neighbor's eyes away from her daughter.

The aunts and cousins held the henna ceremony for Alia the day before and Salma can see flecks of reddish gold in her daughter's hair, brought out by the torch light. It was a squealing, messy affair, the younger women gossiping as they mixed the henna in a tin basin. Each girl took a handful of the goopy paste and kneaded it, trying to remove twigs and leaves. When the paste was blended, the girls tilted the basin into fabric dough sacks, twisted them shut. The older aunts and Salma prepared Alia's skin, reciting Qur'an as they brushed the girl's hair and rubbed lemon juice on her arms and feet. Salma whispered the Fatiha as she massaged the henna paste on her daughter's hands, staining both palms reddish. One of the aunts punctured the dough sacks with a needle, her hand steady as she maneuvered the paste into a design of whirls and flowers and lattices on the tops of Alia's hands and feet.

The henna paste smelled strongly, roughly, of barnyards. The older women spoke nostalgically of their own henna ceremonies, and Salma caught a couple of the younger cousins rolling their eyes. This generation was impatient; it was something the neighbors and aunts discussed at great length over afternoon tea visits. They were becoming reckless. When Salma went to collect a dough sack from the younger women, their chattering stilled, each girl looking at her with wide, innocent eyes. They were speaking of the neighborhood boys, Salma knew, of the men they met at school or the youth clubs. Some might even be speaking of the Israeli soldiers, although she preferred to think that such flagrancy remained outside of Nablus, among the Christian girls or the ones who'd gone to boarding school in Europe. Elsewhere.

It is painful to think of how Hussam would disapprove of the way she raised Alia. Hussam had been a man of precise faith; his was a life of mosques and fasting and austerity. Salma loved her husband in a distant way, mostly because he wasn't a man who inspired anything stronger. In their marriage he remained reserved, chaste even in their most intimate moments. Only after his illness did he begin to yell and curse, and by then his mind was no longer his.

He wouldn't have been prepared for the changes sweeping the youth. The way the West has begun to seep into their cities, the way the occupation divided the generations sharply. The youth drawn to glitter, the elders to bitterness.

Sometimes she has arguments with him in her head, a vestigial habit from twenty years of marriage.

All the girls are doing it, she'd say defensively when Alia began to go out with her friends, when she made it clear she would never veil.

"*And say to the believing women that they should lower their gaze and guard their modesty*." A verse from the Qur'an, Hussam's favorite tactic in arguments.

This is what our life is now, Hussam. The youth are scattered. This is what it is to live under the rifle.

She could imagine him frowning, shaking his head, disappointed with her weakness. *Perhaps if you'd raised her better. Perhaps if you'd read her more Qur'an, taken her to the mosque more.* An imagined pause. *If I were there, she wouldn't be so far from Allah.*

Well, you're not here.

Such is the ease with which one can silence the dead.

"Yamma, have some." Mustafa approaches Salma, a plate in hand. He has puddled the syrup onto the very center of the *kanafeh* slice, just as she likes it. The cheese will soak up the sugar. She looks up at his lanky frame.

"You should see how nervous Atef has been," Mustafa confides. "I swear he changed his tie seven or eight times."

"Gray suits him."

"Gray, blue, orange—who cares! I told him, a suit is a suit is a suit."

Salma smiles, drops her voice to a whisper: "The groom is fussier than the bride."

They laugh together. Only with Mustafa does she banter like this, the two of them conspiratorial. The aunts say he is too attached to her and to Alia, that fatherlessness has stunted him. Selfish as she feels, Salma prays on each of Mustafa's birthdays for the boy to stay with her for one more year, his sports cleats and laundry and dirty dishes cluttering the house.

Mustafa waves Atef over; the other man looks relieved as he moves toward them. His gait is stiffened in the formal clothes.

"What a lovely tie, Atef," Salma says archly. Mustafa laughs.

"You too, Khalto?" Atef asks, mock wounded. He grins down at her, teeth white against his beard. He is handsome in the manner of old pasha rulers, the somber-looking men in history books.

"Will you be going to mosque tomorrow?"

The two men hesitate, exchanging a glance that she catches. "Yes, Yamma," Mustafa finally says. "Only for the prayers. We promised Imam Ali."

"We'll be done by ten. Back in time for breakfast," Atef confirms. All three stand in silence, the unsaid a living thing between them.

"Good," Salma says. She tries to liven her voice: "You boys keep each other out of trouble."

They laugh, embarrassed, looking away. A few months earlier, they were arrested at a demonstration in Jerusalem. In another time, their offense might have earned them a fine, merely a court-issued warning. Instead, both Atef and Mustafa were kept in the penitentiary for four nights.

On the day of their release, Salma sat between Atef's mother, Umm Atef, and Alia in the courtroom. When the boys' names were spoken, Umm Atef's lips began to move, her eyes unblinking. Praying. Salma slipped her hand onto the other woman's lap, interlacing their fingers. Umm Atef's hand lay limply until the boys walked into the courtroom flanked by officers. Then she squeezed hard, her wedding ring digging into Salma's palm. It occurred to Salma in that moment that they were both widows. Atef was the son of a fedayeen, a man who died pointing a gun at an Israeli soldier.

The boys were led with their wrists in cuffs. Alia started to cry. Atef had a swollen, purplish bruise on his cheekbone. Mustafa, Salma saw with great relief, was unmarked, though she would later learn of the contusion over his rib cage, the imprint of a baton that had flecked his urine with blood.

Afterward, the three women waited outside the courtroom. Umm Atef was no longer praying; her eyes sparked like coals. When the two men walked out, she flew at her son. Her beefy fists pummeled Atef's chest.

"You . . . do . . . this to me . . . you son of a dog . . . you son of a dog . . . you think this is what men do?" She wheezed as she pounded at him.

Atef stood still, his eyes shut. He did not guard himself from his mother's blows. Only when her wheezing worsened, her body heaving in sobs, did he move. "Mama," he said softly, taking her into his arms.

Salma said nothing, not outside the courtroom or as they drove home. In the house's foyer, she sat. She pulled her dress to her knees to feel the cool tiles beneath her. She didn't speak for hours, listening to Alia, Mustafa, even Lulwa whispering in concerned tones as they scurried back and forth. She watched the sunlight sluice through the windows, collecting in her lap like water. A cup of mint tea cooled untouched at her side. The light turned red, traversing the length of her body, down her legs. It reached her feet, staining them a bright, unlikely crimson.

Dusk had already fallen when Mustafa knelt on the floor beside her. He cradled her feet in his hands, bent and kissed them on the soles as he wept.

"Never, never again," he promised. "I'm sorry, I'm sorry." Salma hadn't seen her son cry in years. It jolted her into embracing him. He smelled boyishly of sweat and the lemongrass soap he showered with, his long eyelashes spiking with tears as they had when he was a child. Alia appeared in the doorway, her legs longer than her nightgown, the hem hovering midcalf. Salma extended her arm and drew Alia against her brother. She enveloped those two miraculous living creatures, and with them Mustafa's apology—her hungry longing to trust it—crushed them all like a talisman to her chest.

"Save some syrup for the rest of us, Alia," one of the men calls out across the garden. Alia arches her eyebrow at him and ladles another spoonful onto her plate.

"You don't tell the bride what to eat," she retorts to the laughter of the men. She joins the young women sitting on the steps bordered by jasmine shrubs. Alia lifts a forkful of the *kanafeh*, cools it through pursed lips.

The evening is unseasonably warm, the March breeze light. The wind flutters the edge of Salma's veil, tickling her neck beneath the fabric. She tugs the veil down automatically, tightens the edges with her fingertips. In the chaos this morning, she forgot the customary pin on either side, the trick of folding that keeps the veil fastened around her face.

Alia's hair is long, curls coiling compactly beneath her ears. Both of Salma's daughters remain unveiled, a source of shame for her. She'd grown up with a devout father, waking at four to iron and press his finest *dishdasha* before he went to the mosque for *fajr* prayer. Salma would tell herself elaborate stories to try to keep from falling asleep just to catch a glimpse of her father walking down the trail from their hut. The few times Salma succeeded, her vision would be bleary, her father's silhouette barely visible in the moonlight.

During Ramadan, she would spend the long hours of daylight by her mother's side in the kitchen, slicing chunks of cantaloupe and stirring lentil soup. She would be dizzy with hunger when the sun set and it came time to break the fast, all the cousins and aunts and uncles seated around steaming bowls. The first bite, usually bread or an olive slick with oil, seemed to her the most delicious thing her young tongue tasted all year round, and she would be filled with a lush, weepy love for Allah.

Her children, Salma knows, do not have such worship for Allah. Widad, the most devout, prays once or twice a day and never misses a day of fasting, but her piety is steeped in fear, not rapture. Mustafa spends Fridays in the mosque but his attitude suggests it's a social duty, a shared performance with the neighborhood men. And Alia is as mercurial with Allah as she is with all things. For a while after she began menstruating, the girl asked Salma to teach her Qur'an verses, modeled Salma's veils, and spoke of someday visiting Mecca. But she slowly lost interest, drifting over to tight dresses and Egyptian love songs.

Several months ago, Salma overheard a conversation between Alia, Atef, and Mustafa, her daughter's defiant voice rising through the walls.

"Allah might be the most useful invention of all!"

Salma was pleased to hear Atef admonish Alia, tell her to hush.

The *kanafeh* is devoured; Salma's hands are sticky. Mustafa and Atef are seated, one on either side of her. She senses the mosque talk has sobered them. The final smudges of light are erased from the sky.

"The weather's going to be perfect for the wedding," Mustafa says, tipping his head back. Salma follows his gaze. Atef does the same. The night sky is dappled with stars.

"*Inshallah*," she murmurs, and the men, chided, repeat the prayer. Salma rises, takes the empty plates from the men. She walks past the huddle of young women, the children chasing one another. Salma's bladder aches. She turned fifty the previous year, and her body unceremoniously began to murmur discontent. When she bends, her hip throbs; there is a floating curlicue at the corner of her vision, a coil that worsens in sunlight.

She goes in the house and finds Lulwa in the kitchen, ironing a pale silky veil that Salma will wear for the wedding tomorrow. The girl is bent over the hissing metal plate, straining to see any creases in her handiwork.

Salma enters the bathroom and sits upon the porcelain seat with relief. She's been moving and sitting for hours, and her underwear is damp with sweat, mottled with brownish red. It is the body's leftover, as the aunts say, the flush from her idle uterus. Before leaving the bathroom, she pauses at the mirror above the sink.

It is a plain face, recognizable to her as water. She tucks stray hairs beneath the wings of her veil, quietly shuts the door behind her.

AT THE FAR end of the lawn, the men have begun to gather by the fig tree, untangling themselves from the laughter and gossip of the women. The women settle around the table, the torches casting shadows upon their faces.

"I've heard the border might close," one of the women says.

"They're saying Egypt loves a war."

"Egypt loves a good soap opera."

"Speaking of, did you see that last episode . . ."

Familiarly, the talk settles into shows and their favorite starlets. War is war; they are bored of it. The children sit scattered around the women or curled in their mothers' laps. The *ibrik* roasts over a flame in the courtyard's entrance, the perfume of coffee drifting across the garden. The coffee set has been washed and dried, the mosaic tray oiled. Alia sits at the head of the table, a younger cousin settled on her lap. Alia braids the child's hair, smiling at one of the neighbors' stories.

Mustafa and Atef have joined the men by the fig tree. The torch light barely reaches them, and Salma struggles to make out the white of their shirts. One of the young boys at the table squirms from his mother's arms and skips over to the men, arms outstretched to his father. The father kneels down and hoists the boy onto his hip. Salma watches the men gesture. Their hands blur in the dark. Smoke from the cigarettes hovers above them.

She knows without hearing any of it what they are saying, the names they are repeating, the dates. Soon, there will be an argument; there always is. Blisters of rage, which must be drained. And the women, intimate with such scenes, will rise wearily, go to their husbands or brothers or fathers. Speak to them in soothing voices.

Salma can see the bubbling of the *ibrik* at the courtyard entrance. Lulwa rushes toward it carrying the coffee set. Black liquid has begun to spill over the edge, causing sparks in the flame. Salma makes a gesture with her hand, trying to catch Alia's eye. Alia should be the one to serve the coffee, on this last night as a single woman, the cups set carefully on the tray, memorizing who wants sugar and who wants it bitter. Serving the old men first, then the hajis, then Atef. Pausing in front of the man who will be her husband, demurely, one of thousands of times she will serve him coffee.

But Alia doesn't see Salma's beckoning. She has finished the child's braid and is kissing the top of her dark hair.

Salma feels a slow weariness in her limbs. An image of the wedding tomorrow swims, unbidden, before her. The hall empty, chairs toppled, tablecloths stained oily from the candles. Dinner plates abandoned, the feasts now carnage, strewn fish bones and globules of lamb fat. Salma sees her daughter's makeup as it will be after hours beneath hot lights—waxy, crinkles of mascara at the corners of her eyes. The wedding dress, with its beaded bodice and cream-puff sleeves, creased from all the dancing. Across the table, Alia yawns and Salma imagines her tomorrow evening, tired, happy, leaving in Atef's arms.

"God, that breeze is amazing," one of the women says.

"Not that they'd notice." An aunt nods toward the men. "They're starting."

Salma turns. The men are talking more rapidly now. A few look annoyed, shaking their heads. Their voices are audible. She returns her gaze to her daughter. Alia looks at her and smiles, rolling her eyes good-naturedly. The gesture lights the girl's face.

This is why she saw the zebra, Salma thinks. Because it is Alia, darling, baby Alia. Love and fear for the girl have the same metallic taste. Doubt—beautiful doubt—glimmers now. Surely her vision was clouded. Can she even be certain of what she saw? She tries to remember the valley of the coffee cup, can conjure up only the alarm. Perhaps it wasn't even a zebra but a bear or wolf, some other four-legged creature. Alia laughs across the table. Yes, Salma thinks, her hand outstretched to her youngest, miming the lifting of the *ibrik*. The form in the coffee cup flashes in her mind. Yes, it must've been a horse. Not a zebra, but a horse with smudges, a speckled horse. It means travel, perhaps, even a difficult first pregnancy, but luck; it also means luck.

MUSTAFA

NABLUS
October 1965

Brothers, we have come to a crossroad," Mustafa recites under his breath. "We cannot continue as we are."

He pauses at a patch of grass bordering the road and squints up at the sky. The late afternoon is cool, the setting sun disappearing behind the hills. Each morning and evening, he walks along the valley between his house and the school, preferring it to driving. It clears his head. His job is a simple one, teaching arithmetic to adolescents at a nearby school, and though he enjoys it—the elegance of mathematics, the satisfaction of watching pupils solve equations—it feels dull occasionally, rote. The walks give him time to pound the earth with his sandals.

Up ahead is another hill, small houses with vegetable gardens out front. Beyond them are the simpler huts, with cracked windows and pots of water boiled for heat. Aya lives in one of those huts. Mustafa goes by them, keeping his eyes on the top of the middle hills, rising against the plum sky. The view is regal.

"We cannot continue as we are," he repeats.

There is a construction site to the left, and men mill around smoking cigarettes. Mustafa undoes the first two buttons at his neck as he walks past.

"Brothers, we are losing a fight." Too meek. "*Brothers*, we are *losing* a fight." He tries a sweeping gesture with his hand. He is pleased with the effect and does it again, this time with both hands.

"Have you finally lost your mind?" Mustafa looks up to see Omar, one of the mosque *shabab*, walking toward him from the site. Omar wears the green construction uniform, perspiration soaking the collar.

"This is what it's come to, brother?" Omar asks, grinning. "Roaming the streets and talking to yourself?"

Mustafa holds his hands up in defeat, grins back. "We are a lazy generation." It is a well-worn joke among the men at the mosque, a reference to Israeli pamphlets calling Arab men cowardly and indolent. He waves toward the construction. "How's the building going?"

"Starts and stops. Bastards are stingy with permits." Omar spits on the road, a stream of brown. "And if not that, we get hassled on zoning. If we're not getting fucked from one side, it's coming from the other."

Omar pulls out a pack of cigarettes and hands one to Mustafa. They light them and smoke, facing the valley. For a couple of moments they are silent, each lost in thought. Then a whistle cuts through the air and they turn to see the construction overseer gesturing to Omar.

"Let's move it, sweetheart," the man calls out nastily. "You're not paid to chat with your friends."

Omar drops the cigarette. "Piece of shit," he mutters. He nods at Mustafa as he walks away. "Your house tonight, right?"

Mustafa remembers. He told the men to come over after the mosque for coffee and *shisha*. They are supposed to alternate among their homes, but the other men have wives and families.

"Yes, my house," Mustafa says, and Omar walks back to the construction site.

IT WAS IMAM BAKRI'S idea for Mustafa to speak tonight. Imam Bakri assured him that he would be fine, that whatever he said would be *gold, pure spun gold*.

"There are some men visiting from Jerusalem," Imam Bakri told him. "I want them to see us, our congregation, what a fine brotherhood we have here. I want you to speak."

When Mustafa began to ask questions, the imam smiled. "It'll come to you. You'll move their hearts, leave them catching their breath. It's what you do."

From a distance the house appears unaltered, the doorway framed by trees. Only upon closer inspection do signs of neglect become apparent—the untrimmed hedges, the windows streaky with dust, a slackness to the doorknob, which turns too easily in Mustafa's hand. When Salma first announced she was moving to Amman, no one believed it. Mustafa and Alia teased her about abandoning her post, privately assuring each other that she'd never leave. Even now, a year after she'd packed suitcase after suitcase with her belongings and moved into a small house near her sister, Mustafa still half expects her to return.

With Salma gone, the house is his. He has inherited his living mother's rooms and garden and at times is filled with childish resentment, as though given a beautiful trinket that he cannot touch without its breaking.

He walks through the foyer, the sitting room, pauses to unbutton his dress shirt and toss it on the couch. "They want us to crumple. To surrender," he mutters absently as he enters the kitchen. *Crumple* sounds odd, reminds him of paper. "They want us to yield." Better.

The kitchen counters are scattered with newspapers, a bowl of pears—his favorite—and cellophane bags of bread and crackers. A jar of pickles sits atop one of honey; there is a grayish plant he never remembers to water on the windowsill above the sink.

"You know she only left because she thinks it'll jolt you into marriage," Alia said to him once, inciting one of their rapid-fire arguments. He was insulted by the accusation because he knew it to be true.

Every week his mother sighs on the telephone. "I worry about you in that house by yourself. Without a wife, a nice woman to cook you meals, keep you happy. *Habibi*, you are so alone."

During Mustafa's last visit to Amman, Salma and his aunts had transparently introduced him to several women, hosting dinner after dinner where he made strained conversation with the girls and their mothers. His aunts made interjections.

"You know, Mustafa finished university in three years."

"*Habibti*, have you visited Nablus?"

"So pretty, look at that skin. Is your whole family fair?"

The trip felt like one long held breath, him politely smiling and nodding, the aunts and Salma sitting on the balcony afterward and discussing the girls, how Suzanne was a brilliant cook and Amal had a degree in literature and Hind had the loveliest green eyes. Mustafa found himself thinking of Aya, of her long hair always plaited into a braid, the rasp in her voice like burned sugar.

On his last evening, they'd asked which one he liked best. Mustafa answered, "None of them."

His mother's disappointment was palpable. Her voice was streaked with uncustomary anger:

"Go, go back to Nablus. You want to be alone forever? Because that's the life you're building for yourself."

MUSTAFA WALKS AROUND the kitchen scratching his head. He does his familiar dance, opening the drawers, eyeing the detritus in the refrigerator. He takes a jar of olives, peers suspiciously into it. Fuzz grows around the rim.

His grocery shopping is haphazard. Some mornings he wakes early, full of energy and purpose, sets out to the marketplace before work and returns with bags of tomatoes, cheese wedges, pita bread still steaming. Other times he scrounges, making meals of almonds and a handful of figs, a desultory bite of fruit.

The past two weeks have been scavenging, Mustafa pulling together meals of bread and olive oil, at times boiling a lamb chop. Some evenings Atef and Alia come over, Alia occasionally roused into the role of wife, trying her hand at some ambitious meal. *Koussa*, their mother's *warak anab*. It is invariably a failure, Alia a worse cook than

Mustafa. Both of them were raised in the manner of wealthy Nabulsi children, always a maid to cook and clean and wash their clothes, such that Alia's first experience with laundry as a bride was a catastrophe of blanched shirts and dyed socks, now an oft-referenced family joke. *She deprived Atef of his socks, poor man.*

Mustafa finds a half-empty box of spaghetti in the drawer. He smokes while waiting for the water to boil. When he upends the box of pasta into the pot, the strands fan out.

"But who'll cook for you?" his mother had asked when she left, taking Lulwa with her. "Who will clean?" She wanted him to get a maid, a part-time housekeeper at least.

"I will," Mustafa told her. But the truth is the disarray doesn't bother him; most of the time he barely sees the mess. Only after speaking with his mother does the unkempt state of the house come into relief. Those moments, all he can see is the peeling paint, the puff of dust when he stomps on the rug, the cigarette ash in his bathroom sink. He thinks of how, when his mother lived in the house, the rooms smelled of lavender, how he was never allowed to smoke indoors.

When the guilt becomes overpowering, he gathers dishrags and fills a bucket with water. On those days, he scrubs each tile of the kitchen floor, soaps the windows, even dusts the bathroom cabinets.

The cigarette is nearly out. Mustafa flicks it into the kitchen sink, then turns his attention to the pot, the spaghetti now limp and snarled.

He remembers a meal his mother used to make, pasta with béchamel. He tries to recall the ingredients. Cream—a dusty can in the pantry—and oil and salt. There was a fourth ingredient, he knows, but he cannot remember what it was. Cloves? Sugar? Or was it vinegar? Something unexpected. He goes with sugar, two spoonfuls into a bowl with the cream, whisking it until he gets bored.

The pasta looks delicious, steaming and shiny with oil. "Salt," he mutters to himself, then, feeling daring, he rustles around the spice cabinet. A dash of cardamom and several shakes of paprika. He takes a bite and immediately spits it out. It tastes like car fumes.

He surveys the kitchen glumly, as if a roasted chicken or shish kebab might magically appear. He thinks, with dim hope, of his sister. Perhaps she picked something up from the market.

His casual lifestyle is underpinned by Alia and Atef, residing several streets over, their lives spilling into one another's. They all check in daily, usually gathering at Salma's house—Mustafa still refers to it as *beit immi*. Both houses are always unlocked, and they slip easily between them. Mustafa loves the permeability of their days, the way he and the two people he loves most revolve around each other like planets.

As though he has conjured her, Mustafa hears footsteps on the pathway of the house, Alia's trademark heels.

He moves to the sink and starts to scrape the dish, the pasta already congealed.

"Mustafa?"

"In here," he calls out. The cigarette turns the drain water brown.

Alia appears in the doorway, her nose wrinkled. "What's on fire?"

"Dinner."

"I'm starving," she says, setting her purse on the table. She wears a long, peasant-style skirt, and as she walks, the hem trails along the floor, rustling up dust.

"Is Atef here?"

"No, we're meeting at the mosque later."

"I think it's going to rain." Alia lifts the pot lid, frowning. "Another boys-only meeting?"

Mustafa makes a noncommittal sound, busying himself rinsing ash from the sink. His sister is clever, Mustafa knows, clever enough to understand there are secrets, things involving the mosque and men gathering to talk at night. And he knows she resents it, the exclusions, being left in the dark, kept away from a part of her brother's and husband's lives. Especially after the prison.

"I'm sure all you'll be doing tonight is snacking on grapes and discussing the weather," Alia snaps. "No talk at all of Nasser or Eshkol."

Perhaps it is jealousy, Mustafa thinks. Alia has always been sturdy, never afraid of mud or worms, not covering her eyes like other girls during lamb slaughtering for Eid. And while she has been given free rein in Nablus, her life different than other wives'—an easygoing husband, days filled with shopping and tea dates and reading—she is still, first and foremost, a woman. No amount of sturdiness will allow her to become one of the mosque *shabab*.

"No *discussions* in the mosque," Alia continues, taking a bite of the pasta and grimacing. "This is disgusting." She sets the fork down. "No arguments about politics and philosophy."

All Mustafa's life, Alia has been the one closest to him. Atef might be his best friend, the *shabab* his brethren, but he always confided in Alia. They told each other everything, admitting to shoplifting and youthful romances and darker things, such as Mustafa's hatred of his father.

But this he cannot tell her, the kinship he feels in the mosque; this churning of something ancestral and looming—but *what*? Revolution? War?—he cannot speak of.

"Those guys," he says now, casually, "they don't know their Camus from their Sartre." He meets her eyes. Alia breaks the tension first, turning toward the bowl of pears. When she speaks, her voice is tight.

"You want your secrets, Mustafa? You and Atef? Keep them." She moves her hand as though swatting a mosquito. "Anyway, it's all smoke and gossip with you men." Her tone is supercilious. She takes out two pears and begins to peel them.

He is ashamed by the wave of relief.

They throw the pasta out, eat the pears hollowed and dolloped with jam. They talk of the weather, Atef's new job at the university. They swap stories about their mother's recent phone calls, her perpetual worry for their futures. Before she leaves, Alia kisses Mustafa's cheek.

"Enjoy the gossip," she teases. The argument's temporarily forgotten.

Alone, Mustafa rinses the dishes beneath running water. "We have two choices," he says. "Abandon our cause or pledge to it." He likes how the words roll off his tongue, tries raising his voice. "Or pledge to it!"

As if cued, the muezzin begins outside the windows. The echoing tones remind him of the mosque and Atef, whom he is meeting—Mustafa glances at his watch, the face covered in soapsuds—in an hour.

Despite his nerves, he thrills at the thought of the gathering. He leaves the meetings feeling moored, centered, as though someone has finally found the matchstick of his faith and touched fire to it.

Not *that* kind of faith, though Mustafa has a flighty belief in Allah, an avowal that he recognizes in more honest moments as tactical. If there is ever a sweeping of believers into one room and the rest into the other, he doesn't want to be on the wrong side of the door. But he loves the mosque for its dusty smell, for the carpet prickling his feet, for the predictable hum of the muezzin more than anything celestial.

No, when Imam Bakri addresses the men, his arms moving like an orchestra conductor's, when he talks about Allah's greatness and the coming war and the righteousness of land, Mustafa's spine tingles at only one word: *Palestine*.

Atef likes to talk of the overlap of Allah and land, how each is holy in its own way, that, in fact, when one says he loves his country, it is only because he loves his God.

But Mustafa has no patience for such talk, for self-analysis. He prefers the arguments at gatherings, the bickering between himself and Alia. He loves getting angry, that intoxicating rush of blood; his temper is well known—he rips up maps, walks out of dinner parties. He likes the impact of these acts, how people eye him alertly.

"Mustafa, break any teacups lately?" the neighborhood girls like to tease him, referring to one he'd shattered, at age twelve or thirteen, after a particularly fantastic argument with Alia. She'd begun to cry and he, recognizing the cheating inherent in the move—that female trick—had lobbed a teacup across the garden, where it smashed against a tree trunk. The fact that the incident took place in front of dozens of neighbors lent it a legendary air. It was told and retold so many times that some who joke about it are younger than Alia, had not been present or even born when it happened. Mustafa himself barely remembers it.

In his bedroom, Mustafa takes his undershirt off and sniffs it. Smoke and sweat. He chucks it onto the bed, opens his closet door.

"Brothers," he says aloud. "We must recognize the battle ahead." He moves in front of the mirror next to the armoire, repeats the line. He frowns. "We must recognize it will not be fought for us." His dark eyes stare back at him.

He knows he is handsome, although he does what he believes to be a stoic job of hiding this awareness, trying to appear tousled, attractive as an afterthought—the uncombed curls, rumpled shirts. *My honey boy*, his mother would say when he was a child, and the aunts would coo. *Those eyes. That hair*. And once, overheard while playing, a murmur from a neighbor: *A pity, when the boy gets the beauty instead of the girls*. Even as a boy, he understood there was something of an imbalance—Alia's gangly body and Widad's plumpness, both sisters' crooked noses and high foreheads. That he had gotten something not rightfully his.

Six o'clock. Two ties have been discarded; he has settled on a gray shirt and slacks. Outside, the air is cool and pleasant. He is overwhelmed by a sudden desire to walk in the opposite direction, follow the twilight to Aya and her warm bed.

But it is Friday, the one night her family gathers in the hut after mosque, the night she takes her siblings into her mother's room and leads them in prayer. Although he has never seen this, he can picture it—Aya's calm voice, her face in the lamplight, the siblings reciting Qur'an under their breath. She can be hard sometimes, even during lovemaking. But he likes to think of her in moments of softness.

• • •

His mother worries, he knows, about some predilection keeping him from marrying. Some part of her would be glad—or at least relieved—to hear her son has known the bodies of a dozen women, that he is a *man* in that sense.

The girls themselves are far-flung, assorted: Amman girls who studied in British universities, a couple of Europeans working with the refugee camps, even the pretty girls that fill the pool hall with their *oud* perfume and smoke on Saturdays. Whispering incredible, filthy things into his ears, things that leave him both shuttered and pining. *You got twenty? You know what I'd let you do?* He always felt removed with the girls, as though his body were a detached animal, clawing while he looked on.

Aya is different. She lives near the Nabulsi outskirts, where refugee camps litter the land. Her hut is old; damp clothing hangs from wires around the windows. The people in nearby huts work with their hands, the men in farming and carpentry, the women seamstresses and bakers. None of them are Nabulsi. They have come over the past two decades from villages, the ones soldiers set fire to or sowed with salt. They came from cities like Haifa and Nazareth. Their villages are lost, the names already eroded, replaced with new, Hebrew ones.

Mustafa first came to the neighborhood after an imam asked for help distributing resistance posters. The imam told him of a printing shop near the foothills.

The store reeked of paper pulp and ink. Aya worked in the shop, unrolling the reams of paper, capping bottles of ink. She was polite to Mustafa and Atef whenever they entered, always inclining her head when Mustafa caught her eye. She rarely spoke, but something about her infected him—he thought of her incessantly, her half smile, her fingernails darkened from ink.

Their courtship was a simple one, Mustafa returning to the store alone several times, asking her to print various photographs and flyers. Once, he brought a creased photograph of his father's—a view of the sea, a print from their old house in Jaffa—and asked her to copy it for him.

"The sea will be blurry," she'd said, frowning. She leaned over the counter, her fingertips flat against the photograph.

"You have the most beautiful hands," he replied, touching her wrist.

He'd known girls like Aya, poor girls who lived by different standards than his female friends and relatives. These girls had their faith, but their lives were hard and bitter and full of death. The ones that weren't married by their early twenties had a recklessness about them, giving their bodies with abandon. They hadn't been raised on European summers and dinner parties; they had removed shrapnel from their brothers' legs, had washed their sisters after rape. There was no chamber for love in their bodies, and they appreciated Mustafa's banter.

But it is another world with Aya, the only time he has lost his footing, as if suddenly darkness has fallen and he has only his fingers, his breath, to guide him.

AYA IS DEPENDABLE. He always sees her near dusk, as the call for prayer is beginning around them. Rather than making their trysts feel illicit, this seems to sanction them. She invariably smiles upon spotting him and then turns, leading him to the hut where she lives with six younger siblings and a bedridden mother. He has only heard the mother coughing, never met her. At the hut, he waits outside the back door, Aya entering first and making sure the children are playing before gesturing for him to follow—*Quiet*, *quiet*, she mouths—up the stairs to her room. No one ever comes up there, and he understands that this is all Aya has in the world: those walls, those floor tiles.

Even the room is loyal; always the same narrow bed, the armoire, the cracked mirror. Always the same clean lemony scent, the soap with which she washes everything, even her hair. The same Russian dolls on the tabletop, the same empty vase. Their lovemaking is precise, anticipated—Mustafa first sitting on the edge of the bed and, as though signaled, Aya beginning to remove her clothes.

She never does it coyly. She takes off each piece of clothing carefully, pausing to fold the dress and roll up the stockings, even tuck one brassiere cup into the other. And she never looks at him, standing instead in profile, so that he sees her nakedness in halves—one bare leg, one breast, one shoulder. She has the body of an Egyptian film star, none of that tiny-waisted, long-legged nonsense the wealthier girls obsess over. Aya's is voluptuous flesh, heavy-breasted, a roll of fat above her hips. Only when she is finished does Mustafa rise and kiss her neck, then her shoulder, finally her mouth. He removes his own clothes haphazardly and afterward must squint in the dark for his underwear, shirt, socks.

He wonders sometimes what happens after he goes, leaving behind his hairs and scent on her sheets. Whenever he thinks of this, he can dredge up only a single image, like a photograph: Aya getting ready for bed, smoothing down the length of the mattress where his body had been, as though some warmth remains. The image is cheerless, and he puts it away instantly.

Several weeks ago, they finally spoke of it. Aya waited until they'd finished making love. He'd noticed her furrowing her brow during it, a distraction about her. For long minutes afterward, they fell into the pattern of their bodies—Mustafa stretching and lighting a cigarette, Aya settling back against the pillow with her eyes shut.

He thought she'd fallen asleep and started when she spoke, her voice low.

"Someone has asked to marry me."

The pinch in his stomach surprised him. The smoke in his mouth turned sour. He exhaled quickly, wanting to rid himself of the taste.

"Everyone says I should accept."

Another woman might've said such a line coquettishly, with the undertones of a challenge, but Aya spoke simply. Somewhere in the house there was a crash and then laughter. The children had broken something.

"Who is he?" Mustafa asked.

"It doesn't matter." She kept her eyes shut. In the dimness, he could make out the faint wings of her eyebrows lifting. "A neighborhood boy. The son of one of my father's old friends. He wants a wife, children. He'd take care of my sisters and brothers. My mother."

"I can give you money."

"And what would you be giving me money for?" Her voice turned steely. It is their oldest fight, Mustafa trying to leave money—tucked beneath the pillow, inside the Russian dolls—Aya always refusing. Mustafa considered revisiting the arguments, the money left to him by his father, the sheer surfeit of it.

Instead he asked, "Will you marry him?" In the darkness, he couldn't make out the details of her features—the dimple in her chin, each curl. But he knew them intimately. Better than anyone else's face, it startled him to realize.

There was the sound of exhaling.

"No," she said distinctly. Mustafa's relief steadied him. He watched her push her hair back, a rasp against the pillow that he found arousing.

"Why not?"

She sat up, pulling her knees to her chest. Her expression was inscrutable. She spoke the way one might to a dimwitted child.

"Because I would never be able to love him."

The unsaid crowded them in the small room. It was the first time either of them had spoken that word aloud. It seemed to signal something for Aya. The rest—the implication that she couldn't love him because that love, finite, was already elsewhere—she kept silent, gathered with them in the dark.

BUT *WHY NOT*? The question sometimes jars Mustafa awake. It has even been asked directly by Atef, the only person who knows about Aya.

"She's good," Atef said to him once. "Others, they'll see that. They'll look past the rest."

The rest being the hut, the coughing mother, the litter of siblings, Aya's own pliant body bucking under his. His mother's horrified expression at her son marrying beneath him; Alia's perplexity at his choice. The aunts and neighbors would talk for years. Even the men at the mosque, most of them educated and well off, would be taken aback; for all their talk of solidarity with the poor, they are repelled by them.

"They won't," Mustafa replied, his tone signaling an end to the conversation.

MUSTAFA WALKS TOWARD the mosque, the air sobering. He is late for Atef, and his body vibrates with that familiar urge from earlier, to turn and walk in the opposite direction of the mosque, to plead illness or even cowardice.

In these moments, he remembers his mother. Her face in the courtroom years ago. His promise at her feet: *Never, never*. He knows she would never believe that he and Atef did stop for a long time, avoiding the politics and the mosque and spending their evenings together, alone, in the garden at night. They spoke about the future, Palestine, their own fears. But they stayed away from the other talk.

It had been an exercise in futility. Like asking two men living near the sea never to touch the water. The mosque, its thrum of male conversation, the way those walls seemed to palpitate with life and ferocity—what other home was there for two fatherless men?

"We're sitting here like *boys*," Atef once said in a rare outburst. He gestured at the night sky, the garden around them. "While outside, things are happening. The world is *happening*."

Mustafa understood. Every day he woke feeling like he might surge, like he wore his skin too tightly. Every newspaper was splashed with faces of the martyred.

When they returned to the gatherings, the men greeted them like long-lost warriors. Their spell in prison, brief though it was, lent them an air of authenticity. Just like that, they had it back: the sermons, the dust motes swirling during noon prayer, the laughter and fury of the men at evening gatherings. And, of course, Imam Bakri.

• • •

The man is younger than the other imams, in his early forties. While the other imams are aloof, retiring to the offices after prayers, spending their time with one another, Imam Bakri will gather in the courtyard with the congregation, chatting with the men. Now and then, he even swipes a cigarette from them.

"Imam Bakri, Allah is watching," the men tease him and he grins back.

"Allah knows how sweet tobacco is." He is a stocky man with dancing eyes, and he has a gift—one that Mustafa recognizes in himself, though it's a tenth of the imam's—of making the person he is speaking to feel bathed in light.

Rumors coursed through the mosque. The imam was imprisoned for a long time, some said, and was in Nablus to flee some darkly heroic charges. He was a Marxist, others countered, a fighter cloaked in imam's robes. Some—though they were quickly shushed—even hinted that he was an Israeli spy or informant.

His lectures were electrifying.

He spoke of politics, of land lost. "We are pawns in a sick and depraved game," he liked to say. "We can either play or overturn the chessboard."

Mustafa became smitten. The man was awfully magnetic, and more than anything Mustafa wanted to be found, wanted the imam to focus on his face among the sea of congregants and recognize something there.

"He's brilliant," Mustafa told Aya once. "You should hear the things he says. It's like a fever goes through the room. I need to talk to him."

Aya seemed unimpressed.

"Nothing good comes from those sorts of men," she said. "They lure and lure and if you find yourself next to them, what does it mean? That you've got a hook in your lip."

No matter. He felt starved for the imam's attention. For months, he yearned to share a cigarette with him. He rehearsed what he would say, practicing different tactics, from contrarian to sycophant.

I think this country is sinking as well.

We are its only hope.

But doesn't retaliation make it worse?

We need a new approach.

Mustafa fantasized about catastrophes—an earthquake, an assassination—bringing them together, him stuck in the imam's office. Or, better yet, Imam Bakri making an urgent request, perhaps needing an accomplice or somewhere to hide out, and Mustafa coming through, humbly refusing to accept thanks for his help.

In the end, it was merely a rainstorm in August. Mustafa was walking home from work at the school when the clouds bricked over. Rain began to fall. He stopped at the mosque to wait.

Entering, he found it empty, in those lost hours between prayers, the distant sound of a fan whirring. Just as he was wondering why he'd never thought to come at this time, when no one was around, there were footsteps and Imam Bakri appeared, carrying a cup of tea.

Catching sight of Mustafa, he smiled and shrugged, as though it were expected, as though he'd been waiting for months for Mustafa to show up dripping wet. He bobbed the teacup toward him as he spoke. "I'll make one for you."

His office was plain with dark green carpet, nothing hanging on the walls. They sat across from each other, a desk between them. The imam stirred his tea, the metal clinking against porcelain. "My *teta* used to say *maramiyeh* was the earth's cure for everything. Headache, diarrhea." He looked at Mustafa with a quizzical smile. "Even heartbreak."

Mustafa felt driven to honesty. "It's hard for me to sleep," he heard himself saying. "It's like I become louder. I start thinking and it becomes impossible to stop."

The imam nodded. "*Maramiyeh* is good for that as well. Helps quiet the mind."

The men sat in silence, listening to the rain outside. Mustafa grasped for something to say, some glittering insight.

"Are you from Nablus?" he asked.

"My family is from Haifa."

Another silence. Thunder crashed outside. The imam sipped the tea. Mustafa began to notice a faint, animal smell in the room. It turned his stomach.

"From the sea," Mustafa said absent-mindedly.

"From the sea!" the imam cried out. He looked impressed with Mustafa. "Yes, yes. From the sea." It occurred to Mustafa that the imam, at least a decade older than him, must have clear memories of the city he left behind.

"Is it very beautiful?"

Finally—the right question. Imam Bakri's face crinkled into a smile. He leaned forward.

"Beautiful? Beautiful?" He laughed kindly. "In a way that breaks your heart." He took a breath. "My father, my grandfather, his grandfather, his grandfather's grandfather, they were fishermen. They knew the sea as intimately as they knew their children or their own bodies. Every morning they woke before daybreak. The sky would still be dark, and they'd walk barefoot to the water." The imam's voice was reverential. "I'd go with them, as a boy. I knew I wanted that more than anything in the world. That life. Every boy should be lucky enough to have a father that he admires. That he wants to imitate."

Mustafa swallowed the bitterness that rose in his throat. He thought of the wasted body shriveled beneath sheets. What legacy had his father left him? But the imam kept speaking. Mustafa shook his head to clear it.

"They whispered to the fish," the imam continued. "They spoke prayers before throwing fishhooks into the water. The way they'd throw the lines, it was the most graceful thing you've ever seen. And the fish swam to them; I swear they did. They swam like they were grateful. They gave their bodies as though they knew it was sustenance. And my father would always kneel afterward, to the bucket of fish, some of the tails still twitching, and he would thank Allah and thank the fish."

Abruptly, Imam Bakri stopped talking. He eyed Mustafa with a hint of wariness.

"And then?" Mustafa asked. He felt like he was stepping off a cliff, in glorious free fall.

The imam shifted in his chair. He fiddled with the teabag.

"I'll tell you a story," the imam said.

There was a boy, with a mother and a father and a sister. They lived by the sea. The sea was like another member of the household, a recalcitrant child at times, a soothing aunt at others. She crooned them awake; she crooned them to sleep. Everywhere, there was the smell of salt.

The boy's sister was beautiful. Everyone said so. She had golden hair and fair skin, eyes the color of cinnamon bark. And kind as well, baking almond cakes for the family on Fridays so the smell of sugar filled their little house. The father loved the cakes, would pop them whole in his mouth. Every morning the boy's father brought home fish and the mother filleted them. The boy loved watching her in the kitchen, her fingers slitting the fish bodies, removing the bones in one long string like jewelry.

April. The family locked their doors as gunfire blared around them. Many of the neighbors packed suitcases. The boy's father swore he wouldn't leave, that they would stay by the sea. The father wasn't one of those angry men who carried flags and broke glass, and he decided that even with the army, the new country, they would stay. They would stay.

For a while it worked. The electricity was cut. The neighbors left. The news reports said everything was lost. Meanwhile, the boy and his family ate fish and drank stale water. They were waiting, the father said, for everything to settle down.

May. The soldiers came. They knocked on the doors of houses where Arabs lived. They knocked on the door of the boy's home, and when the father opened it, four soldiers came in. Only one spoke, the biggest one. The soldier said the house was built illegally. He used words like *deed* and *eviction*. The father remained polite. He told the soldier he didn't know where the deed was; the house had belonged to them for generations. The soldier began to yell at the father, his face turning red, spittle dotting his lips. The boy and his mother began to cry, but the sister stepped forward. She told the soldiers to sit, asked if they wanted tea. She told the biggest soldier there was no need to shout. They would get him the deed.

The big soldier, he looked at the daughter for a long time. He spoke to the other men. The boy didn't understand the language, but all the soldiers left. The family laughed in relief. *You see*, the sister scolded them, *everyone responds to kindness*. They teased her then, the golden-haired girl who'd tamed the soldier, but they all slept smiling.

Later that night, there was a crash. The four soldiers had come back. They broke the windows in the living room, made the family stand in their pajamas. The biggest soldier shone a flashlight in their faces and the family squinted. The boy found that he couldn't swallow because his tongue was suddenly sandpaper. One of the soldiers held a rifle to the boy's throat. The other held one to the father's throat. The third yanked the mother to the couch and told her if she rose, the same would be done to her.

Of course they all yelled. They all wept for the biggest soldier to stop. The boy tried to punch the soldier and was beaten. The father screamed. After a while, there was nothing for them to do but turn away, cry at the sister's naked body, the soldier against her. The mother howled for Allah. At first the sister whimpered. Out of the corner of his eye, the boy could see her legs twitch. The awful paleness of her thighs. He prayed she was dead. But when the soldier finished, she was silent, her eyes unblinking on the ceiling. She didn't bother to pull down her nightgown. There was blood on her legs.

The family left two days later. They moved to the hills, following the other Arabs, taking their clothes and silver in bags. As they left the little house, the sea didn't crash or froth to the shore. It just came, noiselessly, and went.

The office was silent. Mustafa felt drowsy from the heat and rain. He ached for his house, for Alia and Atef, to smoke cigarettes in the garden and joke. To not have heard this story.

Across the table, Imam Bakri looked lost in thought. He spoke. "The father salted everything after that. Even his water. He would cry out in his sleep for the sea." The imam took a long breath. "He missed the fish," he said simply. "When he died, he was buried beneath the hills he hated, far from the sea."

"What happened to his family?"

The imam looked Mustafa square in the eye. "The daughter—" He swallowed. "Some say she lost her mind. She stopped talking, never married."

"And the son?" Mustafa asked, though he knew.

The imam lifted the teacup to his lips. "The son found Allah."

This time the silence felt endless.

"I try not to remember him like that," the imam finally said. He narrowed his eyes. "My father. Not as that broken husk of a man, chewed up and spat out by the occupation, making a meager life of the remains. Unable to protect his daughter. Watching the soldiers . . . do the things they did."

Something clicked within Mustafa: the imam held the key to *something*. The imam would be the one to change it—everything—for him. In that instant, Mustafa realized just how unhappy he was. How much like a pauper he'd always felt, peering inside a window, watching life carry on while he remained apart, separated by glass. From Alia and Atef, from Aya. He suddenly understood his boredom, the way hours seemed to stretch unbearably in front of him, that, yes, yes, it was all bullshit. The waiting, the talking, the cigarettes, the coffee. What were they *doing?* The thought shook him with its violence. Sitting around while the years piled up, spending his father's money and waiting. Waiting. While their land was gobbled up.

"I like to imagine my father died before that. Before we went to Jerusalem. That he died from an enormous wave taking him while he knelt in front of a fish." The imam's eyes flashed. "They've even taken away our deaths. They've robbed us even of the dignity of death." The imam gestured outside with a jut of his chin. "And our men? They dance to American music and kiss girls in the pool hall. They tell themselves that Palestine is this"—here he waved a hand dismissively—"only this, only the crumbs we've been given."

A peculiar sensation skittered through Mustafa. His limbs tingled. That thing he'd read about in books: the moment when the world seems to sharpen, when colors and objects become vibrant, in focus. He could smell the torched streets, could see the young woman naked and bleeding. The glint of fish scales in the early light.

Finally, he cleared his throat and looked down at his tea. It was cold, an ugly color.

"I want to help," he said.

Mustafa walks toward the marketplace lights. The temperature is still dropping, cool air raising the hairs on his forearms. Alia was right. Clouds are gathering in the evening sky. It is going to rain.

At the marketplace, before the strip of coffee shops and restaurants, there is a trio of ash trees. Atef is already there, leaning against the trunk of the largest tree, a cigarette between his fingers. He takes a drag and catches sight of Mustafa; his bearded face breaks into a smile.

"Abu Tafi," he calls out, smoke trailing as he speaks. It is Mustafa's nickname, earned from a spill during football. Despite Atef's smile, Mustafa can see tension written upon his friend's face; Atef is as nervous as he is.

"How are you feeling?" Atef looks concerned. Atef and Mustafa's meetings before Mustafa speaks at the mosque have increasingly taken on the quality of coaching sessions, Atef treating his friend as though he were some mercurial prodigy. It is a dividing feeling; part of him wants to impress Atef, to make him slightly—in the manner of close friends—jealous, the other part wants to roar with impatience and stalk off.

"Fine." The hours of nerves put an edge in his voice. Atef, always careful, lapses into silence. Past the entryway, men begin to mill into the mosque, and Mustafa squints to make out faces, blurry in the lamplight. Most are familiar: Samir the professor, Imad the engineer, Ahmad, Bashir. The *shabab;* the men that gather in his garden. A vendor sells fruit, his voice hawking his wares across the street.

"*Bateekh, bateekh!*"

Imam Bakri appears, and behind him a group of six or seven, talking among themselves as they climb the stairs into the mosque.

"Must be the Jerusalem men." Mustafa softens his voice, an apology for his earlier curtness. Atef nods.

"They look more *ajanib* than the *ajanib*," Atef replies. Apology accepted.

It is true. Mustafa had expected older men in *dishdashas*, traditional headscarfs, and keffiyehs. But these men are his age and dressed like Westerners, button-down shirts, jeans. A couple have longish hair curling over their ears. Imam Bakri stops at the domed entrance and says something; the Jerusalem men laugh as they walk inside.

Panic seizes Mustafa.

"I can't do this." His voice cracks.

Atef furrows his brow, concerned. "You want to do a round?" It is their habit for years, walking the small pathway encircling the marketplace.

Mustafa shakes his head. He squats, leans against the tree trunk.

"You need water? You want something to drink?"

"I don't know what to say." Mustafa looks up at Atef. The other man's silhouette is outlined in the faint light. "This whole thing—" His lungs feel drained. He is panting. "I think it's become too much. I wanted to be part of it, but I don't think I can. Imam Bakri wants me to talk about fighting. About how things are for us, but I don't *know* how things are. I don't *know* what to say."

"You say what you need to."

"I'm afraid." The word startles him and he repeats it. "Afraid."

"You say what you need to."

Atef speaks with unusual violence. He swoops down next to him. Mustafa recoils.

"They need to hear us. Those Jerusalem men, they need to know we're with them. That we're not all talk. They're going to know they've got brothers out here. Kin."

A thought lights in Mustafa's mind as if ignited by flint. It reminds him of Aya speaking about the proposal. The realization that someone, one you think you know intimately, wholly, has a mystery within. Has thoughts and fears and loves that belong to him or her alone. He remembers it happening with Alia, and with his mother, when he was younger, remembers how alone he felt at the time. But now, watching Atef's angry face—his eyes begging and accusing him at the same moment—he realizes that with Atef, it is far worse.

Atef, son of a martyr. Atef, good man. Comrade. Atef, who'd listened to the same speeches, the same sermons. Atef, who had none of the charisma or ferocity of Mustafa.

I am the roar without the bite, Mustafa thinks unexpectedly. *The empty lion.*

"Listen." Atef speaks more quietly, as if intuiting Mustafa's thoughts. "I know it's hard. We could turn around right now. We could leave. There's always an easier way. Right?" The line filched from Imam Bakri's best sermon.

Friends, there is always an easier way.

Mustafa stands. He brushes his hands on his pants. He recognizes distantly that this moment will matter. "Let's go," he says to his best friend, who is still crouching in the dirt, and begins to walk.

The room in the mosque is overheated. The men sit in rows on the carpet, thirty or so of them, the smell of bare feet souring the air. The fluorescent lighting is harsh and two fans whir above, recycling the same tired air. Mustafa and Atef sit in the fourth row. The imam's sermon has already stretched over an hour and around them men look tired, as though willing themselves back to their cool homes.

Imam Bakri stops speaking, clears his throat. His eyes scan the congregation, and Mustafa sits up taller. The imam sees him, nods. Atef squeezes his arm and Mustafa rises. He makes his way to the front.

Mustafa is thinking of the curtains in Aya's room, a soft teal color that seems misplaced there. Something about those curtains has always saddened him, a color too bright for such a place. He pictures Aya in her bed. Asleep. Or, no—he edits the image—rising to the sound of her mother's cough, dampening a cloth to run over her face.

The Jerusalem men sit in the front row. Mustafa nods at them and one of the men, the long-haired one, nods back.

Aya wearing the creamy nightgown, the one he has glimpsed in her closet but never seen on her. They have never shared sleep. This strikes him as terribly sad, and he looks toward the ceiling.

The imam sits next to the Jerusalem men, mutters something to them. A man sneezes and several voices rise, blessing him.

A small part of him—which he already recognizes as a lost, former self—longs for his mother's garden, the sound of wind rustling the leaves. He takes a breath, his feet flat against the carpet. His right toe itches.

"Brothers," Mustafa says.

In his peripheral vision, he sees a glint, but when he turns to the window, it is gone. A storm. He can feel it in his bones, in the hairs of the back of his neck. *God forbid*, he hears in his mother's voice, that childhood prayer, and he repeats the words to himself. Another crinkle of light; this time he sees it flowering the sky. Seconds later, a rumble. The air is still. Something is coming. He can feel it in his teeth.

In the crowd, Atef moves his hand, a small gesture for action.

Mustafa swallows. Without removing his eyes from Atef—faith, strength, that *quiet*—he speaks.

"Brothers," he says again. "We must fight."

ALIA

Kuwait City
December 1967

Steam rises as water rushes from the faucet. Alia drops her nightgown on the bathroom floor. She kneels at the lip of the bathtub, grazes the water with her fingertip, winces. The water is always hot, too hot. Splotches of mold have begun to appear on the yellow curtain—Widad picked it out, saying the color would be cheery—even though they've lived in the house, Atef and she, less than four months.

Standing beneath the water, Alia keeps her eyes on the small window directly in front of the shower. Beyond it, several inches of Kuwait City are visible—the parking lot of their compound, the other villas, a swath of sidewalk. The relentlessly blue sky. She shampoos her hair then shuts her eyes and steps backward into the stream, the water plugging her ears.

For a moment she is submerged, without breath. She stands under the water until her lungs ache. Afterward, she soaps her body; the thick Kuwait *saboun* is coarse, drying her skin out. She rubs it in circles over her torso, remembering as she always does the white, silky jasmine soap she used in Nablus.

The steam trails her as she steps out of the tub. Atop the toilet is a cabinet, towels folded in neat stacks. She chooses a mint-colored one, her favorite, and wraps it tightly around herself.

"Oh God," she moans. She presses her palms against the sink, trying to quell the nausea.

She leaves behind wet footprints as she walks into the bedroom. The vanity is lined with dozens of bottles and tiny pots, perfumes and creams and makeup, Atef's lone contribution a bottle of cologne. From a porcelain box, Alia takes out several bobby pins, puts them between her teeth, and faces the mirror. Her hair curls damply over her breasts. She begins the intricate, familiar task of pinning it.

When she finishes, Alia lifts her chin and swivels. Wryly, she catches her own eye. She undoes the towel, forces her gaze over her naked body. The bare shoulders, the dark-tipped breasts. Lower still, to the unavoidable: her rounding belly.

The anxiety that arises is habitual, acidic. Alia shuts her eyes and inhales deeply. *Count to ten*, she commands herself. She holds her breath before releasing it with a faint *oof*.

SHE HAS TRIED to tell Atef a dozen times.

The baby was never meant to be a secret. When Alia felt the first ripples of nausea back in October, she thought her body was still recovering from the desert heat. Kuwait remained sweltering well into autumn, and the heat fogged her brain, left her feeling boneless.

Each time, she loses her nerve. The prospect of discussing it embarrasses her—to tell him is to allude to that night in August, when she found him in the bathtub. The only time since his return—not lovemaking so much as something desperate, a frenetic coupling, arching and clutching and biting. For a week after, her lips were swollen; a trail of bruises laddered deliciously on each thigh. Even she understood the sickness of such a crazed night, the nature of Atef's grief. In those early weeks, none of them could mention Mustafa's name without Atef weeping.

Now that months have passed—her body doing her the favor of remaining slender, only a slight plumping below her navel—now that he no longer sits limply in front of the television, no longer moves through the rooms of their new house as a sleepwalker might,

Alia remains too frightened to say anything that might unnerve him. What she knows about her husband, what she thought she knew about the man, has scattered like dandelion seeds beneath a child's breath since he returned from the war.

Alia's trip to Kuwait had been in response to a plea from her mother. Widad hasn't been well, her mother told her, with her myriad ailments and a recent flare-up of arthritis.

"She's always asking about you," Salma told her over the phone. "She asks why you never visit."

"I didn't realize the roads to Kuwait were one-way."

"Don't be uncharitable, Alia. She's struggling."

Finally, reluctantly, Alia agreed to go. Nablus was still flush with the last days of May, the morning cool as Mustafa drove to the airport in Jordan with Atef in the front, Alia sullen in the back seat.

"I hope you didn't pack any of those skirts. Widad says she doesn't even show her wrists," Mustafa remarked.

"How very decent of her," Alia snarled. The flight was an early one, and they'd all woken before sunrise. Her eyes felt dry, gritty.

"Alia," Atef said quietly. All week long their house had flickered with arguments about the trip.

Her sister was effectively a stranger, someone Alia had seen four or five times in the past decade, a woman who dressed in dowdy robes and murmured Qur'an verses when alarmed. The prospect of spending a month—a *month*—with her in Kuwait, a city she envisioned as bare and beige, rankled Alia.

In the airport she pouted. When Atef kissed her, she stuck her tongue in his mouth as punishment. He flinched, looking around, embarrassed at the public display.

"*Habibti*," he said, touching her shoulder. The airport was filled with milling people and the sounds of their farewells. Alia shrugged off his hand. She felt banished, sent off like a child, jealous of the two of them spending her favorite month in Nablus without her. She would be missing two weddings and the birth of a close friend's baby. "Sweetheart, it's only a few weeks. I love you."

"You too." She made her voice indifferent.

Mustafa whistled. "Lighten up."

"*You* shut up," she snapped, turning toward him. She lifted her suitcase and walked toward the gate.

"*Ya* Alia, that's the last thing you're going to say to your kind, handsome brother? Who drove you all the way to the airport? That's what you'll leave me with?" Mustafa called out laughingly as Alia stalked off, pretending not to hear.

From the beginning, the trip was a disaster. Alia used that word over and over in conversations with her mother, with Atef, with her friends; she would become ashamed of speaking so lightly.

"It's been a harsh spring," Widad had said in the Kuwait airport. But Alia was unprepared for the airlessness that hit her when they stepped outside. She felt ambushed.

Alia registered shock before heat. It was dazzling. She hadn't known the sun could blaze with such violence, that air could be so blistering that even inhaling seemed an Olympian task. So absolute was the heat that, in mere seconds, she couldn't recall a time without it.

She was unable to find relief anywhere. During that long month of June, she often dreamed of icy lakes, of walking into an enormous refrigerator the color of lilacs.

She busied herself with the task of cheering up her sister, getting settled into Widad and Ghazi's large but somber villa in a compound of expat Arab families, mostly professors and engineers and doctors. Ghazi himself is an engineer, working long hours at a firm in the city's center. Alia had met him twice before, once at her sister's wedding when she was very young and again five years ago when Ghazi and Widad visited Nablus. She liked him well enough; he was solicitous and careful around her sister. Sometimes he talked too much and there was always a faint odor emanating from him, like cabbage or stale water, but for the most part he struck her as dependable, benevolent.

Her days were usually spent with Widad, often shadowed by the Indian maid, Bambi. Alia took on the role of lively younger sister, encouraging Widad to eat plates of food or go on outings, but such a performance was not in her nature. After a week, her cheeks ached from smiling.

"Let's go to the market," she'd say brightly. And: "Let's visit your friends!"

Those trips seemed endless. Widad had a driver, a sprightly older Indian man named Ajit, and he dutifully chauffeured them to dress shops and other people's villas. They visited with Widad's friends, drank tasteless tea in parlors, the women a decade older than Alia. She was used to gatherings in Nablus, where women laughed and smoked and shared dirty jokes, shocking one another with confidences. But these visits were stuffy, the women speaking of silverware prices and the latest heat wave. Alia would go to the bathroom and roll her eyes at herself in the mirror. In the afternoons, they got sweets from a pastry shop near the compound; Widad loved them, and so Alia would eat as well, queasy from the sugar, the syrup too heavy in the heat. By the time they finally got home, Widad would be cheered, talking a little more and laughing, but Alia would feel drained, so bored she'd nearly kiss Ghazi with relief when she heard his key in the door.

Take her, she wanted to shout. It wasn't that Widad was unpleasant or spiteful. But she was so *droopy*. So sluggish and melancholy and resigned to her life, its tasks of folding sheets, overseeing Bambi's dusting, spending hours preparing dinner as she fretted over spices.

"Should we use cardamom?" she would ask Alia in the overheated kitchen. "Or cloves?" And at the dinner table: "I used yogurt instead of milk—is it too filmy?"

One afternoon Alia watched, exasperated, as Widad spent nearly two hours organizing the pantry. She couldn't comprehend it, this appetite for housework. Her sister was like a mirror of some alternative fate, rolling her husband's socks, scolding Bambi for oversalting the meat, wandering the rooms of her mausoleum-like villa.

Some evenings Alia spoke with Atef on the telephone. "I hate it here," she'd whisper like a hostage. "Everything smells like boiled meat. And the heat. Atef, it's like a furnace."

"Not much longer," he would say. "I miss you. We'll see you so soon." Gone was her anger at Mustafa, at the two of them for their alliance. She missed her bedroom, the sloping hills of Nablus, the sound of the men laughing over her burned meals. She couldn't wait for home.

ALIA'S RETURN to Nablus was planned for the first Tuesday in June. The final week, she was so excited, she willingly put up with Widad's chatter about cumin and starching cotton, even helped her cook *maqlouba*, dropping the slices of eggplant into sizzling pans. She packed her suitcase four days early, stacking gifts for her friends and brother and Atef between layers of clothing.

"You'll come back? Maybe for Eid?" Widad asked over dinner two nights before Alia's flight. She had made *shish taouk*, and the chicken was delicious.

"Why not? Maybe for another month," Alia agreed and was surprised to find that she meant it. Now that she was about to leave, everything—her sister, Ghazi, their cavernous villa—was cast in a kinder light. She had two helpings of dinner and fell asleep happy.

The next morning Alia decided to visit her favorite dressmaker. She'd gone to Umm Omar's store several times during the trip, Ajit driving her to the strip on Salamiyah Road littered with tailors, shoemakers, textile vendors from Bangladesh, Paris, even the Far East.

Umm Omar's shop was on the corner, a nondescript storefront belying the décor inside. Her husband, a soldier, had been blown up in Algeria years earlier, and touches of Africa adorned the store—bundles of rosemary and sage tied with satin ribbons, the skulls of tiny, unlucky creatures on display, Moroccan carpets nailed to the walls. Bright ottomans were scattered throughout, the dressing area shielded by browning palm leaves. Algerian music crooned from the tape recorder near the cash register. Every week Umm Omar lined the racks with new dresses, pushing the others farther back. Unlikely taffeta peeped from beneath emerald silk; all the clothes smelled of Bedouin incense. It was, to Alia, the most wonderful, exotic place she'd ever been. In the monochrome of Kuwait, the store was a dash of vivacity.

Umm Omar herself was wizened, her hair covered in a headscarf though the shop received only women. Her Arabic was harsh, gruffness sanding the words.

"You're too tall for that," she'd bark whenever Alia's fingers lingered over a particularly dainty frock. "You have long bones, ostrich bones; you must wear something that suits them." Umm Omar always chose unfussy dresses with simple necklines, much to the disappointment of Alia, whose eyes snagged on the sequined pieces, the dresses with green and pink tassels.

That morning Alia made for a magenta dress, the fabric mouthwateringly shiny. Umm Omar clicked her tongue and pushed Alia out of the way, selected instead a long gray gown. The silk was unadorned, the only decoration a bow at the center of the neckline. Defiantly, Alia also took the magenta dress to the changing area. The magenta stuck to her hips, the color unflattering against her skin. The gray made her look like a starlet.

"You have a fine collarbone," Umm Omar said when Alia emerged from the dressing room. It was the same remark she made every time. The older woman turned on the small television propped behind the cash register. Every few moments the screen would flatline into static, prompting Umm Omar to swear and swat it until the antennas quivered.

Alia admired herself in the mirror. It was ancient, the yellowed glass making her skin appear unearthly. The dress flared near the ankles, and, after a glance in Umm Omar's direction, Alia did a twirl. She felt bold, like a foreigner in a film. She smiled at her reflection.

In that instant, Umm Omar let out a low, hissing sound.

"Those bastards. Those sons of dogs, *they've done it.*" In her distress, Umm Omar knocked her stool over as she jumped to her feet. She waved her arms around.

"What? What?" Alia rushed over, careful not to snag the dress on the counter. Explosions of light filled the screen, the camera shaking as it followed the arc of a swooping plane. The plane released something from its belly, something that ignited in the air. "What?" Alia stared dumbly at the images.

Umm Omar practically leaped, spittle flying as she spoke. "The Israelis! They've done it. *They've done it.* Tiptoeing like cowards, sneaking around at dawn. They've snuck up on our boys. They're in Sinai."

"Not Palestine." The relief shook Alia's voice.

"Not yet! But we're prepared, you can bet on that! Palestine, Jordan, Iraq. We've been waiting for this. They don't know what they've done, those motherless bastards. They don't know what they've started!" Umm Omar's eyes sparkled. She turned to Alia kindly. "Go on, dear. Let me wrap that up for you. Gray's a good color on you."

Alia meant to protest, the silk suddenly unpleasant against her skin. Instead she walked to the changing room, numbly removed the dress. Her stomach was slick with sweat. She hungered for her bedroom in Nablus, the breeze lifting curtains.

Umm Omar insisted on giving Alia the dress. She called it an early victory gift. Alia watched in a daze as Umm Omar wrapped the silk in brown paper. The older woman circled a ribbon around the package, looped it with a flourish.

When Alia stepped onto the pavement, she didn't recognize the dark sedan, Ajit's familiar figure behind the wheel. For several moments, she was stunned by heat, brightness, bewilderment. The sun blazed above her head. It was still early.

Alia walks naked to the closet. Her hair is heavy atop her head as she flips through dresses and skirts on cedar hangers in the armoire. They are nearly all new, bought in the past few months.

The party had been Alia's idea. It would be good for them all to celebrate the new year.

"We'll invite the Shafics and Mourads and Qiblawis," she told Atef, referring to the families she'd met in the weeks before Atef's arrival. "They were kind to me, during those days."

"Whatever you like," Atef said, and it was this very response, monotonous and listless, that spurred on her planning.

The true reason had nothing to do repaying the kindness of these dull people, most of whom worked with Ghazi, the wives friends with Widad. She couldn't bear the thought of spending the new year as they did most of their nights, in front of the television as politicians roared their dissatisfaction. Or, worse, of trudging through feigned festivities at Widad's house, the four of them forcing conversation and exclaiming over Widad's pineapple cake, as they'd recently done for Alia's birthday. After the birthday song was sung, the slices doled out, Alia fled to the bathroom, where she stuffed a towel against her mouth to muffle sobs. Their straggly, moping foursome; this awful country; pretending to be happy over saccharine cake—it was something to mourn over.

No, better to have people, lots and lots of people filling the rooms of their house, crowding the yard. Better to have voices and laughter, colorful dresses and flashy jewelry, a clatter to conceal the emptiness.

Alia enters the kitchen to find Widad seated at the table, shaggy bunches of mint in front of her.

A bowl brims with water at her side. She lifts a sprig of mint, plucks the leaves, and drops them into the bowl. Leaves skim the water, darkening to an emerald once submerged.

"Good morning," Alia says. Widad has removed her veil, and sunlight from the kitchen windows falls around her, bringing out the amber in her hair.

"I came early. I hope you don't mind. There's so much to do."

"No, it's fine," says Alia, joining her at the table. In the past few months, their companionship has softened, settled into familiarity.

"Want a cup?" Widad nods toward the stove, the new *ibrik* on a burner. The smell of coffee is thick in the air. Alia scorched the old one the first week here; even after the *ibrik* had been scrubbed and soaked in salt, the bottom remained charred.

The smell turns Alia's stomach, and she averts her eyes. "Maybe later."

In the kitchen alcove, Bambi sits with Priya, the maid Widad arranged for Alia months ago. The two women speak their trilling language with each other, a mountain of potatoes, carrots, parsley, and beans on the table between them. Their heads are ducked over it as they chop the vegetables.

"Hello," Alia says to them, and they return the greeting.

"Madame," Priya says in her slow English. "Sir call earlier. I tell him you in shower. He call back later."

"Mmm." Alia busies herself with the radio on the counter. "Thank you." Her mind snarls, as it does whenever it's confronted with her husband these days. The radio knobs are fat and thick beneath her fingers as she tunes.

"Which dress are you wearing tonight?" Widad asks.

"Oh." Alia captures the tinkling of a news station's melody. "The black one," she says. She twists the volume knob. The news music halts, cut by the gloomy tones of a woman's singing.

"Oum Kalthoum." This song is one of the Naksa songs that have cropped up in recent months, sorrowful violins and intonations lamenting the losses of the war. The defeat. Every day on every channel the songs play, haunting the living rooms, the marketplaces, even the schools, all over Kuwait and, Alia knows, other Arab cities. Grieving the death of men, all the land lost, but mostly the defeat itself, the hot, mushrooming shame of it. These tunes are more familiar to Alia than any childhood lullaby now, these songs that seems to skulk everywhere.

Both sisters make a sound at the same instant, a grunt of frustration. Alia turns to Widad, sees her sister's eyes uncharacteristically mischievous.

"Turn it off. For the love of Allah," Widad says.

Alia laughs, surprised. She adopts the droning voice of the newscasters and politicians on the television over the past months.

"Brothers, sisters. This is a period of mourning. Wear your black. Tell your children to grieve." Aping solemnity, Alia sings along with the chorus tunelessly. "Ahhh-uhhh."

"Alia!" Laughter rocks Widad, shocked but delighted. She shakes her head as Alia splays her fingers, tilting her head as she shouts along to the song. Priya and Bambi giggle. Widad lifts her hands from the mint leaves, covers her face. "Turn it off," she says, gasping. "Turn it off."

Satisfied, Alia turns the volume down. She sits across from Widad, picks a bunch of mint. Through lowered lashes, she glances across the table, warmed by the smile on her sister's face, the unexpected expression of pleasure.

"The meat needs another hour or so." Widad squints at the clock above her head. The mint is washed and dried, the vegetables cut into trim squares. "That should give us plenty of time to add the vegetables." She turns to Priya and Bambi. "Is the food prepared for your party?"

"Yes, madame," Bambi says.

The second party was Widad's idea, a gathering for the maids and drivers of the guests, held in the shack—dubbed the Little House—near the villa where Priya slept. Priya and Bambi seem excited, all week long talking about what music to play and braiding bits of tinsel for decoration. Watching them, Alia feels ashamed of her unhappiness.

"Do you have everything you need?" she asks them now in English. She relishes speaking it, the language lost to her since school days. Back then, it was her favorite subject, those melodic, liquid vowels. "Do you need more juice or sweets?"

"No, madame," Bambi says.

"No, madame," Priya parrots. She is petite, barely a year older than Alia, who finds being so close in age to someone this cheery disconcerting.

"Did you say the Awadahs are coming?" Widad asks her sister.

"Yes, and the Khalils. The university dean."

"How wonderful," Widad says dreamily. "They're good people. I'm so happy Atef's meeting people at the university. Ghazi said he's doing really well."

"Yes." Alia stops, not wanting to be disloyal.

"It'll take time," Widad says. "For both of you."

An aphid hides between the mint leaves. Alia holds the wriggling body in her fingers, then crushes it into a tissue. When Atef accepted the professorship at the university, she'd been stunned. She'd thought Kuwait was a transition for them, a temporary sojourn.

"And now you're filling the house with friends," Widad continues. "Building a new life." She reaches across the table and squeezes Alia's hand. Her eyes are earnest. "After Nablus, after—" She pauses. "After Mustafa."

Alia ducks her head. "Perhaps." Her duplicity pounds in her ears. She has told Widad nothing of her pregnancy and—worse—nothing of the idea that has taken hold in her mind, growing lush with time, intoxicating.

AMMAN. To her mother, her aunts, to the cousins and childhood friends who moved there from Nablus after the war. The idea had struck her like rainfall, simple and clear: They should move to Amman.

Instead of staying in Kuwait's wasteland, the endless afternoons of television and heat, let them go to Amman, the coffee shops and vendors hawking fruit, neighborhoods filled with old friends. Yes, everyone was distraught, mourning the houses and cities they'd left behind, the men beneath the soil. Shouldn't they mourn together? Palestine has vanished for them—this knowledge crept up on Alia slowly, a new death every morning: Mustafa gone, Nablus gone—

but they can find the ashes in Amman, collect them to build another life.

The pregnancy is further motive. Amman has knotted like a vine in Alia's mind, her conviction that, if they go, something can be saved. She and Atef could shed the snakeskin of this year, begin to laugh again, lament and heal with their friends in Amman. They could start their family there, live in a house near her mother; *everything could be all right.* She knows in her bones that if she could show Atef all this, could show him the image in her mind—their salvaged life—he would see it and understand. He would go.

Alia watched the war on the television in Widad and Ghazi's living room. Unlike Umm Omar's, their television was new, the screen slick and orb-like. Four knobs adorned the right side, the largest for sound. Ghazi set the volume, twisting it up high, and when the image quivered with static, he was the one who rose heavily from his armchair to fix it. Watching Ghazi swivel the antenna wands, it would occur to Alia that those fat hands had traversed her sister's naked body.

Widad busied herself during the news reports. She clanked her knitting needles against each other, rose abruptly for cups of tea. Irritation scraped Alia as her sister asked repeatedly whether anyone wanted dinner or fruit. Even when Widad finally sat, her back never touched the sofa cushions, her feet remained arched over the floor, as though she might spring up at any second. Alia sat still as a stone. Whatever biscuits or oranges Widad brought languished untouched beside her. Tension clamped her jaw, congealed her muscles. Every few hours she willed her fingers over the telephone, dialing the numbers of Atef, of Mustafa, listening to awful, endless ringing.

Only Ghazi spoke. He seemed excited by the war; there was an edge to his thrill, almost a satisfaction. Alia gathered from his commentary that he'd predicted such an outcome, that these sentiments were well worn.

"I've said it and said it, this was a long time coming. Nasser and his men walking around with their chests puffed out, thinking they're peacocks. Scattered men. What kind of leader promises victory with *scattered men?* An Arab republic. Ha! Look at this—some American money and here's Israel's shiny new toys. What do we have? Flags, songs, dreams. They're going to obliterate us." His enormous body trembled with the force of his words.

Fury rose in Alia's throat each time Ghazi spoke. Swallowing was a measured task. Alia had grown up with angry men—Mustafa, his schoolmates, her uncles, all crowding for protests swathed with Palestinian flags, shouting at gatherings late into the night.

And now war had come, snatches of it harvested in Widad and Ghazi's living room. But it was wrong, horribly wrong. The newscasters spoke of an Arab victory, but no crest of Arab military was approaching, no waving of the green, red, black, and white flags. Alia's packed suitcase remained in Widad's guest bedroom, upright, like an eager child. She would not be returning home. On the third day, tanks rolled into the Old City. Although none of them could have known it, Mustafa and Atef were arrested soon after, when the Israelis entered Nablus, during a sweep of young men affiliated with the mosque. As the fourth day came and went, the Sinai Peninsula fell to the wrong men. The tanks razing through Gaza, Jerusalem, the Golan Heights—even Nablus, even Nablus—and the jets screeching over the Mediterranean, they had not Arabic lettering on their sides but chalky six-tipped stars. *The Israelis were winning.* And for Alia, who had believed the Arabs would conquer, whose only concern was keeping the men she loved on the sidelines, the sweeping victory was inconceivable.

"It's gone. Palestine is gone. The *fools.* They saved nothing," Ghazi said on the sixth day as the sun rose to reveal bodies tossed in ditches. Alia listened dully now. When she dialed, the telephone lines still rang. By sunset that day, Alia no longer startled at the televised images of dropped bombs, the debris clouds swelling out into frothy edges, like something edible.

The same memory assaulted her while she watched the news reports:

When Alia was five or six, Mustafa found a chick in the schoolyard during a rainstorm. The creature was slick with rain, shivering. He fashioned a home from Salma's old hatbox, patiently shredding paper to line it while the chick warmed in his shoe near the radiator. Alia sat by her brother's side, both of them silent as he worked. Every few minutes she bent over the shoe, peering at the quivering bird. Her fingers itched to touch the matted feathers, but she restrained herself. It felt like an honor, sitting by her brave, handsome brother while wind battered the windows with rain.

The hatbox seemed to Alia resplendent, snug, with snowlike carpet and bits of lettuce Mustafa stole from the kitchen. Mustafa lifted the chick from his shoe, knelt beside Alia.

"Do you want to hold him?"

Alia nodded. Her throat caught, making it tricky to speak. She curved her hands, and Mustafa lowered the bird into them.

"Careful," he breathed.

The bird shivered violently, his heart palpitating beneath Alia's fingers. Tiny bead eyes, translucent beak. The claws dug pleasantly into Alia's palm. Pale yellow stood out in tufts, the downy feathers frizzing as they dried. Alia held her breath, forced herself still. It seemed that if she moved she would break him.

"You can pet him," Mustafa assured her. Alia looked up at her brother, her heart pounding. He nodded.

"It's okay, birdie," she said and stroked carefully, the skull solid beneath her forefinger. Mustafa smiled at her, his teeth straight and white and beautiful. Alia felt big, bigger than ever before, the chick's heartbeat calming in her palm.

THE BIRD, MUSTAFA, bombs, Atef, Nablus.

That almost-week jumbled everything as Alia sat before the television, images searing her hour after hour. Her mind raced. She was parched, but whatever she drank tasted sour. When Widad called them to dinner, Alia had to force her teeth over the meat, the spinach. When they returned to the living room, the images on the television seemed stolen from another time. The men's faces, brown, dirty, the features so alike, they could've been photocopied.

She kept her body still. It had never occurred to her before how similar they looked, the two men. To each other, and to the men in uniforms. Once they were broken down into parts, she could see how those parts could be ignored or hated—grimy faces, dark eyes, beards.

ON THE FIFTH day of the war, President Nasser's face was drawn and somber as he told Alia and the rest of the world it was over. The Arabs had lost. Reels of Israeli soldiers pointing their rifles at truckfuls of captured Arab soldiers played over and over. The prisoners held their hands up, looking childlike and absurd without their weapons, just sweaty men, the same men who had played war as children in neighborhoods just like Alia's. Then, as now, the captured didn't speak, kept their heads bowed; the victors ran around waving their guns, imaginary or real, heavenward, spraying celebratory bullets to the sky.

Widad peeled potatoes during Nasser's resignation speech and the reels of captures. After the images of grinning Israelis looped around for the fourth time, Ghazi rose and clicked off the television.

"Well," he said to the blackened screen, grimly. "Well."

Nobody said Mustafa's name, or Atef's. It was clear there were more capture sites, dozens, maybe hundreds more. And the dead bodies, the piles of corpses feasted on by flies, stacked in the desert—the camera had whizzed by them, Alia's eyes neither fast nor willing enough to scan for faces.

She sat in the yard for hours that evening. The June night was muggy and hot, but she didn't move. Above her head the sky was clear, stars like salt tumbled onto a tablecloth. She tried to count them but finally gave up.

ATEF HAD WARNED that no one would want to come to a party. *Everyone with Arab blood is mourning.* But the guests arrive with flowers and trays of sweets. Many of the women wear iridescent dresses, the men well-tailored suits. They kiss Alia's cheek and ask when Atef will arrive.

"Soon, soon," she says laughingly and prays it is true. She ushers them into the house, the living room with an archway leading into the dining room. Other guests are gathered inside, sitting on couches or standing around the table, plates balanced in their hands. Chicken and lamb are arranged on platters of jasmine rice, little burners beneath to keep them warm. Ghazi laughs in the corner with one of his engineer friends. Alia feels a brief envy toward her sister for her noisy, unaltered husband.

Throughout the house, Bambi and Priya have placed vases of roses and gardenias, giving the rooms a heady perfume. Shallow bowls of nuts and cherries cover the tables. Even the yard behind the dining room, normally desolate and untouched, has been swept. Through the large windows, Alia sees a constellation of chairs, candles dancing between them.

The house fills. Widad puts on a record, and some women begin to sway in the living room. It looks like a home, Alia thinks. She asks people if they want pomegranate juice, laughs at their stories. Yes, some of the men have gathered outside, where Alia knows they are discussing the war. But otherwise it feels as though she has stumbled into someone else's living room, where everyone is having a perfectly pleasant time.

At half past nine the doorbell rings, and Alia smiles at the group of guests she is speaking with.

"At last."

She pauses at the mirror in the foyer, finds her wild-haired reflection satisfying. Arranging her face in a half smile, she opens the door. Samer, Atef's coworker at the university, and Samer's American wife, Maryanne, beam at her from the doorstep. In the corner is a blur in the dark. Alia squints.

"Hello," she says in English.

"Look what we've brought you." Samer grins, holding out a vase with one hand and pulling at the blurred figure with the other.

"Oh, how beautiful, thank you," she says, taking the vase. Flowers spill from the edge, tangled in delicate nets of baby's breath. And: "You!" she says gratefully as the figure steps into the light.

"Your husband's quite the dedicated professor," Samer says. "We found him in his car still thumbing through books!" There is a pause while Atef glances at Alia, his eyes inscrutable.

"My little bibliophile," she says dully.

"You look beautiful, as always," Samer says, and Alia forces a smile.

"What a dress," Maryanne joins in, then tries for Arabic: "Like the moon!"

"Please." Atef holds an arm out, and the couple walk inside. He steps in himself and kisses Alia on her forehead.

"I'm sorry," he begins. "The thought of coming in . . . all these people—"

Alia shakes her head, lifts a hand to his cheek. The gesture feels illicit; they rarely touch these days. "I know."

At the archway, they stand watching the guests laugh and talk.

"They're having fun. Can you believe it, the lamb's almost finished."

"I see Majed's here," he says, nodding toward the young, hairy man laughing and snapping his fingers at the dancing women. He is from the university, Jordanian, a bachelor.

Alia smiles. "I don't think there's a girl over thirteen he hasn't flirted with." Atef lets out a roar of laughter, like his old self.

"It's a wonderful party." He pulls her to him, and she instinctively places a hand on her belly. Soon.

"Wonderful," he repeats.

"Atef!" one of the men calls out.

"The host has finally arrived!"

"Come, Professor, the meat has gone cold."

Atef looks down at her questioningly, and she laughs.

"Go," she says, warmed by his pleasure, and watches him walk to the men.

• • •

Alia and Widad are dancing together. Their feet are bare, and the blue Persian rugs are soft beneath them. The other women dance around them, the air rippling with dozens of perfumes. The lights are dimmed, candles in silver candelabras casting shadows across the walls. The maids have cleared the dishes and trays, setting fruit and little cakes atop the dining-room table.

"That's plenty," Alia told them afterward. "Go enjoy your party."

The music is lusty and fast. Alia is dizzy with it. She twirls once, twice, then lifts her arms for Widad to do the same. Above the archway, the clock reads nearly eleven. In an hour, it will be a new year. The thought brings an unexpected lump in her throat, the sobering thought of Mustafa. She will become older than him. She will watch the world tumble into yet another year. Without him.

"*Ya habibi.*" Widad sings along, her face close to Alia's, close enough for Alia to see the lashes coated in mascara, the reddening from her eyebrow threading this morning. She looks younger, girlish, with her flushed cheeks and bare feet. Impulsively, Alia leans in and kisses her cheek.

Widad smiles, startled. "*Habibi inta,*" she sings even louder. Around her, the women laugh and clap.

You have your sister, Alia, her mother says on the telephone when they speak. *And your husband. You cannot forget them in your grief.*

"*Aywa,* Widad!" Majed weaves his way between the women, snapping his fingers and wiggling his bushy eyebrows. Widad blushes but continues singing and moving her arms back and forth.

Slowly, Alia stops swaying. Her arms drop to her sides. She steps out of the dancing circle, away from the living room. Her chest aches with want; it catches at her throat, dwarfs her.

She misses Mustafa. Like a city after a tsunami, the earth is altered without him, wrecked. They never found out how he had died, just that he had, somewhere in an Israeli prison. And yet she continues eating éclairs and gathering hairs from the shower drain. In the back of her mind, that terrible, treacherous voice, the one that possessed her while she watched the war on the television screen—*If one of them has to die, if I could pick*—a voice she hates. She clamps the heel of her palm against her rib cage as though to quiet it.

You are surrounded by the living, her mother says. *Housing one of them too*, Alia thinks. Her hand flutters over her belly and she wills movement. Anything. But it is just a hand atop silk. Last week at the doctor's office—the kindly man she has been seeing furtively—she listened to the heartbeat through a stethoscope. At four months, the doctor said, the eyelids are fused shut; sound cannot yet be heard. The thing—sightless and cloaked in fluid; does she feel her mother's grief? Does she drink it like soup?—sleeps, will not turn for weeks.

"God." She pants. She knows these moments well; the despair is a lake she must move across, water in her lungs. She thinks of Priya and Bambi, the maids and drivers dancing in the Little House, stirring pots of spiced stew. The thought of their happiness steels her, and she finds her shoes before moving quickly toward the yard.

She fumbles for a second with the sliding door, the bottom slots jamming. Through the screen door's mesh, Alia sees Atef sitting with the other men. Smoke from their cigarettes rises into the night. They talk animatedly but stop as the door opens, greet her.

"Alia!"

"The lady of the fortress!"

"Is Majed still making a fool of himself in there?"

Alia smiles and leans against the door frame. She feels a craving for men, familiar from girlhood, a need to sit with them and listen to their talk. Behind her, the music is loud, brassy.

"He certainly is. And all of you, still cowering out here?"

The men laugh appreciatively.

"She knows us too well."

"We are unfortunate men, Alia. We can't dance!"

"Nothing terrifies us like music."

Alia laughs. "And you?" She turns to her husband, his face relaxed in the candlelight. "Are you also afraid?"

Atef grins at her. "I'm the biggest coward of all."

His smile fills her with nostalgia. It is like seeing a ghost. Alia extends her arm to him, palm upturned. "Just one."

"You're a lucky man," one of the men says. "My wife wants me out here."

Atef stands. "I am lucky," he says softly, walking to Alia, his own hand out until his fingertips close over hers.

"Come dance," Alia says. "Those shoulders." She brushes his shoulder lightly. It is a tease, a reminder of their wedding day, when he'd jounced them to music.

Atef chuckles and brushes her forehead with his lips. "I'm a terrible dancer," he says. He takes a drag from the cigarette, smoke trailing as he speaks. "You go on." His fingers unlace from hers and he lowers his hand, grazing the dress over her hip, giving her a secretive smile.

"What romance!"

"Oh, the perils of young love," one man says.

"You were young once?" another man asks him.

Atef glances at the men and turns back to Alia. "You go on, *habibti.*"

Alia forces her lips upward. When she is back inside, the disappointment capsizes, suddenly, into anger. She strides through the house, pausing at the living-room archway. The women and Majed have made a *dirbakeh* circle, shoes—magenta, blue, silver—strewn by the couches, the faces flushed.

The kitchen is a mess, gloriously so, the kind of mess that implies something *happened.* Stacks of dishes, platters of uneaten rice, a large bowl of tabbouleh.

"For the love of God, someone put some Fairuz on," Alia hears Majed call out, then a bout of female laughter.

She picks up a dirty spoon and plops it into the rice, suddenly ravenous. She eats quickly over the sink, swept with an urge familiar to her these days, as though her body is a cavern to be filled.

"I always loved watching you eat."

Alia startles and the spoon falls on the counter. Grains of rice scatter. She turns to find Atef in the doorway, smiling sheepishly.

"From that first dinner, in your mother's garden," he continues, walking toward her slowly. "She'd served soup and *fassoulya.* You ate like you were going to battle."

Alia smiles, remembering. "I'd been with Nour all day, in the shops." Atef had worn a white shirt that evening, lending him a swarthy air. When she'd finished her mango juice, he'd poured her some more, rising to reach her glass. Being near him woke something reckless in her.

He comes to her now, kisses her once, twice, full on the lips. "I'm a fool," he says. "You still want to dance?"

Love rustles her. And gratitude, for this miracle of a man. The one who returned to her. She feels ashamed of that earlier voice. She kisses him back hard and turns to face the sink. Atef wraps his arms around her and pulls her against him. The counters and walls are beige. The window above the sink frames a view of the driveway, the sky, a film of dust clouding the glass.

"Darling."

Her eyes prickle, the window swimming.

"You look beautiful tonight."

They fall silent, listening to the music and laughter in the other room. *We're like castaways from a shipwreck*, Alia thinks. One of the glasses in the sink has red lipstick on the rim.

"It's like a circus in there." Atef's lips move against her hair. "Even Widad! Did you see that?"

Alia smiles and turns to him. "She looks so happy."

"I couldn't believe my eyes. Went back outside and told Ghazi he had to see his wife. It's amazing what a little music will do to a person."

"I miss him."

Alia hears her voice as if from a distance. The words hang like tiny detonators in the air.

Beneath her head, she feels Atef's chest rise and fall. There is a long silence. He holds her more tightly, his arms hurting her rib cage. Alia thinks absently of the baby, cramped between their two bodies.

"Atef," she begins tentatively. "In Amman—"

"We'll be happy here." Atef's voice breaks. He sounds desperate. "The people are kind; my work is good. We're near your sister and it's safe, no one will bother us here. It's a little bare, I know, and the heat can be hard, but after a few years we'll be settled. We can start a new life. In Amman, it's the same people, the old neighbors, the people we grew up with. How can we return to that? How can we look at them without remembering"—he lets out a sound, laughter or a sob, into her hair—"what we lost."

Alia turns to face him. His expression is frenzied. As she looks into his imploring eyes, a truth alights: All is lost. There will be no Amman. *He believes Kuwait will save him*, she realizes. *Us.*

"Go in the summers," he pleads. "You could go every summer."

The finality of it steals her breath. Since Atef's return, she has lived what feels like centuries, reimagining their lives, one fantasy after another of untying the war from themselves, shaking it out like sand from hair. It hadn't occurred to her before this moment that there might be something waiting for her in Kuwait, years with their summers and mornings and birthdays stretched out in front of her. Watching her husband's face, Alia feels something deep and instinctive within tell her this will be their life.

"Yes," she manages. "In the summers."

She excuses herself to the bathroom and leans against the sink. The porcelain is smooth and cool, and she places both hands flat upon it. She sees Atef's frantic eyes.

From the other room, the women's voices begin to call out the new year. Alia flees the house.

Outside, she moves quickly down the pathway of the compound, past the cars out front, the palm trees skeining above her, toward the small hut. Foreign, lilting music is playing inside, punctuated by laughter. Alia knocks on the door, lightly at first, then pounding, until, at last, she hears the sound of a lock unclicking and the door swings open.

It is Priya, her moon-shaped face peering at her. Behind her Alia sees a swath of colorful candles, dark women and men dancing. There is a table covered with plates of rice, the leftover meat and chicken and fish from the villa.

"Madame?" Priya says, a furrow of concern on her forehead. She looks different, and it takes Alia a moment to understand why—the maid's uniform is gone. Instead, Priya wears a sari, peacock blue, her hair in waves over her shoulders. Shame drops over Alia, for interrupting the party, for standing here like a madwoman.

"Ajit," she blurts. "I need Ajit."

"Madame?" Priya asks again. "Is something wrong? We will come now if you need us to clean—"

"Ajit," Alia repeats and begins to cry. "Please, bring me Ajit." Priya looks alarmed. She turns and calls out something in her language.

Within seconds, Ajit appears in the doorway. He wears a silver-threaded robe; a white hat caps his bald, brown head. He is carrying a teacup.

He looks at Alia for a moment without speaking and seems to understand. He turns to Priya, speaks in low tones, and hands her the teacup. Priya nods and glances once more at Alia. The door shuts behind Ajit, his eyes not leaving Alia's face. She is no longer crying, feels oddly soothed.

"Please," he says, bowing his head. Alia follows him down the pathway. They pass the parked cars, Alia averting her eyes from the villa. For the first time, she notices the noise the palm leaves make as they rustle against one another, like the sound of lace against lace. In the moonlight, Ajit's robe seems to glow.

When they reach the sedan, Ajit pulls the keys from a hidden pocket in his robe—are they always with him?—and holds the backseat door open for Alia. As she climbs in, her heart is pounding, her throat dry. *Like a fugitive,* she thinks.

They sit in silence for a while, Ajit in the front, the engine murmuring. Finally, Ajit clears his throat.

"Where would you like to go, madame?"

The question dangles in front of Alia and her mind blanks, then races off. Lemon-colored bedrooms, an armoire full of summer dresses. A hidden pathway behind a schoolhouse, the sound of boys yelling, her own feet bare over cool, moist earth. Garden—before its ravaging—at sunset, mint tea. Running wet cloths over tiles, the marble sparkling like gems.

"The water." Her voice is astonishingly clear. "Take me to the water, please."

"Yes, madame."

Ajit drives through the compound. The identical villas blur by, the boulevard swallowed into darkness as they turn onto the main road. Streetlamps are interspersed at wide intervals, and for whole minutes at a time, all Alia can see are the shadowy edges of palm trees, telephone poles, the occasional villa.

Impulsively, she rolls down the window. The wind is cool, rushing against her face, swirling her curls against her cheeks, her lips.

On the seventh night after Atef's return, Alia had woken to find the bed next to her empty. She walked through the dark, silent rooms of Widad's house looking for him, finally seeing a strip of light beneath the guest-bathroom door.

She'd hesitated outside it. It occurred to her that he might wish her away. Since his return, Atef sat for hours without speaking.

"Tell me," she would say to him. "Tell me." She wasn't sure what exactly she wanted but longed to hear it.

Instead, Atef was silent. He rarely ate, his cheeks hollowing. He slept until afternoon and seemed to move as though underwater. When he spoke of Mustafa, his voice was flat, detached.

"I don't know when they killed him. Or where. They just told me he was dead."

This is what Alia thought as she stood in front of the bathroom door: *Mustafa, dead.* Every incarnation of him, young and old, had to be folded away. What she had, then, what remained, was on the other side of that door. Atef was hers; he was alive. The sound of rushing water was audible. Alia opened the door.

Blood was everywhere.

This was the first thought Alia registered: a marveling at the blood, crimson around Atef in the bathtub, streaming down his chest. She blinked, her eyes adapting to the light. The blood wasn't from a single wound, she saw. No. It had gathered in the bathwater where Atef sat naked. Dozens of cuts ornamented his back, his shoulders, his chest.

Glass was her next thought. But Atef turned to her, his eyes not crazed but soft, staring up at her with a childlike helplessness. Looking down, Atef lifted his arm from the pinkish water and found a healing wound on his chest—Alia saw that between the streaks of blood were long, scraggly scabs—dug with his nail, and let out a sigh as he tore the scab, ripping it carefully from his skin.

Instantly, red flowered. He dropped the scab into the bathwater, where it floated on the surface. He'd been doing this often, she understood in that moment, the gesture practiced. The strips on his torso were raw and pink. It occurred to her that she hadn't seen her husband's body, his nudity, since his return; she hadn't known this new skin.

Alia made a sound—stifled, aghast. A wave of nausea. She felt a powerful urge to turn away. Return to the bed or leave, the fantasy coming to her unbidden, the desire to walk out into the blank, desert night, walk until her feet blistered, walk until she reached the dunes.

Shame composed her. It sobered the sound in her throat, moved her legs toward her husband, the door shutting behind her.

As Ajit drives, Alia keeps the window open, watching the city go by. Something about the landscape, transformed in the dark, is haunting; she has never seen it so late at night. Kuwait is usually a metallic blur of sunshine to her, the ugly buildings and concrete exposed in the light. Midday, the city is absurdly male—the local men draped in robes, street vendors, taxi drivers, construction workers—all men, all turning to Alia with alert, hungry eyes.

But now, in the first hour of the new year, the city is ghostlike, almost tender. As they drive past the banks and the university, the buildings seem welcoming. Alia is comforted by the lights of the mosque, the surreal quality of the streets. Emptied, the city is feminine.

Ajit drives past the city center, past the roads where the royals live. The globes of palace turrets rise into the night sky, lit from within, grotesquely beautiful. Inside, Alia imagines, servants are clearing massive tables, silver bowls of rice and camel meat and fruit, the princes and princesses lounging in airy, gilded rooms.

When Alia first arrived, Widad told her stories about the Bedouin, how a mere thirty, forty years ago, none of this had existed, none of the villa compounds or courtyards or even the pearl-hued mosques. Men, women, children—all had traveled from dune to dune, enveloped in linen cloth as armor against the sun, walked the scalding sand for days. Some royals had servants who carried their dwellings on aching backs until they arrived at an oasis—lustrous fabrics swelling into tents beneath the trees. The miraculous trees. When they prayed, Widad said, they did so by the slant of the sun, no muezzin audible for miles. If there was no spare water, they did their ablutions with sand, rubbing their wrists and feet with handfuls of the clear, rough grains.

As the car moves to the city outskirts, Alia thinks of the palaces. For the younger generation, nothing is lost. But the elders—Alia feels a pang of sorrow for the older generation, the men and women who still remember the desert before all the construction. It reminds her of the aunts and uncles in Nablus who spoke of a Palestine before the big war, before soldiers and exodus. Easier, she thinks, to remember nothing, to enter a world already changed, than have it transform before your eyes. In the palaces, the grandparents must sit in their extravagant rooms, remembering sand.

Nostalgia is an affliction. Someone said that once in front of Alia, and the words reach her now, years later. Like a fever or a cancer, the longing for what had vanished wasting a person away. Not just the unbearable losses, but the small things as well. Alia thinks of her bedroom in Nablus. The seashells she filled with bobby pins. The tangerine dress she'd bought right before her trip to Kuwait and never worn. Photographs, necklaces, the glasses and silver *ibrik* her mother had given her.

You cannot forget them in your grief.

The lot in front of the beach is empty and dark, eerily lit by two streetlamps. The smell of the sea gusts into the open window. Ajit pulls in across from a boarded-up shack with a sign shaped like an ice cream cone. A metal chain is woven across the service window. Rows of rocks rise like hills at the edge of the parking lot, blocking the view of the water.

Ajit turns the key and the engine hushes. The sound of the sea moves around them and Alia feels shy for a moment, alone with this kind man. It occurs to her that Atef and the others must have noticed her absence by now. She imagines Atef's stricken face, then pushes it out of her mind. For moments there is no sound aside from the thundering sea. Finally, Ajit speaks.

"Would you like to go down?"

Alia is grateful for his asking. "Yes."

"I will come."

"You don't have to," Alia says, but Ajit is already opening his door. She is glad. Beyond the light of the streetlamps, the parking lot dissolves into darkness. Alia shivers in the cold air.

They walk wordlessly to the rocks, Ajit behind her. Alia's heels click as she steps. At the rocks, she moves carefully, her shoes snagging in the crevices as they climb down. She nearly trips, and Ajit's arm shoots out; his fingers wrap around her wrist.

"Perhaps it would be easier without the heels?" Ajit says. When she looks up at him, his eyes are mirthful. The mood of their trip seems to lighten, an audacious air about it. They are having an adventure, Alia thinks.

"Ajit, you are correct," Alia says merrily and slips the shoes off, dangles them from her fingers. Her feet are clammy, and once she makes her way down the rocks, the sand is surprisingly velvety. She tosses her shoes near a clump of dried seaweed. For a moment, the two of them are still, facing the sea, which is suddenly everywhere, a living, snarling, barreling thing. Waves foam against the lip of the shore.

"It will be cold," Ajit calls above the sound of water.

"Oh God, please let it be," Alia says. She laughs bitterly. There is a desire to start talking, to tell Ajit about her hatred of the summer, the heat, how breathing had been like drinking steam. She wants to talk about the unremitting dampness of her skin, the loamy odor everywhere.

But it would be betrayal, she recognizes, betrayal to speak those words, though she is uncertain whom she would be betraying. To keep herself silent, she walks toward the waves. At the water's edge, she pauses before stepping forward.

Ice. The water felt like ice—needles of it. Alia gasps and turns to Ajit, who stands watching her. "It's freezing," she marvels.

Ajit smiles, nods. He joins her, holding his robe bunched in his fists; the two of them move until the water reaches their calves. The ocean rocks around them, the sand shifting beneath Alia's feet, a vertiginous sensation. Suddenly, a wave breaks, unexpected, sending them both stumbling backward. Water sprays, drenching Alia's dress, neck, hair. She can hear Ajit laughing beside her, and she begins to laugh as well. She tips her head back, the moon above them a bonfire in the sky. She remembers, for the first time since standing in the kitchen, her body, the rustling within it; she laughs harder.

Alia turns to Ajit, standing with his soaked robe, droplets of water beading his bald head. She places both hands over her belly, her laughter tapering. She speaks not to Ajit but to the sky, eyes lifted to the moon.

"So this is the beginning."

ATEF

Kuwait City
May 1977

The soldiers call to one another in Hebrew. There are seven or eight of them, loosely forming a circle around Abu Zahi, who is on his knees, a line of blood trailing from his nostrils.

"Let go of me!" Mustafa tries to move toward Abu Zahi, but Atef tightens his grip. "Are you blind? It's Abu Zahi," Mustafa says.

"It's a trap," Atef whispers. His voice shakes.

"Have you lost your mind?" Mustafa is furious. "They're taking him."

"Mustafa." Atef swallows, trying to steady his voice. "Mustafa, they're arresting him at dusk. Minutes before prayer. It doesn't make any sense. Why would they do it in front of everyone, out in the open?"

Mustafa frowns, gazing in the direction of the soldiers. A look of comprehension dawns upon his face.

"They want to see who steps forward."

Suddenly Atef is in a dim room, his wrists in handcuffs. Across the table sits a soldier with a scar above his lip.

"You camel-fucker," the soldier snarls at Atef. "He's dead."

"I don't believe you," Atef says. He tenses his shoulders, preparing to flinch. But the soldier's hands remain flat on the table. Something gutters in the soldier's face—malice, humor—and he leans back, lazily crosses his arms over his torso.

"Believe what you want." The soldier shrugs.

The room changes. Atef is lying on the floor. There are sounds—men coughing, spitting, the rasp of blankets against concrete. Some of the men are masturbating with loud grunts. Someone weeps.

"You talk or I take this." Gruff, broken Arabic. His fingernail held between metal pliers. A faceless man tugs.

The snake is coming.

"You want to stay silent? Fine." Somewhere, someone has spilled ethanol, the smell piercing Atef's nostrils. Metal is wound around his head and his wrists; he wants to scream but cannot. "*Ya Rab*," he mutters, and spears of fire shoot up the length of his arm. "*La ilaha illa Allah*," and electricity snakes into his jaw, binding his teeth shut.

"Drink," a male voice says in Arabic, and Atef sees a metallic shape—a flask etched with calligraphy. Atef reaches for the flask and suddenly he is gripped with the most fear he has ever known, fear that has nothing to do with the soldier or death but with some abstract loss, with the sudden knowledge that he is dreaming, just as the flask begins to fade and he loses his breath and, catching it, wakes.

Atef lies in bed for several minutes, heart thudding. The flask glints in his mind. He places a hand over his chest and breathes deeply, as Dr. Salawiya, his physician, has advised.

"The mind is a mystery. Give it time to catch up." The doctor always says the same thing, has since Atef first went to him a decade ago. The Six-Day War was over and Atef had been released from prison, stumblingly finding his way to Amman, where he stayed with Khalto Salma for a few days before continuing to Kuwait, the tawny desert looking like a hopeful face from the airplane window. He and Mustafa had been arrested soon after the Israeli invasion of Nablus, the fifth day of the war, and swept up along with dozens of their neighbors, men from the mosque, cousins. The charges were spurious and arbitrary: organizing protests, pamphlet distribution, inciting violence. *Planning infiltration* was the charge for him and Mustafa. *It's not true*, he'd wept to the guards once they were separated. Yes, they went to the mosque, Mustafa made his weekly speeches. They were angry. *But they hadn't done anything.* He shook during those unceasing days of prison, having imaginary conversations with Mustafa, who had been taken elsewhere.

"It's like a shadow life," Atef once tried to explain to the doctor. "Like there's another me, and that me is still stuck, like a skipping record."

"It'll get better. The dreams will come less frequently."

It is true. No longer is Atef afraid to fall asleep, as he was for years, jerking awake from the edge of consciousness, convinced his palpitations were a heart attack, his dry mouth the result of a stroke. The dreams have lessened as the years passed, from several a week to once a week, now once every few months.

But though less frequent, the dreams have sharpened in focus. Atef hears his breath over the whir of the air conditioner, thinks of the electric shock buzzing his teeth. His jaw hurts.

He once read about a young woman who often dreamed of drowning, water rising above her, filling her mouth. One night her parents woke to the sound of gurgling, a muffled cry. They fell back to sleep. In the morning the girl was dead, her lips blue. Her lungs had filled up with water, an ocean of fluid from her own organs drowning her.

Such are the ways the body believes what we tell it.

Snatches of the dream—electricity, blankets, smoke from a soldier's cigarette—spark in his mind, the images already dissolving, tamed in the quiet bedroom. Beneath the damask curtains, swaths of morning sun peek through, the bedroom like an aquarium.

Alia lies sleeping at his side, and Atef watches her for a moment, reassured by the sight of her splayed arms. She always sleeps on her stomach, face burrowed in the pillow, snarls of hair surrounding her head.

She'd cut her hair off while pregnant with Souad. That pregnancy, the third, was the worst, the heat leaving her dazed with nausea. Even in cool bathwater, which Atef would fill with ice cubes, Alia spoke of heat.

"It feels like wool," she'd tell Atef, moaning, gathering her curls in fistfuls.

Atef was mournful when he saw it shorn, his wife's shoulders suddenly bare. He loved the weight of her hair, the citrus scent he could bury his face in. But Alia liked it short, said it made her feel airy. Now, she cuts it every few months.

Atef swings his legs over the side of the bed. His body feels stiff, as though he has walked for hours. He squints at the clock on the bedside table. Nearly forty years old, Atef can feel the complaints of his body begin to gather momentum—the twinges, the blurred vision in the mornings, the occasional headaches. He blinks, and the numbers on the clock sharpen: 7:20 a.m. The plan he half formed last night before sleep returns to him: go to the market before Alia and the children wake and buy strawberries for Riham.

Atef walks down the hallway, his feet bare against the tiles. To his left, the bedrooms are lined up, one for each child—Souad's an eruption of sorbet colors, toys strewn around the four-poster bed; Karam's in navy and white, his wooden figures arranged neatly on the shelves; and Riham's pristine, a bookshelf lined with spines of novels and encyclopedias.

When anyone asks about his children, Atef recites the names like a talisman, his voice full and grateful over each one. "Souad is five, Karam is seven, Riham is eight." And now the talisman will be adjusted, for today is Riham's birthday, her ninth.

Nine, he wrote in his last letter. *The age fills me with sadness, for the solidity of the number, its cementing of her foray into adulthood, a lifetime of double digits. But I keep such thoughts to myself. I know Alia wouldn't approve. She'd just look at me with that frown of hers and shake her head.*

Atef hears Priya's humming before he enters the kitchen, the toneless noise she makes while working, like a children's lullaby. She stands with her back to him, the ironing board in front of the windows. He watches her lift and press the iron to a pink swath of fabric, one of the girls' dresses. Steam comes out in tiny puffs.

"Good morning," he says.

Priya glances over her shoulder and smiles. "Good morning."

She still looks girlish, the years plumping out her cheeks and arms. Atef likes to think of Priya as a pillar, the center of the house, all of them crowding around her, coming for bandages and tea and laundry. Every two years she returns to India for a month, packing suitcases full of clothes and treats to bring to her husband and two children, children Atef imagines as miniature versions of Priya. The weeks she is away, the villa feels empty, all of them restless, aimlessly moving through the rooms. Someday, Atef knows, she will return for good. The prospect is a bleak one.

Now, Priya turns the dress over, smoothing the fabric on the ironing board. She speaks above the hiss. "There is coffee; would you like a cup?"

"I'll get it." Atef chooses a maroon mug with hearts on it. A birthday present from the children last year. "I was thinking of going to the market. Picking up some strawberries."

A small, approving nod. "For Riham."

Atef smiles as he pours himself coffee from the *ibrik*. "Yes, and some figs if they have them."

"Good. I can make a fruitcake."

"For the party at Widad's? Riham will love it." Atef likes these exchanges, the moments he shares with Priya while the family sleeps.

Priya lifts the dress, shakes it firmly. She makes an appreciative sound. "If you buy some cane sugar, I can make pudding."

"I'll buy ten kilograms of sugar," he declares theatrically and Priya laughs her low laugh, shaking her head.

He takes his coffee into the study they furnished last year, the wooden desk and tightly packed bookshelf. At the doorway, he waits for a second, looking down the hallway, before shutting the door behind him and moving to the books. He finds the brown spine and pulls it out, his heart quickening familiarly at the touch of the smooth cover, the book opening in the middle like a mouth, revealing the sheaf of papers. They are held together by a rubber band, a blue Bic pen tucked under it.

He turns the last page over—*April 29, 1977*—the ink spidery through the paper, and sits at the table. He glances at the door before beginning to write.

> *I wake up and it feels like my lungs are dropped in ice and I have to count, one two three four, listen to myself taking in air. Sometimes I wonder if this is really the waking world: coffee in a red mug, three children sleeping in three rooms, the television blaring in the background.*

Years ago, when the pills and diet changes and vitamins didn't work, Dr. Salawiya recommended letters.

"They say it can help. It's a way to organize your thoughts, explain what you've been through. Write them to your wife, your family back in Palestine."

But when Atef sat down, it was Mustafa's name that tumbled out, his eyes that he saw. At first he wrote just about the dreams, the whittled faces of the soldiers, but then he began to talk to him about other things, daily things, always starting the letters with his friend's name, writing about Riham winning the spelling contest, how Souad upended a glass of milk during a tantrum. He told him, delicately, about Alia, how neither of them ever spoke of Palestine.

I'm crazy, a part of him realized. *If anyone finds this, they're going to think I'm crazy.*

But it was the only thing that helped. Pretending that Mustafa was still somewhere in the world, still in Nablus or, better yet, in Peru or Thailand, living one of his dozen lives, pretending that a rickshaw was delivering Atef's letters to a doorstep somewhere, his friend laughing and sucking his teeth as he read them. Sometimes—in his more reckless moments—he even bargained with himself: *They never gave us a body, it's not impossible, lots of men left Palestine during those months, what if, what if.*

Atef pauses before finishing the letter. *They always make me say your name. I was afraid I called it out in my sleep, that Alia might've heard. But when I woke, she hadn't moved.* Even though it feels unnecessary, he still signs his name, in a complicated flourish at the bottom of the page.

He has chosen a particular book for this job: *A Lifecycle of Plants.* He tucks the letters in, then replaces it in the far left corner of his bookshelf. The spine is drab and brown. He knows no one will ever touch it.

Atef drinks the rest of his coffee too hot, and as he steps outside the house, his tongue feels raw. He moves it over his front teeth, winces, does it again. The car, a silver sedan, is new, a gift he bought for himself after his promotion at the university last year. What pride that letter had brought, seeing his title embossed in golden ink—*Honorable Professor*—with precise handwriting. A far cry from his childhood in Nablus, from the rice his weary mother ladled, the clamor of his six brothers in their house. His brothers are far-flung now—Amman, Istanbul, the youngest two lost in the bowels of Israeli prisons.

In certain moments, Atef feels the small miracle of his luck perched on his shoulder like a parakeet—something alive, trilling a new song. He feels it even now, fluttering in his chest as he pulls out of his driveway. If left unaddressed, the whirring becomes torrential, threatening to spill over into tears as it often did those years after the war. And so, as he steers the car down the road, passing the rows of white villas and palm trees, Atef quietly recites: It is spring. He has a lovely home. He has three healthy children and a wife. It is his elder daughter's birthday today, and he is going to buy strawberries for her.

This remembering, this gentle recitation, calms him, gives him something to focus on. These are facts, the obelisks of his life, and, gleaned, they glow for him—sturdy, true, his.

Over the years, the compound has grown, as have others in the neighborhood. While theirs remains mostly Arabs, other Palestinians, and Syrians, the nearby compounds—admittedly nicer, with pools and frantically watered lawns—are luring in more Westerners. Atef sees them in the grocery store and the shops, their golden hair hypnotic.

Atef complains, as the rest of their friends do, of the influx of Americans and British, of the ways the "international"—primarily Western—schools have become mixed, teaching English and French just as vigorously as Arabic. Of the increase of English shows on the television. And yet, when it came time to enroll the children in school, Atef fought with Alia to put them in one of those international schools.

"So they can share lunch with *ajanib*?" Alia had asked. She felt distaste toward the foreigners, found them greedy. "And learn their ABCs? What for?"

Atef thought for a while before replying. "There are sides," he finally said, because he could think of no better way to put it. "And I want them to be on the right one."

Sometimes he imagines a series of time-lapse photographs, like the ones of a tree undergoing changes in foliage or a seascape during sunrise. Only this is of Kuwait City. Although it has happened bit by bit, Atef can picture it after years of driving the same streets. Over and over and over, the whole city bursting into life.

In Atef's imaginary photographs, the transformation is astonishing. In the beginning, a stark desert, the landscape sparsely decorated with industrial buildings and compounds. And then, *whoosh*, years pass and things begin to crop up—restaurants, Indian, Pakistani, Lebanese, with bright signs; the newer mosques; the billboards cautiously advertising toothpaste and banks; and, slowly, the cranes and concrete pillars, dunes of sand turned into construction sites.

Whoosh. The photograph trembles and changes once again. More years pass. The cranes and pillars are gone, and buildings appear in their place, a telecommunications center. The outskirts of the desert, reddened with sand, are becoming compounds with swimming pools, their villas blooming like flowers. More restaurants are opening downtown, so that driving past them at night gives the impression of tangled light, neon comets. *Whoosh.* More years. It's the late seventies, and even Kuwait is feeling it. The billboards are bolder now, showing toothy women advertising veils, travel-agency images of the Eiffel Tower. Driving through the city no longer feels as contradictory as it used to—certain areas sand and air, others fully urban; it feels like a city now, with a distant melancholia about it, like all cities.

Atef pulls in to the entrance of the Mubarakiya souk and parks. Over the years, most of his friends—and Alia as well—have come to view the marketplace as outdated, a holdover from the old days. Sprawling and loud, its mazelike stalls and shops fill the air with saffron and cinnamon. Men's voices hawk goods with an energy so ample it seems to fill one's mouth.

Atef loves it.

When he first arrived in Kuwait, he would weave between the stalls like a sleepwalker. Here was a place where nobody wanted anything from him except coins. He began offering to pick up spices and bread and rice, spent hours walking the kiosks, stealing touches of camel-skin rugs, accepting samples of olives and goat cheese, overwhelmed and comforted by the cacophony of vendors. It was the only place he felt relief those first months, and he came to view it as a sort of haven, a makeshift mosque.

Even now, ambling past stalls, nodding at various vendors, he feels warmth at the familiarity of their cries.

"Sir, good morning, sir, sample the melon?"

"Three for ground coffee! I'm giving it away!"

"Buy perfume for the madame? Jasmine, gardenia, *irfil, irfil!*"

Atef ignores them all, walks to the corner stall where an older man hunches over a radio, a splinter of khat dangling from his teeth. He is muttering under his breath, surrounded by an arrangement of fresh fruit, baskets of dewy berries and apples.

"Morning of luck, Abu Mohsin," Atef greets the man.

Abu Mohsin grunts without looking up. "Is it Friday already?"

"It's my daughter's birthday. I came for some strawberries."

"You know where everything is." Abu Mohsin fiddles with the antenna, curses. "Goddamn American piece of shit. They can take over the world, they can't build a radio?"

"Might be good for you if it's broken," Atef teases. "All those Egyptian soap operas are going to melt your brain."

Abu Mohsin looks at him blackly. "Bah." He spits the khat on the ground and rises as though Atef is an unwanted houseguest who must be entertained. "Strawberries, you said?"

As Abu Mohsin rifles through the baskets, he asks, "Which girl is it? The lighter one or the one with the curls?"

Atef smiles, then rearranges his face as Abu Mohsin turns to him with a basket. Now and then the old man slips up and shows his hand, reveals that he pays attention to the tidbits Atef shares during these visits.

"The lighter one. Riham."

Abu Mohsin hands him the basket. Atef touches the strawberries, picking a plump one. The strawberry is warm from the sun, specks of dirt clinging to the fine hairs. The fruit seems to throb with redness. Atef is pleased by the color, knows Riham will admire it. Riham, who is forever tugging his arm to show him a particularly yellow flower or the sky swirled with pastels at sunset. Sometimes she brings home drawings from school, underwater scenes with violet jellyfish, sketches of girls dancing on a beach. He tapes them up in his office at the university, the pictures placed next to his framed diploma and teaching awards.

"You going to taste it or commune with it?" Abu Mohsin folds another wad of khat between his teeth.

Atef bites into the strawberry—sweetness, ripe, with a hint of tart. It is perfect.

"I'll take four baskets," he tells Abu Mohsin.

The older man looks pleased for an instant before his eyes sharpen, shrewd, as though he's remembering he is the vendor of all this unlikely fruit. "You want some cherries? Arrived this morning. Sweet as a virgin's thighs."

Atef laughs uneasily. Such talk makes him uncomfortable. "All right. One basket." Abu Mohsin's eyebrows knit together. "Okay, okay. Two."

"Sugar from Morocco," Atef calls as he walks into the kitchen, sets the bags on the floor. "Are they awake?"

"The girls are getting ready," Priya says, hefting the cloth sack of sugar. "Karam is in the sunroom. You want more coffee, sir?"

"Sure," Atef says. "And, please, those cherries."

The sunroom is actually a storage room. Three windows cover one side, filling it with sunlight. It is unofficially Karam's playroom, where he spends hours coaxing figures out of wood.

The boy sits at the desk Atef bought for him. Slats of wood are scattered around a small birdcage. In the sunlight, his curls are nearly golden, his hair lighter than the others'. Karam had been born in February, not even two years after Riham—Alia's pregnancy a blur, her drawn, sleepless face, the flurry of Atef's academic projects—and it was as though he sensed the chaos he was being brought into. He was a calm infant, an agreeable toddler. Whenever Atef entered the room, Karam would babble with joy: "Ata, Ata." Even when he fell or was jostled in play by Riham, he didn't cry; his eyes went liquid, but he made no sound.

The fascination with wood came two years ago, when Atef took the boy to the market during Eid, stalls lined with toys and Bedouin goods—crafted jewelry, satchels of soap, and wooden figurines carved with perfection into limbs and grave faces. A Bedouin man sat on the ground, paring a piece of wood impossibly fast, tossing the shavings to his side. Karam was awestruck, his mouth pursed in transfixion. He insisted on staying until the man finished. The figurine was a swan with a graceful neck, which the Bedouin gave to Karam, telling him gruffly, "This is for luck."

The swan still rests on the shelf above Karam's bed, along with a myriad of objects and figures the boy has since created, in varying stages of skill. A duckling, an elephant with a drooping trunk. The creations are rudimentary but solid.

Atef feels a pang at times watching the neighborhood boys play soccer on the compound lawn, elbowing one another in dirty shirts. His own memories of childhood involve camaraderie—a scraped knee, the elation of making a goal, playing games of tag.

Alia defends their son's quietness, his solitary play. When she speaks, Atef watches her face cloud over, knows she is remembering the boys in Nablus.

"He doesn't steal; he doesn't fight. He's never in trouble like the other boys."

Of the children, Karam is her favorite. It is unspoken, but Atef can hear it in her voice, the way she spends hours admiring his handiwork. In less forgiving moments, Atef mentally supplies the reason: The boy demands less than the girls. He is unobtrusive, his moods easier to manage than Souad's tantrums and Riham's anxiety to please.

"So you went for the birdcage."

The boy looks up, a smile unfolding across his face. Grinning cartoon wolves dot his pajamas, which, Atef notices, are too small, inches of skinny ankle exposed. "And this. It's still drying."

Karam lifts something near the birdcage. Atef leans in. A wooden bird, the size of his son's hand, with a tapered beak.

"Kiki," Atef breathes out. "It's beautiful."

"Blue's her favorite." Karam's face is radiant. "I know because she always picks blue notebooks for school."

"It is," Atef agrees. "She's going to love it." He feels a tenderness toward his son, happy in his sunlit closet. *Karam's a gentle heart*, Alia likes to tell people.

"But I still need to paint the cage." Worry ripples his voice. "She can't see before Khalto Widad's party tonight."

Atef suppresses a smile. "Don't worry," he says. "I'll distract her until breakfast."

In the living room, Priya has placed a silver tray on the table, along with a bowl of cherries and the hearts coffee mug. Atef sips his coffee. Years ago, Alia decided the living room was too beige and changed nearly all the furniture. Now, the room pops with yellow and green and blue. Each of the pink couches is strewn with overstuffed pillows the shade of banana peels. Even the walls are painted an unearthly pearl. To him, the effect is garish; he'd found the beige soothing. The colors make the room glisten, as though everything—the varnished wood, the walls—has not quite dried.

The cherries are fat, beaded with water from Priya's washing. Atef decides to wait for Riham and turns on the television. The news is on, and Atef resolutely changes the channel. Not on Riham's birthday, he tells himself—he is careful with the news; an image of flags burning or a row of corpses can set him trembling for hours. He switches to a soccer game.

As the jerseyed men jog onto the lawn and begin kicking the ball back and forth, Atef hears the familiar padding of feet—light, careful. Each child has his or her own stride, a concerto as distinctive to Atef as their voices. He hears the steps get louder, pause, Riham's voice calling out, "Good morning, Priya," and Priya's muffled reply.

Finally, she appears in the doorway, her hair wet and already curling. Atef's heart fills—she wears a dress he bought her, the lilac silk tied in a bow around her waist.

"All this sugar!" Atef cries, leaping to his feet dramatically. The shameful truth is that Alia isn't alone in having a favorite—he loves Riham beyond reason, a love tinged with gratitude, for when she was first placed in his arms, tiny and wriggling and red-faced, he felt himself return, tugged back to his life by the sound of her mewling. The arrival of Riham restored something, sweeping aside the ruin of what had come before.

"You look like a queen! A thousand happy returns." Riham ducks her head, embarrassed, but a smile sneaks across her face. Atef bows to her, extending his hand. "My lady, may I request a twirl?"

"Baba!" She giggles, the taffeta rustling.

"My lady, I must insist." Atef mock frowns. "Such beauty cannot be allowed to pass without twirling." Riham shakes her head, still giggling. Finally, she takes his hand, and he twirls her once, twice.

"Cherries!"

"And strawberries for a certain someone's day." They sit on the couch and begin to eat. "So," Atef says, spitting a pit out. "We have Auntie Widad's at five. Before that, the day is yours. Anything you want."

He watches her chew. She is the plainest of the children, with a high forehead and slightly bulbous nose. But her eyes are extraordinary, flecked with honey and green, a fringe of thick eyelashes. *Bit of a waste, those eyes on that face*, Atef once overheard Alia say wistfully to Widad, and he'd wanted to shake her.

"Anything? Mama said so too?"

Atef remembers the argument last night after the children had gone to sleep, one of those spats that blaze in their marriage like grease fires. *You spoil them, Atef.* He'd countered, *You barely notice them.* Her hurt, furious face floats back to him now.

"Yes, *habibti*," he tells Riham. "Anything you'd like."

Riham chews her lower lip, stained red. "Even if it's far?"

He knows in a flash what she is thinking of: the dunes. Last month, he went with some of the men at the university far beyond the reaches of the city, where the sand stretched uninterrupted for miles and miles, gilded with sun. Some local Kuwaitis joined them in the evening, building a fire and roasting chunks of camel meat. Atef had told Riham about the starry sky, the way the locals plucked scorpions from sand and flung them into the fire, causing sparks. The girl listened attentively, the way she always did to him, her eyes spellbound. Afterward, she'd pored through her encyclopedias, looking up *scorpions* and *Bedouin.*

"Even if it's on the moon."

Riham looks at him solemnly. "We would die. There's no oxygen." Atef eats another cherry, hiding his smile with splayed fingers.

"That's true. So no moon."

"Could we go to the dunes?" she asks, looking down at her hands. "Is it too far?"

"That's it?" Atef feigns relief. "I thought you were going to say Istanbul, Hong Kong. Paris!" Riham giggles. Atef tucks a strand of hair behind her ear. "Of course we can."

"And we don't have to worry about scorpions, because I read that they hate lavender, so we'll take that spray Priya uses for laundry." Her face lights up. "I'll tell Karam! He'll be excited." She is nearly out of the living room when Atef remembers the birdcage.

"Riham!" She turns. At a loss, he blurts, "Can you do my shoulder?"

Atef sits at the edge of the couch, his left arm held out like a scarecrow's. Riham balances on the cushions behind him and holds on firmly to his elbow. Like a seesaw, she pulls and pushes.

"*Akh*, you're getting too strong," Atef says. For years, his children have done this, yanking at his limbs, pulling and hefting like tiny construction workers. Sometimes Atef imagines how he must appear to them, enormous and long-limbed, with his backaches and creaking joints. Especially his shoulder, an old dislocation never properly healed, from where a soldier yanked him to his feet. The children never ask him why or how. They accept it, like air or bread, their father with his ailments.

Riham puts forth a burst of strength and, surprisingly, his shoulder pops, air resettling in his joints.

Riham's eyes widen. "Baba, did you hear that?"

He rotates his shoulder gingerly. "It doesn't hurt," he marvels. "You should become a mass—"

A cry interrupts him.

"No!" The voice is small but strong. From the other side of the house, a door slams. Then flat-footed, decisive strides: Souad's. Of all the children, her footsteps are the loudest.

"Your sister's up," Atef says to Riham and they both wait, listening. Atef can make out angry tones—Souad defiant and Alia's voice rising in return.

"Nooo!" Atef braces himself. Souad rampages into the living room, running in that absurd, leggy way of hers, her hair riotous, sticking nearly straight up. She is wearing underwear, a yellow sock on one foot, and nothing else.

Still hollering, she runs straight for Atef, in the manner of someone seeking her protector. "Baba!" she howls, her fingers outstretched. When she reaches the couch, she wraps her arms around his neck like a vise. Atef lifts her, smothering a smile at her tear-stained face.

"You banshee, what's all this?"

"No dress!" Souad yells. She buries her head in his neck as Alia appears in the doorway. Alia's lips are set in a tight line, a frothy dress hanging from her fist. She shakes it in Souad's direction. A pale ribbon jounces maliciously.

"Atef, you tell that barbarian daughter of yours to put on this dress or she's spending the day in her room."

For a moment Alia glares, then catches sight of Riham. Her face softens; she tosses the dress toward Atef—slightly too hard, he notices, and remembers again the previous night's argument—and holds her arms out.

"Darling, happy birthday."

Riham hugs her mother, smiling as Alia brushes the shoulders of the dress. As they speak, Atef turns to Souad.

"Turtle," he whispers. "Why won't you wear the dress? See how pretty Riham looks." This grabs Souad's attention and she examines Riham. She shakes her head.

"Too itchy," she declares. She has a bizarrely older voice, nearly sensual, a lounge singer's voice, hoarse, as though she has spent all of her five years drinking whiskey and lighting cigarettes.

In Souad's features, the dead flicker. His father in the almond-shaped eyes, the color of wet bark—a father Atef barely remembers, knows through old photographs his mother kept in Nablus, the man looking directly into the camera. And in the mouth, the quirk of lips when she smiles, is Mustafa.

She is the child they hadn't intended to have, surprising them and toppling the neat symmetry of their family—Karam and Alia, Riham and Atef—so that even in babyhood she arrived in mutiny, with reincarnated features. Atef furrows his brow as though pondering this. "Where does it itch?"

"Here," she says, pointing at her neck. She grimaces. "I want the mermaid." A polyester nightgown adorned with mermaids, Souad's favorite garment.

"But Turtle," he says, "it's Riham's birthday. Don't you want to make it special for her?"

Souad's brows lift together. "The mermaid is special," she says flatly.

"It's okay," Alia sings out. "Souad can stay in her bed*room* while we all go o-*uut*."

Desperate, Atef reverts to a timeworn practice—bribery.

"I'll give you two dinars if you wear the dress," he whispers to Souad. She considers, a shrewd expression on her face. She nods. Atef cheers. "She'll wear it!"

Riham applauds and Alia snaps up the dress from Atef's lap. "Finally," Alia says, holding it toward Souad. "Hands up."

"Baba does it!" Souad cries out. Atef sees the brief wounded look in Alia's eyes, but she moves her head.

"Mama, can you braid my hair?" Riham asks, always astute.

"Fine," Alia says, "let's go to the bathroom."

After they leave, Souad scrambles down and lifts her arms in a V, like a gymnast. "I'm going to buy a camel with my dinars," she informs him.

Atef cannot quell the blossom of pride in his chest, though he knows it is wrong, wrong to feel so pleased with being the chosen one among his children.

ALIA IS NOT like most mothers. She is rash, impulsive, sometimes settling into daylong pouts when things don't go her way. Compared to Widad and the other wives they know, Alia is childlike, sleeping late in the mornings, sprawling with Karam in the sunroom to paint his wooden creations. She is carelessly affectionate, brushing her lips against Atef's beard at random moments, swooping down to kiss the children on their foreheads. But there is an absent-minded quality to her love, as though she is only just remembering this is her home, her husband, and her three children. Other times, she moves through their house with impatience. Atef had thought at first it was a temporary reaction to leaving Nablus, or to her first pregnancy, that she was overwhelmed with it all. But the preoccupation never quite abated.

The children, Atef believes, sense it. Even as babies, they seemed to understand—intuitively—the restlessness of their mother.

Several weeks after Riham was born, Atef arrived from work to the baby's wails reverberating through the house. He panicked, thinking that Alia had fallen and couldn't get to the child, but when he entered their bedroom he found Alia standing over Riham's bassinet, watching the bawling infant.

At his entrance, Alia turned around. "I don't know what she wants," she'd said, her hands balled up at her side, genuinely at a loss.

• • •

Priya has sliced some strawberries for breakfast, the table spread with pita bread and *labneh* and jam, a bowl of cut tomatoes with cucumber in the center.

"Look at this!"

"Omar at school wants me to make him a dinosaur."

"Just make sure you have your father cut the wood."

"I know, Mama. Omar wants it to be green and yellow."

"Souad, have some strawberries."

"Strawberries have worms."

"Suit yourself." Alia turns to Atef, pops a piece of bread in her mouth. Flour dots her lower lip. "What's the plan for today?"

Atef catches Riham's eye and smiles.

"We're going to the dunes," he announces to the table.

"What?" Alia frowns; Atef immediately sees his mistake. He wishes he'd spoken to her earlier. "In this heat? The car ride out will take so long. And the scorpions."

"Scorpions sleep during the day," Riham says quietly and Atef's heart clenches.

"I want to take her," he says, harsher than he intended. "It's still early."

Alia gives him a sidelong look, a glint in her eyes. *You want to do this in front of the children?* After years, the two of them are fluent in this wordless language.

"Riham." Alia turns to the girl with a coaxing smile. "Wouldn't you rather go someplace else? Like the toy store. Or the shops? We can buy you a new dress." She reaches over and tucks a stray hair into Riham's braid.

"We go to the zoo!" Souad upends a cup of orange juice.

"Souad!" Alia swats Souad's hand and begins to blot the juice. Souad's face turns thunderous. Karam intervenes from across the table, leaning forward on his elbows.

"You want to see the peacock?" Karam asks. "Or the camel?"

For an instant, Souad's face wavers between tears and curiosity; curiosity wins out. "The camel," she says. "With the big head."

"Even the zoo will be hot," Alia says. "I think somewhere indoors is better."

You're unbelievable, you know that? Atef turns to Riham. "Don't worry, duckie. Today's your day."

"Zoo!" Souad cries out, but Atef keeps his eyes on Riham. The girl shreds the pita bread, a nervous habit. She looks up at Atef.

"It's okay, Baba," she says. "I like the zoo."

"We're going to the dunes," he says helplessly to the table. "It's Riham's birthday."

"It's *my* birthday!" Souad calls out.

"Hush," Atef says. "We'll do whatever Riham wants today. Mama knows that."

He widens his eyes at Alia. *Temporary cease-fire. It's her birthday.* Irritation travels across her face, then passes. She pushes the napkins away from her, leaving a slick trail on the table.

"Of course," Alia says primly. "*Habibti,* whatever you want."

"I want to go to the zoo," Riham says, her eyes on the torn pieces of bread. "The dunes are really far. Besides"—the perky, bright voice that breaks Atef's heart—"this way we get to see the deer again."

"But the zoo's going to be hot—" Alia begins, and Atef glares at her. *You've done enough.* She falls silent.

"Camel! Camel!" Souad turns to Karam and demands, "Make the lion noise." The boy obligingly growls.

Atef leans over and taps the table in front of Riham. She looks up. "I'll take you next weekend," he whispers. "Just us. We'll get shawarma for the trip." The girl's eyes shine.

"Souad," Riham calls out. "Do you want to see the elephant or the tiger?"

Souad considers. "I want," she says slowly, "to see the tiger eat the elephant." In spite of themselves, they all laugh, even Alia, who reaches over to ruffle Souad's curls.

"You barbarian," Alia says, and they laugh even harder.

• • •

The zoo is at the outskirts of town, past the marketplace. The children pile into the back of the car, Souad in the coveted middle seat, dangling her feet. Alia fidgets with the car radio, turning up the volume too loud and humming along. As he drives, Atef peers into the rearview mirror, stealing glances at the children as they chatter.

"I'd be an eagle," Souad is saying. "No, a bear."

"Bears live in the forest," Riham says patiently. "Think of something in the desert."

"Bear!"

"What about a snake?"

"Okay! A snake." Souad makes a hissing sound and the other two children pretend to cower.

He is lifted, as always, by the sight of so many people in the car, bickering and talking and laughing, this family, *his family*. Atef's own father had been more mythical than real for him, his mother made zealous with grief after he died. The only memories he has of his entire family together are at funerals and Eid dinners.

"*Take me with you*," Alia sings along to the radio. Despite her sunglasses and the way she bobs her head to the music, he knows she is furious. With him. He feels a pang of remorse, for breakfast and the quarrel last night. Their arguments have the quality of a monsoon, gaining momentum, as they batter against each other until, finally, they flounder uselessly as shorn branches.

"We won't stay long," he says now, as a peace offering.

"Widad said to be back by five." She raises the volume more.

He tries another tactic. "Priya's making that fruitcake," he says in a stage whisper. Alia turns to him. In her large, glossy sunglasses, he sees his face duplicated.

"She'll like that." Her tone turns mischievous. "But Widad's going to be annoyed."

Atef grins. "Remember the party for Ghazi?"

"'*I told you* not *to bring a* thing!'" Alia mimics Widad's high, anxious tones perfectly.

"And the thing about the chicken." Atef laughs.

"'What are we going to do with *two* of them?'"

They laugh companionably. Alia settles back into the seat, her curls unbrushed around her face. In profile, she still looks young, all angles—cheekbones, square jaw, strong nose. As she tilts her head back and begins to sing again, he glimpses her former self, the girl who teased him for ironing his ties. The likeness is breathtaking. He plucks these moments when they come, gathers them as proof—though of what, he is unsure. Love? Permanence?

Years ago, in Umm Mustafa's garden, Atef had been dazed at the sight of Alia. Sitting with her unbrushed hair, her feet propped on a chair as she cracked pumpkin seeds with her teeth, he'd been jolted by a memory of sitting in the mosque as a boy, sneaking his eyes open during prayer to watch dust motes sparkle in the sunlight. The two things merged in his mind—Alia, the memory of the mosque—making the meeting seem holy, a manifestation of fate.

This is why he writes the letters, he knows. Thousands of times he has thought of coming to her, dropping them in her lap. Begging her. *This is what really happened, all those years ago. It's all in there. This is why we don't talk about your brother. You always said you wanted to know, and now you do.*

When he remembers that afternoon, he can forgive her everything—the resentment, the detachment, the way she is cruel at times, going off for long summers in Amman and returning tan and happy, sighing when she walks through the house as though she has been on furlough and is now returned to her prison. But he has known Alia for half his life, and with those years is the understanding that if she knew the truth about Mustafa, she would never return to Atef.

At the entrance of the zoo, families line up in front of the ticket booth. The gate is covered in chipped paint. Up ahead, children skip in front of their parents, yelping and laughing. The sky is blue and clear, unfurled like satin.

"Five," Atef tells the young Indian man at the booth. As they walk ahead, the children discuss where to go first. "Riham chooses," he calls.

"The monkeys!" Her favorite. When she was younger, he'd perch her on his shoulders to pitch grapes into the cages. Once, a larger monkey swatted some baby monkeys for eating them and Riham began to cry.

After the monkeys they go to the deer, then the jackals. The cages are halfheartedly decorated with painted backgrounds and fake plants. The animals stare back at them with bored, unfathomable eyes. Atef feels bad for them, listless from the heat. The sun is dizzying, and when they pass the ice cream shack, he buys the children shaved ice.

"I should've let her wear the pajamas," Alia says as Souad dribbles red ice onto her collar.

"We'll wash it." Atef smiles down at Souad's sticky face.

"What's gotten into you?

"What?"

"You're so"—Alia wrinkles her nose—"*chirpy.*"

He feels a childish hurt. "It's a *beautiful* day," he says spitefully, then raises his voice. "Isn't it, kids? Isn't it a beautiful day?" The children turn and nod, clamoring to get to the elephants. He tilts his head to Alia. "See? Everyone's happy." *But you.* He cannot help but feel satisfaction at the annoyance on Alia's face. It quickly dissolves into shame. *It's Riham's birthday*, he tells himself.

"It's good to see them so excited," he says, contrite. "It makes me happy."

Alia's face softens and he feels an urge to kiss her. *You love that woman too much*, his mother had told him before the wedding.

"That's nice," Alia says now, trailing her fingers on his wrist. She speaks loud enough for the children to hear. "But Karam's already getting sunburned. Did you see his cheeks? I knew it would be too hot."

He pulls his hand away. "Your daughter's enjoying herself," he mutters. "That should matter more than being right." Even beneath the sunglasses, Alia's expression is a kaleidoscope of hurt and anger and, finally, retreat.

You look beautiful in red. I miss you. Remember that afternoon in your mother's garden? I was watching you earlier. You look exactly the same.

After circling the zoo twice, they pile back into the car, Souad punctuating the trip to Widad's house with various animal sounds. Alia turns the radio on, stares out of the window. At Widad's compound entrance, Atef turns left and goes past the villas. There are already several cars parked in the driveway.

"That's Sahar's dad's car!" Riham calls. "And Miriam's. So many people!"

At her happy voice, Atef and Alia glance at each other and—as though galvanized at once—Alia turns off the music, Atef cuts the engine, and they turn to their three children, smiling.

"There are, sweetheart," Alia says.

"Ready to have some fun, everyone?"

The children laugh and say yes. Doors clank open; seat belts are unbuckled. The fight, formally, is over.

For the cake, they seat Riham at the head of the table, Souad and Karam at either side. Widad has decorated the table with garlands of flowers and silver balloons tied to the chairs. The guests have piled gifts with colorful wrapping paper and ribbons. There are children from Riham's school, Atef and Ghazi's coworkers, the circle of friends they've made over the years. The girl looks dazed with joy, shy from the evening's attention, the adults complimenting her dress and calling her *aroos*.

Alia lights the nine slender candles on the cake and nods at Ghazi standing in the doorway.

"To the birthday girl!" Ghazi calls out as he turns off the light. Everyone cheers, suddenly bathed in candlelight. Souad stands on her chair and claps.

"Chocolate," she calls out.

"Hush," Alia says, smiling, and begins to sing. "*Happy birthday to you.*" The others join in. Atef stands and watches: Karam hugging Riham as he sings, Souad's grinning face. And Riham—she leans toward the cake, exquisite in her delight. Emotion engulfs him, tears springing to his eyes, his view a tangle of candlelight and figures. *Mustafa, you should see the way they sang for her, Alia's voice carrying above all the others.* He takes a breath and recites: He has a daughter. Three healthy children. A safe home. He is here, surrounded by these lovely, warbling voices.

The singing ends and everyone applauds, whistling and calling as Riham leans toward the cake, blows through her pursed lips. The candles waver and go out.

"More fire!" Souad cries and the adults laugh. Ghazi turns the lights back on, and the women begin to slice the cake, calling the children to sit and eat. After several moments, Alia walks over to him, balancing two plates of cake.

"Those children are savages," she says. "There's nearly none left. I managed to salvage this." Atef notices that she has lined her eyelids with kohl.

"Thanks," Atef says, taking the plate.

"I saw you," Alia murmurs. Atef looks away, swallowing. And yet, buried beneath the shame is a tentacle of hope—she watches him. He is touched by this.

Unexpectedly, she leans her head on his shoulder. How infrequently they touch, really touch, not brushed fingertips but their bodies aligning with each other's, naked and feverish. When they were younger, newly wed, every second alone had been stunning. It felt like a stolen galaxy, the kisses, lips trailing skin.

He sighs and eats his cake. Against him, Alia's body is relaxed, rising with each breath. It is unnecessary, to always lust for the past. He knows this. There is no good in greediness.

AS GUESTS BEGIN to leave, Widad and Alia wrap up the food and the remaining men go outside.

"A smoke?" Ghazi asks but Atef shakes his head. Instead, he walks through the house, looking for an empty room. The clamor of the evening has tired him. His head is beginning to ache, the tendrils of a migraine unfolding. In the guest bedroom, a group of children play in a semicircle. Karam is helping Souad build a tower with Legos, one of Riham's birthday gifts. Atef catches Souad's eye and blows her a kiss.

At the end of the hallway is Ghazi's study, the scent of leather and smoke pungent as Atef opens the door. It is dark, and it takes him a second to see the figure sitting on the windowsill behind the desk, her silhouette outlined by the open window.

"Riham?" The girl startles, turns around. "What are you doing here?"

"I'm making a wish." Her voice is small.

"You forgot to make one earlier?" He smiles as he walks toward her. "What did we pile that cake with candles for?"

"In the old days, people used to do this," Riham says, turning back toward the window. Outside the moon is a crescent, slender as a fingernail in the sky. "I read about it. They'd make their wishes by the moonlight. They believed that smoke carried the wish all the way up."

She taps the windowsill beside her, a white candle next to a box of matches. Atef moves closer to catch another glimpse of the moon.

"How'd they do it?"

Riham leans her head against the window frame. "They would light a candle and hold it up to the moon."

"And then?" Atef asks. He is drowsy from the food and the dark and Riham's voice.

She smiles beatifically, her face suddenly much older. "And then you blow it out."

They both look up at the thin moon. Atef thinks of his bookish daughter reading about the old days and birthdays, hoarding that knowledge like a jewel until today. It saddens him, the thought of her slipping away to make wishes.

"Can I stay?" he asks.

She nods and takes a match out, strikes it against the box's side. As Atef watches her touch the flame to the wick, her face illuminated, he suddenly thinks of Mustafa. Before the war, before the prison. There had been a girl, Atef remembers. He'd completely forgotten about her, a girl Mustafa mentioned at times. Atef tries to hunt the grottoes of his memory for her name. Something buoyant, delicate-sounding. He thinks of the stacks of letters without an address.

Riham holds the candle up to the window, peers through the flame to the moon. Atef is awash with love for her, her thin lips, her thick nose, all the awkwardness of adolescence beginning to crowd her face. He imagines time-lapse photography of her—her youth, then womanhood, wrinkles creasing her forehead, the years whirling by.

He will write to Mustafa about this moment, about her silhouette against the window, how he saw her years come before his eyes. He will tell him about the ways the world has changed. He can see the blank paper in front of him, his fingers curving instinctively. *I'm addicted to this*, he wrote a while ago. *My confessional.*

She takes a deep breath and exhales; the flame disappears in a wisp of smoke.

"What did you wish for?" he asks his daughter.

"I'm not supposed to say, Baba." She hesitates. "For nothing to change." Her eyes shine up at him.

"That's a good wish," Atef says. He imagines Mustafa in a small bungalow in Latin America, tanned, wearing leather sandals. That long-lost girl with him. "A very good wish, duckie."

How tiny our lives are, he thinks, *swelling to impossible size with love, then shrinking again.* He puts an arm around his daughter and pulls her close, this girl he will lose eventually to something. She settles against him. For long moments, they sit together in the dark, watching the sky and smelling the sulfur around them.

RIHAM

AMMAN
July 1982

Of the dozens of things that Riham dislikes about spending summers in Amman, the worst is the noise. She has been making a list all morning on the inside cover of her tattered *Gone with the Wind*, sitting in the kitchen of her grandmother's house, the quietest place she can find.

It isn't the mosquitoes that leave itchy welts in the cruelest of places—her eyelids, the space between her toes—or the soap operas the aunts watch compulsively. Not the vague smell of rotten meat when they visit Khalto Mimi's, a scent Riham attributes to their two cats, of whom Riham is shamefully afraid—once when they leaped onto the dining-room table, Riham jumped and Khalto Mimi's daughters, Lara and Mira, stared at her—or the fact that her father isn't with them. Not even that Karam stayed in Kuwait this summer, part of a sports club at his school.

It is the noise. The tireless clamor that Riham cannot escape no matter what she does. Back home in Kuwait, she has her bedroom at the corner of the house, with her rows of books. Any sounds, Priya's cooking or her parents talking, are always muffled by distance.

Here, the noise is like another creature in the house.

"It's not *mine!*" Souad is yelling.

"Now," their mother says. She is standing in the kitchen, an open pouch of pita bread in her hand. "I'm not saying it again."

There is the sound of thumping and Souad appears in the kitchen doorway. The early morning light filters through the window above the sink. Alia points at the clutter of blocks and dolls near the entrance. "That's not mine," Souad says again, although her voice wavers.

Their mother closes her eyes and takes a deep breath. When she opens them and speaks, she sounds falsely cheerful.

"Riham," she croons. "Are you ready to go? *Mama,*" she calls. "We're going. But I'm leaving Souad here."

Souad hoists herself onto the kitchen counter, dangles her bare legs. "No, you're not," she says.

Their mother's cool shatters. "God*damn* it, Souad, every day with you. All I ask is for you to pick up your toys, because someone could trip on them and break their neck. Is that what you want?"

"But they're not mine!"

"Stop lying, Souad. Whose are they? Teta's?"

"I don't know—"

"Fine."

Riham looks up from her book and watches with interest as her mother begins to clear the toys. She makes for the door. "Since they don't belong to you or Riham, then they're just trash, and I'm throwing them out."

"You can't do that!" Souad jumps down from the counter.

"Why not? They're not yours, why should you care if—"

"They're mine," Souad says sullenly. Their mother continues to walk away. Souad raises her voice. "They're mine! They're mine! Give *me.*"

"Then *clean them up.*"

"Okay!"

"Is there a reason everyone's hollering like maniacs?"

Riham's shoulders instinctively relax at the voice. Her grandmother walks into the kitchen, a robe the shade of eggplant fluttering around her. She is wearing the paisley veil, Riham's favorite. Her grandmother is the one bright spot of these summers.

Alia looks abashed. "Everything's always a battle with her," she grumbles. "We have a long drive ahead of us and she's already making trouble."

Salma picks up a stray doll and hands it to Souad. "Sousu doesn't mean it, do you, sweet? She's sorry."

Souad looks down. She nods. "I'm sorry."

Alia touches Souad's hair and says, her voice softer, "Should I make honey or cheese sandwiches for the beach?"

Riham writes down *the beach* on the list in her small, tidy handwriting.

Summers, they stay with Teta. Her building, which overlooks the city, belongs to the family, Riham knows, and her great-aunts live on the other floors. Her grandmother's apartment, where each of them has a room, stays the same from visit to visit, filled with framed photographs of their younger selves. At night from the balcony, the city looks like a distant, smoldering thing.

"Your second home," her grandmother says when they arrive. Every year she gets fatter, her face crinkling up. It saddens Riham to think of her grandmother alone during the year, moving through the large apartment.

But Salma never seems forlorn or lonely. She spends her days cooking with her sisters or in the garden, an enclosed area behind the house sprawling with plants and flowers and one large, gnarled olive tree. She weeds and waters the plants herself, waits for the tomatoes and cucumbers to grow large before picking them. Sometimes she asks Riham to help her clean the vegetables and Riham gets grit beneath her nails.

"Now *this* is food," her grandmother likes to say, beaming at the colorful salads on the table. "From the soil to our mouths."

There was another garden, Riham has been told, though the details of it are hazy to her, almost fictional. All she knows is this garden was in Palestine, and it burned down. It is linked to the war she learned about in school and to her father being away a long time ago. The adults rarely speak of these things, giving vague responses to questions. It is clear they find this talk painful, and Riham isn't the type of girl to ask for more.

This summer, her mother's cousin Khalto Mimi is here. Khalto Mimi's husband died the previous year and now they spend much of their time at her small house. Riham had envisioned a silent, somber home, everyone draped in black, but instead Mimi and her daughters wear bright dresses and laugh often.

There are dozens of photographs of the father, a handsome man with a thick mustache—kissing a pudgy toddler Lara, his arm around Khalto Mimi, smiling in front of a cake dotted with candles—and the girls bring him up casually in conversation.

"It was when Baba first got sick," Lara corrected Mira once while talking about an old family vacation. They are both sunny and beautiful, with sleek black hair. Riham is envious of their trim bodies, the easy way they tease their mother.

"How wonderful," Alia says often, "that Lara and Mira are so close in age to you." Karam's absence means that Riham has no excuses not to spend time with them. She wants to explain to her mother that Mimi's daughters are a different breed of girl, akin to some of the ones in Riham's private school in Kuwait, pretty, daring, streaking their hair with henna and lemons.

She knows Lara and Mira are aware of this, but they are nice to her, politely inviting her along. They have the magnanimity of the innately beautiful.

"Would you like me to straighten your hair?" Lara asks her sometimes. They eye her with an optimism—as though she is a ratty car with a decent engine—that Riham finds alarming. In the shops they coax her to try dresses on.

"Hmm," they say. "Flowy designs definitely suit you, with your . . . body type." She knows they are trying not to say *fat*.

Afterward, they get ice cream cones and sit on the balcony, their brown legs stretched onto each other's chairs. Lara and Mira speak voraciously of the future.

"Paris," Lara says, as though she were a woman in her twenties. "Definitely Paris. It's the only place to become a real dancer."

"Ugh, Paris. Too cold. I'm going to move to Spain. Or California." Mira, fifteen years old, with a waist so small Riham could wrap her hands around it.

"What will you do there?"

"Sing," Mira always says. She sometimes sings for the adults when they gather for tea. She winds her hair into a bun, tilts her long neck back, and parts her lips. It is like watching someone paint the sky.

"What about you, Riham?" the girls ask her. "What do you want to do?"

The answer is complicated. Riham is mousy and shy, her body pudgy in the thighs and hips. Her left breast is treacherously larger than her right one. A smattering of acne mars her forehead, and her limp hair never curls like her sister's.

Still, she burns with daydreams of growing up and moving to Europe. Riham has never been there but imagines a life with a studio apartment, eating jam on baguettes and drinking green tea, days filled with reading novels and drawing.

When Riham thinks of her future self, it is of a person transformed, so removed from her current self that the only remnants will be phantomlike. In her daydreams, future Riham simply erases current Riham, forgets her entirely. And if this causes a twinge of preemptive mourning or protest, the smallest tendril of sorrow for herself now—with her love of soggy cereal, the way she drapes strands of hair like a mustache over her lips while reading, her thrill at the scent of old books—it is slight and she resolutely ignores it.

But, of course, she cannot say all of this, and so she quietly replies,

"I want to live in an apartment by myself," and the girls exchange glances of confusion and pity.

In the past few months, she has amended her fantasies to include boys, someone kissing her full on the lips. It happened without warning; suddenly she was dreaming of faceless boys touching her, dancing with her. She always wakes breathless and ashamed, a dampness between her legs. During the day, her thoughts race and circle, heliocentric, always returning to boys.

Well, one boy.

Lara and Mira speak frankly about boys, in a way that Riham's friends in Kuwait—girls Riham has known since kindergarten, shy girls who like to swap books and talk about films, their only transgression an afternoon when they bought cigarettes and smoked until they became dizzy—never have.

"So luscious," Mira croons about a rock star. "Those eyes are like caramel drops."

In the afternoons, Lara and Mira gather with their friends at a neighborhood pastry shop. They buy *kanafeh* and sticky rolls, gossiping and laughing. Sometimes boys from their school come in, sweaty from playing football. They are rowdy with one another, teasing when the girls, demurring, call out for them to be careful.

Riham watches these interactions with fascination, an anthropologist observing a new tribe. The girls toss their hair and smile at the boys.

"You're disgusting," they say when the boys spit. And the boys grin.

Sometimes one of the braver boys, usually Rafic, will catch an insect and chase the girls around with it, but slowly, giving them time to escape. The girls shriek and run away, flushed with attention.

"Stop!" they call. They punch the boys playfully on the shoulder.

Of all the neighborhood boys, Riham likes Bassam the most. He is Lara's age, one year younger than Riham, and yet oddly poised. He never roughhouses or spits, like Rafic, and she has seen him smoke a cigarette only once. He isn't handsome like Rafic either—slightly chubby, always wearing the same scuffed sneakers. His face is oval as an egg, and his eyes are faintly slanted. Tufts of curls stick out around his head. The other boys call him Romeo, and Riham can tell he is well liked.

"Why do they call him that?" Riham once asked Lara.

Lara rolled her eyes. "Oh, Bassam." She explained that he'd once, on a dare, kissed a girl in the middle of the playground.

"Anyone could have seen it. The teachers would've kicked him out."

"Did he get in trouble?" Riham asked. She felt jealous of the girl.

"No," Lara had said. "But he's been Romeo ever since. Which is hilarious because he's so chubby and has all that weird hair and he barely speaks. You know?"

"Definitely," Riham replied, her plainly affected indifference giving her away.

"We're going to be late for Mimi," her mother says. "They headed out an hour ago. Everyone ready? Souad, help me wrap these up." On the kitchen counter there is a stack of sandwiches her mother has prepared. Souad begins wrapping them in paper towels. She wears a cotton dress, and when she turns, Riham can see the outline of her hipbones. Riham is dreading the car ride, the long day at the beach.

"If you're going to pick any more shells," her mother is telling Souad, "you need to wash them *before* you get in the car. Teta's car is full of sand."

"The shells are for Karam—"

"I'll wash them with her," her grandmother interrupts smoothly. "Right, Sous? We'll get a nice bagful for your brother."

Riham feels a sudden longing for her brother, doe-eyed—though in the past few months his features have begun to elongate and harden, several scraggly hairs prickling his chin—her ally during these summers.

Her mother kisses Riham on the forehead. "Enough with the melancholy." She winks at her. "The beach will be fun."

Amman transforms her mother. Back in Kuwait she complains of being tired and snaps at them when the television is too loud. She wears slacks and T-shirts, kohl around her eyes. But here, she keeps her face bare, wears short dresses that cling to her thighs. Her skin browns the way Souad's does, while Riham's turns red and peels in itchy flakes.

In the evenings, they sit on Khalto Mimi's balcony and visit with the neighborhood women, women that Alia went to school with years ago. They eat figs and pour tea and cut thick wedges of orange-peel cake. No husbands ever come, no fathers or brothers. Only children, laughing and playing as dusk falls, the light turning first red, then orange, then purple. Her mother looks radiant in the evenings. The other women call her Aloush and tease her about her school days. Riham perches on the balcony railing, watching them. They seem like strange, mythical creatures to her, with their laughter and talk. They speak of soldiers and husbands and love.

"Come here, *habibti*," Alia will say sometimes, her arms extended, and Riham goes to her mother gratefully.

"*Aroos*," the women call her. "Little bride."

"We're going to marry you off," they tease.

"Good God, so long as he's not Kuwaiti." Alia wrinkles her nose, and everyone laughs.

"Are they so bad?"

"They're awful. With their terrible country. Not a single decent restaurant!" Her mother likes to imitate the locals, their harsh Arabic and mannerisms. Riham feels her ears burn when she does this, angry at her mother for speaking this way of their life in Kuwait, for the disloyalty to her father.

Her father, with his ink-stained fingertips, his slow chuckle. The way he pops peppermint candies in his mouth that clank against his teeth as he drinks tea. His habit of retiring to his study after dinner sometimes, the door only slightly ajar, so that Riham has to flatten herself against the wall to see the familiar silhouette of him, bent over his desk, writing. She loves the sound of the pen scratching against the paper, the way he always looks so solemn in those moments, unaware of her watching.

She misses him terribly, even more than she does Karam, misses talking with him about books, the way he quizzes her on characters and plot lines.

"And Anna Karenina?" he would say while cracking a pumpkin seed—her favorite, though she only sucks the shells until the salt is gone. "Do you think she made the right choice?"

If he were here, her father would understand why Riham wished to stay home, why she preferred to be alone rather than trailing Mira and Lara—as though she is some leper, some babysitting charge—and why she hates her polka-dot bathing suit, the one her mother bought when they first arrived. It is the exact same one as Lara's and the contrast is depressing, how it clings perfectly to Lara's thin frame, bulges and strains on Riham. She always wears a shirt over it.

So far, she hasn't entered the water once. Even on the hottest days she remains in the shade with her book. When anyone asks, she says she has a stomachache.

In her fantasy, Bassam notices her suddenly. There is a lull in the chatter at the pastry shop and their eyes lock, like the click of a clock's hand snapping into place. He sees her and nods.

"Want to walk to the sea?" he asks, taking her hand. Everyone in the shop watches them go, surprised at the mousy girl from Kuwait. As she heads out with Bassam, Riham turns and smiles at Mira and Lara.

They walk together until the sun goes down, night settling around them. He tells her she is pretty as the moon—Riham edits herself liberally in her fantasies; she has a trim waistline, curls the shade of mink—and she tells him about Scarlett O'Hara, how she made men fall in love with her in minutes.

"I never thought I'd meet you," he says, and this is when he turns to her. In the distance, lights from the fishing boats glitter. Riham dips her head and looks up at him through her eyelashes—a trick she learned from watching her mother—and smiles without speaking. Bassam places a finger on her chin and tilts her head upward. They kiss.

Here the fantasy always stalls. All that Riham knows of what bodies do together is gleaned from passages in novels and ambiguous biology lessons. She understands there is nudity involved, and some complicated incursion—an upward motion, the woman below, usually clutching the man's neck—something enormous and final.

There are times she feels a tremble, tiny quakes within her body, feels the firecrackers beneath her hipbones and shakes. She knows it is sin.

"I think Lara and Mira are going to a party tomorrow," Alia says to Riham in the car. She glances at her in the rearview mirror.

"Hmm." Riham makes a noncommittal sound. Next to her, Souad is humming to herself and rolling up a tissue.

"I think it's a birthday party. Mimi said you should go with them."

Several hours at some girl's house, sweating and discreetly lifting her arms to smell her armpits, struggling to think of things to say while the other girls giggle and chat.

"They've assigned us books for the summer that I have to read." It is partly true; the books exist, but Riham has already read each one twice.

"Good for you, *habibti.*" Her grandmother twists back to smile at Riham. "Keeping up with your schoolwork."

"She can read them after," her mother says. From the back seat, Riham sees her bright red fingernails drumming on the steering wheel. In Kuwait her mother never drives, never paints her nails.

"I need to start tomorrow," Riham says desperately.

Her mother sighs and waves her hand out of the window, letting another driver pass. "Riham, we're here for only two more weeks. Every minute you spend with those girls, you act like your teeth are being pulled out. This is what girls your age do, they go out together, they have fun, they talk and—"

"Aloush, leave her," her grandmother says. She turns the car radio on. Riham sees her mother's brow furrow in the mirror.

"Mama, I'm not punishing her. I'm trying to get her to enjoy herself."

"She is enjoying herself. Aren't you, dear?"

"Yes," Riham says as enthusiastically as she can.

"I'm not!" Souad calls.

"Listen." Salma holds up a hand, and they all fall silent. A newscaster's voice fills the car with urgent tones.

"In southern Lebanon . . . Several shot dead . . . Tanks have rolled over . . ."

Her grandmother clicks her tongue and lowers the volume. "That poor country. All that slaughter, and now Israel's joined the party."

"They said an entire village was burned to the ground. The bodies stacked high."

"Mimi's cousin is saying they're lucky if they get an hour of electricity a day there. Most of the time it's just candles. Even the water's filthy."

"Riham," Souad whispers and Riham looks over. Her sister is smiling mischievously as she chews on a strand of hair. Between her fingers is the rolled-up tissue, twisted and elongated to look like a cigarette. Souad puts the tip of the paper between her teeth, still chewing on her hair, and purses her lips. At ten years old, Souad is all curls and full lips: Riham has begun to envy her sister. Souad pretends to blow out smoke.

"Don't chew your hair," Riham says automatically. Souad has always chewed on pens and toys and her fingernails. For a while, her mother dipped Souad's fingers in hot sauce, but Souad stubbornly learned to like the taste.

Souad lets the curl fall out of her mouth. She clamps her lips around the fashioned cigarette, pretending to inhale. "*Wooooo.*" She exhales, tilting her head back like an actress.

Riham laughs in spite of herself. Her sister is a foreign, beguiling creature. Last year they'd all gone to an aquarium, and one of the rooms had an enormous tank lit from within. Inside there was a jellyfish and several other fish rippled by. One fish was purple, veined with brilliant, iridescent scales. Watching it dart through the water, Riham thought: *Souad.*

"I'm making smoke rings," Souad says, oblivious to tanks or burned villages, oblivious to her mother and grandmother deep in conversation about war, to anything but her lips releasing invisible coils of smoke.

The car ride takes hours and by the time they reach Aqaba, Riham is already tired and vaguely nauseous. At the beach, families have laid out bed sheets and towels, fruit and sandwiches spread between them. Groups of boys kick around a ball, the air punctuated with their cheers and groans. A flock of veiled women have pulled up their skirts and ventured into the water up to their calves. Riham's stomach knots at the sight of so many slender bodies.

"There." Alia points. They follow her toward a trio of colorful towels, Khalto Mimi and the girls lying on them.

"The water is incredible," Lara calls out as they approach. She has rubbed oil all over, her skin shimmering. Between the towels are an assortment of oils and lotions, a large bottle of water.

"Honey and *labneh* sandwiches," Salma says, setting the basket down.

"Bless your hands, Auntie," Khalto Mimi says. "I'll be starving soon." Her mascara is clumpy and the roll of flab around her midsection, bulging against her Lycra bathing suit, reminds Riham uncomfortably of her own.

They roll out their own towels, and Khalto Mimi rummages through her bag for a pack of cigarettes. "Did you hear about Beirut?"

"I was telling Mama, this is exactly what the Israelis want," Alia says.

Souad kneels and picks up a bottle of lotion. There is a smiling coconut tree on the front.

"You want some, *ma belle*?" Lara asks. One hand shields her face from the sun. Mira and Lara's nickname for Souad—"my beautiful."

"Yes," Souad says. "I want a lot."

"Off," Mira says, smiling, and Souad lifts her dress over her head and tosses it on the sand. Her bathing suit is green, faded.

There is a tightness in Riham's chest as she watches her sister flop down onto Lara's towel, brown limbs everywhere, then lifts her hair with both hands so Lara can rub oil on her shoulders. Souad has fit in easily with the older girls; they seem entranced by her. Riham lies down on her towel, careful not to let her dress rise up.

"Gimme," Alia says, turning toward Khalto Mimi with her arm out. Riham notices the tightness of her mother's thighs, only the slightest puckering when she turns, her compact torso beneath the bathing suit.

"Your lungs are turning black, girls," her grandmother chides as Alia lights a cigarette.

"I know, Auntie," Khalto Mimi says with mock shame. "We're terrible."

"Only in Amman, Mama," Alia says, blowing out a ribbon of smoke.

"They're leaving," Khalto Mimi says as her daughters get up. "They can't sit with their poor, overheated mother for more than a half hour."

Mira rolls her eyes and turns to Riham, the tiny divot in her collarbone beautiful, collecting a pool of oil. "We're going to get some lunch. You want to come?"

The question has an artificial lilt to it and Riham knows Khalto Mimi instructed her to ask.

"I need to get some reading done," she says, gesturing uselessly at her bag.

"That's too bad." Riham hears the relief in Lara's voice.

"Riham," Alia begins pointedly, but Salma interrupts her.

"It's hot," Salma says, rising. "I need some water from the shop. Riham, will you help me?"

"Mama, you should let her— "

"Are you okay with that, dear?" Salma speaks over Alia, looking at Riham. She can see her grandmother understands. The way her father would if he were here. Riham nods.

The shop is at the corner of the parking lot, a hut with a metal roof and a man selling drinks and falafel sandwiches.

"This weather," her grandmother says as they walk across the sand. Riham can feel the heat, like fire, between her toes.

"Thank you." Riham keeps her eyes on her toes. She sees her grandmother glance toward her. Salma clears her throat and speaks gently.

"Are they mean to you?"

Riham shakes her head, tries to think of the right words to describe it. "It's like we speak different languages."

Salma laughs. "When I was your age, I knew girls like that. They would call me names and I'd cry and cry. Sometimes they pulled the ribbons from my hair and threw them in the trash."

"Really?" Riham loves being alone with her grandmother, the snippets of her life that are revealed. She loves to imagine the life her grandmother had, a peasant girl by the sea, before everything changed.

"It was because I was different. They knew it. I didn't, not until later."

"Different how?" They reach the shop and her grandmother gestures to the man behind the counter.

"Dear, a large bottle of water, please."

"Yes, Auntie."

"Ice cold, please."

While they wait, her grandmother has a distant look in her eyes, remembering. "I cared about different things. I prayed a lot. I spent time alone."

"Like me."

Salma smiles. "Have you been reading the suras the imam told you about?"

"Yes." Riham hesitates. There is something she wants to ask her grandmother, about whether she prayed after her own son was killed. The adults rarely talk about him, but Riham gathers details about him like a magpie, snatched from overheard conversations: his name was Mustafa; he was five years older than her mother; he died in Palestine and no one—not her mother, not Teta—got to say goodbye. "All those deaths, the bloodshed. And then I think about what's happening in the world now. Sometimes it seems—" Riham falters.

"That Allah is cruel."

Riham nods. Her grandmother leans down and, unexpectedly, kisses Riham on her forehead. She speaks lightly.

"There's nothing wrong with having questions for Allah. It means you're taking Him seriously."

Since Riham can remember, her grandmother has been her favorite part of the Amman trips. She is like Khalto Widad, warm and loving, always cooking Riham her favorite meals. When Riham was younger, her grandmother would bathe her, sprinkling scented oils into the water, and braid her hair afterward. At the end of every school year, Riham tucks her report card in the sleeve of her suitcase to show her grandmother.

"You brilliant girl," Salma says every year, hanging the report card on the refrigerator. When people come over to visit, she introduces Riham as "my smart one."

Salma's faith lends her a dignified air, authentic and stately in a way other veiled women are not. During Ramadan, her grandmother breaks fast not with mouthfuls of meat but rather a single olive and a sip of water, a restraint that Riham marvels at.

Sometimes she takes Riham to the mosque near her apartment, a domed edifice with a marbled courtyard. There is an imperial archway of grape leaves and vines, an inscription reading *There is no Allah but Allah.* Riham knows the phrase from school and is always happy to see something she recognizes.

Her grandmother gives her a scarf to knot around her head, and a long robe, white with red embroidery. Although it's too large, the sleeves past her fingers, the hem tripping her, Riham always feels strangely beautiful following her grandmother up the stairs, into the suddenly cool, dark entrance. They step out of their sandals before entering the mosque, place them alongside the others. The carpet is scratchy beneath her bare feet.

Inside the mosque, women speak with her grandmother eagerly, and Riham understands that Salma is loved.

"Pretty scarf, Khalto."

"How are the tomatoes this summer, Khalto?"

"Fine, fine. Strong and red. You should come by and pick some for your children."

"*Inshallah.*" Last week, an elderly man approached them. "Dear Salma, is this your granddaughter?"

"It is." A smile unfolded across her grandmother's face. "This is the lovely Riham. Riham, this is Imam Zuhair."

"Riham." The imam smiled, thousands of wrinkles crinkling his eyes. Riham instantly liked him, the way he inclined his head slightly to her. "It's an honor."

"Your mosque is beautiful." The words came out stammered, and Riham blushed. She sounded stupid to her own ears, childish.

He looked around at the rows of Qur'ans lining the walls, the green carpet, people sitting in the corners, praying. Light poured in through the large windows.

"Why, yes." He spoke as though startled. "It is beautiful." He turned to Salma. "Your granddaughter sees beauty even in the well worn. This is a gift."

Later that day, when they were praying, and Riham touched her forehead on the carpet, kneeling and rising with the other bodies; she shut her eyes and let herself be carried by the sounds of the mosque, the rustle of feet on the floor, the fragrance of incense, carried and then returned gently to the earth.

Alia and Khalto Mimi smoke one cigarette after the other as they talk, the smell thick in the air. Riham watches their mouths, every few minutes looking up from her book.

"I can't believe the summer's almost over."

"I know, back to Kuwait."

"Do you think you'll be able to return for Eid?"

"Probably not. The children's school—"

"I hate school," Souad says.

"Sous, your turn."

Souad returns her attention to the game of chess with her grandmother, the pieces streaked from wear, weeks of salt water and sun eroding them.

"I'm roasting." Khalto Mimi sighs, inspecting her shoulders. "Remember how awful returning to school was? The girls are positively depressed about it."

"Not Riham," Alia says. She eyes Riham thoughtfully. "Are you looking forward to starting school?"

Riham thinks about her school, the air-conditioned classrooms, the way the teachers love her, especially Madame Haddad, the librarian who saves the new books for Riham to read first. She thinks about her friends, who are quiet and awkward, never telling her to straighten her hair.

"I can't wait," Riham says softly.

"Bravo." Khalto Mimi blows a stream of smoke. "Teach my lazy girls."

"Exactly," Salma says. "That's what will last. A good brain, hard work."

"Yes," Alia says with an uncertain smile, and Riham knows her mother is thinking of Mira and Lara, off somewhere getting lunch in their sundresses, giggling about boys. "Yes."

• • •

ALIA AND KHALTO MIMI begin unwrapping sandwiches. Souad, bored of the chess game, wanders over to the water and comes back with handfuls of shells.

"Look!" she calls, standing over the towels. Sand scatters over them. "I found a bunch of big ones."

"Goddamn it, Souad." Alia shakes sand off the sandwiches as Souad sits.

"I'm trying to keep myself busy. That's what you said to do." Souad imitates their mother's voice perfectly. "'Souad, Mimi and I are talking. No, you can't go play with Mira and Lara. Keep yourself busy.'"

The tops of Khalto Mimi's large, greasy breasts jiggle. "That's pretty good, Aloush. She should be an actress."

Alia pulls her sunglasses off and slits her eyes toward Souad, but Riham can hear the laughter in her voice. "Mannerless! I need to raise you all over again."

"You can raise her after you feed me," Khalto Mimi says. Alia unwraps a foiled sandwich.

"Honey or cheese?"

"Cheese."

"Mama?"

"Half of each, please."

"Those boys are getting louder and louder." They all turn to watch the group of boys kicking a football near the shore. One kicks the ball straight up and uses his head to jounce it, sends it soaring in the direction of their towels.

"I can kick better than that," Souad says, scrambling to her feet.

"Don't," Alia warns, and Souad sits again.

Two of the boys chase after the ball, laughing as they run. Their figures get closer to the group, one tall and lean, the other small and stout, their features slowly visible.

Bassam and Rafic.

Riham shimmies her body up, ducks her head, mortified, as they jog past. Her mind spins: Bassam isn't supposed to be here, so far from Amman. She is excruciatingly aware of her body, the dampness under her arms, her smell.

"*Ya* Riham." Her mother waves something silver in the sun. "Your sandwich."

Riham's face burns; she's horrified at the thought of Bassam watching her eat, especially something so huge. "I'm not hungry," she mumbles.

"What?"

Lower your voice, Riham wants to scream. From the corner of her eye she sees Rafic reach the ball, then the two of them running back to the group. "I'm not hungry," she says louder.

Her mother frowns, waves the sandwich again. "You haven't eaten since breakfast."

"I want to swim first." As soon as she speaks the words, Riham regrets them—what is she *thinking?*—but surprise crosses her mother's face. She looks relieved, and Riham suddenly puts together the sharp, furtive looks her mother has been giving her all summer, that scrutiny—*concern*.

"Oh." She lowers the sandwich. "Good. Swim first, then come eat." Riham catches her grandmother's quizzical eye. Alia gestures toward the sea. "Go, go."

Riham rises reluctantly. She eyes the water, dread knotting her stomach. In her peripheral vision, she sees Bassam and Rafic with the group of boys, kicking the ball toward each other. She can't walk to the water without crossing their path, she realizes with a jolt.

"I'm going swimming too." Souad stands up, all leg, sand sticking to her skin. She looks like a dirty, beautiful urchin in a Victorian novel. "I'll be back soon," she informs their mother.

Without looking up, Alia clicks her tongue and points to the empty spot on the towel where Souad had just been sitting.

Immediately, Souad begins to whine. "That's not fair, you're letting Riham go. I want to swim too."

"You," Alia says to Souad, "sit your little butt down. You can go after you finish your sandwich."

"I can just stay," Riham offers desperately. "I'll take her after."

"You go have fun, *habibti.* She'll be fine."

Souad eyes her mother, hands clamped on her hips. For a moment they glare at each other. Finally, she kicks at the edge of the towel and sits down, pouting.

Riham begins to walk toward the water. Her heart pounds and she is painfully, overwhelmingly, aware that she is on display. It feels like a thousand eyes watching her. She feels an impossible hush settle over the beach, every single person—families, all of the boys, Bassam—stopping and turning to her.

She takes one step and then another, sand hot beneath her feet, suddenly conscious of her arms, how they swing unnaturally against her hips, how her knees knock together as she walks. All of them, she knows, are holding their breath, watching this agonizingly slow walk, this walk that is taking forever, years, really, because the water, even though it seemed so close from the towels, is far, far away. Sweat trickles between her breasts and that spongy scent is stronger.

And then, at last, she is there: at the edge of the water. She takes a quick look behind her and is stunned to find that no one is watching her. All the people are eating and talking. The boys are still kicking the ball around, jogging as they call out to one another. Bassam kicks the ball neatly through the air.

She watches him for a second, so lovely as his leg arches midkick, and, as if charged by her gaze, he turns and looks directly at her. The air leaves her lungs. He lifts his hand in greeting, his face brightening into a half smile.

She moves rapidly, taking off the dress and throwing it on the sand, then scrambling, mortified at the sight of her own naked arms and legs, toward the water quickly, quickly, before he can reach her, before any of them can see her in this awful bareness.

The only place away from the boys' laughter is the water, and so she propels herself in. For the first few seconds she is so charged with adrenaline, her heart pounding at Bassam's eyes, his smile, that she doesn't even notice the water as she wades in. But then it hits her, the water freezing against her sunburned skin, so icy and unexpected that she gasps. She keeps her back to the shoreline—is he still watching?—and moves, her feet catching and slipping on mounds of seashells and tiny rocks and something slimy that makes her shiver.

She used to love the water when she was younger, would swim for hours during the summer, she and Karam racing each other to the little red buoys. She'd loved the way her hair still tasted of salt even after her grandmother scrubbed it with shampoo. Alone in the water, she was something magical, her limbs suddenly graceful as she pirouetted, pretending to be a mermaid floating in the sea.

But now she is filled with hatred toward it—at the water unfurling and undulating like some enormous tongue, aquamarine and gleaming with malice. Even though it terrifies her, she keeps her eyes on the sea ahead. To turn around would be disastrous, she thinks; to turn around would be to see *him*, and she imagines his gaze burning across the beach, skipping over the water to find her. She continues to wade deeper, moving messily in the water, aware that her skin is visible to those on the coast until she—quickly—blankets herself with water.

The water now reaches her upper arms, covering her breasts, the sea like a towel. She starts to swim. One arm after the other, she slices the water with her body. After taking a breath, she dives her head in, swims as far as she can until her lungs begin to burn. She lifts her head and sucks air thirstily. Her legs tread water and she notices that she isn't cold anymore.

The only sounds filling her ears are the waves and her breath. Her back still to the shore, she moves her arms, making circles. A faraway memory jars her—her mother carrying her into the ocean as a child, a glimmer of seawater beneath her tiny hands.

"It's like bathwater, see?" her mother had said, cradling her. Riham, looking up at her, saw the sun haloing her head. She remembers now what her four-year-old mind had thought: *The most beautiful woman in the world.*

Just as the memory is filtering through her, Riham understands that the water does, indeed, feel like bathwater, no longer icy, and not just from the effort of swimming—the water itself swirls warm. She turns at last to face the shore.

It is a distant smudge of gold.

This is the thought that comes to her first—that the shore is now a blur—and panic begins to squeeze her. She realizes the voices and laughter and splashing are barely audible from here, that the slapping of waves means she is far, really far away. Even the other swimmers are distant, their heads dots in the waves. She squints toward the shore and sees the yellow of her family's towels. This calms her and she takes a deep breath.

"O-kay," she says to herself in the singsong voice she uses with children. "Time to swim."

She takes another breath and begins to kick, one-two-three, strong thrashing motions, knowing in the back of her mind she must look so stupid, thankful that no one can see her. Her breath comes heavily, moistly, water bubbling against her lips, and she tries to part the water with her arms like two knives, as she'd been taught years ago in this very sea. She holds her breath until her chest explodes, then lifts her head for air.

It is then, as she is gasping for air, that the second realization comes, far worse—*she is not getting closer to the shore.* No. She is being pulled away from it, trying to slice the water when, in fact, she is lashing against it uselessly. Something invisible in the waves is pulling her quietly but urgently back into its arms. She feels her body being eddied, the water around her warmer now, and she begins to panic in earnest.

With the panic comes motion; Riham begins to kick and claw and fist at the water. She forgets the knives, the graceful diving; her body—her arms and legs—and her mind seem to fuse into one screaming thought: *land.* She feels the drag of the current and remembers dimly someone once telling her, years ago, in another lifetime, that if you felt the ocean pulling, you should never fight against it, but wait until you were out of the current. But whoever said that had never been here, Riham thinks, had never felt this terrible, magnetic tugging, as though there were nets and she was being swept up into them, swept into the water's mouth.

Riham hears distant screams. She tries to blink as she looks toward the shore, but the sun is too bright, and she cannot see anything but the sea, the salt in her eyes, the rush and pull of water.

There is a flare of blue, and she is suddenly under the water, her head beneath it. Riham opens her mouth but gargles salt, sputters. Up. She needs up. Her thoughts come in brief, choppy phrases. *Up. Lift head. Kick.*

Her head surfaces and Riham gulps air, her ears full of her rattled breath. She will break, she knows, she will flop and sink to the bottom of the sea if she doesn't move. Her arms are so tired, heavy as stone, but she knows she must lift and slice, lift and slice, even as her body shakes.

"Now, now," she yells to herself, but it comes out hoarse. She forces her legs to kick and hears the screaming once more, falling and rising above the waves.

She sees herself, a flimsy string floating through the water. Then another image—seeing herself from above, looking down at her struggling, airless body. A swath of light and some blackness, a splotch of it. Riham thinks to herself, conversationally, *She needs to scrub that out.*

Again there is the calling out, thudding against the waves: *Riham. Riham.* Startled, she recognizes that is her—Riham, Riham—that some essence of her is here, threading through the water, far from sand. She takes shaky gulps of air and tries to remember Riham. That was so long ago—why, she is an old woman now! It is a peculiar thought, but decisive, with the same conviction she would say yes, of course her eyes are brown, or yes, she loves her father—but she is certain, absolutely certain, that she has lived for decades, that she is an old woman dying now, elsewhere, and this is just a memory.

She doesn't have a chance to dwell on this. Another undulation of the sea and she rocks with it, her shoulders knocking against the crested wave, her arms furious with pain, and she understands suddenly that if she doesn't call out, if she doesn't open her mouth and speak and say—anything, *anything*—then she will die, the old woman and the little girl, she will die and she will be dead, and the water will take her. And with that fear Riham opens her mouth and speaks against the salt water the only name that leaps to her lips.

Allah.

Him, oh, Him, oh, that warm rush at the mosque, that hope that quickened her heart when her grandmother fitted the veil around her head and they sat on the carpet, surrounded by the perfume of incense, the roof above her like a green sky. She thinks of it and is overcome with a hot, liquid love.

Someone is shouting, the sound reaching over the waves, but Riham is shaky with exhaustion, fatigue that petrifies her limbs. The arms rock her again but suddenly they are different arms, arms that are not water but, impossibly, human, and there is something warm, breath against her neck, someone saying, *Hold on, hold on*, and Riham rests her head—on the wave? on the arm?—and the water stretches and glitters and blackens.

There is a dark room where Riham is lying down and she can smell cake. Around her, she understands, is a magnificent party, and that is where all the noise is coming from, dozens of voices chattering. They sound scared, but Riham knows it's a trick; they are just pretending to be frightened because they haven't invited her. She wants to cry because now there will be no cake. All of a sudden, stinging sears her nostrils, and she is coughing, salt, salt, it seems like it will never end, the water in her throat. A light shivers and claps, stretching into a creature with many arms, an octopus, she sees, an octopus moving his body in a flashy dance and saying something. Qur'an, she thinks, recognizing the frantic verses, but the octopus is doing it wrong, garbling the words.

Riham opens her mouth to scold the octopus but before she can, salt shoots through her once more and she is coughing, arms are pulling her up, someone is slapping her on her back and she is retching, suddenly yanked out of the water, akimbo on the gritty shore, and she is vomiting, stream after stream, clumping the sand with globs of white. *Cheese*, Riham thinks, recalling the warm bread and cheese, her breakfast this morning.

She lifts her head unsteadily. Blinking in the sunlight, she looks around at the people gathered. Her mother kneels in front of her, sobbing. It occurs to Riham that she hasn't seen her mother cry in years. Khalto Mimi is hugging her mother. Souad stands beside them, her face white and afraid, her eyes trickling tears. The towels have been wrenched around, and food is scattered everywhere, and for a second Riham thinks her mother will be furious, all that sand in the food, but then she remembers that her mother is crying, and crying for her.

"Riham." Her mother chokes out her name like a talisman, a prayer, and suddenly Riham is enveloped in her mother's arms, smelling the musk of her skin. She peeks around at the people surrounding her, the other picnicking families and the boys, too, Bassam standing to the side with the group of them. He suddenly looks very young, afraid. The voices merge.

"She's alive, she's alive."

"Uncle, I've never seen anyone swim so fast, you *saved* her."

"When I saw her on your shoulders, limp like that, my God, I thought—"

"Shh, we all did, but she's fine."

"She's a tough little girl, she was carried so far out, but she kept kicking."

"She's breathing, right?"

Riham contemplates this last question, recognizes that she has never had to wonder about such a thing before, never had to consider her breath—what a remarkable thing to think about, *her breathing*, that thing she does without thinking—but now she becomes aware of how her lungs feel, tight and ragged in her chest, of how it hurts to inhale, like there are tiny spikes in her throat. She turns away from her mother and vomits promptly on the sand.

"*Move*," her grandmother's voice commands above the rest. "Everyone, give her space. She needs air." A hand appears near the sand, holding one of the bottles of water. Riham looks up at her grandmother's face, ashen beneath her veil but strong. She nods at Riham. "Drink this, slowly." Riham brings it to her lips and her stomach cramps, but she sips.

A drop of seawater trickles into her eye, stinging. She blinks and is aware of her body, the flab beneath her bathing suit, her bareness while throngs of people watch her, while Bassam watches her. Watch her vomit too, they all saw it, she thinks, mortified at the lumps of white on the sand. Ancient, familiar shame begins to throb but she hears her grandmother breathing and realizes that this, the strings of vomit, *this* is what saved her, it is what kept her alive, what returned her to breath.

Suddenly she doesn't care at all who sees her, who watches as she lifts her head and looks not at the picnickers or boys or swimmers but her family, at her mother still weeping. They are all, Souad and Alia and Salma, looking at her as though she is a ghost and it dawns on Riham that she did something, that she has accomplished something just by living, just by kicking and kicking in the water.

"Riham." Her mother's voice catches. "Riham, this is the man who saved you." Her mother points to a young man from one of the nearby picnicking families. His trousers and shirt are wet, plastered to his body. Riham sees for the first time that her own mother's dress is wet and caked with sand. She tried to swim as well, Riham understands. *It's like bathwater, see?*

"You're a strong little girl," the bearded man says. "You kept kicking." Riham tries to imagine this man carrying her, her body in his arms, but she feels no embarrassment.

"Thank you," she says, and everyone starts laughing, even her mother, the hysterical laughter of the relieved.

Riham pushes her hair back, her hands less shaky now. She squints in the sunlight, people's voices around her.

"It's a miracle."

"They need lifeguards here."

"That water can be so dangerous."

The sun glints and Riham sees, for the first time since waking, the water between the legs of people, that astonishing blue. She says something under her breath. No one hears except her grandmother, who bends down. She rubs a rough, callused hand through Riham's hair as the voices around them continue.

Her grandmother's arms are firm around her body. "Yes," her grandmother says quietly, so no one else hears. "Yes, He saved you."

And Riham remembers, as her grandmother holds her, she remembers, as though in a dream, how she'd been an old woman in the water, how somewhere she was dying and this would be part of that story. How, when the waves rocked her hard enough, she had called out for Allah and no one else.

ALIA

Kuwait City
April 1988

Alia stirs the spoon in her teacup vigorously, though the sugar has long since dissolved. She finds the clanking comforting. A distraction. Outside the living-room window, night has fallen; the streetlamps are on. She glares into the night as though she can will a car—and from it, a lanky, disobedient body—into appearing.

"She's still not back?"

Atef appears in the doorway. He frowns, dozens of lines around his face springing to life.

Alia shakes her head. She is tired but somewhat invigorated, her mind still buzzing from the fight hours earlier.

"It's nearly eleven," Atef says. "You should sleep." Though it is slight, Alia can hear the accusation in his words. Atef loves the calm, listening to Oum Kalthoum in the evenings as he reads over his students' exams. He finds such conflict unnerving.

"*You* should be more concerned," Alia shoots back. Instantly his face falls, and she regrets her words.

He sighs. "Fine."

Gesturing for her to move over, he joins her on the couch. For moments, there is silence, and she feels the anger radiating from her skin. On the television screen a Lebanese music show plays, beautiful girls taking the stage and singing.

"She may just go to Widad's again," Atef finally says.

"Widad makes it worse!" The outburst is cathartic. "She just coddles her, cooks her meals. What the girl needs is discipline."

"Widad can't just turn her away." He sounds expressly unhappy to be having this conversation again.

"Oh! God forbid," Alia says sarcastically. She lifts the teacup. It has cooled and fills her mouth with lukewarm sweetness. They fall silent once more, watching a young woman move around the stage in a blue dress. The audience applauds.

Several moments later, Alia erupts:

"Never, *never*, would something like this happen with the others."

"Alia—"

"Never, Atef! Not once. Karam is a boy, he's supposed to be the one that stays out late and gets into trouble. But no, never. He studies and sees friends, he goes to the university, he comes home and sleeps in his bed."

"Comparing them gets us nowhere."

"And Riham," Alia continues, aware of the shrillness in her voice but unable to stop. "Can you imagine? She doesn't even sneeze out loud."

Atef clears his throat; Alia pretends not to hear. "Only Souad," she finishes triumphantly. "Only her."

"Different personalities, Alia. You know that," Atef says. He is careful during these talks not to say the thing she knows he wants to. She knows this because she heard him say it, last year after an argument between her and Souad. She'd overheard him speaking with Widad, his voice low:

"I've never seen two people more alike."

The earlier argument was about sugar. Souad eats it sprinkled between slices of bread, and she leaves trails on the kitchen counters, attracting ants. Priya is constantly killing them, using a sponge spotted with their bodies.

Over and over, Alia and Atef have told Souad to use a plate. Atef is good-humored about it, making jokes about unwanted guests, but Alia has been sharper, bringing up Priya's arthritis.

"We're going to have an infestation," she told her.

The girl never listened. Still she ate the sugar sandwiches, still the trails appeared, followed eagerly by the ants. For weeks, Alia stewed—the thoughtlessness! The selfishness, the entitlement. Unwilling to inconvenience herself even in the smallest ways.

So when Alia happened upon Souad that afternoon, taking a bite out of a half-eaten sandwich, the sugar crumbs falling *right in front of her eyes*, she'd snapped, screaming something about the girl being a brat and poking the embers of their ancient, age-old fighting until it roared a brilliant, unrelenting red.

"You're insane," Souad had hurled later as she tugged her shoes on in the doorway. Crumbs of the now-forgotten sandwich clung to her lips. "Absolutely insane." Then there was the slam of the front door, and she was gone.

The clock above the television blinks nearly midnight. On the TV, the dancers behind the singer move their hips suggestively. They no longer wear the short skirts and feathered hair of previous decades, the style Alia had grown up with—tight sweaters, eyeliner, frosty lipstick—and still favors.

Instead the women dress as Souad does, in too-tight jeans and leather. Alia finds it unattractive, pushy. Perhaps fashion reflects each generation's women, Alia thinks, and she is pleased by the thought. She wants to tell Atef, but there is still a distance between them, his kindly silence an affront. His face is illuminated, the dancing women causing ripples of blue and green across his face.

The singer finishes and bows, applause surrounding her. The dancers exit the stage and the lights dim. Another singer walks on in a long dress, a hijab wound around her head. Alia recognizes her—the Moroccan singer who'd abruptly announced her faith a few months ago, swapping her trademark short dresses for a veil.

"I wonder what *her* mother thought," Alia comments. She keeps her voice light, glances sidelong at Atef. It is a peace offering. The volatility of their marriage, when the children were younger, has cooled over the years, yielded to camaraderie.

He clears his throat, considering. "Maybe she had another daughter to make up for it." They both laugh and Alia scoots closer to him on the couch.

In some ways, it is truly comical. *The Miniskirt and the Veil*, she likes to quip to her friends. Quick nicknames for her daughters, well intentioned but occasionally ringing caustic to another's ears.

The truth is that Alia can scarcely make sense of it—the two daughters, years apart, one godless and unruly, the other veiled and earnest and *married.* Though both are intense, Alia thinks at times, prone to immoderation. In some ways, not so dissimilar, a restlessness drumming through them that has them rifling through selves like dresses on a rack.

It is not that Alia dislikes Riham's faith; rather, she is vaguely uncomfortable by its *visibility.* Riham was always a quiet girl, and in her adolescence signs began to emerge, the girl asking about veils, saying she wished to fast for Ramadan. And Alia and Atef, proud but perplexed, exchanged worried glances.

"I'm happy about it, I really am," Atef said once, "but it's just so—"

"I know," Alia said.

Watching their daughter avert her eyes from food during Ramadan, overhearing the splashing water in the bathroom as she prepared for prayer, listening to her footsteps before dawn as she rose with the muezzin—it was like having a mirror held up to their household, and in the reflection, they saw themselves as lacking.

Alia had grown up with her mother's praise of Allah, her gentle faith coloring religion a soft hue for Alia so that she loved the muezzin, the Eid festivals, the verses of Qur'an. For Alia, after the war, after Mustafa's death, these things had not been lost so much as quietly, intentionally misplaced.

And then, years later, Riham wrapped faith around herself as effortlessly as a shawl, never once mumbling a complaint about rising early for prayer, never sneaking bites of bread—as Alia always did—during Ramadan. What could she and Atef do but encourage Riham even though over the years faith seemed to engulf her? To do anything else seemed inconceivable.

In that way, Riham has worn them down as much as Souad, both daughters pushing until Alia and Atef surrendered, in small ways at first, and then bigger ones.

"We need to support her," Atef would say, his voice uncertain. It was his refrain when Riham veiled, when she took Islamic studies courses at the university, when she began to volunteer at the hospital.

So last year, in the early days of May, when Riham sat her and Atef down and told them in her slow, wistful way that she was to wed one of the Jordanian doctors at the hospital, an older religious widower with a young boy, there was nothing left for the two of them—stunned, they who had made a vow of their silence—to say.

THE DOCTOR — this is how Alia still thinks of him, though the wedding was in January, though she should think *Latif* or *Riham's husband*—is a dull man with kind eyes. When he first came to their house for dinner, Alia was struck by how soft-spoken he was, how calm and refined, even his shoes polished.

"I have only the finest intentions toward your daughter," he'd told them in a voice cultivated by years of reassuring the ill and dying, and the two of them exchanged looks.

"He's old enough to be your father," Alia hissed at her daughter afterward and Riham shrugged, unblinking.

"He's good, Mama. You know that. You can see it." An enigmatic smile traveled across her face.

"Also," she'd said, her voice final, "Teta would've loved him." Salma, dead in the ground for nearly a year. Alia felt the fight leave her.

Surprisingly, it was Souad who spoke up the most.

"A child!" Souad stood in her sister's room, fists on hips as Riham packed her clothes in large suitcases. The doctor was returning to his native Amman after the wedding and would be taking Riham with him. "He has a child, Riham. You're going to be that kid's *mother*. Do you understand that? *You still sleep with your stuffed animals.*"

Alia silently cheered her youngest on, but Riham bore all their comments with that same patient smile.

"He's a good man," she repeated throughout the months and again on the evening of her wedding as Alia adjusted her daughter's dress and cried predictably. Though she wasn't crying from happiness or because her daughter was leaving, but rather from the dreariness of it all, the white dress stretching around her chubby daughter's waist, how ordinary she looked as she beamed at people during the wedding. How old and uninteresting the husband looked, the pouting child with his bow tie askew, the life her daughter was inheriting. How badly she wanted to shake her eldest and cry out that you don't have to marry the first person who likes you or who says he'll take you away.

Even the wedding had been boring and had dragged on, guests kindly complimenting Riham's dress and kissing Alia's cheeks, the dance floor empty until Souad stood up in her fire-engine-red dress, grabbed her brother's hand, and began to move her hips in a way the guests would talk about for days.

Atef falls asleep on the couch, his head angled against cushions. Alia watches him. Thousands of times she has done this, and she is struck by the thought. He appears older in sleep, the lines between his nose and mouth deepened. It frustrates her, that he can sleep when she is so wound up, but she knows this is unfair. Sometimes she envies his composure, the way he is able to draw the children to him with his stillness. *What are you really thinking,* she sometimes wants to yell when he smiles mildly at traffic or goes to his study for hours. Once or twice, she has stormed into his study even though the door had been shut, hoping to catch him in the middle of some depraved nameless act—masturbating? Speaking to a mistress?—but all he was ever doing was writing. This would irrationally annoy her sometimes, all those hours, hiding away in his study, smoking cigarettes.

What could he be writing? His mother had died years ago; he rarely spoke to his brothers.

A door shuts within the house. Karam appears in the doorway, his tufted hair betraying sleep.

"Still not back?" He stifles a yawn.

Alia shakes her head, glances at Atef. "God knows where she is," she whispers, her temper rising once more.

Karam smiles at her. "She'll be fine, Mama." He gestures at his father. "Should I wake him? Get him to bed?"

"He'll wake on his own. How is the studying going? You're going to wear yourself out."

Karam rubs his eyes. In his sweatpants and cotton shirt, dark hair covering his arms, he looks like a man. "Not great. I've still got a couple of chapters left."

"The exam's tomorrow?"

He nods, and she makes a sympathetic noise, feels keenly for his tired face. His life is a mystery to her, the architecture classes at the college, sketches of buildings that she sometimes glimpses on his desk. He told her once that he wanted to build skyscrapers in Kuwait City, to make it like Paris or Manhattan. She feels a rush of warmth toward him. Her easy one.

"Good luck, *habibi*."

She listens to his footsteps recede. When he hit puberty years ago, it had been awkward, the soft-eyed boy suddenly transformed into a gangly teen. Adam's apple, straggle of facial hair, the lush, fertile smell of adolescent bodies. She became afraid of touching him for a while, afraid of what would be appropriate and what not. It seemed remarkable that his tall, unfolded limbs had come from within her.

Perhaps that was the divide, always, between her girls and Karam. The girls, in a way, were predictable. Made in the image of her—tiny breasts that grew, blood that spotted their underwear, hair that sprouted between their legs. But Karam, with his masculinity, his foreignness, his *otherness*—he was the miracle that she had borne.

• • •

The music show ends and a sitcom begins, some American program with a family, a husband and wife laughingly arguing. There are Arabic subtitles below, but Alia likes to listen to the English. Her English is decent from years of listening to the children talk but especially strong on the esoteric—*gorgeous, mind-blowing, bungalow.*

Next to her, Atef shifts, his head falling abruptly on his chest. He blinks awake, disoriented for a moment.

"Who?" He is panicked whenever he's woken suddenly.

Alia places a hand on his shoulder. "You should go to bed."

He yawns, shutting his eyes. "Will you come?"

"No." She keeps her voice light. "I'm going to watch this a little longer." Atef squints at the television.

"An American sitcom? That's what we've come to?" He laughs fondly. "*Ya ajnabiyeh.*" A phrase Alia's mother used for the children when they taught her English and French words during the summer. *You foreigner.*

The mention of Salma is still sobering, even with the time that has passed, time that Alia counts in pairs. Two summers, two birthdays, two Eids. Atef places a hand on Alia's forehead, as one would with a child.

"May Allah keep her in rest," he says, his eyes solemn.

"May Allah keep her in rest," she echoes and is overcome with that familiar sorrow.

He kisses her before he leaves the room, his breath sour. He has become more chaste over the years, touching her less, and she suspects it has to do with some misguided sense of decorum, as though, now that Alia is nearly forty-five and has to studiously dye the gray streaking her temples, she needs to be treated carefully, as though she is a matron.

She would shock him if she ever said, *I loved it when you'd leave marks on my body. It was like touching fire, the heat from those bruises.*

He would blink at her, in that good-natured way of his. He would be hurt. Atef probably remembered those nights of lovemaking after his return with shame. Never would he believe her if she told him she has dreamed, in the two decades since, of being touched that way again.

Alone in the room, Alia watches the television family laugh. She feels a heaviness, awakened, she knows, by the mention of Salma. She touches the thin strand of gold she wears around her neck, a gift from her mother at her wedding. Her fingertips still on the metal, pain shoots through her. Like a wave, it passes, the sharpness dulled to an ache.

Salma died in winter, on the eve of a momentous thunderstorm that raged over Amman for three days, three nights. Alia had traveled to Amman the previous week by herself at the urging of her aunts.

"She's not well," they said. "It's getting worse." For years, Salma's health had been failing, a mysterious illness that afflicted her lungs, muscles, even her sleep.

During that week Alia brewed her mother tea, sliced cantaloupe onto platters. At night she curled childlike in her mother's bed, her dreams slashed with tigers and floods, caves of burning lanterns.

Whenever her mother let out moans of pain, Alia rubbed circles on her back. When her mother's breathing steadied, Alia continued to rub until her wrists ached, lost in thoughts about her mother dying. It was the most awful thing Alia could imagine, a fate that filled her with sharp, peppery fear. When Alia envisioned her mother dead, she couldn't imagine anything beyond that—the boiling of rice, the trimming of hair. It was, simply, incomprehensible.

Men later referred to the storm as biblical, talked about the sickly shade of rainclouds, the bolts of lightning that forked the sky. The afternoon it began the two of them were sitting in her mother's garden. Salma was feeling better and berated Alia for traveling to Amman.

"You have children to care for," Salma scolded. "Your aunts are a bunch of worriers."

Alia watched her mother pick at her cheese sandwich, pushing the tomato slices aside, breaking tiny bits of bread to eat.

"The jasmine came out nicely," Salma said. Above them, clouds hung low and gray in the sky.

"It's the late winter," Alia said. "Shall I cut some for the vase?" She rose as she spoke, brushing crumbs from the djellaba she wore, one of the old garments from her girlhood. She liked wearing them around her mother, the musty smell tugging at something wistful. At the jasmine shrub, Alia stood on her tiptoes until she pinched a stem with several flowers, the petals startlingly white against the green leaves.

Twirling the stem, Alia brought the flowers to her nose and inhaled. Perfume, heady, a sweetness she could nearly taste. Something fat and wet plopped on her wrist.

"Oh!" Alia heard behind her, turning to find her mother's arm extended to the sky, eyebrows raised. "It's raining."

Alia walked back to her mother. When she reached the chair, Alia lowered her own arm, carefully presenting the raindrop—still a perfect half-sphere—to her mother. "I know."

Salma touched Alia's hand, lightly dabbed the raindrop with her fingertip. Around them, rain began to fall softly but adamantly, plunking into the half-drunk tea, moistening the bread of the sandwiches. Her mother's face creased into a smile, rain splashing her hair. She looked up at Alia, her eyes impish, joyful.

"Let's go inside."

Salma died later that evening, after the sky had darkened, drizzle giving way to a downpour. Wind and rain obscured the view as Alia drew the bedroom curtains.

"Recite for me, *habibti.*" Salma's voice had been muffled beneath the blanket, slightly out of breath. Alia lay next to her. Thunder exploded in the distance.

"*Bismillah,*" she began. Slowly, she recited the Qur'an verses, keeping her voice steady. She chose her mother's favorites—al-Fatiha, al-

Kursi—feeling shy as she spoke. When she finished, her mother's breathing had evened.

"There is no Allah but Allah," Alia said softly and turned to her side, her forehead touching Salma's shoulder. The sound of rain surrounded them as they slept.

Alia woke first to the thunder. Only then, disoriented, did she realize that Salma was talking in a low voice.

"You must remember." Salma spoke urgently. Sitting up, Alia saw in the dark that her mother's eyes were wide open, staring past Alia, toward the window.

"Mama?" Alia willed her voice calm.

"When it happens, you must find a way to remember."

"When what happens, Mama?" An icy fear seized her. She had never heard her mother speak this way before.

"I was wrong. I thought I could make myself see something that wasn't there. But it was a lie. I saw the houses, I saw how they were lost. *You cannot let yourself forget.*" Her mother began to cough, her voice frenzied.

Light, Alia thought. She needed light to see her mother, the dark suddenly terrifying for her. In panic, she rose and stumbled to the window, pulled at the curtains until they finally gave and slid open. Outside, rain churned in sheets, blurring the streetlamps. Above, nothing was visible, the sky dark.

When she turned back to her mother, Salma was dead, her face tilted toward the window. Her open eyes glistened in the limp, streetlamp light.

AND THEN SHE was gone, the ordinary dullness of death taking Salma as it took everyone, Alia stunned and heartbroken at the predictability of it all. What followed was banal, excruciating—the funeral, Atef and the children flying in from Kuwait, the body washed and wrapped in white, being reminded of other deaths, of Mustafa, of her father, loss after loss after loss, as though rehearsed.

But since that evening, there remains a mystery, a question that plagues Alia: What remembering had her mother meant, what lie?

Alia doesn't realize she has fallen asleep until she wakes, a sound of tires screeching from outside. She jolts upright, blinking in the glow of the television. As she stands—already the anger is flooding her body with adrenaline—she remembers some scenery of water, pillars shooting out of the ocean. A dream she was just having, or a painting she'd seen somewhere?

From the foyer come muted, shuffling sounds. There is murmuring, a low laugh. Alia cocks her head and listens. Budur, Souad's closest friend since grade school. They walk slowly, one hushing the other, past the entrance of the living room.

"I can't believe—"

"I know." More laughter, and Souad flips the light on; Alia squints at the sudden glare. Her daughter wears jeans and a shirt so tight Alia can make out the lace of her bra.

"Mama." Souad looks caught out but quickly rearranges her features to convey irritation. "What are you doing standing there in the dark?" She glances at the television. "What are you watching?"

Alia looks at the grandfather clock on the wall. "It's *two in the morning.*"

Both girls fall silent, a glance exchanged between them. Budur looks scared; it is Souad who speaks up. "We ran a little late. I didn't realize the time."

"Where were you?" Alia feels the fury clog her. She crosses her arms over her robe.

Souad shrugs. "Out."

"Out, Souad? Out where?"

"Yes, Mama." Souad rolls her eyes. "We went out for a bit, it got late, now we're home. Budur, let's go to the—"

Alia begins to scream. "Out? *Out?* You think that's what other girls are doing? Staying out till all hours of the night?" There is immense relief in yelling.

Souad slits her eyes at her mother, and, though her daughter is smaller than she, Alia nearly steps back. Since girlhood, there has been something queenly about her, formidable.

"That sandwich," Souad says viciously. "This is about those stupid crumbs. You stayed up to yell at me for it?"

Next to her, Budur bites her lip, looking as though she might cry. "I'll go to the room."

Alia softens toward Budur. Poor thing. Souad is perpetually the culprit in that relationship, Alia knows. The one that pushes her to do things. When they were twelve, she'd caught them smoking cigarettes in the yard. Budur had instantly begun to cry, saying, *Sorry, sorry.* Souad had taken another puff before she stamped the cigarette out with her sneaker.

"Go, Budur, *habibti*," Alia says.

"No, you stay," says Souad.

Both of them speak at the same time, then glare at each other. Budur hesitates for a moment before retreating, her footsteps quiet and light in the hallway.

"I want you to be happy." Alia changes tactics. "Acting this way isn't good for you."

Souad snorts, and Alia wants to slap her. "*Happy?*" She drops her purse onto the floor with the languor of the unaffected, but Alia sees her daughter's jaw tensing and it satisfies something small and petty in her. "You mean like Riham's happy? Or like you're happy?"

"Oh, oh, this again? It's like living in a theater. You want everyone to be unhappy so we can be like one of your American films." In recent months, Souad's disappointment with the family has been a keen, living thing.

"Don't talk to me about living in a fantasy."

"What—"

Souad smiles like someone about to sweep a poker table.

"You've been pining over Amman like some jilted lover."

This halts Alia. "I'm waking up your f-father," she stammers.

"He'll deal with you. He should know what time his daughter traipses home."

It is an empty threat, and they both know it. Atef is a tepid disciplinarian at best, too soft with the children. Souad arches an eyebrow.

"Wake him up."

"I'm happy," Alia shouts. The childishness shames her.

"No." Souad speaks slowly, picking up her purse. "You're not. You're a liar, and you're always lying. And you're just angry because I can see it."

Souad walks out of the room. She switches off the light as she exits—a final insult—leaving Alia in the dark, with a slack mouth and anger pulsing through her rib cage.

It takes Alia a while—ten, fifteen minutes—to calm herself down. She fights the urge to follow Souad into her room, to yank her by the shoulders and demand, if not an apology, then more fight. The urge to scream, to say terrible things, lances her. Her entire life, she has been denied a good fight; Widad too mild, Salma too good, Atef too kind, Karam gentle, and Riham withdrawn.

Only Souad has the ferocity. And her daughter is a smart girl—funny, how bitterly one could think such a thing about one's child—who knows perfectly well the potency of walking away.

There are times when Alia cannot bear to look at her daughter. Not only out of anger, but also out of the peculiarity of recognition. No one had warned her of this, that she would see herself so brazenly in her child. It is alarming, watching Souad filch her gestures, the scowls and hair flicking and lopsided smile. Alia can see her own spitefulness in the girl.

There is, of course, the other likeness, the shiver of someone darting across her daughter's face. Mustafa in the dark limbs. Mustafa in the twitch of her mouth, the lips pulled downward when she is impatient or afraid.

Watching a news report years ago, a newly adolescent Souad

cursed at the television, her brows drawn in a glower. Salma had shaken her head, marveling. She spoke so quietly Alia barely heard her:

"Allah have mercy, she has your brother's blood in her."

Across the room Alia winced, watching her daughter, all those likenesses, those hurts—scrawled plainly on her pretty face. Mustafa, whose name they go entire years at a time without speaking. It became a tacit rule between her and Atef: *If it hurts, leave it.* Their marriage had a glove compartment, a hollow, cluttered space where emotional debris went—Mustafa, those first months in Kuwait, Nablus. Palestine tossed in there like an illegible receipt, keys that no longer opened any door. *Why would we,* Atef seemed to beg her silently in those early years after the war, his face tightening with pain when she spoke of Nablus, when she cursed Meir and Rabin and the day they'd been born. So she spoke of it less and less, everything they'd left behind, her dreams of walking into her childhood bedroom, the way her entire body drummed when she thought of the place that was, suddenly, not hers anymore. She folded it away.

SOUAD'S AMMAN REMARK was a punch in the face. So Souad knew.

If Alia put her discontent away, it wouldn't stay. Her wanting disobeyed her, needling over the years, nudging her awake. *If not Palestine, then Amman,* it whispered. *Anywhere but this hot, unwelcome country.* Alia's one wicked secret, the one she thought she'd hidden from the family—that on each of those summer trips, finding herself surrounded by friends and family, the same thought pinched her.

I could stay.

It was not in and of itself a betrayal, but the implications were. *Stay here and what? Be with my mother, my cousins. And my children?* So it would go, the silent argument, back and forth in her mind until she loathed the sight of herself in the mirror. What kind of mother, or wife, would consider such a fate—living apart from her children, moving to Amman.

"Atef wants you to be happy," Mimi argued with her once. Only she knew everything; Alia had broken down one summer and told her. Late into the night they'd talked, the children asleep in their rooms; Mimi thought Alia should stay even if Atef kept the children. "He must know how miserable you are there."

"But he would hate me."

"No, he wouldn't. He'd forgive you."

She was right. The simple truth was that Atef would've forgiven her if she remained, the same way he would've forgiven her if she divorced him or fell in love with someone else. Because his love for her—and her understanding of this was tenuous, the way one snatches at the wisps of a memory—had always been straightforward. Uncomplicated.

That summer, she'd spent long hours with Mimi smoking cigarettes and crying, nearly telling her mother about it. While Alia fed the children, while she combed their hair after baths, her mind churned with plans.

It might have happened differently. She might have returned to Kuwait and told Atef everything: How she hated the heat and dreaded the summer, had nightmares of being buried in hot sand, how she found the city oppressive, always felt numb, as though moving in swamp water. But then they'd gone to the beach one afternoon, and Riham had almost drowned. Nearly died. And Alia, clasping her shivering daughter as she heaved, holding her so tightly the girl had tugged for air, as she wept and grabbed at her daughter—as the drowning lunge for wood or flesh or tire—for the rest of the day, Alia understood that she'd very nearly been punished.

It is not that she believes Allah is vengeful or cruel. The opposite. When she thinks of Allah, she imagines only love, magnified and multiplied into a room of marble, blinding white and then traveling with synaptic speed onto the earth, into her mother's voice as she prayed, into the breath of those around her. And it was this love that made Allah so dangerous, so terrifying. Because the sin, the real sin, she'd learned that summer, was to forget it or take it for granted. No,

Allah hadn't punished her out of spite or malice. He'd been warning her not to forget.

Alia flips through the television channels in the dark, the screen a kaleidoscope of newscasters, music videos, soap operas. She finally settles on a program about elephants and lowers the volume. The couch cushions are soft beneath her as she sits, adjusting a pillow between her knees. She feels the anger quiet into a briny resentment. The bitterness floats like an inkblot in her mind's eye.

Suddenly exhausted, she drops her head back onto the couch arm. The steps to her bedroom seem impossible. Screw them all anyway. Let them wake and find her. Let it be her final protest on this night.

Bastards, she thinks and sleeps.

She dreams of a foreign city. A marshland and some women walking throughout it. Someone is speaking in another language. French, or Spanish. Somehow Alia can understand it. The person is telling her to turn around, that it is about to rain. She follows the voice. There is hail. Someone is dying.

It is morning when Alia wakes, her consciousness still pulling at the marshland, the foreign language. Sunlight pours into the living room. Alia's head is angled uncomfortably against the cushions. The television screen is blank; someone—Atef, Priya—has turned it off. She sits up, flooded with déjà vu, the sensation of waking on this couch—then recalls the night before, Souad's words, the fight. Not déjà vu, then. Memory.

She walks into the kitchen. Atef is drinking coffee at the table. Alia can hear Priya's humming in the laundry room, the whir of the washing machine.

"Good morning," she says.

Atef sips his coffee, suppressing a smile. "I didn't want to wake you."

"That couch is a nightmare."

"We'll have to buy better furniture. For nights you stand guard." His voice is mischievous, and Alia laughs, feeling the tension break. She cracks her neck with the heel of her hand, a satisfying pop.

"My back's killing me," Alia admits. A mess of papers are scattered in front of Atef, his briefcase open. "What's all this? Are you finally divorcing me?"

He glances at the clock above the oven. "The staff meeting's today." He starts piling the papers up. Alia remembers vague talk of changes in the department.

"The British professor?"

"Professor *Roberts.*" Atef says the name with uncharacteristic sarcasm. "The liberal. Coming in to change everything. Those British, they still think Arabs are impressionable. Starving to be *saved.* We're having a meeting on his proposal today, some referendum vote. He even wants to take out smoking in the classrooms. Says it gives people asthma."

"He sounds awful. Maybe they'll have him oversee the construction projects."

Atef grins. "We'll just give him Souad to deal with. He'll trip over himself rushing back to England." He finishes the coffee and sets the cup on the counter. "*Au revoir.*" It is their little joke, begun when the children started taking French in school.

"*Au revoir.*"

On his way out, he places a hand on her shoulder and grazes her temple with his chin. Another ancient gesture of his, from the days when they first wed. She watches him from the window above the sink, walking down the driveway, his familiar silhouette dark in the bright sun.

Priya makes her some tea and boils an egg. When the water froths, Priya cracks the egg with a spoon and carefully peels it. Two pinches of salt, a sliced tomato.

"Thank you," Alia says. She eats absently, her mind still on her daughter.

"Chicken today?" Priya asks as she wipes the counters. Her hair is pulled back into a gray-streaked braid.

"I was thinking lamb. With a nice stew."

"We finished the lamb yesterday. I can walk to the store?"

"No, no. The chicken's fine. Priya?" Alia says impulsively. The other woman turns, the dishrag in midair.

"Souad . . . she never listens. I talk, I yell. Nothing works. Do you know how she—why she . . . does the things she does?" she finishes lamely.

Priya's gaze is sympathetic but resentful, as though she was hoping she'd never be asked. "Madame, children are not easy to know." She pauses for a moment before resuming the wide, swooping circles on the counters. Alia feels ashamed for asking, as if she has admitted some shortcoming in her maternal abilities.

Alia sops up the remaining yolk with bread, places the plate in the sink. She begins walking to her bedroom but hesitates in front of Souad's closed door. The urge to pull it open and yell is fierce, but she forces herself to walk on.

In her bedroom, Alia restlessly trails her fingers along the cosmetics atop her dresser. Much of them are old and unused, dust filming the covers. Her favorite is the burgundy jar, a cream that smells of lavender. She dabs it onto her face, rubs circles on her forehead and cheeks.

She is still attractive, somewhat. At dinner parties she catches glimpses—from the men, an aloof appreciation; from the women, scrutiny. She can feel them scanning her neck, the flesh of her arms, with hawkish eyes.

"What a tiny waist!" they exclaim. Or, "Your skin is so smooth."

And Alia—capriciously superstitious—finds herself fumbling for some wood to rap her knuckles against. She remembers her mother in such moments, how Salma used to recite Qur'an whenever anyone paid her children a compliment.

Alia likes her body in the same way she likes her bedroom, or her car, or the lovely green curtains in the living room—as a commodity, something she can smooth over with her hands, a working machinery. Nice legs, firm abdomen, even after the children, though she'd held her breath at each pregnancy, dismayed as her body stretched and flared.

The irony is that the features she loathed twenty years ago have become her assets. The dark skin that remains unblemished. The square jaw and broad shoulders that now give her a certain stateliness. And her height, which has become suddenly fashionable, women in magazines and films teetering in impossibly high heels.

We never want it when we have it, Mimi likes to say.

The restlessness grows. Souad's words return to her. *You're a liar, and you're always lying.* Alia showers and chooses slacks and a T-shirt. The bed looks warm and inviting, and she flops onto it, feeling like she did as a child on rainy days.

But the sun streams ferociously into the room, and she is a grown woman, she reminds herself. The house ticks with the unexploded arguments of this afternoon.

"Goddamn it."

She kicks the covers, suddenly hungry again. The kitchen is empty save for the scent of baking chicken, a cutting board of chopped vegetables. Abruptly, Alia envies Priya her daily tasks, the constant motion of dusting and folding laundry. Priya rarely sits still for more than a few minutes; she certainly doesn't mope in bed past noon.

Alia filches a chopped carrot, feeling once more like a child. A memory floats to her, unasked, of her mother's kitchen in Nablus: sunlight streaming through the windows, tangling in the coriander and mint plants on the windowsill. The image hurts, and she shakes her head to clear it.

Alia rustles around in the cupboards. She craves, irritatingly, something. A precise, elusive wanting. This has been happening to her since her first pregnancy. Her mother told her to expect curious cravings: pickles with dried dates or yogurt milk and cinnamon. But what happened instead was haunting, daylong cravings for something *unknown.* Alia would hunt in the supermarket for hours, trying to locate the source of her longing, until, magically, like a remembered word, it would appear and she'd want to weep from gratitude—watermelon with cheese! Falafel mashed and topped with hot sauce!

Alia places a teabag into a mug, then leaves it unused on the counter. She gnaws on a wedge of bread, scoops apricot jam with her fingertip and licks it. No, no. She peers into the refrigerator, debating whether to eat leftover lentil soup, when she is struck by inspiration. Figs. She wants figs and cheese, the sheep's-milk cheese with rosemary.

In the refrigerator, she finds a wedge of the cheese wrapped in wax paper but no figs. Apples, grapes, cantaloupe . . . but no. It must be figs. This is how her mind is at times, something she could never explain to easygoing Atef—the stubbornness like a lock, once bolted, impossible to move.

Outside, the short walk to her car fills her mouth with humid air. It is only April, but the sun is already overpowering, stark in the clear sky. Atef bought the second car several years ago, a blue thing with a powerful engine. Even now, after so long, Alia thrills at the engine revving, the humming life she orchestrates with a flick of her wrist.

Sometimes she thinks of Ajit, Widad's old chauffeur, who returned to his country in the early seventies. Alia had become fascinated by India for a while, watching reports on the fighting, the men rushing the streets, dropping like dolls when gunshots rang out. There was a wild-eyed man who'd speak, his robes falling to his elbows when he lifted his arms. Alia would try to imagine Ajit there, among the crowds or throwing flaming bottles, but it was impossible; for her, he existed solely in the front seat of the sedan.

She'd felt sadness at Ajit's departure, but also relief. He'd always seemed like an ally of hers, the one who would watch her in the rearview mirror. He was the one who'd seen her lapse, the only person in this country who knew she was capable of fleeing.

• • •

The supermarket is flanked by a row of restaurants and shops, directly facing benches and the marina. Atef hates when she shops at the supermarket. He says fruits from the marketplace taste fresher, but Alia prefers the efficiency, the rush of air conditioning that hits her now as she strides through the sliding doors. No one calls out to her here as they do in the marketplace, no one asks if she wants mangoes or spices as she walks the aisles. The employees, Pakistani, Filipino, work quietly, not even glancing her way as they stack cans and arrange the fruit. She can come and go unnoticed.

She finds the figs easily, packaged in plastic boxes next to a pyramid of oranges. Over the speakers a Fairuz song is playing, the one about love and summer. Alia sings along to it under her breath as she walks to the cashier. Her mood has lifted, and she curves her fingers against the box in anticipation.

Ya Mama, her mother used to say, *everything in its place. There is a time for anger, a time for sorrow. You have to learn to distinguish.* A lesson Alia never learned. Emotions swirl within her like the complex dish of *maqlouba* the aunts used to make in Nablus, the raisins impossible to pick from the rice.

Halfway across the parking lot, Alia changes her mind about going home and walks instead toward the sea. The marina is mostly empty, a couple of people sitting on the benches, a man walking along the railing. Alia chooses a bench fringed by palm trees. The water roils in front of her, several boats bobbing in the distance. Over the years, such things have become acceptable, little freedoms that would've been impossible a decade ago. An Arab woman alone, sitting on a bench and unwrapping a parcel of figs.

Years ago, when she'd flung her body into the sea as Ajit watched, Alia had felt outrageous, the most defiant woman in the world. The sheer audacity of the act had subdued her for months. But such an act would be laughable to these new girls, the ones in skintight leggings, girls like Souad and Budur who smoked cigarettes during harbor parties with foreigners—she has heard whispers about these parties, whiskey and dancing on yachts—let boys touch their bodies in the dark. In the face of such girls, a woman swimming at night is a small, trifling thing.

Alia bites into the flesh of a fig and shuts her eyes. Even without the cheese, the taste is perfect, her favorite fruit. She eats contentedly, the sun hot on her face. For the first time since she saw the crumbs fall from her daughter's mouth yesterday, she feels calm.

In the distance, a girl walks on the sand toward the marina. She is dressed simply in a black dress falling below her knees, the neckline low, revealing the tops of her shoulders. She walks past the other benches and sits on Alia's. The girl—not a child, Alia now sees, but probably Riham's age, though small and thin—hooks one leg over the other and glances over at Alia. They exchange the quick, shy smile of strangers.

Though the calm feels broken, Alia is curious. She glances at the girl, the sharp edges of her cheeks and jaw. Thin earrings dangle from her earlobes. The girl looks decent, but there is something feral about her. An unwashed odor rises from her.

The girl speaks first. "Morocco or Beirut?"

"Pardon?" Alia is startled by her voice, gruff and low.

"The figs."

"Oh." Alia lifts the basket. "Casablanca," she says.

"They're even sweeter than the Lebanese ones. May I?"

Alia is surprised at her forthrightness, the girl's hand extended. Four or five bracelets circle her wrist. Alia holds the basket out, and the girl takes several, peels them. For moments, there is silence.

"I'm Telar." Then, as if just remembering: "Thank you."

"Alia." Though the girl is significantly younger, though it would be appropriate for her to refer to herself as Tante Alia or Khalto Alia, something about the girl makes that seem unnecessary.

"Are you a student at the college?" Alia finally asks.

The girl looks animated, as though Alia has asked the correct question. She begins to talk rapidly, her bracelets clanging as she moves her hands. "As if the dogs would let us go to school. My education?

Mortar and gassing. One hundred nights of death, while that bastard sleeps in his marble bedroom."

Alia's mind whirs. She puts it together, guesses.

"Saddam."

"That *dog.*" The girl spits, as though the very name is something bitter in her mouth. "He drove us to the wasteland; he took the gold from our flesh."

So the girl is Kurdish. Alia watches her, sidelong, with interest. The reddish hair, kohl thick beneath her lower eyelashes. There are stories about the Kurds, whisperings about magic and gypsies living in the underbellies of cities. The girl eats the rest of her figs, sucking at the skins before tossing them onto the sand. She lights a cigarette and speaks again, her voice vehement.

"We came a while back, my mama and siblings. Seven of us. Baba died, of course. All the men did. The army rounded them up, slit their stomachs in front of our houses, shot the knees of anyone who cried out. To the women—" The girl spits again, slitting her eyes toward the sea. "To the women they did awful things. They made husbands watch. They made little children watch."

"I'm sorry," Alia says. Telar ashes her cigarette and Alia sees that her nails are bitten, blackened around the edges. Something like revulsion stirs within her.

"He's a godless, motherless bastard," the girl is saying. "Left us starving. We ate paper when there wasn't any rice left." She takes a long breath. "But at least we left before the gas. Poison! You hear about that? He dropped poison on children. They're saying the dead smelled apples and fell to the ground."

Alia's stomach lurches. Suddenly she wishes the girl would stop talking, would leave her alone. She thinks of the teabag left carelessly on the kitchen counter. Odd, to be nostalgic for something that has gone nowhere; she feels melancholic thinking of her stovetop, her teapot, as though it is all a country she has dreamed up. She tries to think of how to offer money delicately to the girl, who seems like the kind for whom charity is censure.

"You know what it's like to be hungry?"

Alia blinks at her, this girl with dirty nails and cigarettes. What would Souad think of her? she wonders. Would she furrow her brow, step to the side? Or would she be enchanted, as she is by parties and the new hotels in Kuwait? *Souad.* Alia says her name silently. *Taken by the* ajnabi *men with their accents and tailored suits, taken by the attention—daughter, it is awful—that a girl with tight jeans and a devastating smile can attract.*

"Pardon?" Though she heard the question.

"Hungry. You ever been hungry?" The girl continues before Alia can respond. "I don't mean late-dinner hungry. Or having to wait for your maid to finish cooking a meal." She lets out a quick, angry laugh.

Alia remembers with shame the bread back in her house, the crust she threw in the sink. The years of uneaten chicken and rice, chucked into the trash. The utter waste.

The girl, Alia suddenly knows, would have no patience for Souad. For either of her daughters. The children of a professor—well fed, spoiled, ungrateful. Alia is oddly gratified by the thought.

Alia shakes her head. She opens her mouth to say no, admittedly not, and is surprised to hear herself say, "Once."

The girl turns to her, eyes disbelieving. "When I was pregnant," Alia says. "When I gave birth to my youngest." And Alia remembers with rocking clarity that pain, coiled and endless in her abdomen, the labor that had lasted nearly two days. "It's like it was yesterday or, no, just this morning. Like it just happened. Everything I ate, for days, I couldn't keep down." Not even water. The doctors had said it was the difficult labor, the bleeding and ripping, her body unable to digest. "The first two days it was awful, like a long fast. But then." Her hospital room always darkened by a curtain. Atef begging her to eat bread. Outside, a warm, bright winter and fires burning in the desert. "Then . . . it was like madness. Every inch of me begging for food. And my body refusing it."

The girl smokes, considering. "I know it's not the same," Alia says in a rush. "I know it's not. But it was still—you asked if I was ever hungry."

Telar nods. She adjusts a silver chain around her wrist. "What happened?"

"My daughter was born." Alia tries to remember, really remember. "And everything was suddenly loud and sharp." Riham and Karam were quiet children. Those early years, Alia thinks, newly in Kuwait, newly a mother, she'd been a sleepwalker. "It was like being shaken awake." Only with Souad did everything change, that screaming, selfish child.

"I never forgave her," Alia says slowly. "But I also never thanked her."

"When we came here, my sister, the littlest one, she'd cry and cry for rice pudding." The girl drops the cigarette and steps on it. "It was terrible. Here she was, this tiny thing, no memory, just wanting and needing." Telar laughs. "When she's old enough, I'll tell her that story. Of how she cried and cried, then cried harder when we told her there was none."

Alia remembers her mother telling her, back in Nablus, that she used to cry for something when they left Jaffa. Though she cannot remember what. She has now forgotten twice.

"Coming here was terrible. I didn't think we would ever survive it."

"What else could you do?" Alia says.

The girl nods. "For weeks, we touched each other's faces, trying to make sure we hadn't dreamed it. We drank water slowly. Everything we did was like that. Slow, careful." Alia thinks of Atef's chin against her temple this morning, watching him walk down the driveway. How there is something precious in those gestures, and tragic, too, accumulated over the years. Her daughter is still sleeping, she thinks, her long limbs akimbo like in girlhood. Next to Alia, Telar has fallen silent, watching the water. Alia holds out the figs for the girl to take another, and she does.

SOUAD

PARIS
August 1990

Souad wakes with a start. The sound of a French news channel trumpets through the rooms. She has been sleeping fitfully since the invasion, at odd hours. Everyone in the house has been doing the same, Khalto Mimi and her brother Ammar taking long naps after lunch, Lara sleeping through the afternoons and waking at night.

She blinks against the pillowcase, squinting toward the open curtains. The streaks of setting sun stain the wooden floors red. From the television, the newscasters' words drift through the room in bursts.

"Troops . . . vacillating . . . the borders."

Not a nightmare. Each waking, there is this moment—the clearing when she remembers everything, realizes once again what has happened.

Souad sighs and turns, pulling the thin blanket around her. She is a messy sleeper, the sheets always twisted when she wakes. Shutting her eyes, she buries her face in the pillow.

"Sleep, sleep, sleep," she whispers to herself. She wishes to sleep for hours, until it is midnight outside. But it is too late, her mind is already crowding with everything, the invasion and Elie and her mother's dreaded phone call. Of the three, the invasion feels, ironically, least pressing.

Souad sits up in bed, wincing at a twinge in her back. She is thirsty, her muscles sore.

An image of Elie comes to mind, his silhouette beneath the streetlamp last night, after the whiskey and dancing. He'd shrugged. *Think about it.*

Souad's art professor at school, Madame Jubayli, had recommended her for a summer program at the newly opened L'Institut Supérieur des Arts Appliqués, but when Souad brought up the idea at home, it had caused many arguments, what Karam referred to as "the Paris impasse."

"They teach painting and textiles; it's perfect. It's exactly what I need," she said, over and over, to her parents. Her father vacillated, diplomatic but reluctant, while her mother outright forbade it.

"You want us to send you to Paris by yourself, like some street girl?"

The months churned on. There were charges and pleading and nightlong fights. Souad convinced Madame Jubayli to meet with her parents and speak about the program, its reputation, the colleagues she knew who taught there. Souad requested a copy of the brochure, went through it line by line. Still her mother refused to let her go.

"You're just jealous!" Souad finally screamed one evening. "Because you're stuck in your little life, you want everyone as miserable as you!"

Her mother's face stormed, and her father finally intervened, telling Souad to go to her room. Souad went, paced, kicked her door and walls, then finally stomped back out to the living room, ready to scream at them both.

But when she drew breath, she collapsed. Falling onto the sofa in front of her parents, she wept like a child.

"Please," she said between sobs. "Please, please, please." She finally lifted her head, looked her mother straight in the eye. "Mama. Mama, *please*."

Where yelling and bargaining had failed, tears worked. Within a week, Khalto Mimi, who'd moved to France years ago, was called; she agreed to have Souad stay with her for the summer and, like magic, Souad found herself on a plane headed to Paris.

Souad kicks the covers off and gets out of bed. The blue and white room, with lacy curtains and small porcelain figurines, is the elder daughter's old room, Mira now living in her own apartment near the Sorbonne. In the drawers of the armoire are playing cards, a nightgown, an old notebook covered in stickers.

She is in awe of the girls and their European lifestyles. They are each in their twenties, Lara still living with her mother, both sisters leading sophisticated, unmarried lives. Every Sunday, Mira comes over, and they eat brioche thick with warm berries and watch television, the girls chattering in their alluring fusion of French and Arabic. They wear knee-high boots even on sunny days, and tight, short dresses above them, their hair barely grazing their shoulders. And as much as they coo over Souad's slimness, her curls, she cannot help but feel unmodern around them, with her skinny legs and long hair. It is the same on the streets of Paris, Souad—who was always the voguish one in Kuwait—feeling plain among the swarms of elegant women smoking cigarettes, their lips painted the color of apples.

But here, at least, her restlessness has found a place. She loved Paris from the beginning. The people were neither friendly nor particularly welcoming, for the most part treating her coolly. It was part of the Parisian appeal, Elie told her. He has summered in Paris since babyhood and has a French passport; he knows the quarters and streets like an old lover. It was Elie who pushed her to do the program at L'Institut so they could be together for the summer.

Their last summer. Then he would remain in Paris for university, and she would return to Kuwait, their lives forking apart. That was their unspoken agreement. Or it had been, until the invasion. Now everything, *everything*—her family's house, Karam's engineering program, Souad's own reluctant plan of beginning courses at Kuwait University—was suddenly suspended, uncertain, like sand lifted by malicious hands and tossed everywhere.

Souad dresses impulsively. Black leggings, oversize black shirt—in Paris, she retired colors—a cat's-eye swipe of kohl. Outside, the sun has nearly set.

She walks toward the sound of newscasters, into the living room. At the doorway, she stands for a moment, unseen. Mimi and Ammar sit on the large sofa. Lara's legs are stretched onto the coffee table; she is painting her toenails. All three of them watch the screen.

"Here she is, Sleeping Beauty Liz Taylor!" Ammar says, catching sight of her. His nickname for her, the absurd moniker for her constant napping and thick eyebrows. "Sit, sit."

Souad sits next to him, and Mimi speaks, her eyes not leaving the screen. "Your mother called."

Souad bites her lip, waiting. This is what she has dreaded since the other calls, the first to say they were safe, the second to say they were leaving for Amman as soon as her father organized finances and passports.

"What did she say?"

"Oh." Mimi sounds distracted. "I told her you were sleeping; it's been a rough couple of days. That she should let you rest. She said they'll call tomorrow morning."

Souad feels a rush of gratitude toward Mimi. "Thank you."

"Asshole," Lara blurts as Saddam's expansive, grinning face appears on the screen, a repeated clip. *Oh, God Almighty, be witness that we have warned them,* he is saying. The room falls silent, all of them watching the man raise an arm, not a shred of fear on his swarthy face.

The news report cuts to flames, bulldozers. The fires on the television screen—Souad thinks of her neighborhood, the auditorium she walked across in a graduation gown two months ago, the shopping mall. She feels a rising nausea. There are moments, these last few days, when she has felt as lost as a child, the urge to scream like bile in her throat. Souad averts her eyes, fixing them instead on the Persian rug, a landscape of spirals in shades of green.

"He's insane," Mimi says.

"No," Lara says deliberately. "He's an asshole." Ammar snorts with laughter.

There is a lived-in feeling in the apartment, one of camaraderie and airiness, a nonchalance among them that reminds Souad of those Amman summers, how envious Souad would be of Mimi's lackadaisical upbringing of her daughters. There were times in the past weeks when Lara lay her head on her mother's lap, and Mimi braided her hair. Souad cannot imagine ever doing such a thing herself with Alia. With her mother, Souad is her prickliest self, a cat stroked the wrong way.

During yesterday's phone call, her mother had yelled. The line was staticky and her voice kept being cut off.

"Goddamn this phone! Souad—Atef, I can't hear a damn thing."

Souad's mouth was dry as she repeated into the receiver, "Mama? *Mama?*"

"Yes—Souad—can you hear me?" A coarse sound, like the rustle of leaves, muffled the line. This alarmed Souad, as though the sound were somehow pulling her mother away. Suddenly her mother's voice broke through, clear. ". . . goddamn reception. Can you hear me?"

"Yes, yes!" Souad stood on her tiptoes, pressing a palm against the counter in Mimi's kitchen. The granite was smooth and cool. "How are you? What are you all doing?"

"Souad, we're leaving. In a couple of days, I think. It depends on how quickly . . . with the car . . . the airport's gone . . . Your father's trying to sort things out with the bank—not sure how long." Her mother spoke rapidly, in fragments, and Souad had a difficult time understanding. "We can take only a few things," her mother continued. "Small enough to carry. I know you have some clothes, but is there anything you want me to—that I should take." Only at these last words did her mother's voice falter; there was a distant clicking sound, like a swallow.

Souad was confused. "Take where?"

"Take with us." A familiar irritation crept into her mother's tone. "Souad, we're leaving Kuwait. We have to. Everyone is."

"But on the news they said it'll be over soon. That Europe or America will help." Even to her own ears, Souad's voice was childish, whining.

"*Habibti.*" Her mother's tone softened. "We don't know what's going to happen."

"But they're saying—"

"We're leaving." Alia ignored her, kept talking. "Things are bad, they're getting worse. What do you want me to take?"

Their house rushed through Souad's mind. The rooms, the photographs on the walls, the sunlight through veranda windows. Her own bedroom, suddenly empty—she knows the room as she knows her own body, and she couldn't conjure a single image of it.

"Nothing," Souad heard herself saying. "None of it."

"Are you sure?" Her mother sounded startled. "What about your jewelry? Clothes?"

"Nothing," Souad repeated, firmly. "I'll see it all when we go back."

"Souad," her mother said. "Souad, no one knows what will happen. We have to get to Amman as soon as possible." There was static on the line, and then her mother's voice returned. ". . . so we'll send you the ticket as soon as we get there. Probably next week."

"A ticket to where?" Souad felt slow, muddled.

"To Amman, Souad," her mother said. "I don't want you so far away while this is happening."

"But Mama"—a wild, spinning panic rose in Souad's throat, Elie appearing in her mind, *so few nights left*—"Mama, the program isn't over for three more weeks."

"Souad!" Her name hurled like a knife through Alia's teeth—disgust, pity—and Souad fell silent. Her mother took a deep breath, and when she spoke again, it was with finality, the way one speaks to those in shock. "Souad, there is a *war.*"

Souad sits impatiently in the living room, jiggling her leg. She glances at her watch every few minutes. It is only eight, and the Elie nights, as she has come to think of them, with their sidewalk cafés and bars and glasses of sherry, begin around now, everyone gathering at Le Chat Rouge to start the evening.

The phone call looms ahead of her. And with it her old life, slung, no longer hers and morphing into something unrecognizable: Amman, a new house, Riham and her family.

And Karam—her ally, the only one in her family she feels close to—when she spoke with him yesterday, his voice somber: "Sousi, I might be going to America. The architecture program in Amman isn't strong. We called a university in America, one where Baba's dean went, somewhere called Boston. They said they'd consider an emergency application. They're calling it asylum."

As a child, Souad hadn't been afraid of the same things her brother and sister were—spiders, heights, sandstorms—and she'd known wordlessly, from a young age, that people thought her intrepid. She was the only girl in the schoolyard to squat next to a lone scorpion and, later, the first one to light a cigarette, to sit daringly in the front seat of a boy's car, the wind raising her hair into a cloud. People wanted her like this, she understood. They loved watching the fearless.

This was why, as a girl, she'd never spoken of what she *was* afraid of. Never said that she was in fact *jealous* of her siblings, jealous because their fears had such specificity to them, could be labeled and confronted and dismantled.

What Souad spent her girlhood afraid of was incalculable, nameless. Not a creature so much as a shadow, a room emptied of lighting. She hated dusk; it filled her with dread. Hated the last few stairs when coming down from the roof of her grandmother's building.

When she was in bed sometimes, her small heart pounding just before she fell into sleep, she felt an endless plummet, as though someone had pushed her. Her fear had something to do with not being able to breathe, her mouth filled with water, with some enduring want. A suffocation. It was something like pursuit, something like not being fast enough.

This is what Souad thinks of as she watches the army tanks roll into the desert in tidy green rows.

In the living room, Souad watches Lara closely. Since her arrival, Souad has learned to blend in, to act nonchalant and follow the older girl's lead. They haven't become close, though Souad has joined her for drinks, met her intellectual French friends, all young professors like Lara. They laugh and tell stories, but, having taken English throughout school, Souad has a meager command of French. Lara's Arabic is broken after years in Europe.

Souad knew instinctively that Mimi wouldn't ask Souad's mother about rules and curfews. Still, she is careful, always slipping out with Lara, pretending that she spends her evenings working on art projects for her program.

Ammar flips to an Arab channel, where an American reporter speaks, her words dubbed in Arabic.

"The United Nations has released its strongest condemnation," the ethereal voice says as the reporter moves her lips out of sync. Her blond hair is cut above her eyebrows, straight across, like a doll Souad once had.

Lara stands and stretches, her midriff visible beneath the shirt. "I'm going out."

"Okay." Mimi continues frowning at the television. "With?"

"Luc," Lara says.

"Have fun."

"Be safe," Ammar says.

Souad watches the exchange, as she always does, with a fascination that still hasn't abated. In her own home, this would never, ever happen, the topic of boys—even harmless, friendly ones—a minefield of arguments with her mother.

She knows this is her moment; stands. "I'm going too," she announces, then holds her breath.

They barely look up. "Be safe," Ammar repeats, his eyes on the tanks and bombing onscreen.

On the street, she fumbles for a cigarette from her purse and smokes as she walks into the evening. She feels a sudden urge, now that she is outside the apartment, to clear her head. This is her favorite thing about the city—the ability it gives you to walk, to literally put space between your body and distress. In Kuwait, nobody walks anywhere.

Mimi lives in a quiet part of the city, mostly residential, with small, pretty apartments, each window like a glistening eye. The streetlamps are made of wrought iron, designs flanking either side of the bulbs. There is a minimalist sense of wealth in the neighborhood, children dressed simply, the women always adjusting scarves around their necks, their hair cut into perfectly symmetrical lines. Souad walks by the manicured lawns of a grammar school, empty and discarded for the summer. Next to it a gray-steepled church. She tries to imagine that, elsewhere, there is smoke and destroyed palaces and men carrying guns. It seems impossible.

The night is cool, and Souad wraps her cardigan tightly around her, crosses her arms. A shiver runs through her. She is nervous to see him, a familiar thrill that he always elicits in her. Even before last night.

Le Chat Rouge is a fifteen-minute walk from Mimi's apartment, but within several blocks the streets begin to change, brownstones and Gothic-style latticework replaced with grungier alleyways, young Algerian men with long hair sitting on steps and drinking beer from cans. One eyes her and calls out, caressingly, something in French.

She can make out the words for *sweet* and *return.* Bars line the streets with their neon signs and she walks directly across the Quartier Latin courtyard, her shoes clicking on the cobblestones.

"My mother's going to call tomorrow," she told Elie yesterday. She wasn't sure why she said it, but it felt necessary. "They're taking me to Amman." In the near dark, Elie's face was peculiarly lit, the sign making his skin look alien.

"You could stay here," Elie said. He smiled mockingly. "You could get married."

Souad had blinked, her lips still wet from the kiss. "Married?" She wasn't being coy—she truthfully had no idea what Elie meant. Married to whom? For a long, awful moment, she thought Elie was suggesting she marry one of the other Lebanese men, that he was fobbing her off on a friend in pity.

"Yes." Elie cocked his head, as though gauging the authenticity of her confusion. He smiled again, kinder this time. He closed his fingers around hers so that she was making a fist and he a larger one atop it. They both watched their hands silently for a few seconds, an awkward pose, more confrontational than romantic, as though he were preventing her from delivering a blow. It occurred to her that he was having a difficult time speaking. She felt her palm itch but didn't move. Elie cleared his throat, and when he spoke, she had to lean in to hear him.

"You could marry me."

Now, even in re-creating that moment, Souad feels the swoop in her stomach, her mouth drying. It is a thing she wants in the darkest, most furtive way, not realizing how badly until it was said aloud. *Eighteen years old*, a voice within her spoke, *eighteen.* Too young, too young. And her parents, her waiting life.

But the greater, arrogant part of Souad's self growled as if woken. Her steps clacked with her want of it. The self swelled triumphantly—*Shame, shame*, she admonishes herself, thinking of the war, the invasion, the troops and fire, but she is delighted nonetheless.

• • •

They met at the Shuja'a café in Kuwait a year ago. It was a space near the university where the intellectuals went to smoke cigarettes and talk about the war in Beirut and the Intifada. People sat around circular tables and drank Turkish coffee. It was a favored spot for those who considered themselves Communists, the young men wearing all black.

Souad loved it. She felt like an academic, crushing her cigarette neatly when she was finished with it, the lipstick stains around the butt unspeakably elegant to her. In the Shuja'a café, she felt like a version of herself that was nearly complete, someone whom others would want. Would envy. She spoke in a low, murmuring voice, batted her eyelashes. It was different than the boat parties and dancing, where the *ajanib* fluttered around her. There, she got more attention but it felt too easy, those blue-eyed men hungry for her laugh. At the café, women were poets or working on manifestos. They wore baggy pants and cursed like the men.

The pity of it, then, was that she felt out of place at the café. She hated to admit it but knew it was true. Souad had never been a strong student; she didn't have a sturdy sense of history or politics. Frankly, the topics bored her. She just wanted the sickle necklaces and the berets. Still, she faltered through Marxist writings and began to read the newspaper. She learned to laugh when the men finished a sentence with a sardonic arch of their eyebrows, for this signified they'd said something they found—in a self-defeating way—funny.

Souad began calling Elie's group of friends the Libanais, a nod toward their French-infused upbringing, and they seemed taken by her. Elie was the center of the group, with bushy eyebrows and an egotistic charm about him. He was the quintessential Libanais, leaving Beirut after the violence began, summering in France since boyhood, and attending the Lycée Français in Kuwait. When he argued with the other men, he switched to French, the language silky and eruptive in his mouth. Three years older than Souad, he had already begun university, studying political science, though his true passion was writing.

"I'm moving to Paris," he told her the night they met. "At the end of this year, I'm transferring there to study writing." He spoke to her about his dead mother and overbearing father, how Elie had finally struck a deal with his father, after much argument: Elie would move to France after two years at Kuwait University.

"How can you know you'll still hate it here in a year?"

He'd looked at her pityingly, as though she were a child. "Some things you know, *poupée*." The nickname, meaning "doll," stuck. Souad hated it, but she learned not to throw tantrums. In Elie she'd met someone, finally, who was more volatile than she.

He has many faults. He becomes grandiose when he drinks, is prone to exaggerated gestures and endless, solipsistic speeches. He winks at waitresses. He emanates a certain smell, not entirely unpleasant but slightly baked in, like leather or day-old bread, especially after a night of drinking. He seems not to see her sometimes, blinking when she speaks to him as though he'd forgotten she was there. And Souad, accustomed to attention—the youngest of her family, the liveliest of her friends—is scathed by such indifference.

Still, when he kisses her, pulling her summarily against him, she feels all of her selves scatter and then, exquisitely, repair.

Souad walks the length of the courtyard until she sees the fountain, two teenage girls sitting at the marble lip and smoking cloves. One of them wears large, black-framed glasses and is speaking rapidly in French while the other girl nods. Souad crosses them and sees the red of the Chat Rouge sign.

She pauses outside of the entrance, watching her reflection in the dirty, reddish glass, her chest split by the curve of the *g*. She is afraid. Though Elie mystifies and infuriates her in many ways, Souad understands him well enough, she realizes slowly, that she will know instantly whether he meant what he said last night. She will know as soon as he looks at her.

For a moment, Souad remains outside, listening to the girls, catching the words *jamais* and *collier* and *merde*. It is like listening to an orchestra. She wishes she could walk up to them and take a seat, ask them if she should go home, ask them what will become of Kuwait, whether she should trust Elie.

A couple stagger out of the bar, laughing and carrying beer cans. The air from the bar whooshes outside—music and chatter—and Souad steps in.

The bar is always crowded, chain smokers seated around small tables. One side of the room has a long wooden bar, the bottles behind it twinkling like jewels. Ivan, the bartender, pours glass after glass, his silver hair cut into a pageboy, a gold hoop dangling from each ear.

The group, Albert, Sami, Marcel—the Libanais who spend their summers in France—sit on stools, their usually boisterous tones muted, glum. Elie is at the edge of the bar, his eyes on the television, another news story about Kuwait—already the flames and bulldozers are familiar to Souad—his expression grave. The television flickers on his face, his eyes hollowed and somehow older, much older.

Watching the forlorn expressions, Souad feels something click within her and she knows that she will remember this moment, that she will come back to this as the crux of her life, the instant when she fully understood the gravity of it. There would be no return. Her clothing—so much of it borrowed from Budur—the large evil eye dangling from her window. The map she'd hung after an argument with her mother years ago, enormous, spanning an entire wall with blues and greens. Her old school, the chalk on her classroom floor, the market her father likes to buy melons from. She suddenly recognizes it all as lost. It is enough to make her weep, and she walks to them, wishing to tell Elie, praying that he will be kind.

"Souad!" Albert says, and voices tangle in greeting. Souad keeps her eyes on Elie, watching him as he turns. She sees the truth assemble itself on his face. And she knows: He meant it. He meant what he said last night, and he means it still.

"Do you see this bullshit?" Sami asks her.

"It's awful," she says, trying to keep the joy out of her voice. *He meant it, he meant it.*

There are murmurs of assent, and Souad walks to Elie's side. A horrible thought crosses her mind, a doubt—that he would never have asked if Saddam hadn't invaded—and she is briefly, disgustingly, grateful for the flames on the television. She shakes her head to banish the thought.

"You came." His voice is low, full.

"They've burned everything."

"I know."

Souad watches the news, a pretty reporter speaking, though the sound is muted. Behind Elie and Souad, people are having lively conversations in French. They wouldn't be able to find Kuwait on a map.

She orders a whiskey sour, eats the cherry first. The alcohol is harsh on her tongue, but she drinks gratefully. She and Elie talk carefully, predictably, about other things. The airport closing, his father going to Lebanon.

"And you?" she asks, her heart filling with the question. She is afraid, suddenly, of saying yes or no.

"Fuck Beirut," he says, a glimmer of his old self showing. "I keep telling them. Makes no sense, trading one war for another. My aunts say the mountains are fine. But Jesus—a village life? Sheep and chamomile tea every morning? *Non, merci.*" He squints his eyes at the television in a gesture Souad recognizes as studiously casual. "Your mama still going to Amman? Did you talk to her?"

"I missed her call," Souad says, her mouth dry. This is it; they are coming to the heart of it. "But it's still Amman. Amman for everyone."

She holds her breath as Elie swallows his beer, turns finally to her. His eyes fill with recognition, then transform entirely. Gentling, dark and warm. He looks luminous.

"Hey," he says.

Souad turns. Fucking Séraphine. She is a childhood friend of Elie's from the summers he spent in Paris. She stands, a shot glass in each hand. A blue scarf is twisted attractively around her torso, slithers of pale skin showing. Tassels fall against her hips. Eyes like a cat's, bottle green. Her nose tiny and sloping, a smattering of freckles across her cheeks. Over the weeks, Séraphine appeared at various parties and bars; Souad befriended her with the wariness of one who wishes to keep a threat close.

Okay, boys, okay, one at a time, Séraphine will say at last call when the Chat Rouge men clamor to buy her another drink. She seems to pick favorites arbitrarily. Sometimes Sami, one of the Libanais visiting from Kuwait; sometimes Émile, a thin bearded Parisian. A slew of other artistic, handsome men. On any given night, she focuses almost exclusively on one man, often letting him kiss her before reapplying her lipstick right at the table, with everyone watching her.

"Whiskey," Séraphine says now. "For this shitty night."

She sets down one for Souad and one for herself, and Souad lifts hers. They clink glasses. Souad swallows, welcoming the fire in her throat.

"*Assieds.*" Elie stands, and Séraphine smiles at him, taking his chair. Now she and Souad are next to each other, one of her tassels against Souad's thigh.

Séraphine clicks her tongue. "*Horrible, c'est incroyable, ce qu'ils ont fait.*" She glances at Souad, switches to English. "He is a terrible man, Saddam."

Rage inexplicably bubbles within Souad. How dare she, this tiny exquisite thing, click her tongue and look sad? Séraphine's face is grave, her eyes on the television, on images of troops barricading the city. Souad wants to shake her. How dare she gaze mournfully at the screen?

You can't leave me, she'd told Karam yesterday, her voice breaking. *You can't.*

Sousi. You can't imagine what it's like here. Everything's gone.

"They've burned everything" is all Souad says now, repeating herself, and the other woman hugs her, abruptly, enveloping Souad in the scent of something spicy, like cinnamon or pepper.

• • •

One news report replaces another. The volume remains muted while French-language updates about the invasion travel across the bottom of the screen. As the rest of them watch, Souad looks around at the faces of the Libanais. She remembers her bitterness toward Séraphine and feels ashamed, small. Sami, she knows, went to college on a scholarship; his family lives in a small house in the city's center. They would have no money to leave. Marcel's brother worked with the royal family—no one has heard from him since the day before yesterday. *Missing, assumed dead;* Souad remembers the phrase from history class, the line that emerges during any catastrophe. She says, again, a quick prayer for her family, her friends, her aunt Widad, Budur, all those still alive.

Everyone talks of news back home, stories of their families, the people they know in Kuwait. The French, Émile and Séraphine, remain respectfully silent, listening.

"I heard they're looting the hotels."

"They're saying the soldiers barricaded the roads."

"My sister can't get out. They've shut down the electricity."

"The water too. He's making the sick die of thirst in the hospitals."

"And in the outskirts? They're going to start eating sand out there."

"America will come in."

"Fuck America. It's because of America that son of a cunt has power."

The voices swirl and become louder, people arguing, their eyes never leaving the television. Ivan pours them shots of vodka, refusing to take their coins. Souad wonders what the other patrons must think of them, with their raised voices and Arabic.

Hours pass. The men continue their talk; Séraphine braids the tassels of her scarf. *Turkish blue*, Souad thinks. She drinks one, two glasses of wine, stealing glances at Elie. He has fallen strangely silent. She needs to get back to Mimi's. It is nearly two. Her aunt and uncle will be worried, and she is suddenly tired of it, tired of going back, always going back. She wishes she could have, just once, an entire night for herself, a blank stretch of road. The way the men do, the way Séraphine does.

Amman darts into her mind. Her drunken head throbs. A life with her sister and parents, without Karam, the endless arguments about curfew and college classes. She thinks of Riham and her quiet garden, little Abdullah with his anxious eyes, Riham's boring husband. It makes her want to scream.

The television shows another scene, a new one. A park, blazing.

"*Vous êtes certain? Je peux le changer. C'est trop triste.*" Ivan speaks to Elie, his brow furrowed in concern.

"*Non, non, c'est bien.*" Elie keeps his eyes fixed on the television screen.

They fall silent watching the fire. A sentence moves across the bottom of the screen: *Le parc a été dans les premières heures de ce matin.*

"Bastards," Sami says in Arabic.

Séraphine drains her glass. She frowns as she stares at the screen. "It is sad, of course," she says in accented English. "But what is a children's park when homes are being destroyed?"

Souad is suddenly angry. She remembers an afternoon during Eid, when she was six or seven, when her father took her to the zoo, as he always did—she loved to feed the giraffes, thrilled at the sandpaper tongues on her hand as she fed them crackers and seeds—and then afterward to the park.

"There are these little statues in the park," she says, and then fumbles in French. "*Comme des anges. Avec des petits chapeaux.*" Everyone is watching her and for once she doesn't care about her meager French. The eyes of the Libanais men are afraid, she realizes, like children's. Dwarfed in the face of this. "*Je les aimais.*"

"*Des figurines,*" Elie adds, then switches to Arabic, speaking only to Souad. He looks grateful. "We used to go as children as well. You remember the entrance? That little gate."

"The latch always stuck." Souad feels his sorrow. "My father would have to jiggle it loose." She has something that Séraphine doesn't.

Only she knows what is being burned, what is being taken in Kuwait. Elie shares this with her alone.

"My father too." Elie smiles at her. "I'd forgotten, all these years."

They spill onto the streets. The men roll hash cigarettes, the air pungent with the scent. Séraphine takes a puff and in the ethereal light of the streetlamps, she looks like something mythical. It is late. Far too late. Khalto Mimi will know she stayed out later than Lara; there will be questions in the morning. And they might smell the whiskey on her.

She lights one of Elie's cigarettes, leaning into the flame in his hand, and smokes as they walk down the narrow, fairylike streets. Kuwait is burning; her mother is packing their house right now, as Souad walks.

Séraphine does a little skip, loops her arm through Sami's. The tassels of her scarf sway back and forth, her hips moving like water. It reminds Souad of Khalto Widad, how she plaits her hair into one long braid after showering, the tip like a serpent's tongue. They will go to Amman as well, Khalto Widad and Ammo Ghazi, everyone. Except Karam, who will go to some faraway city. Souad sniffs. It is too much.

They reach the Quartier Latin courtyard, where a woman is playing the violin next to the fountain, and two other women are singing. In her tipsiness, Souad first mistakes them for the women she saw hours ago, but, of course, they are different. Different beautiful women in this city of beautiful women.

"Let's sit," Séraphine suggests and they do, sprawling on the stone steps across the courtyard. The stone is cold, and Souad lifts her knees to her chest, Elie at her side. He puts his arm around her shoulders.

The women are singing Pink Floyd, their French accents shaping the English lyrics into an elegy.

"*Your heroes for ghosts*," they croon. Souad thinks of the map on her wall at home. For the first time, she realizes sharply that it isn't her wall anymore. The house is gone.

The music dips and rises, their little group swaying to the rhythm. One of the singing women wears a loose dress and she twirls, the skirt flaring, during the chorus. "*Wish you were here.*" They finish with a flourish, and the men whistle, their applause echoing down the street. The women curtsy.

"'Je ne regrette rien,'" Séraphine calls out and when the violinist plays it, they all begin to sing along. "*Ni le bien qu'on m'a fait.*" Even Souad, with her deep, graceless voice. She watches the musician, the singers, the fountain burbling water in the streetlamp light. Kuwait is a planet, a lifetime, away.

"*Je me fous du passé.*" Elie's voice, baritone, by her side.

She glances at him through her eyelashes. His eyes are shut, and a pure, boyish delight fills his face as the music drifts around them.

And she feels not love but detachment, an odd calmness as she watches him, as if she's appraising a house she's not sure she wants to live in. *I wouldn't have to leave*, she thinks. The realization settles over her, imagining tomorrow, her mother's fingers dialing the phone, a lifetime of *Souad, Souad, where were you, when will you be home.*

After the song is over, she decides. After the violinist bows and smiles, and the applause scatters, she will walk him over to the fountain, will slip her body against his and lean into his ear. Will whisper, *Yes.*

RIHAM

AMMAN
October 1999

Riham stands straight and leans over, grazing her toes with her forefingers. She straightens and mutters, "Six," before repeating the stretch. Once she reaches ten, she stands and begins to do lunges. Farida and the other women recommended them for the twinges in her lower back.

"And they won't hurt your behind either," Farida quipped, too refined to say *ass.* Riham knows that the other women do these exercises for the results, the tightening of calves and elongated spines. But she likes the process itself, hearing her joints pop, feeling the tendons and muscles stretch and tense, the quiet of her bedroom as she counts aloud.

After the lunges come the sit-ups, then the long, pointy-toed stretches with each leg propped on the windowsill. She likes to pretend she is a ballerina warming up before a performance, though she is over thirty and corpulent, to put it nicely. Still, she tells herself—in defiance of the body she was given, the tepid Amman morning outside the window—for these few minutes she is transformed, a Russian soloist prepping for the stage, her hair sweeping against her knees as she bends, as far as she can, an audience of well-dressed people waiting for her to walk into the spotlight.

• • •

Her favorite part of the day is this—late morning, after breakfast, the men out of the house, Abdullah at university, Latif already at the hospital. Last May, he was promoted to medical director, and Riham had invited all their friends over, cooked a feast of chicken and lamb and rice with the maid, Rosie, to celebrate. People milled around until midnight; afterward, Latif kissed Riham and said he felt like a celebrity.

Next to the windowsill is a notebook with a blue pen. Half the pages have already been used, and Riham opens to today's list. Latif likes to tease her. "A to-do list for the president," he says. The mockery stings but Riham just smiles. "A clear mind is a clear heart," she tells him, and she loves to examine the day before her, still not begun.

Today, the list is short: Breakfast, exercise, hemming her dress, the garden, basting the chicken, tea at Farida's, dinner. With satisfaction, she crosses off *breakfast* and *exercise* with tidy swipes. She wraps her veil around her hair as she makes her way to the living room. Walking past the kitchen, she can hear Rosie's voice, the young girl singing songs about flowers and men in her language.

The house is a large one. It has the high ceilings and tiled floors of a space that seems to multiply itself, giving the impression of something vast and swelling. When Riham and Latif first moved in after their wedding, it had been smaller, with three bedrooms and the living room, which opened to a garden. The other bedrooms, the study, the veranda, came later, as the years went on.

Riham thrilled at each addition, finding a certain magic in the renovation of the house, the weeks and weeks of construction, laborers scurrying around, the thin coat of dust that layered everything, *everything*, until she couldn't take it anymore, would be on the verge of telling everyone to leave when, finally, the workers would step back and reveal another room, gleaming and white, belonging to her.

It reminded her of gardening, the crop of new spaces, walls and floors blossoming, the way the house—and in this she took matriarchal pride—grew.

Except the Fixture. She avoids the wooden shed near the garden, entering it only if she must. Over the years, they took to calling it that—the Fixture—as though it were temporary. She never told Latif that part of her joy last year—part of the extravagance of the dinner party—was in his retiring the Fixture, the plain space with five cots and drawers full of medical instruments that he'd used less and less frequently as time went by. There had been spikes, of course, after wars, invasions, when it seemed the Fixture was swarming with people, the desperate and moneyless coming to Latif's door, sent by family in other countries. Latif would suture wounds, clean out gunshots, without taking a single dinar.

"Please, the doctor," they would say when she opened the door at their knocking, sometimes in the middle of the night. "We were told to come here. They said he would help. They said he helps everyone."

Certainly it was something to be proud of—the distinguished doctor husband who felt so keenly for the fallen, he tried to heal them all. And for the first few years, Riham *was* proud, making soup and tea for the men, offering them fruit when they got strong again and walked around her gardens.

But eventually another side of her shone through, a side she was ashamed of and so never shared with Latif—the irritation, the utter boredom of it. Selfishly, she wanted her house, her husband to herself. She watched the lives of her friends, wives of other doctors, with envy—the men home for dinner, no stink of unwashed bodies in their yards.

She never spoke of it. It was a stain, she recognized, an unclean part of herself, what Latif would call a faltering. So she did what she always did in those moments. She prayed. The men came less and less often, going instead to government clinics as Latif grew older. But Riham kept praying, exhausted, wishing she could stop the resentment. And when Latif accepted the position at the hospital, announcing he would end the home practice, she felt a full, rushing relief: if she couldn't change the faltering in herself, at least she wouldn't be reminded of it anymore.

• • •

In the living room, she catches sight of one of Abdullah's *dishdashas* on the couch, spilling over the arm. He has worn them more frequently over the past year, the European T-shirts and jeans unused in his closet. Riham folds the garment, smells the metallic scent of him. Every hour, it seems, the boy finds a way to enter her mind, some reminder, and then it starts up again, like a faithful Ferris wheel: her worry for him, her fear.

She glances at her watch and starts. Past eleven. She rushes toward the garden. Each morning, like clockwork, her father walks the mile from his house to his favorite café, where he and the other neighborhood men meet for coffee and talk. Since retiring, it is the one thing he does religiously, saying it helps him stay fit. At precisely eleven o'clock, he passes by Riham's garden, and if she is there, they sit and drink tea. It is Riham's time with her father, the only gatherings without her mother or Latif or Abdullah.

"Damn," she curses softly as she stumbles on the lip of the rug. She kicks it loose, then hurries out of the door and down to the garden. Riham smiles at the figure walking along the fence around her yard.

"I thought I'd missed you," her father calls, unlatching the gate. They meet at the clearing between patches of wildflowers and black irises. There are several chairs and her father chooses one next to the jasmine shrub.

"I was daydreaming in the house." She smiles at him. "Tea?"

Her father shakes his head. "Already had some?" she asks. She doesn't mind it, Atef's reticence. It comforts her, her father's ability to stay quiet, reflective, when it seems like everywhere—the news, the marketplace, the streets—is one endless soundtrack of prattling.

He examines the jasmine plant, a sapling, by his side. He touches a browning leaf.

"You were right," she says. "I should've just planted acacias."

"They'll be fine."

"They're *drooping*. It was the heat this year. It killed everything. The poor darlings dying of thirst." She gazes at the shrub ruefully. She hates summer.

"Prune them anyway," he says. "Who knows, winter might be late. It's still warm out."

"Dinner tonight, yes?" They do it twice a week, her parents coming over for dinner, Rosie cooking *koussa* or *maqlouba*, her mother's favorite.

He hesitates. "Perhaps later in the week."

"What happened?" Riham catches his pause. "Mama?"

"Well." He sighs. "There was a bit of an incident yesterday."

"Incident?" Riham knew that *incident* could refer to any of the assorted episodes over the past few years—her mother's arguments with a maid or neighbor, a misunderstanding with her husband, or something with Riham's siblings. Riham guesses it's the last one, for her mother's favorite topic is her two wayward children, living in a cold city across the world. Karam had moved to Boston, and after Souad moved to Boston as well, their alliance was sealed: Karam and Souad *got* each other. Riham has never visited them in America, never gone with her parents on their trips for children's births, Souad's son, Zain, and Karam's daughter, Linah, born months apart. "Karam or Souad?"

A smile dances on her father's lips. "Not Sousi this time."

"Surprising." Of all Alia's topics, Souad's behavior is her favorite rant: her reckless marriage, her wasted youth, the impulsive move to Boston a few years ago. *The girl lives a vagrant life with a husband and two young children, barely ever visiting us, spending her days getting that thankless degree in design like some adolescent.* When Souad wed, only their father had gone. Their mother refused, saying she wouldn't show her face at such an abomination.

"What happened with Karam?"

"Ay." Atef sits back in the chair, stretching his legs out. Riham settles back as well. She loves these moments, loves being the only child near her parents. The one who never left. She feels a camaraderie when her father brings news of her siblings, those mysterious, unfathomable creatures living lives she cannot imagine. She was planning to go for Karam's wedding, but they wound up having it in Amman, a brief affair. Riham was not completely over the shock of seeing the elegant, dark-haired woman who was Budur—*Budur*, the skinny girl from Kuwait, flying to visit Souad in Boston and tumbling into romance with Karam—by her brother's side, kissing him full on the mouth, both of them so happy that the aunts had whispered about decorum between two young adults.

"They can't do the December trip anymore," her father says. "Budur has her thesis defense scheduled then, and Karam can't take time off in January, so they're putting the trip off till the summer."

"*Akh.*" Riham lifts a hand to her head. It is a sensitive topic to her mother, how infrequently her other two children visit, the rare times she gets to see her grandchildren. *All my cousins live with their grandchildren; I'm lucky if I see mine once a year.* Riham is torn. She knows her mother is demanding. But she feels her siblings are feckless, wayward, not considerate enough. "Did it get bad?"

He grimaces. "I came in too late. I could hear her yelling from the kitchen." A sigh. "She brought up the land."

"Oh, Mama." Riham groans. The land is a tense topic. Two years ago, Budur's uncle passed away and left her a plot of land near Erbil. Through relatives still living in Iraq, the land was sold, raking in a tidy sum. The matter of the money was one that Alia spoke about constantly. *She could've bought stocks or saved for her children's tuition or helped Karam with the mortgage.* Instead, Budur had signed up for courses at Tufts.

"Which led to the topic of Beirut . . ."

"Oh no."

The Beirut apartments were another point of contention. The money for the apartments came from childless Khalto Widad, who'd died several years ago, quietly, Ammo Ghazi having passed a decade earlier. It had shocked them all, the amount of money she left, equally divided among Karam and Riham and Souad, kept in a Swiss bank, no less. Through a Lebanese lawyer, Riham bought one apartment, Karam the other. Souad used the money for her mortgage in Boston. But Alia was furious with them for buying the Beirut apartments, since the chaotic, lively city was more alluring to her children—and therefore more likely for them to visit—than Amman. *Now I have to spend my summers in that land of whores instead of my home just to get a glimpse of my grandchildren.*

"Then she told him Budur was wasting money on a hippie degree, studying literature."

Riham shakes her head. "Did Karam get mad?"

"He was polite. I spoke with him afterward. He seemed worried about her. He said he might try to come by himself, or perhaps with Linah. I told him not to worry, that your mother was just disappointed. He sends his love."

"Allah keep him," Riham murmurs automatically. They lapse into silence, the only sound insects buzzing and, far off, cars rushing along the main road.

Riham thinks of her brother, how his knuckles must have whitened on the telephone, hearing his mother speak that way about Budur. He wouldn't have said a word, she knows; she and Karam are alike that way. Only Souad ever speaks up, yells back. Karam would have listened, then gotten off the phone and smiled at Budur, pretended all was fine. Poor gentle Karam, mild-mannered like their father. Years ago, when he'd announced he was going to marry Budur—they'd gotten engaged quickly, within weeks—her mother had been inexplicably furious.

"I don't understand you children!" Riham heard her shout over the phone. "There's a war, and suddenly everyone has to get married? Look at Souad! Look at your sister, Karam. She's raising an infant in an attic. Is that the life you want for yourself? What did we send you across the world for? God, at least if you married an American, you'd get the passport."

It was the greatest insult. Only Karam's love for his mother kept him from responding. He politely got off the phone and did not speak to her again for a month.

Riham makes a mental note to call him tonight or tomorrow. Their telephone conversations are always brief, Riham muttering platitudes about faith, coming off as vacuous and dowdy. She feels dwarfed near her brother and sister, small and pudgy and boring, even though they are kind to her, as one is to the slow or elderly. She knows her life is dull to them. She sees her life, sometimes, the way an eagle would, circling overhead—herself a tiny dot, moving predictably, making to-do lists, laughing, pouring cups of tea.

"Can you imagine," Riham once overheard Souad saying to Karam, "that sort of life? The doctor's wife. Spending your days doing laundry and cooking." She sighed. "I'd kill myself."

Karam and Souad, by contrast, are their own worlds. Cavernous, chaotic, beautiful. All she knows of her siblings are her memories of them as children and then, abruptly, snapshots of adults whom she sees every couple of years. Listening to conversation between those two—living minutes apart in Boston, sharing their lives and children—is like listening to a foreign language. When they attempt to include Riham—explaining their work or the city, with its college bars and bookstores—it feels wooden, forced, like they're trying to help her understand something she simply cannot.

Connecting with the children is easier. Manar and Zain and Linah. Like a charm said thrice over, darlings, all of them, with olive skin and unruly hair. They look like siblings. Riham sees the children in snapshots as well, as infants, then chubby toddlers, then young children. They love her guilelessly, wholly. She holds for them the allure of the exotic; she's the aunt whose veil they can unfasten to play with her long hair, the aunt who feeds them zaatar, takes them through her garden as though it is a magical land.

With them she is transformed, buoyant, playing with dolls and singing aloud, all of it threaded with jealousy, reaching for the children with a longing closer to hunger than love.

After a while, her father rises. "Don't forget the pruning. And water them a little more."

"And tonight?"

He sighs. "We'll come. She may be a bit much to handle."

"I'll make *maqlouba*."

"Ah!" Her father laughs. "That might do it."

She watches him walk, his shoulders thin against the linen of his shirt. "Wait!" she calls out, remembering. "Abdullah. Did you speak with him?"

Her father pauses. "I did," he says. He seems reluctant to say more.

"And?"

Atef runs a hand through his silver hair, a nervous habit all three children inherited. "The boy is lost, Riham."

"Did you ask him about the men?"

"He says they're just friends. That he met them at university. When I pushed, he admitted they were political. That's who he's been spending his time with."

Riham had asked her father to speak with Abdullah. The boy has been staying out late the past couple of months, since he began university. Another mother might suspect girls. But several times, she has glimpsed older men dropping him off at the house, found political pamphlets in his clothing. With Latif's father dead and his mother's family in Syria, the boy's only grandparents were Atef and Alia, who—after their initial bewilderment with Riham's marriage—loved Abdullah fiercely. But it was Atef the boy seemed most connected to, becoming attached to the man who was around while his father worked endless hours. They walked to the library together, went to Petra. Riham knew it was unfair, asking Atef to speak with Abdullah, taking advantage of the boy's love and respect for her father. But she was afraid.

"Why is he doing this?" she wonders aloud. "What does he need that we don't give him?"

"It's not that simple." Her father looks pained. "Those sorts of men, those meetings, they give you something that can't be replicated."

"So what can I do? I worry about him. Latif worries about him."

"There's nothing to do, Riham. He has to learn on his own." He starts to walk, then pauses. "Those gatherings, they make boys feel like *giants*."

• • •

She remains in the garden for a while, thinking about Abdullah. When she goes back inside, she crosses *chicken* off her list and writes *maqlouba.*

"We'll need to soak the rice," she tells Rosie in the kitchen. "And defrost the lamb."

Rosie raises her thin eyebrows. "No chicken?"

"*Maqlouba.* Mama's coming tonight." Rosie shrugs, not particularly interested. Riham likes her indifference. She finds it liberating, a relief from the false cheer and formality of previous maids.

"Please make sure the meat isn't overcooked. I'm going to Madame Farida's house in a bit but will be back in time."

Riham gathers the soft nest of yarn and needles from the basket in the living room. Knitting calms her, reminding her of her grandmother. She turns the television to a popular Turkish soap opera, the voices dubbed in Arabic. While she knits, Riham shakes her head and talks back to the characters.

"He's going to leave you," she says to the starlet, blond and slate-eyed. "He's in love with your sister. He's just after your inheritance."

But still the starlet rushes forward, gasping at the crimson flowers, saying yes when he pulls out a ring. The camera zooms in on the ring, alive with sinister sparkle. *I'll love you until the sky is no more.*

"Stupid," Riham says to the screen. "Stupid, stupid girl."

The air fills with the muezzin's call for prayer. Three o'clock. If she keeps dawdling, she will be late for Farida's lunch. Riham winds the leftover yarn, clicks the needles together. On the way to her bedroom, she passes the framed photographs lining the hallway. Her family, in various poses of smiling and laughter. Souad with an infant Manar; Karam and Budur on their wedding day; Latif and Abdullah on the beach.

She performs *wudu* instinctively, done thousands of times, her hands moving of their own accord, splashing the cool water over her wrists, her ankles. Her lips move soundlessly with prayer. She cups the water, smoothes it over her face, behind her ears.

When her grandmother taught Riham to pray years ago, Riham asked her about this part, the ears. It struck her as silly, detracting from the gravitas of the ritual. It was because people rarely washed there, Salma had said. *It's easy to overlook.* Through some network of synapses and cells—once, Latif explained to her how memories formed, the elegant cells shaking with potentiation, synapses in the curved temporal lobe hooking onto one another—it is this memory that has taken hold, latched onto the very act of touching water behind her ears, and she remembers her grandmother, briefly, each time.

As Riham stands over the prayer rug, the curtains in her room drawn—she prefers to pray in dim light—she begins the task of trying to keep her mind pure and focused. Every prayer, it is a struggle. Oftentimes, her mind returns to a single image: her struggling body in the water decades ago, the black splotch she saw in herself. "*La ilaha illa Allah*," she begins, the words effortless off her tongue, just as her grandmother taught her.

Her mind skims between her grandmother and her son, Abdullah's face drifting in her mind's eye, his stiff back at the dinner table. She prays as snippets of memories drift across the backs of her eyelids like snow. An image of the *dishdasha* tossed on the couch. Abdullah's beard, Latif's tightened lips when his son stays out late. Her grandmother bent over a coffee cup, reading the dregs. She would do it only for guests, refused to do it for Riham and Souad, though they would beg her during the summers.

"*As-salamu alaikum wa rahmatu Allah*," Riham murmurs first to her right shoulder, then to her left. "*Ameen.*" She slackens her body. She recites the names of everyone in her family, asking Allah to bless them, as always.

". . . Karam, bless him. Linah, bless her. Mama, bless her. Latif, bless him." She finishes and rises, then drops back onto the rug again, aghast.

"Oh, and Souad, Souad, bless her."

• • •

She is stepping into her shoes when the telephone rings. She hears Rosie pick up, speak inaudibly, then a pause.

"Madame!"

"Yes, Rosie."

"It's Madame Alia. She says to talk."

Riham sighs, eyeing the front door. "Okay." She walks to the kitchen and takes the cordless phone from Rosie. "Mama?"

"That girl is ruining your brother."

Riham rolls her eyes upward, berating herself for taking the call. "I'm pretty sure you said the exact same thing about the American girl he dated."

Her mother sniffs. "That was different. That girl had an excuse—she was raised American, mannerless, no culture. She couldn't help herself."

"Mama—"

"But Budur," her mother continues, undaunted, "why, we practically raised that girl! She was with us most of her childhood. Good parents, good upbringing. That whole mess with the first husband, I'll grant you, wasn't pretty, but these things happen. But what—"

"He was terrible to her."

"—what I don't understand is why on *earth* she would start putting on these airs. Going for her undergraduate degree, wonderful. I'm happy about that. You know I've always supported women getting an education. I pushed you and pushed you. And Souad! I was devastated when she had Manar instead of going to college and so happy when she finally got her degree—"

"You called her pretentious, Mama."

"Well, art *is* pretentious. But Budur, she took her courses, she got her education. She has a small child, for God's sake. Even the master's, I can understand. But in literature! And now, it's taking away from her family, depriving Linah's grandparents of seeing her."

"Baba says they're coming in the summer."

"I knew it! You and your father have been gossiping about me," her mother accuses. "This always happens. You sit in that garden and talk about me, like I'm some pariah."

Riham sighs. "Mama, you know that's not true. He was just telling me the news. We're all disappointed about it."

"Good. If you're so disappointed, you'll call your brother. Tell him this is unacceptable. Talk to Budur if you have to. Tell them they simply have to come."

The thought of Riham issuing commands to her brother makes her smile. She softens her voice, uses the one she reserves for her mother. "Okay, Mama. I'll see what I can do."

"You're the only good one, dear. The only one that listens. Allah give you grace." Even though she knows her mother is mercurial, that Riham is praised only because she never talks back, she cannot help but feel a small glow at her mother's words.

"I'm worried about Abdullah," she says impulsively.

Her mother snorts. "Finally. It only took you and Latif a year to catch on. I've been telling you since that boy turned sixteen, something's off. He's too easily taken in. I talked and talked, and no one listened. You see? Maybe if you and your father spent less time gossiping and more time listening, the boy wouldn't be in trouble now. And Latif's no help. A good man, yes, but too quiet. A father needs to speak up, needs to take charge. Not like your father, mind you. I had to be the father for you three. We let you kids run wild with your American cartoons, playing, and reading novels. We let you all become soft."

Riham sighs. "Mama, I have to go."

The last time Souad and Karam visited, they both seemed taken aback by the change in Abdullah. "It's like he's a jihadi," Riham overheard Souad joke to Karam once. The evening of their final dinner, they sat in Riham's garden, swatting mosquitoes and eating watermelon. The conversation drifted, predictably, to politics.

"The Americans and their missiles," Atef had said to Karam. "Can you please tell your boy Clinton to take it down a notch?" It was an inside joke, Karam's fondness for Clinton.

"Tell your fundamentalists to stop first," Karam countered. The conversation turned to Monica Lewinsky, then the situation in Palestine.

"They're saying it's getting worse."

"The Intifada didn't stop the settlers."

Abdullah spoke suddenly, with violence. "You're all wrong."

"What do you mean, son?" Latif asked gently.

"All of this, all of you, this *joke* of a conversation. A group of middle-class Arabs, most of them more American than Arab"—here he looked pointedly at Souad and at the tank top that showed the tops of her breasts—"from the comfort of a *mansion*, speaking about the plight of the poverty-stricken. As if any of you have stepped foot in a refugee camp. You barely speak Arabic with your children." Again a glance toward Souad, Budur, Karam. "You're fair-weather Arabs, all of you."

"He's got a point!" Karam tried for a joke. "We're addicted to American television, that's true, but I don't think it's a crime." Uncertain laughter rippled. Riham caught Latif's eye; he looked away.

Abdullah turned to Karam. "Do you know the words to the Fatiha?"

"Abdullah!" Both she and Latif spoke at the same time.

"What? Is it wrong of me to ask? To be concerned about the spiritual fate of those around me? My *family?*" The word dripped from his tongue. "If I don't speak, no one will. This is exactly the problem. Arabs go over to the West, fall in love with their fake gods, their starlets and music stars, drink their poisoned water—"

"We have a Brita," Souad muttered.

"It's disgusting." Abdullah ignored Souad. "We lose our culture. We sell our souls. Instead of getting fat off of their land, we should be fighting them, arming to the teeth. We should be returning to Allah. The people who are going to save us, they aren't those spineless politicians. It's the men inside the mosques."

Abdullah sat back in his chair, looking satisfied. He lifted his teacup and slurped. Silence.

"If you think that, you're a *fool.*" Alia's voice rose, sharp. Riham was shocked by the ferocity in her voice.

"Mama—"

"Those men hand out lines like candy; they're trying to brainwash our boys."

"Mama—"

"No, *no.* You listen to me, boy." Abdullah lifted his eyes reluctantly to meet Alia's. "You listen to me. What those men are trying to do, what they're trying to sell you, this idea that you're lost and they're saviors and the rest of the world is evil, that what you need is to bow and surrender and fight, they've been doing that for decades. You think you're their first one? They'll pick up anyone hungry enough to listen. So don't sit there thinking you're special. Don't sit there thinking you have some great secret. We're all a mess. Iraq's a mess, Lebanon's a mess, don't even get me started on Palestine. But if you think those hypocrites are going to save anything, those *liars* wearing God like some gold to attract boys . . . well, then you're an idiot."

No one spoke. Latif eventually cleared his throat, asked about Boston, and Souad answered with visible relief, told him of the children's school. Rosie brought out coffee, and everyone spoke of other things. Abdullah remained silent, ashing his cigarette into the wildflowers, though they'd asked him dozens of times not to.

Riham didn't say anything. She watched her mother. She remembered her uncle, dead for decades now. Riham remembered how, when she was a girl, she would listen for mentions of him, would look at photographs of the wickedly handsome man smiling in the sun. She fell in love with him, in a way. She would wonder about his voice, if he'd ever loved anyone, what songs he'd sung when he was happy.

Abdullah was five when she wed Latif. Latif had spoken about him matter-of-factly, telling her about his son just as he'd told her about the house that waited for her in Amman. At the time, everyone thought her mad.

"But he's so *old.* And with a son . . ." her childhood friends would say, trailing off uncertainly. Her father suggested that she might wait before deciding. Souad was most direct, telling her she was making a mistake.

"You can't just enter a child's life and pretend you're his mother."

But they had been wrong. For years and years, they were wrong. Within a few months in Amman, Riham learned tidbits about the woman before her, Abdullah's mother, dead for most of the child's life. Whatever memories he had of her must have been dim and few. Somehow, the fact that she wasn't Abdullah's biological mother didn't dampen her love for him. It made it fiercer. As he grew, she'd look at him sometimes, watch his dark head bent over the dining table, and her chest would fill with love. Latif worked constantly; the boy had been raised by a string of maids. No father, no mother. He was hers, hers alone.

She fretted, as Abdullah grew older, about what she wanted for him. More and more, it seemed like the fate of mothers was to lose their children to other cities, to London or Istanbul or Los Angeles. She spent years worrying that she would lose him to the place she'd lost her siblings, to America, that he would grow up without Allah.

She needn't have worried about Abdullah leaving. She should have worried about what was happening right in front of their faces. The Fixture, the mangled bodies.

It was 1991. The Gulf War had ended, and Riham was always afraid. Every night she dreamed of islands, something shining—necessary, *imperative* for her to reach—across the water. The world, as she knew it, was over. So much of her parents' money was lost, the Iraqi forces shutting the banks down. They used the inheritance that Salma had left behind, selling her apartment and buying a small house in Amman, filling it with new furniture, carpets, teapots. Karam was in America, speaking of snow and highways over the staticky telephone line. And Souad had taken the most bizarre turn of all, remaining in Paris, a hasty wedding, moving out of Khalto Mimi's house and into an apartment with Elie.

In the evenings, Riham gathered with her parents and Latif, watching news reports. Abdullah usually fell asleep with his head in her lap. Latif began speaking about the influx of refugees, how the hospital was swamped.

"People are rotting waiting around for antibiotics," he'd say. "Something needs to be done." Riham watched his jaw clench and knew something was coming.

In the end, how could she not love him for it? For his generosity, for his power, this man who put his hands on others and healed them. These refugees entered their lives abruptly, bringing lice and night terrors, the endless smell of antiseptic soap and Dettol. They slept in the Fixture, where Riham unrolled carpets and laid out clean sheets. She made pots of stew. How could she begrudge them—with their open mouths and ashamed eyes—Latif?

She couldn't.

(But the truth is that she begrudged them anyway. They reminded her of the black splotch on her soul that she'd glimpsed that day—years and years ago—in the water, the ways in which she was impure. She has been scrubbing, after all. Every day since.)

She tried to treat them all the same, not to get too involved in their stories, instead playing the role of young wife, slicing bread and cutting tomatoes. But occasionally one of the women would insist on helping her in the kitchen, would speak of cities left behind. At the time, the refugees seemed endless, though there was a lull after the Iraq war, for a while. But every year or so, another conflict erupted, and they'd appear at the door, with different dialects and darker skin. Anytime Jordan opened its doors, Latif opened theirs.

So intently was Riham scrubbing blemishes from her soul that it seemed the refugees affected only her and Latif. Only now, in the past year, has her memory shifted, her mind's eye fracturing and refocusing on the invisible character, the overlooked.

Abdullah.

There he is, in her revisited memories, in every single scene. The refugees given soup, Abdullah in the kitchen, doing his homework. News reports raging on the television, Abdullah watching. Midnight cries from the Fixture as Latif cleaned wounds, Abdullah in his bed, awake. And the children, the grimy children, Abdullah playing with them in the garden, sharing his toys. At the time, Riham barely noticed it, feeling only a fleeting pride in him.

But now she sees it all. Abdullah's questions as he watched the refugees: *Why are they hungry?* he'd ask. *Why is God making them hungry?*

Why did he have a pillow while they did not? Why would a soldier stab a child?

It started off as ordinary, a little boy fretting. Abdullah asked only Riham, who'd become Mama, soothing him when he woke from nightmares. She didn't tell Latif; it never occurred to her there was something bigger, that Abdullah would put things together, connect dots to form a chilling picture. The anger came later.

Farida's house is impressive. The furniture is gilded, and the rooms are filled with imposing, untouchable antiques. Whenever she hosts, her two Filipino maids cover the table with food, grape leaves stuffed with meat and nuts, pastries, three different types of *kanafeh*. Today, there is a platter of watermelon, sliced into triangles.

"The last of the season," Farida says, handing them plates. "Enjoy, enjoy." Farida, like her house, is assiduously regal, her hair pulled back to showcase a long, lean neck. Twice a year she goes to Paris, returning with trinkets for the women, perfumes or ribboned *macarons*.

Most of the women are doctor's wives, their friendships forged from necessity, and their solidarity is comforting to Riham. She had few friends growing up, and these gatherings remain a novelty, even after a decade. Some of them met their husbands while volunteering at hospitals, as Riham had. Others, like Hanadi and Lujain, had been nurses themselves before they got married and had children, though these former lives are rarely mentioned.

"This breeze is divine," Lujain says, nodding toward the open balcony doors. "What a summer."

"They're saying it's going to be a brutal winter."

"Good, after all that heat."

"You won't be saying that after the first snow."

There is laughter, and the women fill their plates with fruit and sweets. Of them, Riham is the youngest and most devout, the only one veiled. Riham sometimes gets the feeling they view her as a child.

"Did you hear the news last night?"

"Let them rot," Hanadi says. She pops a grape into her mouth. "To the gallows, I say."

"What about the women? The children? Not everyone's a militant."

Over the years, the conversation has evolved. There was a time, eight, nine years ago, when it revolved solely around the children—diapers and breastfeeding, concoctions of peppermint and olive oil for teething toddlers. Nothing was taboo, and in this way their meetings became sacred. They spoke of cracked, bleeding nipples, of the slackness between their legs after childbirth.

The women would ask her about Abdullah, inviting her in as a mother. *Tell us about his grades*, they'd say, or *What do you do when he won't eat?* In this way they were kind to her.

But the sting of it—no children of her own, Latif surprisingly unwilling to budge on the matter, saying he was too old—never left her. So the recent years have come as a relief. No more is the talk of pregnancy and toddlers, but rather the tribulations of adolescence. It is a different generation, they comfort one another.

"I find brochures," Yusra says. Riham turns to her attentively. "In Samer's jackets."

"PLO?" Hanadi asks.

Yusra shakes her head. "Something else. An Islamic group."

"Those dogs," Shahd says. "Going straight for the young ones."

"What is the draw, I wonder." Farida purses her lips. "How do good boys get caught up in it?"

"The money."

"Or maybe the community. There's that comradeship."

"It makes them feel like giants," Riham says slowly. The women nod. The maids circle the room, pouring fresh tea in cups. The women fall silent, contemplating.

"Sons," Hanadi says. A birdlike woman, she has three of them. "Trouble, trouble, nothing but trouble. You spend your life trying to protect them from everything—fights, women, now political parties." She shrugs. "And then they grow up and leave you anyway."

"Nothing's more difficult than sons," Lujain agrees.

Farida lets out an elegant snort. "Please. At least sons are predictable. These days, the girls are wilder than the boys."

The women murmur assent and the talk turns to friends of friends, second cousins, girls led astray. The stories always involve a girl from a good home and some bad influence—a boy or a wayward classmate. So short, they commiserate, is the fall from grace to liquor and cigarettes and sex.

"And after what happened to Maysam!" Farida tsks. "Her Farah went to visit family in Beirut for a week, *a week*, and now she says the girl is impossible. Going out at all hours, rolling her jeans up. Just last week Maysam came home to find Farah had cut off her hair *by herself*."

"No!" Lujain cries out. "Those beautiful curls."

"The girl said she wanted to be like Britney Spears. I mean, really, these girls are disasters."

"I say let Farah do whatever she wants with her hair," Hanadi says, "as long as she keeps her legs crossed."

"Hanadi!"

"What? Come on, let's not act like fools. You know what happened to Jehan's daughter. Nisrine." The women grow somber, thinking of how the girl had looked wan amid rumors of pregnancy, the family abruptly moving to England. "The truth is these girls aren't just bobbing their hair and wearing skirts. They're giving themselves up."

"That's terrible."

"Times are just so different."

Riham thinks of her sister. She wonders whether Souad was a virgin before she married, if she'd saved herself for the wedding.

"What frightens me is the secrets children keep."

"I just thank God my Hania isn't like that," Farida says. "A good girl, well behaved."

The women agree, but Riham remembers the last time she saw Hania, her nails painted a too-bright red. Not that she'd ever say that aloud to Farida.

Is this what happens with her and Abdullah? she wonders. A denial of what is apparent to others? Does love cloud the picture, give us blind spots? Though she is able to see more clearly than Latif. Perhaps that is the advantage of being the substitute mother, one step removed. She can see things Latif cannot.

The driveway is empty when she returns, Latif and Abdullah still not home. The house smells of eggplant and meat. Rosie is stirring something when Riham enters the kitchen. On the counter, there is a plate of eggplant slices. She lifts one with her fingers. It is perfectly fried.

"Wonderful," she says. Rosie nods without lifting her eyes from the bowl.

The muezzin rings out for prayer. Riham does *wudu* quickly, knowing that Abdullah and Latif will be home any moment. As she prays, the women's words echo in her mind. She shuts her eyes and, seeing Abdullah's face, makes a decision.

Without finishing her prayer, she rises. She moves down the hall, past Latif's study, to Abdullah's room. The evil eye amulet hanging from the door stares at her accusingly. After a second, she pushes the door open.

She can feel the guilt pulse with each heartbeat. It is a bad habit of hers, vestigial from Abdullah's youth, when she'd rustle through his drawers, searching for—what? She didn't know exactly. Evidence, warnings.

Abdullah's is one of the original rooms of the house. When he got older, they asked if he would prefer a different room, but he demurred, saying he liked the view: trees that bloomed with orange blossoms every April. Riham steps into the room gingerly, as though he is hiding in the closet, furious.

In the boy's childhood, his room was filled with rows of action figures, toys lined up with military precision. Now the toys are gone, as are the mystery novels he used to love, the schoolbooks. Several versions of the Qur'an appear on his shelves, and books with long titles about divinity and the Prophet, as well as history books and textbooks for the University of Jordan, where he enrolled last month.

One book catches her eye—the blue spine of *An Encyclopedia of Insects*, which she gave him when he was twelve. He'd been stung by a wasp and became obsessed with them, as well as spiders and ants and scorpions, constantly asking her: "What do they eat?" "When they poison you, where does the poison go?" "Do they dream?" She finally bought the book and he read aloud passages for months.

It warms her heart to see the book still there. She always scans the shelves for it. What she'll do when it vanishes—discarded like the others—she doesn't know.

There is a stack of pamphlets on the bedside table, the outline of a minaret and below, in calligraphy, *How do you serve Allah?* What is he doing with so many of these, dozens of them? Riham answers her own question: distributing.

She flips through the pamphlet; well-worn, tiresome paragraphs about the *lost ways* of the world, the golden days, returning to Islam in its *pure form*—*Shari'a*, Riham thinks—the evils of the West defiling their youth.

She sits down and reads on, engrossed in spite of herself. She agrees with some of the points—religion *has* become a side note, an afterthought, people *are* far too entangled with material things. But, she thinks, it is cowardly to coax rage, to turn to condemnation. Prayer is as good as bread, as simple as the dirt she turns over for seedlings. It was what her grandmother used to say in her garden: *Allah is in the stem, in my fingers, in the water, and in the drought.*

Meaning good *and* bad. Meaning it was too intricate to be whittled down to something one could point at. This was the aversion Riham felt toward those shrewd, bearded men on television—they spoke of the greatness of Allah, of servitude and humility, but they were cloaked in fury, preoccupied with it. They were simply angry.

And it was too easy to blame the West—though certainly their music was all cursing and their films just one nude woman after the other—or greed. That becomes convenient, Riham thinks, just an excuse for bad behavior. There were kings who, five times a day, removed their jewels and silks and knelt, silent and humble, to pray.

Isn't that what she does? Each day she cleanses and bows, revealing herself, utterly, for Allah. Or perhaps this is what makes her uncomfortable; the pamphlets seem like an attack on her, on Latif, their material comforts and trips to Beirut, the air-conditioned house. *But we're grateful*, Riham argues with an invisible jury, *so grateful*, though she feels herself sometimes clutch this gratitude as if it might prevent it all from being taken away.

She is jolted by the sound of tires on gravel and drops the pamphlet. Outside, the noise of Latif's footsteps, the door opening, and she rises, following the sounds, his voice, deep and known, calling her name.

He is sitting on the sofa with a newspaper. When he catches sight of Riham, his face creases. He is getting old, she knows, his hair already entirely white. With each passing year, he loses a sliver of his former self, the olive-skinned doctor that she first met. His age is showing and will continue to. The spots freckling the backs of his hands and feet will spread, the veins will get more spidery. Rather than being repulsed, Riham is comforted by his fading looks; this makes him fully hers. It makes her own flaws—the hips, the smattering of acne on her shoulders—more forgivable.

"How's the to-do list today?" he asks, grinning.

"Crossed off every one," she reports.

"Bravo. And Farida? How were the madames?"

"Good; they asked about you."

Latif folds the page back. "They've arrested a dozen more in Ramallah."

"Mama and Baba will be here in a bit. Rosie's making *maqlouba*. Another scandal arose."

"Let me guess." Latif smiles. "Souad."

"Karam." Latif glances up in surprise. "I know," she says. "Poor boy. He can't come because Budur has exams, not till the summer. But you know Mama. She's furious, she's saying they're selfish, that no one considers her."

"Mmm." He shrugs. "A bit right this time, no?"

Riham feels a ripple of defensiveness. "But she's not being realistic. They're busy, Budur's about to graduate—"

"So let him come with Linah."

Riham sighs. "You sound like Mama. Please, when she brings it up, just don't say anything."

"You know I never do."

"Where's Abdullah?" she asks timidly. How infrequently they speak of their son, she realizes.

His brows draw. "I don't know, perhaps class—" There is the sound of the front door opening and shutting, footsteps.

They look at each other for a second. "There he is." Relief flickers in Latif's eyes, and she lets out the breath that she holds whenever the boy is out of their sight.

They make an almost normal tableau, Riham thinks. A small family in the kitchen: mother, father, son. Father reading the newspaper, son sitting in silence, and mother—mother placing olives, nuts, dried apricots in porcelain bowls near the sink, the setting sun making the plants on the windowsill glow emerald. Stealing furtive glances at the two men behind her, identical in their reticence.

It is almost seven. Her parents will arrive any minute. She can practically taste the chill in the room, yearns for Rosie to return to the kitchen, fill it with her uninterested energy. Abdullah sits two chairs from his father. He has lit a cigarette, and the kitchen is filled with the smell of smoke. He looks like a surly prince from a former era, the beard stark on his young, delicate face.

Riham pictures the pamphlets in his bedroom, that sinister minaret. He's angry with his parents, with everything. Angry in a way that frightens her.

"How were classes?" Latif asks, folding the newspaper away. His voice is gruff.

Abdullah keeps his eyes down. He lifts a shoulder.

"Are you learning anything interesting?"

There is a silence, then Abdullah's voice. "No."

Latif looks at Riham. He shakes his head.

"I'm going to clean up," he says, defeated. "They'll be here soon." He leaves the kitchen. Riham returns to her work, a quickly moving shape catching her eye on the windowsill.

"Oh!" She draws a sharp breath. "Oh!" She sees Abdullah tense. "Come, Aboudi, come see." What frightened her, she sees, is on the other side of the glass. A beetle. Horns, shiny black shell, a grotesque mouth.

Abdullah walks to her. They watch the insect pause, then turn and scuttle the opposite way, its body surprisingly agile.

"The khapra beetle," Abdullah says. The encyclopedia. Riham is silent with hope.

"You always knew them so well," she tells him. A smile glimmers beneath his beard.

"It's easy," he says. "You just learn the armor." He filches an olive from the bowl, pops it in his mouth.

"Hey!" She slaps his wrist and they smile at each other, shyly. It is like learning music, she thinks, getting him to come to her. Trying not to startle a wary creature. Thoughts swarm her mind, all the things she might say right now, to bring him back.

She follows his eyes past the window, to the garden, to the Fixture. They both watch it for a moment.

"Your father was saying we might put a greenhouse out there," she says.

"It's strange." His voice is boyish. Soft for the first time in months. "Isn't it?"

And she knows exactly what he means. At last. They were joined in this, after all, weren't they, in the aftermath of strangers' lives, the detritus that Latif brought to them. It emboldens her, to see something Abdullah does.

"Yes," she hears herself whisper. "It's like I can still hear them. I think of them all the time, Aboudi." She is too afraid to lift her eyes or speak louder, as though he is a moth in her palm that even breath will frighten off. She inhales, takes a gamble. "I know you think you're the only one that does, *habibi.* But I do too. All the time."

He turns to her. She meets his eyes and sees—to her surprise—fear. "No one ever talks about them. We never say anything. It's like they were a dream, like we're all pretending."

She knows Abdullah is waiting, knows Rosie will return any second and the doorbell will ring. She knows she must speak now. A memory glints in her mind, one of the refugees helping her rinse parsley years ago, over this very sink. The woman's fingers had been dark with henna, Riham remembers. She'd spoken of her husband hanging from a tree. How strange, that Riham should remember her now. To think of this woman she'll never see again.

And how strange that the only person she wants to tell is Abdullah. Perhaps she will. If not now, then after dinner. Or tomorrow morning. She will tell him about the dreams she still has, how people can leave their mark even after decades. She will tell him her fear, the one she found in the water years ago.

"Listen," she says, and the boy looks at her, his eyes asking her to say everything.

SOUAD

BEIRUT
June 2004

Souad stirs one spoonful of sugar into her coffee, sighs, then spoons in another. The day and its tasks loom ahead of her. She carries the mug into the dining room, where Manar and Zain sit, eating cereal at the long wooden table she purchased several weeks ago, along with beds and silverware and the azure couch. The essentials, as she keeps telling Karam. She and the children have been here for nearly a month, and the apartment still looks unlived in, the pale blue walls undecorated. Light floods through the curtainless windows.

There is the sound of clunky footsteps and Alia appears, clicking her tongue. "I should just burn them all."

"The boxes?"

"Tell me, what human being needs six astronomy maps? Six! I told him, 'Atef, you're not an astronaut, pick one.' But he says he can't decide. And then he makes me promise not to throw anything away."

"There's certainly room, Mama."

"Room isn't the point!" The topic of the boxes is a touchy one. She arrived in Beirut last week with seven of them, filled with old books and clutter from the Amman house. "The point is waste."

Manar and Zain continue eating their cereal, familiar with their grandmother's outbursts. Alia came from Amman to help Souad and the children settle in, but mostly she just complains about Beirut and makes oblique comments about Manar and Zain's Americanness.

"There's enough space," Souad repeats. "Just put it all in the storage room. I can help you when I get back today." On cue, Manar sets her spoon down.

"I'm not coming," she says. "I don't need another capricious shopping trip."

Capricious. In spite of her irritation, Souad smiles at her daughter, owlish in black-framed glasses as she scowls. They weren't able to find any of the cereals the kids ate back in Boston, and she's been buying Rice Krispies, which Manar smothers in sugar. Watching Manar sprinkle sugar on her cereal now makes Souad feel guilty.

"You don't have to come," she says now, using the cheerful tone she has adopted since their move. "You can stay here or go downstairs to Budur's. But I promise, if you come, you can pick out anything you want for your room."

"Anything?" Manar's eyes sharpen, and Souad sighs. She knows what this will mean—giraffe-print curtains, carrot-hued lampshades. At thirteen, Manar is smart and incisive and sly, the kind of girl who will suffer to make a point. The old Souad would've snapped at her, set out rules, but that was before, before everything, and so Souad just sips her coffee and promises:

"Anything."

"Spoiled *ajnabi* children," Alia grumbles in Arabic. Souad ignores her.

"Can Linah come with us?" Zain asks.

"Yes!" Souad tries for enthusiastic, her impression of a soccer mom. "It'll be fun. We can go to that shawarma guy afterward, maybe get some sandwiches. Manar, we can fix your bangs." Souad reaches out to touch them, but the girl recoils.

"I like my hair like this."

"Souad," Alia says, "those shawarma places are filthy. They use rat meat."

"*Mama.*" Souad sees Zain's brow crease.

"I love that shawarma place, Mama," Zain says in a rush. "Those fries are the *best.*" Zain smiles, eager and shining. It breaks her heart to hear it—that tone, that enthusiasm, carefully prepared for her.

They walk down one flight of stairs to the apartment where Karam and Budur are staying for the summer. The building is old, with a shabby but charming façade. Near the Corniche, it overlooks shops and endless, winding traffic, and it's steps away from the American University. The apartments are full of professors and their families, most of whom have been friendly to Souad. Their two apartments, on the fifth and sixth floors, are high enough for them to glimpse the Mediterranean between telephone poles and buildings.

"It's a summer house," Riham had said about the Beirut apartment when she called Souad. "I barely ever use it, Mama and Baba go for only a couple of weeks every year. It's just sitting around, collecting dust. You'd be doing me a favor."

The doors to the two apartments are identical, both with intricate woodwork. Souad knocks once, twice, though she knows it is unlocked.

Alia lets out a snort. "What is this, America?" She pushes the door open and calls out, "Karam!" Souad looks, briefly, heavenward. "Karam!" Alia strides in and the children and Souad follow her into the foyer.

"Karam's not here." Budur appears, wearing her bathrobe, hair disheveled. "Morning of lovelies," she exclaims. "Linah's inside, *habibi.*" Zain darts past her, and Manar walks toward the balcony in the living room. Budur gestures for Souad and Alia to follow her into the kitchen. Where Riham's place is painted blue, the walls in Karam and Budur's apartment are a lush green, and they refer to the apartments as *the green one* and *the blue one.*

"The house smells like cigarettes."

"I'll tell Tika to open the windows, Auntie," Budur says smoothly.

Souad admires her equanimity, the way Budur steps deftly over conflict as she would an overturned shoe. "Tea?"

"With sugar." Alia sits at the kitchen table. "Souad's glasses are filthy."

"They're not." A vessel throbs behind Souad's left eye.

Budur slips by Souad as she gets a mug, squeezing her arm. "Easy," she says in a whisper. Raising her voice, she tells her, "The dress looks good, Sous."

Souad tugs the hem. At the store last week, Budur insisted she buy it as Souad cowered in the dressing room, aghast at her cleavage.

"She looks like a hooker."

"Mama!"

"What?" Alia shrugs innocently. "You do."

"I think she looks lovely. Vibrant."

"*Vibrant.*" The word is lethal in Alia's mouth. "What divorcée wants to look *vibrant*?"

Budur holds a hand up. "Please. Have you seen the women in this city?" She pours a cup of coffee for Souad. "It's practically a niqab compared to what they wear."

Alia snorts. "A city of whores." Their distaste of Lebanese women is something that unites Alia and Budur.

"You two," Souad says, taking the mug, "are single-handedly murdering feminism." More caffeine can only help, she thinks.

From somewhere farther inside the apartment, there is a crash, followed by silence, then an explosion of laughter. Budur and Souad catch each other's eye.

"Linah," Budur calls out.

Linah appears in the doorway, still in her pajamas. Nine years old, she is only months younger than Zain, though she looks much younger, petite for her age and skinny, with hair so fine it is always slipping out of her braids and ponytails, scattering across her shoulders. *Little button nose and those enormous eyes,* Riham always says. Even when Linah was a baby, Souad felt drawn to her, with her tantrums, her wolfish grins, difficult but so dear, so *touchable*, in a way Manar—whose body went slack when held—never was.

"What was that noise?"

Linah hides a smile. "Nothing." Zain appears behind her.

"Zain, *habibi*, what was that noise?" Budur asks.

Zain hesitates, looks at Linah. "We dropped a picture frame. But we're cleaning it up."

Linah glares at him. "*Shhhh*."

"Good boy," Budur says. "Linah, what did we say about lying?"

Linah ignores her mother. "Can I have some of your coffee?" she asks Souad.

"It'll give you a mustache," Souad says. She remembers that line, oft repeated by her mother and Khalto Widad in Kuwait. It used to terrify her, the idea of waking up with a bristly mustache like her father's.

"No, it won't!" Fists on her hips, legs splayed out. Even Alia laughs.

"It's hot," Souad says, tipping the mug carefully toward her little face. Linah purses her lips, drinks. Grimaces.

"It tastes like dirt," she announces.

"The last thing that child needs is caffeine," Alia observes.

"Caffeine!" Linah yells. "Caffeine, caffeine, caffeine." She jumps up and down, hopping toward her mother like a rabbit. Zain laughs, delighted at the antics of his younger cousin. Budur doesn't yell or rebuke the girl, just shakes her head and opens her arms. She holds Linah, still hollering, between her legs and redoes her braids, the dark hair flashing quickly between her fingers. When she finishes, she lays her cheek, briefly, against the top of Linah's head, then releases her. Linah dashes out of the room, Zain following her.

"Get dressed," Budur calls. "Souad wants to leave." She looks at Souad, raising an eyebrow. "That girl is a terrible influence on Zain."

The building is fourteen stories high, with an apartment on each level and an ancient, wrought-iron elevator that skids between floors. In the lobby, it stops an inch higher than the floor, and Linah and

Zain make a production of jumping down. Manar follows, ignoring their chatter.

Souad's hope is that somehow Beirut will fix whatever hungry, invisible malaise she felt in Boston after Elie left. At first she'd thought it was because she was aging, at the end of her twenties, but no, it was something larger, an epiphany at a gas station one February evening, as she stood holding the gas pump, breathing in that addictive scent, and suddenly she understood that *this place* was the malaise. It was in the sprawling malls, the highway lights, the tax season, suburban America itself, in whose veins she'd lived and slept and woke for years.

Beirut called to her. She wanted somewhere new. She wanted to go home, she told Zain and Manar, though Manar just stared at her and said flatly, *What home.*

Home as in somewhere familiar, somewhere people look like us, talk like us, where you guys can learn Arabic and be near your grandparents and never come home asking what raghead *means.*

The route to the mall is a combination of glitzy buildings and unkempt roads. Souad had visited Beirut in previous summers, but when she and the children arrived a few weeks ago, past midnight on a Friday, it felt different. Exhausted, they'd woven through airplane lines, endured the long wait in airport control, which concluded with the security officer saying, as soon as Souad spoke Arabic, "You're not Lebanese," as plainly as though he were stating the sun was hot. When they finally made it to the arrivals gate, Karam was waiting. It was a striking, ethereal landscape as they drove home—the bullet-riddled buildings, glimpses of coastline, billboards whizzing by, the pictures alternating between women posing in lingerie and grave-looking men.

It is the same here, on the road to the mall. One advertisement shows a woman holding a cigarette with the lines *La belle époque est arrivé* emblazoned below, while other buildings are papered with flyers of men with liquid, haunting eyes. Martyrs, she thinks.

Of all the things in this new country—the precipitous streets, the electricity cuts, the war still etched into the city's skin—this is what frightens her most. The men on the posters—the dead, or the ones hungry for death. Their frenetic, glassy eyes are identical to the hijackers', whose faces are burned into her memory as though it happened yesterday, Elie coming home early, huddling in front of the television with her, both watching the ash and fire and collapsing buildings on a loop.

Souad watched the towers fall for days. The world was addicted to watching; over and over, they were reborn, made whole and silver and resplendent, only to crumple into themselves again. Each time felt like the first time, the destruction so immense it bordered on the majestic. Souad watched the dust-fogged streets, people's panicked faces as they shrieked for those they loved. She felt her heart move with the shaking cameras. Smoke and fire spilled from the buildings like blood from a gunshot wound, and people began to jump, their little bodies unreal as they lurched from the sky, dolls in someone's nightmare. One newscaster played the recording of an emergency call, a woman's voice frantic as she begged the operator for help. Souad tried to imagine what she could've said to this woman, what anyone could say, what the operator himself finally said. *I'm sorry, oh God, I'm sorry, I'm so sorry.* For weeks, Souad touched her legs, ears, face, her aliveness, imagined herself in that building, looking out of a window, wondering how it felt to realize that you were dying. That you were already dead.

Souad felt the falling of those men and women; she felt the human ache of watching that plummet. *What does any of it mean*, she wanted to ask, *when you are a body, a body you suddenly love, a body that is tumbling through the air?*

"They're jumping" was all she'd actually said to Elie that long-ago night, and he shook his head, his eyes red. He clutched her body to his—for weeks they were fine after that, a second honeymoon, though it proved temporary, which must've happened in many homes across the country—and kissed her temple, whispering something she hadn't caught. *I love you.* Or *Wouldn't you?*

If we go, Souad had told her children, *we'll be free. We'll make a new life.* An old friend of hers helped her find a job at the American University, as an adjunct lecturer teaching an English introduction course to freshmen. It is a straightforward syllabus, uninspiring, with a meager salary, since she doesn't have a doctorate—has, in fact, only a barely completed undergraduate degree in design, which she cobbled together over a string of nighttime classes and online workshops, a thankless task that took her six years—but still she is grateful.

Sometimes she sits on the balcony floor, smoking alone, smoking not for the nicotine but for the simple pleasure of watching smoke rise into a series of helixes and curlicues in the dark. The noise downstairs, even in the middle of night, of honking cars and people arguing and laughing doesn't bother her. Her heart rises with the sound of Arabic. If she shuts her eyes, it is as though she is sitting in the café downstairs, men having conversations around her, and she doesn't have to speak, doesn't have to say a single word to be with them.

She had missed the muezzin, the food, even her own tongue faltering in Arabic. In Beirut, she has gone back to being Palestinian. To everyone from the cabdrivers to the bank tellers, her accent exposes her. It reminds her of Kuwait. As a girl, this cataloging of origins never struck her as strange; Kuwait was a place of expatriation and everyone seemed to come from somewhere else. Elie had his Lebanon, Budur her Iraq. Even if a person's heritage was flimsy, unused for years, you were where your father was from.

America wasn't like that. You became what you coveted. Memories were short. She met Mexicans, Germans, Libyans, who spoke accented English but responded, *From here,* whenever asked. Souad became brown. People's eyes glazed over when she tried to explain that, yes, she'd lived in Kuwait, but no, she wasn't Kuwaiti, and no, she had never been to Palestine, but yes, she was Palestinian. That kind of circuitous logic had no place over there.

After the towers fell, other passengers on the T eyed her, but living in a liberal suburb meant people were kinder about it. *Tell us if you need anything*, the playdate mothers would say. *If anyone's rude to you.* Outside of Boston, she felt it more. During a trip to Texas once to visit a friend, she and Budur stopped at a gas station for cigarettes. Souad felt the clerks' gaze—two young Midwestern men, eyes like icepicks—on them the entire time. One of the men flung the change at her, several coins falling to the ground. Souad's fear was like a bell, waking her. As they were leaving, she caught the words *terrorist* and *bitch* and a burst of laughter.

"The Undertaker is going to win."

"No way! He's so weak. Triple X is going to beat him."

"Nuh-uh. You'll *see*, he's a loser."

"Only because he cheats! Remember last time, he hit Shawn Michaels with a chair and the referee didn't see him."

"That referee was stupid!"

"*You're* stupid!"

"Guys," Souad says. The clamor in the back seat quiets, Linah and Zain continuing their argument in whispers. Souad makes out the words *idiot* and *champion* and *chair* several times in rapid succession. For the past year, wrestling has been Zain's favorite thing, and since their arrival, Linah has quickly caught on. They've always been like this—Linah and Zain, born months apart, devoted to each other. In Boston, they grew up together, wore each other's clothing, Linah inheriting Zain's overalls and toys, the two of them inventing games involving pirates and robots.

Souad arrives at an intersection, pauses at the oncoming cars. The jeep behind her honks, and the car behind that as well. The man in the jeep makes a gesture for her to drive. "Just wait," she mutters. She inches toward the turn, then loses her nerve. "Oh, go, go," she says, waving the driver on.

"He's probably cursing you out," Manar informs her, taking an earbud out. Ominous music thumps from the headphones.

"He probably is," Souad says cheerfully.

"He was right," Manar says. "You should've gone." Manar puts the earbud back in and leans her head against the window frame. Her wiry hair—not thin like Elie's or curly like Souad's but some unfortunate in-between, a charmless frizz—halos around her, and she shuts her eyes.

Paris had transformed for her after the wedding, its vivacity turning leaden. The days became shorter, colder; the permanence of the invasion sank in. On particularly icy mornings, Souad caught herself daydreaming about Kuwait. For a summer, Paris seemed infinite, vast, with its shops and museums and cafés. But as her new home, the city chafed, the cobblestone streets always crowded, the sky pocked with clouds.

Elie cajoled his father for money as a wedding gift; within a month he'd conjured an apartment for them in a dark, ugly building in the Belleville neighborhood, sandwiched between a Chinese restaurant and an Indian fabric shop.

Souad was charmed by the doll-like rooms at first, clapping her hands with delight at the pink-tiled bathroom and the skylight above their bed. She twirled through the bare apartment that first day, awash in morning light, mentally constructing their lives—lace curtains for the tiny picture windows, the kitchen stocked with French cheeses and spaghetti. They painted the walls yellow and bought vanilla-scented candles for the living room.

In the end, the vanilla smell was overpowering and the yellow nauseated her, especially after she became pregnant; the color reminded her of egg yolks. Elie had a life outside the apartment. He had his novel, his university courses, which he loved, long nights of debate and conversation with other students in wine bars. Souad had nothing. She couldn't explain it to Elie, her random bursts of tears. Her irritation. Restlessness. She went to classes reluctantly and then the afternoons stretched, interminably, ahead of her. The longing of the day, the object, was him coming home to her. For a year, this went on. Soon, another winter came, her second in Paris, and she swelled with Manar.

One day, many months after the invasion of Kuwait, he came home to find her weeping in front of the television.

"They used them as target practice," she said, sobbing.

She'd just watched a report on the invasion, bursting into tears whenever the animals were mentioned, the way the Iraqi troops unlatched the cages, shot the fleeing creatures. There was one image of a giraffe, bullets buried in its torso. Souad remembered the giraffes of her childhood, wondered if this was one of the ones she'd loved as a girl.

"Shh. Let's turn it off." He put his arms around her bulging belly, nuzzled her neck.

But it was freezing, and she had been crying for hours, and his breath was sour against her face, turning her stomach.

"Don't touch me," she said miserably.

He stiffened. The arms disappeared from around her waist. They had a fight, the first of hundreds that would follow in the coming years—at restaurants, during the children's birthday parties, after an evening of drinking, *before* an evening of drinking—fights that would eventually become commonplace, predictable. But that time, they'd never yet been as cruel with each other, Elie's voice vicious, calling her pitiful. And Souad, trembling with anger, heard herself yell awful things back, about her regrets, shrieking that she'd made a mistake. It was terrible and frightening, what they could do.

But also—a relief. Such relief, after months being the too-young wife struggling to learn French and getting lost in Parisian alleyways. The anger was bracing. It reminded her of herself.

He stomped out eventually, slamming the door. She prepared dinner in tears, cursing him as she stirred spaghetti in a secondhand copper pot. The cream sauce clotted into lumps. A realization: she hated Paris.

It wasn't the animals she was weeping for, or the lost city; it was herself. Her mother was right. She missed everyone: Karam, her father, Budur. Cradling the mound of her belly, Souad shook with a perverse, hungry longing for her mother, for Alia's coolness; she ached for her to stroll into this cramped apartment and lift a single, sarcastic eyebrow.

That was where she drew her strength. The image of that lifted eyebrow. Her mother's voice. *Well, Souad, look what you've done.* She thought wistfully of the bracing anger she'd felt earlier.

And she let the pot scorch.

This is what Souad thinks of these days. That night, when she saw too late her mistake, all those moments that make love and destroy it. Her younger self, almost a mother, brimming with rage. The smell of burned copper.

There was the *after*, of course. The house, Elie's graduation and teaching job, their move to America. In some ways Boston came as a relief, even with its snow and broad accents. Souad left Paris easily, the city she'd never learned to love. In Boston, their life was quieter, constructed around their having small children. They lived in a series of cramped apartments near Suffolk, Souad taking the children on playdates with the kids of other young mothers in the neighborhood, spending her afternoons pouring apple juice and making small talk about teething. And the weekends were full of birthday parties and barbecues in the park with Budur and Karam, building snowmen during the winter. Every couple of summers, she booked flights to Amman with them and the children—Elie always begged off, saying he needed to write. They trudged through airports with huge suitcases duct-taped together on the impossibly long journey to visit Alia and Atef. Then two months of *shisha* and arguing with her mother and swimming in salt water, the children becoming ropy and brown, in need of haircuts.

They eventually moved into a house with a small lawn and narrow hallways, a staircase with slanted ceilings Souad was constantly bumping into. They argued about bills, vacations, which extracurriculars to enroll the children in. Whether to salt the driveway before or after it snowed. They fought about Elie's novel, the same goddamn novel Souad had heard about as a teenager in that Kuwaiti café. It was like an unwanted houseguest that haunted her marriage. It was never-ending. Elie would speak at times of being nearly finished, then something would shift, and he'd call the whole thing rubbish and spend weeks morosely staring out of the study window. Twice, he set hundreds of pages on fire in their bathtub, and she yelled at him for days.

The years went on. Their marriage died a thousand deaths before Elie finally caught on and left.

The Spinneys market is one of those all-purpose centers, a huge building filled with furniture shops and book kiosks and even a grocery store. The four of them walk through the entrance, a sign in French advertising laundry detergent.

A Sri Lankan man stands beside rows of shopping carts and unlatches one for her as she approaches. Behind him, other Sri Lankan men carry grocery bags, wearing ridiculous uniforms in primary colors, like children's clothing. Everywhere in the city, there are reminders of servitude, the maids trailing families, the men working at gas stations and construction sites.

Even Budur has a maid, Tika, that she hires for the summers, but Souad finds the idea unappealing. She is awkward with Tika, awkward with the maids at her mother's house in Amman—her mother, after Priya, being exceedingly picky—always fumbling and uncomfortable, prefacing any request with *If you have time, maybe, at some point, could you possibly . . .*

She pushes the cart to a map of the market adjacent to a candy kiosk with colorful sweets in jars.

"I want one!" Linah reaches toward a bouquet of lollipops in a vase.

"Careful."

"I want a purple one."

Souad sighs. "Linah, it's eleven in the morning."

"Please?"

The girl's smile is disarming. Souad shakes her head. "Really, Miss Linah? Sugar and chemicals?"

"Mmm." Linah grins. "I love chemicals. De-licious!"

"Yum," Zain chimes in.

Souad smiles down at the small, upturned faces. She cannot imagine sorrow in their lives, cannot bear to think of the ways they will love and hurt and fret. *Motherhood doesn't suit me*, she once confessed to Budur, drunk. *I don't have the stomach for not knowing what comes next.*

"Okay," she says, and they let out cries of excitement. "Okay, okay, okay."

"You're supposed to set limits," Manar grumbles.

Souad counts, silently, to three. "I'm a terrible disciplinarian," she sings out.

Linah and Zain pick out lollipops and bounce ahead, chattering. Past the bookstore, there is a small wine shop, the bottles dark and glossy on the shelves. She averts her eyes.

She can sense her children watching her carefully at times, even as she's doing the most ordinary things: folding dishcloths, pouring tea, yawning. She knows they are scared—though Manar's fear has metamorphosed neatly into anger—that she will lapse, go back to the days of sobbing, drinking the way she did for months after Elie left, staying up past midnight and calling Elie. *How could you do this? I gave you everything*, she would scream over and over into the phone and, when he stopped picking up, into his voice mail, sometimes even getting into bed with Zain and asking him to stroke her hair.

That self is still so recent, so alarming, that it makes her shiver with shame.

"I know you're mad at me," she'd said to Zain and Manar the morning after telling them, yes, yes, they would be leaving Karam and Budur and Linah, would be leaving Boston for good. "I know you're mad. You should be mad. I haven't been doing this very well.

And I know you're scared of moving, I'm so sorry, I'm so sorry to do this. But I promise—"

Here she paused, tears prickling her eyelids. She looked at her children, Manar silent and reproaching, Zain with trust in his eyes, and she began to weep. Zain rose, embraced her, but Manar watched scornfully as Souad shrank into her son's arms.

Moments later, she composed herself enough to speak again, but when she did, her mind blanked and she just said, lamely, "I promise to do better."

They walk upstairs to the indoor play area with toys and cushions and a makeshift library. In America, a place like this would never work, leaving your children on their own while you shopped. Kidnappers, perverts, murderers—every street pulsed with threat. Her time in Boston had felt like one long held breath.

"Okay, guys," she says to Zain and Linah. "I need to buy a few things. Can you sit here and not break anything?" She pauses. "No wrestling." They nod, lollipops in their mouths. She turns to Manar. "You want to come with me? Help me pick some things out?"

"No. I want to look at bed sheets. I don't like the flowery ones."

Souad feels her temper rise, takes a breath. "Okay. Let's just meet back here—*guys*, I said no wrestling—in an hour? Good?" A shrug. Souad tries for a joke. "Do you want a lollipop, Manar, to cheer you up?"

Not even the trace of a smile.

Souad watches Manar leave. Her daughter has become unrecognizable to her. She used to hear people talk about their teenagers and think, *Nonsense.* How could your own child become a stranger to you, this creature you had fed and soothed and sung to?

But, now, here it is. Her daughter, unknown to her. The body she had nourished inside her, held for hours at a time. She knew every scar, every miraculous bone, had spent whole nights watching her chest rise and fall with her breath. And now Manar plodded that body around like luggage, her thoughts a mystery.

Part of it, Souad thinks, might be the weight. Her daughter had been a fat, dimpling baby, then a pudgy child. It is shameful to admit, but Souad worried about it, praying her daughter would slim as she got older. It was impossible not to look at her daughter with sharp eyes, out of necessity, out of *love*, the way one surveys a landscape for wires, traps, a hidden net in the trees.

And now, at thirteen, Manar's body is plump, hips flaring, her breasts large and hanging. She has the physique of an older woman, with fleshy arms and thighs, though a startlingly slender neck and attractive face—Elie's wide, sardonic mouth, Souad's nose and almond-shaped eyes.

The girl has noticed. Over the past year, she has bought a closetful of black—jeans, tank tops, shirts, even socks. Souad knows that Manar must have overheard someone saying carelessly, *Black makes you look thinner*, and taken it devastatingly to heart.

"It's the age," Budur says often. "We were all like that."

Souad never tells Budur her fear, that she had lost Manar in some irrevocable way after Elie left, when Manar would come home to find Souad two vodkas in and no meal prepared, when Souad would ask Manar to make her brother a sandwich—or to brush his teeth, help with his homework—while she went upstairs to lie down and cry. *How could she* not *hate me*, she wants to ask Budur but is too afraid.

The home-decoration store is divided into long aisles of candles and lamps and kitchen utensils. Souad pushes a cart through them, dropping in towels, a teapot, several pans. *For pancakes*, she thinks. Zain loves them with cinnamon and bananas.

The dress is tight against her hips as she walks, and she tugs at it. Budur was right. The other women, followed by maids pushing shopping carts, all wear bright, revealing clothes. Souad watches as one woman waves at another, and they rush to each other, kiss each cheek loudly.

"*Bonjour*," they cry. One woman wears lipstick so red it glows.

When Souad used to think of Beirut, in the months before their move, she envisioned a version of Jordan. The same quiet, languid lifestyle, tea in the garden, long calls for prayer.

Instead, the women here are fiery, wear themselves like banners. They are bolder than women in Paris, even the older ones dressing in neon colors and tight skirts. It is startling, after so long in America, where she often wore the cigarette jeans and workman shirts that Elie found sexy, everything in black.

She touches the sumptuous fabrics of a curtain display, plucking items off the shelves as she walks. Throw pillows, a juicer, picture frames. It is the third time, she realizes, that she's buying furniture for a house, the third time she's piecing together scattered, unnecessary objects, trying to build a life around them.

In Boston, she'd kept the walls a dull white, thinking it would be soothing, infuse some calm in her marriage. She hates white now. It became oppressive, like living in perpetual mist. White couches, white carpets, white plates.

Now she wants color. Colors so vivid she can taste them. She wants dishes the color of watermelon; glass tumblers that catch light and splash blue, green; yellow on the walls while they eat. She is starved for iridescence.

Clean slate, she told herself as the plane landed in Beirut. Her life in Boston already feels so distant, a smudge barely visible on the horizon, as do all the people who populated it—her mailman and neighbors, the redheaded cashier at the local grocery store, the women she went to happy hours with. All the little things that made a life, spent. It reminds her of Kuwait. It has felt like a pitch-black hallway, these past few months, this unknown she has pitched herself into; it's as if she is feeling along with her feet and her fingers, knowing nothing beyond the little that she touches here and there.

AFTER AN HOUR, she pushes her shopping cart back to the play area. Manar is seated on one of the beanbags with a shopping basket at her feet. She has her earbuds in, and her lips move along with a song. Linah and Zain jump up from their toys.

"I won the tournament," Linah says.

"She cheated," Zain says. Souad touches Zain's sweaty forehead.

"To the register, *habibi.* Manar?" Her daughter reluctantly pulls an earbud out. "You ready?"

"Manar's getting frogs!" Zain cries out. A small smirk appears on Manar's face and she brings the basket over.

"And rainbows!" Linah says.

The shopping cart is a multicolored fuck-you. Curtains covered with giant, kitschy rainbows, a sparkly unicorn decal for a small child. A ceramic frog, blue tongue extended.

"Manar—" She catches Manar's triumphant eye. *It's the age*, she reminds herself. "So this is how you want to decorate your room? Frogs and unicorns and rainbows?"

"Yup." The word clips from Manar's mouth. "I think rainbows are *terrific.*"

"Terrific," Linah echoes.

"Great." Souad forces a smile. "Great. That's it, then. Let's go."

The cashier is an indifferent woman with long, French-manicured nails. While she waits for an item to scan, she taps a nail on the punch pad. Souad watches the colorful tumblers, the silky curtains and picture frames skim by on the conveyor belt.

"And the basket?" The woman gestures to Manar.

Manar catches Souad's eye. "Manar," Souad sighs. "You sure you want this stuff?"

Manar nods bravely, but Souad catches the hesitation.

"Well, okay. You made some fine choices; that unicorn will go beautifully with the blue walls." They continue to eye each other. It is clear Manar had expected a fight. *Not today*, Souad thinks.

"Madame?"

"Manar, this nice lady is waiting."

Manar's eyes dart between the basket and the conveyor belt. "Maybe—maybe I don't need the curtains," she says reluctantly. Souad tries to keep her face neutral but can't help grinning. There is a beat of silence, and the two of them erupt into loud laughter.

"Madame?" The cashier taps a nail impatiently.

Linah and Zain begin to bounce around, excited by the laughter.

"The unicorn's wearing a bow tie!"

"I want one too!"

"Green . . . plastic . . . lamp?" Souad gasps, rummaging through the basket.

Manar giggles. "It goes with the frog." Souad pulls out the ceramic frog, its massive red eyes bulging.

"It looks *homicidal.*" They collapse with laughter, Manar holding on to her mother's arm for balance.

"Madame, there are people waiting—"

"We'll come back later," Souad says, wiping her eyes. "Just the things you've bagged for now. Sorry."

The cashier rolls her eyes. She takes the basket from Manar and places it on the floor behind her.

"I want the frog!" Linah calls out.

Zain agrees. "Get the frog!"

"We'll take the frog," Souad tells the cashier.

In the car, the atmosphere is light, playful. Manar keeps her earbuds in her lap while Souad flips through the radio.

"I saw this white-and-black comforter. I was thinking I could get that," Manar says as they drive. "Like that hotel we stayed at in Manhattan. Baba said it was modernist."

The mention of Elie is like a tiny lash, but Souad keeps her voice steady. "That sounds beautiful. We can get a black bed frame, some sheer curtains."

"And a rug," Manar adds. Souad fights the impulse to kiss her daughter.

"Like a Prayer" comes on the radio and Souad puts the volume up, starts to sing. When she glances sidelong at Manar, she sees her lips are moving as well. In the back seat, Linah and Zain are dancing, bobbing their heads. Souad rolls the windows down; the warm, humid air rustles around them.

"When you call my name," Souad yells, and the children erupt in laughter, even Manar. And her heart, her heart, rising with the sound. These are her loves. The hope returns. That treacherous hope, which rises and falls, she can taste it on her lips like salt. She will fix it. She will fix it all.

Once they're back home, the living room is a mess within an hour, bags and bubble wrap strewn everywhere, Zain and Linah making capes of the packaging paper and running in and out of the rooms.

Souad is putting together a dish rack in the kitchen, immersed in the task of metal links clicking into place, when she hears a thud. A string of curses. She follows the sound into the storage room next to the living room.

Alia is sitting on the tiled floor, her skirt bunched up around her knees, surrounded by partly opened boxes. There is a bookshelf against one of the walls, half filled. Strands of hair curl around her face; she's flushed and huffing. One of the boxes has tipped over, books spilling across the tiles. "I'm going to divorce your father," she grumbles.

Souad suppresses a smile. She squats down.

"What's in them?"

"Who knows? Useless things he collects over the years. They're just sitting in his study in Amman. You could write in the dust. He can't throw anything away! Look at this." She plucks a bulky-looking book filled with loose pages from the nearest box. *"A Lifecycle of Plants."* The book falls back into the box with a thump.

Souad sinks to the floor next to her mother, suddenly exhausted. Alia looks at her sharply.

"Are you sick?"

"Just tired."

"I told you not to drink the water here."

"Mama, I'm not sick."

They fall silent. It occurs to Souad that she and her mother rarely sit together; one of them is always trying to get away.

"The kids got stuff from Spinneys," she says. "We got curtains and plates and new sheets."

"Good," her mother says. "This needs to start feeling like their house."

Souad thinks about her mother's absence at her wedding, how it seemed like a bad omen, as ominous as an evil godmother's presence at an infant's cradle. *You're going to remember this,* Alia had told her on the telephone when Souad announced her engagement. *You're going to remember this moment and wish you listened.*

"They hate it here." Souad is surprised to hear herself say this. Her throat tingles. "They miss Elie." She suddenly feels limp.

The air is stiff between them. Alia looks intently at her lap.

"They're children," she mutters. "They'll get used to it."

Souad feels tears spring. Without looking up, her mother reaches out, fast as a rattlesnake, and takes her hand. She squeezes it, once, hard.

"You will too."

Once everyone goes downstairs, getting ready for dinner, Souad walks out onto the balcony. The light is the color of chamomile tea, pale against the floors and walls. This is the trickiest hour for her: dusk, the sun already vanished—that halfness. It is the hour she wants to drink the most, before the dark crushes the city, her longing for a finger of vodka, that first sip like stepping into bathwater.

Enough. Enough. She steps to the balcony railing, watches the nearly vanished sun, a pool of red above the water's horizon, the air salty and moist.

She still loves him. This is the fact she wakes up to each morning. She checks it, sometimes, a tongue probing an aching tooth, making sure it still hurts. This seems most shameful of all, that she would still love someone who didn't love her, who had left her—sometimes that very word dazes her; she was *left*—in fact. But she cannot help it. She hates him and she loves him and she will never forgive him. These three verdicts line up for her like soldiers. It is her truth.

She'd never loved him more than when he'd left. Of those days after his departure, she sees only gray—that endless Bostonian winter—and evenings that seemed to last for weeks. She found herself playing old songs, songs from their days in Paris, singing along in French. In the afternoons—those dead, wasted hours, the children at school—she would flip through photographs, tracing the planes of his face. Aware, even as she did, that there was something vaguely ridiculous about the act, filched from the movies. On the rare evenings that she cooked, she made Elie's favorite dishes and cried as the children ate.

What Souad marvels at most is the time. Squandered. The whirlwind that swept her life since she was eighteen—*eighteen*, that night at the fountain, and then the hasty marriage and then Manar and those years trying to be a mother, a wife—Time. That is how she thinks of it, as a person, Time, as something terrifying and tremendous. What else could account for it? How the years had spun by, the 1990s in their entirety now one big blur of Paris and Boston, of shitty neighborhoods and cheap restaurants and the kids getting colds—there were certain winters, *entire winters*, that were captured in her memory as the single, swift motion of swooping down with a wad of tissues and squeezing little noses, squeezing so that the snot ran green and viscous—and the fights, she and Elie yelling for hours. It was Time, whirling her along, spinning, spinning, until it finally stopped, and she looked around, blinking, and she was thirty-two.

Enough. She says it aloud, softly, to herself on the empty balcony.

"Enough." The word is its own heartbeat.

She walks down the stairs carefully. There is a slight chill in the air. Tomorrow she will swim, she decides, before summer is over. She will wear the black bikini she bought with Budur, will stay until the sun begins to set, then eat those tiny fried fish from a restaurant along the coast.

At Budur's apartment, she pushes open the door and steps inside, takes off her shoes and walks barefoot toward the dining room. The voices are loud, Karam saying something, Budur laughing. For a moment she pauses in the hallway, watching them—Karam and Budur, one at each end of a table covered with a cream tablecloth on which is a tray of lamb and rice. Her mother sits halfway down, flanked by Linah and Zain; Manar is on the other side, breaking a piece of bread.

Manar says something and Linah laughs, imitating the way Manar brushes her hair out of her eyes, and a smile lights Manar's face. Souad's heart swells with gratitude. She feels a fierce urge to tell her daughter how beautiful she is, how beautiful she will be. She takes a breath, suddenly starving for the delicious-smelling meat, and steps into the dining room. There is a clamor, faces turning toward her from the table, hands holding out plates, voices rising, telling her to take a chair, asking if she wants sugar with her tea, telling her to sit, sit and eat.

LINAH

Beirut
July 2006

"We could be back in ten minutes." On her bed, Linah stretches her leg out toward the window, toward a swath of late-afternoon sun. There is a spider climbing up the curtains. She moves her bare foot; the dust dances.

"They'll know."

She sprawls on the pillow, speaking against the fabric. Her voice is muffled: "I'm going to die of boredom."

"No one *dies* of boredom," Zain answers. "It's not like cancer."

Linah shoots her leg out and kicks him, sharply, in the shin.

"Ow!"

"Help me," she groans. She turns over, flinging her arms over her head. "I'm dyyyying."

Linah waits. Finally, she sits up, frowning at Zain in her desk chair, where he's playing a game on the computer. She scoots to the edge of the bed and peers over his shoulder. The label of his T-shirt is sticking out and he needs a haircut, his curls falling past his ears.

"So," she says, irritated. "You're backing out."

"I'm not," he says evenly. On the computer screen, he shoots a trio of zombies.

"You said you'd do it."

"I said okay to the cigarettes." His voice drops at the last word and they look toward the shut bedroom door, though Linah knows they shouldn't worry about anyone walking in. The adults are always in the living room since the airport was bombed last week—huddled around the television, cursing when the electricity cuts out, taking turns running to Hawa's for platters of greasy baked chicken, which they've eaten for lunch and dinner for days. "Not going to Abu Rafi's."

"If we take them from your mom, she'll know it was us."

The zombies fall to the ground, green blood oozing. Zain turns to her.

"I don't know."

"We haven't left the apartments in a week. They won't even let us walk to the *dikaneh*. It's like we're prisoners." If her father were here, he would tell her to stop being a drama queen. But Zain just nods. "It'll be fun. We'll leave when everyone's watching the news."

Zain looks unconvinced. "I guess."

"You promised," she accuses him. She'd come up with the idea weeks ago, before the war started, when she saw a group of older girls leaning against the railing on the Corniche. Their long brown legs dangled as they smoked. They looked glamorous and mysterious, the smoke drifting from their lips.

"Okay, okay," he says.

Linah recognizes Zain's tone—he's convinced. She leans back in bed, satisfied, the insect still scrambling up the curtain.

The last two weeks have been mind-numbing. The electricity cuts out every few hours, like it does every summer, but she and Zain can no longer wander outside, go to the video store down the street, where the AC is always on, delightfully freezing. Nor can they go to Malik's to get ice cream, or down to the beach. The adults have even forbidden them to go onto the balcony. They still sneak out sometimes, for the breeze. When the adults are in one apartment, they migrate to the other.

Watch television, the adults keep telling them, but whenever they put in a movie—drawing all the curtains and sitting on the tiled floor, where it is coolest—they rarely get to finish it. They'll be halfway through when the adults rampage in, ordering them to move and open the curtains, yelling at them for the crumbs on the floor. The cable has been shaky the last few days; sometimes one apartment will abruptly stop receiving a signal.

Go to the other apartment, they'll tell them. Everyone is distracted and upset, the trashcan full of cigarette butts.

Summers aren't supposed to be like this, Linah thinks. Summers are supposed to be about swimming at the beach, spending nights bowling and going out to dinner, staying up playing video games. And this summer, this summer was supposed to be the *best*, because she was finally eleven, and the adults were allowing her and Zain to go to the beach alone, without Manar there to babysit.

But now it's ruined. The summer is just heat and mosquitoes and the bombings that sometimes make the windows shake. All the adults do is talk about evacuation and warships and explosions. They watch men yell on the television and shake their heads.

It's been nine days. Nine days since Linah woke to Zain saying her name, his face afraid.

"Something's wrong."

Her first thought was the adults had found the ants that she and Zain were catching with sugar cubes inside plastic bottles.

"The ants?" she asked, sitting up.

He shook his head. "Something happened to the airport. Your mom says to get up. Everyone's freaking out."

The next few hours were chaos. Noises of traffic and honking below them, voices carrying from the street. The adults watched television and yelled at Linah and Zain whenever they went near a window.

"We don't know what's going to happen," her mother said, her voice taut.

The day was spent in the living room of the green apartment, the adults insisting the children remain nearby. The news reports showed the same images over and over: Streaks of smoke from the airport. An old man talking about prisoners. Airplanes dropping bombs like eggs from their abdomens. Khalto Riham made plates of bread and *labneh*, and they ate on the couches, eyes fixed on the television. The conversation was cryptic and urgent.

"You don't think they'll fight back? It'll be suicide."

"Thank God Latif and Abdullah aren't here."

"And Mama and Baba! Can you imagine Mama here?"

"They should return the men."

"I can't believe you'd say that!"

"Without the airport, how could—"

"Hush, not in front of the children. People are driving through Syria."

"The UN won't let this continue."

"When has the UN ever done anything?"

One of the men on the news wore a white robe. He had twinkling eyes and a long beard. Linah recognized him from posters near the mall. The billboards showed him speaking, his hand outstretched as though about to swat a fly, and behind him a landscape of mountains. Once, when she was at her friend Susan's house in Boston and they were playing in the living room while her father watched the news, the bearded man came on.

Barbarians, Susan's father had said, spitting the word from his mouth like an olive pit.

Her understanding of it all is half formed, hazy. She knows there are good guys and bad guys, like in Spider-Man movies and the Sherlock Holmes books that she and Susan swap. She has heard her parents talk about Israel and Palestine, wars and land and people dying. Linah knows that someone is wrong and this is why everything is happening—the airport burning and the men on the television, the shouts on the streets below them, the rumbles that resound every few hours when night falls, just yesterday shaking a bathroom window so hard they woke to its shattering. She is afraid that she might die but more afraid that everyone else—especially her father and Zain—will die, and then she'll be alone, like that girl in the movie she watched a while ago who was by herself after a plane crash in the tropics.

The adults won't elaborate. Only Khalto Riham pays any attention to them, asking if they'd like to sit with her and recite Qur'an. It is something they do with her in the summers—Linah's earliest memory is of curling up with Zain in Riham's bed in Amman for an afternoon nap, the air smelling of almonds and mothballs, Khalto Riham reciting the Fatiha. Even then Khalto Riham seemed separate from the other adults, as though the rest—Linah's mother, Souad—were children. It is the reason they call her Khalto instead of her first name—it seems sacrilegious with Riham.

Several days ago, Khalto Riham found them on the green apartment's balcony, swaying on the porch swing. Instead of scolding them, she sat down and read verses from her small, worn Qur'an.

"There's a war," she told them. "People are fighting, bad things are happening. People are dying. We can't do anything but wait. And pray."

They'd sat out there for nearly an hour, the sun setting over the water, the sounds of traffic screeching below, but Khalto Riham didn't flinch once, her voice strong and even as she went over the suras.

"O Allah," she said, at the very end. "Please keep these darlings safe."

During the summers, Linah plays with Zain's friends from school, all neighborhood children: Camille, Alex, Tony. Zain has been friends with them since third grade. Before the war, the five of them would hang out on the Corniche, talking about video games and movies, as waves crashed behind them.

The connection among all of them—something Linah has suspected for a while but been unable to put into words, something she's been understanding more and more—has a lot to do with difference. There is something about them that feels unlike the other kids, especially those back at her school in Boston. Tony spends a lot of time in trouble. Alex has a sister with Down syndrome. And Camille, who is beautiful with long blond hair, is painfully shy except in their little group, spending her time drawing seascapes in her notebooks.

They all come from elsewhere. Alex's father is Jordanian, Tony's is Swedish, and Camille's mother is British. They are all mishmashed and mixed up, which draws them together, Linah sees, just like the siphonophores she studied in biology last year.

As for Linah, she feels her difference glow through, something phosphorescent beneath her skin. Weeks ago, Linah and Camille were getting ice cream at Malik's when the most popular girl at Zain's school, Marie, overheard Linah talking about Jbail.

"You're not even Lebanese." Marie's voice rung out loud and sharp, several patrons in the store turning to stare.

Taken aback, Linah stammered through an answer. "W-we have an apartment here, we come every summer—"

The other girl's mouth twisted meanly. "You think that matters? With your weird accent in Arabic." A couple of girls behind her tittered. "You think your people deserve to be here? My mom told me all about them. Palestinians killed my uncle during the war." Linah felt dozens of eyes upon her, heard whispering. Camille froze like a deer.

And Linah felt confused, was speechless, wanting to say something about how no one ever really talked about being Palestinian in her house, the same way no one talked about being Iraqi, that when either set of grandparents came over, they spoke of things like villages and bombings with a sort of mournful resignation, as though the places in question had vanished into thin air. She wanted to say something about how she'd never been to Iraq or Palestine, that she knew only Boston and Beirut, that this was her home in the summers, and Marie must be wrong, because whoever it was that killed her uncle, it wasn't Linah's *people*, whatever that meant.

But her voice felt ghosted and so she said nothing at all.

• • •

THERE IS THE SOUND of footsteps in the hallway, and, a moment later, the door opens and her mother appears.

"Lunchtime." Her hair looks greasy; dark circles smudge her eyes.

"Is it more chicken?" Zain makes a face.

"I'm not hungry," Linah says.

"I think there's some rice too. Linah, you haven't eaten since the morning. Come on."

In the kitchen, Tika stands over the sink, rinsing a pot. Budur pulls out two dishes and sets them on the table, slightly too hard. "Tika, please, can you fix them something to eat?"

"Chicken?" Tika wipes her hands on her apron. "There's some underneath that foil. I'll heat it up."

Linah peels back the foil, eyes the cold, greasy chicken. She gestures to Zain and they grimace.

"Can we have pizza?" Linah asks as her mother turns to leave.

"No, Linah, you can't." Her voice is tense. She takes a breath; Linah watches the guilt travel across her face. Her mother brushes several strands of Linah's hair from her eyes. "Maybe tomorrow, monkey."

Tika heats up two plates, places the food in front of them. Linah and Zain peel the crispy skin off the chicken and eat glumly. "It tastes like rubber," Zain says.

Tika laughs. Zain turns to her and asks, "Can you make us potatoes and eggs?"

"Yes!" Linah slips out of her chair, rushes to her. Tika is tiny, barely Linah's height even with the small stool she uses to reach the sink. "Please. Please, please, please." She ducks her head and bites Tika's arm lightly, a gesture from when Linah was younger. Linah loves Tika, sometimes dreams about her in Boston. "Please," she says through her open mouth. Tika's skin tastes like soap and sweat.

Tika yelps, shakes her arm. "Get off of me, savage child." She grins. "You want mild or spicy?" Linah and Zain look at each other.

"Spicy," they say in unison.

• • •

Sometimes, if Linah begs enough, Tika will show her photographs of her home. Her town is named Matara and Tika once wrote it for her using Tamil letters and then gave Linah the slip of paper. It looked like dancing lines, a curlicue of beetles, not an alphabet.

In the photographs there are rows of huts with moss-covered rooftops and gardens of leafy plants. There are palm trees, some bent over so far the leaves graze the houses, as though they are kissing their cheeks. A group of people stand in front of the huts, all dark and tiny like Tika, the men with thin mustaches, the women wearing stacks of bracelets all the way up to their elbows. Last summer, after Tika went home to visit, she returned with boxes of rainbow-colored bracelets for Linah and Manar, made of glass and metal, dotted with rhinestones and small mirrors.

Because this is my job, not my home, Tika told Linah when she asked why Tika never wore any bracelets herself. She said it gently, but the words still stung Linah. She knows there is a boy, Manar's age, back in Matara, reedy-looking, wearing glasses in the photographs—Tika's son.

Manar never wears the bracelets, always dressing in flannel shirts and jeans, even in the summer, so Linah took hers, stacks them all on both arms. Linah loves the sound they make, like an orchestra, whenever she moves. The colors, watermelon pink, lemon yellow, vibrant purples, make her mouth water.

Tika sets the plates of bright red potatoes and eggs on the table, then two glasses of milk.

"For the spice," she says, smiling.

The eggs are delicious and peppery, a welcome change from the chicken and bread they've eaten all week. Linah's eyes water and Zain's face mottles.

"God," he sputters, gulping the milk.

"It's not that bad," she says, shrugging. Her throat is on fire. She sips the milk nonchalantly.

"Liar." He coughs. "You're crying."

"I'm not *crying*, it's just a little hot." She waits until Tika walks into the laundry room adjacent to the kitchen. "Okay, so the balcony. I was thinking we could do the blue apartment, your mom's room. She smokes out there sometimes, right? There would already be old butts around."

Zain spears a forkful of eggs. "She stopped doing that after the *natour* spoke with her. The ashes were falling into Mr. Azar's plants."

"What about Manar's balcony?"

"No way. She'd kill us."

"Yeah." Linah slumps against the chair. "Anyway, Manar would tell if she saw us."

"Would tell what?" They turn. Manar strolls into the kitchen, her book dangling from her hands. The pages flutter as she walks. Her T-shirt has a shamrock on it, a dancing leprechaun on either side.

"What are you reading?" Linah asks, trying to distract her.

"Faulkner." Manar cocks her head. "Would tell what?"

"None of your business."

"It's personal," Zain says.

Manar laughs. "Personal?" She opens the fridge, pulls out a Coke. "Like the bad-word club?"

"Go away!" Linah says, embarrassed. They'd made the fatal mistake of telling Manar about the bad-word club they'd started a couple of years ago. When Linah and Zain got into fights with the adults or were just bored, they would sneak off to one of the balconies and say bad words aloud, words they'd heard from television or their parents or the older kids at school. They delighted in them, like little knives in their mouths. When they told Manar, she laughed, called them juvenile.

"You're a jerk," Linah says to Manar's receding back. "I can't stand her," she informs Zain.

He nods. "She thinks she's a grownup." It is a betrayal, Manar who used to play with them, write and orchestrate plays for the three of them to put on for the adults during school vacations.

"Are you guys finished?"

Linah jumps. Her father and Souad walk into the kitchen. Like Linah's mother, they look worn out, exhausted. Souad is tossing a pack of Marlboros from one hand to another. Her shorts are frayed and there is a stain on her T-shirt.

"Hi, kiddos." She smacks the pack against her palm, pulls one out. "Tika made you eggs? Karam, did you talk to the *natour*?"

"Not yet." Linah's father runs his fingers through his hair. "Yesterday he said the generator is broken. And the electricity is failing throughout the city. He thinks they must've hit some electrical plant last night. Pretty soon we're going to run on a few hours."

"Motherfuckers." She perches herself on the kitchen counter, near the open window, and lights a cigarette.

"Souad! The children."

Souad wrinkles her nose, takes a drag. "Go to the blue apartment, kids."

They both protest at once.

"That's not fair."

"*You're* the one who told us to come down earlier!"

"Je*sus*." Souad slaps her palm on the counter, a thwacking sound. The gesture startles them, and they all fall silent, even her father. Of all the adults, Souad is the most relaxed, the one most like a child. When they build forts, she helps them make flags out of newspapers. In the plays they used to put on, she would always be the evil witch, making shrill, cackling noises.

"Enough. No more nagging, no more complaining. Linah, if I hear you bring up the beach one more time, I'm going to scream. And Zain, enough with the puppy eyes." Souad's voice breaks and she clears it, taking another drag. "Please," she says. "Please. For me. No drama today. Just go upstairs, watch a movie. Didn't you just get a new one, about that group of lawyers or something?"

"They solve crimes," Zain says quietly.

"Okay." Her voice gentles. "The group that solves crimes. Please, just go upstairs and watch it. Please." She smiles. "I'll run to the *dikaneh* later and buy you a tub of ice cream if you just don't argue."

Linah and Zain glance at each other, silently conferring. Zain nods, and they rise from the table. "Chocolate swirl," Linah reminds her aunt. Souad sticks her tongue out at her.

Her father laughs, his voice carrying as they walk away. "They're little masterminds, those two."

"Little mobsters, more like."

Linah waits until after they've walked through the living room, Khalto Riham and her mother barely glancing up from the television, until they are outside the green apartment, free in the hallway, before she nudges Zain.

"Now?"

He looks at her, hesitant. Then he nods. "Let's go."

THEY SNEAK DOWN the stairs like the spies in their favorite movie, tiptoeing down each step. At the front entrance of the building, they peek around for Hassan, the doorman, but he is nowhere in sight. Linah steps out first, stands for a moment on the pavement, marveling at how easily they did it.

"We're actually outside. What?" she asks, noticing Zain's frown.

"It's . . . empty," he says, looking at the street around them, many of the stores shuttered, parking spots bare. The road is usually bustling with university students and older couples, men on mopeds zipping between gridlocked traffic. But now there is a lone car driving along, hurriedly, as though not wanting to be caught here. Linah thinks of the girl in the plane-crash movie.

"It's like something from a zombie film," Zain says.

Where the world has already ended, Linah thinks. She swallows. "We'll go to Abu Rafi's real quick and come back. He's always open." As she turns left, walking toward the ribbon of shuttered storefronts, she can feel Zain's pause, his eventual capitulation, then hears his footsteps behind her.

They walk along the sidewalks, past the fancy hotel with lushly flowering plants flanking its entrance. The bellman catches her eye, tilts his head quizzically. *What are these children doing out here?* She looks away, quickens her pace. The air is queasy, a tarlike tension in the warm dusk. The few people that cross their path are men, scruffy-looking, as though coming from a day in a mine somewhere, their hair rumpled, clothes dirty.

When they reach the enclave of delis and bakeries, she thinks for a moment she was mistaken, everything's closed, but then sees the door—a cracked white sign above announcing *Abu Rafi's*—slightly ajar, the usual display of flowers and fruits outside missing.

Inside is an unkempt brown woman standing in front of the cheese aisle. Somehow, unmistakably, Linah knows she is a maid, Sri Lankan, although she is dressed oddly, in neither a uniform nor one of the pretty saris Linah has seen clusters of maids wear on their days off. This woman wears an ill-fitting dress, falling past her knees, the shoulders and bust too large for her. It is as though she just tried it on to see what it would look like. Her dark hair spiders past her waist, a handful of liras in her fist.

The store is empty save for the woman and Abu Rafi, looking grim and cheerless behind the cash register. Many of the shelves are bare. Sometimes, when she and Zain come here, running errands for their parents, Abu Rafi slips them a Snickers or a Fanta, but now he looks at them blankly.

"What is it? Tell your parents we're out of meat. Milk too. Sold the last of it this morning. Those idiots at the port promised a new shipment, but the bastards have blocked the ships."

Linah finds she cannot speak. Their adventure suddenly seems so stupid. To her astonishment, Zain clears his throat, steps forward.

"A pack of Marlboros. The green ones. For my mom," he adds when Abu Rafi hesitates. The man shrugs, pulls out a pack.

"One fifty," he says.

Zain offers him a trickle of coins. Linah watches with amazement as Abu Rafi slides the cigarette pack across the counter and into her cousin's hands.

"Now, run along. This isn't a babysitting service. *Hey!*" Linah and

Zain jump. They follow Abu Rafi's glare to the dark-skinned woman fingering a packet of peanuts. "No more wait-wait, you understand?" he says in broken English. "You pick something, you leave."

Linah has never seen an expression like the woman's: frantic, vehement. They watch her grab a motley of items—spicy nuts, a bag of pita, a wheel of soft cheese—with a brisk nervousness, an animal foraging during drought.

Something keeps Linah frozen in the doorway, Zain by her side now, the pack of cigarettes in his grip; something keeps them watching as Abu Rafi piles the groceries in front of him, punches numbers into a large calculator. The woman stares at a spot on the floor.

"Fifteen, twenty-three—forty-eight thousand lira," he concludes. Then, in condescending English: "Now you pay."

The woman drops the crumpled bills on the counter, her eyes still downcast.

"What is this? A joke? This is just *ten.*"

The woman remains silent.

"Speak up, girl. You think this is a charity? You go tell your madame that she has to—"

"No madame!" the woman suddenly explodes. Her hair shudders around her as she snaps her head up. "No madame, no sir. They leave."

"Well, that's none of my business," Abu Rafi grumbles in Arabic.

"They leave five days ago." Now that she has begun talking, it is like a levee breaking, crests spilling from the woman's lips, her hands moving wildly. "I wake up, they gone. I wait. Wait for lunch, then dinner, then sun goes down. I stay awake one night, two nights. I wait. I take the laundry down, soak the rice. But they no come back. They hear the war and they go. They go—" Here, her voice falters. "They leave me behind. Here. I look everywhere for passport, no find. I try to call embassy, they say no one can help. They say stay inside, away from windows. I cannot call my children. I cannot go home. The food is finishing. There is no electricity."

"We should go," Zain whispers. But Linah is rooted in the doorway, her flip-flops glued to the linoleum. Abu Rafi and the woman stare at each other.

"There is no money," the woman says simply. "They left."

The man's face darkens with anger, disgust, exhaustion—exhaustion at his store being the only grocery open, at another long day of telling people there is no more flour, cursing the Israelis every time the rumbles begin from the south.

"Forty-eight," he repeats. Linah wants to punch him. "Or get out."

"But madame and sir— "

"Forty-eight! You think I don't have children?" He lets outs a long string of Arabic curses. "You want help, you find it somewhere else. Not here. Look around." He gestures at the paltry supplies on the shelves. "Someone wants bread, they pay. Eggs! Apples! Cheese! They pay. They pay!" Spittle dots his lips. "I help one Sri Lankan, ten more at my door tomorrow."

The woman flinches. She stares at the crumpled bills. With one hand, she smoothes her wiry, bristling hair from her face. Her profile could be on a coin, the nose straight, the forehead uninterrupted.

"The bread," she finally says. "Only the bread." Her voice could cool molten glass. *This is who you are,* she seems to be saying to the man, *look at this wrinkled bill on the counter, my unwashed hair. For the rest of your life, you will remember this moment.*

It is not until the woman has paid, swung by Linah and Zain with her bag of pita—she smells of sandalwood, perspiration—as though they are invisible, and left, the door slamming shut behind her, that Abu Rafi finally notices the two of them. He looks at them for a long moment.

"Go," he says. "Run along home."

They rush down the streets, the pockmarked asphalt and snarl of telephone wires overhead suddenly unfamiliar. *What an ugly place,* Linah suddenly thinks. She longs for Boston, the manicured lawns that light up during December, the community pool with an ice cream stand, her classrooms' perfume of chalk. At the hotel, the same bellman catches Linah's eye. This time she doesn't look away.

At the building entrance, the *natour* is carrying a jug of water. "What are you two doing?" Zain crosses his arms to hide the pack of cigarettes.

"Errands," Zain manages, then ushers Linah into the entrance and up the stairs. She has the vaguest sense of vertigo.

"Blue apartment," she reminds him. This whole time, they were supposed to be watching a movie.

The apartment is empty and dark. "Quick," Zain says. "Make it look like we're watching something." They draw the curtains shut and turn on the television, put the detective movie on. They toss the cushions on the floor, arrange them between small piles of unwashed clothes—Souad is a dreadful homemaker—but there is a funereal quality to their movements, like children playing children.

Zain is still holding the cigarette pack. "Gimme," Linah says, taking it and stuffing it in her shorts pocket.

The room is gloomy and hot. The movie begins, but Linah's attention wanders; the image of the woman's downturned mouth, her dirty hair. Halfway through the movie, the electricity cuts off abruptly. The television hums off. Neither of them speak for a moment. Linah can feel Zain's eyes on her, his concern.

"We could set off the sparklers."

Linah looks at him with respect. When he wants, Zain can get interesting. They'd bought the sparklers last summer. Her father and Souad lit them on the rooftop. *Stand back*, they'd called, and the sticks made a *shh-shh* sound, dissolving in a shower of embers. *Yes*, she thinks. The sparklers would change things.

"They'd freak out."

Zain shrugs. Linah wants to hug him. "You still have them?"

"I think my mom put them away somewhere. Maybe in the kitchen cupboards."

But the cupboards are filled with cans and coffee tins, stale boxes of crackers. The sparklers aren't under the bathroom sinks or in the cluttered bedrooms. They open every last drawer. Now that they finally have an idea, they both seem spurred by it. Suddenly, Zain snaps.

"The storage room. It's where she puts anything she doesn't know what to do with."

Linah wrinkles her nose. "It stinks."

"So hold your breath."

She follows Zain down the hallway to the little room next to the living room. It is the size of a closet, strewn with crates and boxes and a half-filled bookshelf. The mess is glorious, sprawling across the floor like an animal whose limbs they have to step around. The room is a museum of their old lives.

"It's like Narnia," Linah breathes.

The sparklers are soon forgotten as the two of them dig through the boxes, finding stuffed animals and broken jump ropes, toys they couldn't remember ever having. For the first time since the war, Linah feels buzzing, alive as she plucks through the mess. One basket is filled with old scarves of Souad's, and Linah tries one on, tossing it over one shoulder. *I'll call you sometime*, she says silently to a young man.

"My Game Boy!" Zain leans down to pick up a weathered console. An entire shoebox is devoted to old Beanie Babies, and Linah pulls the plush bodies out, the fabric smelling of dust.

The electricity comes on; the sounds of the movie float in from the living room. But neither of them move. Zain is taking books from a cardboard box.

"God, these are so old they're falling apart. Look at this." He lifts a purple-spined one, the cover in Arabic calligraphy. A lone page falls out and drifts to Zain's lap.

"Do you think your mom ever comes in here?" Linah likes the image of Souad sneaking in after everyone falls asleep, lining up the Beanie Babies and wearing her colorful scarves. "To look at this stuff?"

There is no reply. When Linah turns to Zain, she sees that he is frowning down at a book in his hands. "This one has something in it," he says.

Linah cranes her neck. The cover of the book is a dull brown, an image of a plant turning toward a painted sun. From inside the cover, Zain pulls out a bundle held together with an old, tawny rubber band. They both huddle around it. There is page after page of ancient-looking paper, lined with someone's neat handwriting. Some of the handwriting is in blue ink, some in black. The paper is creamy, thin with age.

"It's in Arabic," Zain says, disappointed. Neither he nor Linah can read Arabic well. "There's, like, a hundred pages."

"I think it's someone's journal." Linah sits upright. The prospect is dizzying—access to secrets; a thousand times better than being a detective. "We found someone's journal!"

"No." Zain squints at the writing. "They're letters. Look, there's the heading, and a signature at the end of each one."

Linah's mind whirls. Letters from her parents to each other? From Elie to Souad? From old friends?

"And dates at the top. This is from 1998," Zain says.

"That's a seven, idiot."

"Okay, from 1978." The moment is broken by the front door opening. Voices call out for them.

"Linah! Zain!"

"Where are they?"

They freeze. Footsteps. Zain mouths the words *Oh no*, and Linah thinks instantly of the *natour*, the adults finding out about their excursion. They rise, dusting themselves off. Zain slips the bundle of papers under his shirt.

But when they walk back into the living room, the adults—Khalto Riham, Linah's father, Souad—are talking about the news. They barely glance at them. Even Manar looks concerned. Karam opens the curtains, letting in the last of the dusky light.

"Hey!"

"Where'd you guys go?" Souad says.

Zain glances at Linah. "The electricity went out."

"Well, it's back. The TV reception froze downstairs; the channels aren't working. We need to try this one."

"Sorry, kids, you'll finish your movie later."

"Put those cushions back. What is this, laundry?"

They reluctantly stack the cushions. Zain moves carefully, bending awkwardly at the waist. He holds a cushion in front of him.

"This *is* laundry. Jesus, Souad, when's the last time you—"

"I keep telling her!"

"Not now, Manar! Karam, I'm sorry, there's been a *full-fledged war* going on outside, I've put household chores on hold."

"Apparently." Linah's father speaks under his breath, but Souad glares at him.

"Channel eight," Khalto Riham says and Manar flips through channels.

The newscaster looks frazzled, headlines in Arabic whizzing by on the bottom of the screen. Linah catches only a handful of the newscaster's words: *military, shelling, security.* Linah tries to read the sentences, but they glide by too quickly. Whenever she goes to Amman, her grandmother scolds her father and Souad: *You've raised these children as Americans. They barely understand what their grandmother is saying to them.* Linah likes her grandmother but is slightly afraid of her, her razor-sharp nails and the way she glances over whatever room she is in, like she is bored.

The newscaster says something about an announcement, and the camera shifts to a wall with green banners. A bearded man walks to a podium and begins to talk. Linah thinks of the wiry-haired woman, the way she had said *Only the bread.* The man says something about justice. His eyes snap when he speaks.

"Oh, for God's sake." Souad scoots to the edge of the sofa and slides the living-room balcony door open. She lights a cigarette, holding up the other hand, palm first, toward Khalto Riham and Karam. "Not a word, I'm serious. My living room. Not a word."

"So what have you kids been doing?" Linah's father asks her distractedly.

"Watching a movie," she says. Her voice sounds strange to her ears; she wonders if the adults can hear it. Perhaps her father does because he doesn't say anything else, nothing about their lungs or going to the other apartment.

"Monkey," Linah's mother says over Souad's head. "I was thinking we should order that pizza tonight. What do you think? If I have another bite of chicken, I'm going to cluck." She laughs again.

Suddenly Linah cannot bear to hear the newscaster's voice, her mother's laugh. It is wrong, all of it. She stands, Zain's worried face blurring at her side.

"I'm taking a shower," she announces.

"Linah, the hot water."

Linah turns to her father. He looks so sad, so *ordinary*, all of a sudden, his eyeglasses smudged. *I'm getting old*, he'd joked the day he got them, and Linah shivered at the thought.

"I'll only use the cold," she says to him gently. "Promise."

THE GREEN APARTMENT feels empty, deflated, though Linah can hear plates clattering in the kitchen, Tika's steps. She wants to run to her, embrace her.

Her bathroom is colorful, the only room her parents let her decorate. There is a mirror over the sink with soccer decals from when she was younger framing it. A shaggy, rainbow-colored bath rug on the floor, the bottom of the bathtub covered in stickers.

Linah turns on the hot water, pulling the handle all the way to the left, to the very hottest. She removes and drops her clothes on the bathroom floor and stands for long minutes in front of the mirror, steam beginning to billow around her, examining her body. This seems to her a necessary task, something she must endure. Her body is fascinating. In the past few months, she has secretly peeped through the keyhole and watched the women in her household as they prepare to shower, inspecting their bodies: Manar with her excess flesh and a triangle of dark hair between her legs; Souad small-breasted, hairless everywhere; and her mother, a trimmer patch of hair and with bigger breasts than the others.

Her own body is predictable, unchanging. Skinny. Flat, flat, flat. Like the landscape of tundra that they studied in geography class.

"Miss No Tits," she says aloud. She heard an eighth-grader say it once, when the boyish gym teacher walked by in the hallway.

WHEN SHE HAS USED up the hot water, Linah walks to her bedroom, leaving a trail of wet footprints in her wake. From her closet, she chooses a nightgown her grandmother brought her from Amman.

"They left," she says aloud, echoing the maid's words. She wants to go home, although the thought makes her feel babyish. Why do the adults like this city? If it were up to her, she'd never come back. She would go to summer camp with Susan in the Berkshires, where the girls stay up late telling scary stories and make friendship bracelets. There's horseback riding and theater and water-skiing; Linah stole one of the brochures from Susan's house last summer and read every page.

Instead of going upstairs, Linah walks down the hall into her parents' room. Like the rest of the apartment, the walls are painted green, and the ceiling has a white, curling trim. A Persian rug the shade of persimmons spans the room in front of the bed. This is where they used to rehearse their plays, she and Zain and Manar, the space perfect for jumping and dancing around. Above the bed, there is a painting of an Iraqi souk with stalls of silver jewelry and spices, one man holding out a palmful of fruit.

Linah walks through the room, lifting things and returning them—the jewelry box, a small wooden bird her father made years ago. She feels hungry for touch. She opens her parents' closet and trails her fingers through the clothing, her father's khakis and T-shirts, the two silk ties he brings every summer, her mother's dresses. She ducks her head to the turquoise gown her mother wears to parties, inhales. Gardenia, a tinge of sweat. The smell makes her sad, as though her parents were in another country instead of just upstairs.

When she was a child, she used to wear her mother's dresses. She would mimic the things she overheard her mother saying on the phone about work and the family. Sometimes her mother would help, on rainy weekends when they were both bored, draping pearls around Linah's neck. Her mother would dab her Dior perfume behind Linah's ears, calling out, *There's a lovely lady here for you, Karam*, and her father would come into the room. He would always stagger and clutch his heart when he saw her, pretend not to recognize her, until they all laughed, and she would twirl, feeling beautiful.

She steps onto the balcony of her parents' room barefoot, the night air warm and heavy. There are several potted plants with large, purplish leaves that her father waters every morning. Souad never remembers to water the ones upstairs. Her balcony is strewn with dead plants.

Her parents' balcony is large, with an iron rod railing that overlooks the traffic and slivers of sea between buildings. There is a chair and table with someone's empty mug on it. Next to the table is a jasmine plant, her mother's favorite. Something about those eager, white-faced flowers makes Linah's chest ache.

She sits next to the plant and lowers her face into the tangled leaves as though into a pillow. It hurts, a branch poking her in the ear. Still, she stays like that for a moment, breathing in the sweet scent.

Eventually she disentangles herself, leans back against the wall. She tilts her head up, sees the night sky. It occurs to her she hasn't been alone in the past two weeks. The sky is clear tonight, a crescent moon shining. A reverberating sound rumbles from the distance. Bombing, from the south. She remembers the world outside, the burning. *They're slaughtering us*, a woman had said into the news camera. A lone siren rings out.

A part of her hopes they will come looking for her, the adults, their faces anxious. It was something she used to do as a child, though her mother would scold her: She would hide in closets or under the bed and hear their voices break with fear until, finally, she'd appear. She never understood the anger that would bloom then, the yelling. *I'm giving you a gift*, she always wanted to say. *You thought I was lost, but I never was.*

Something is different. There are streaks of light cleaving the night sky, punctuated by low rumbling that feels close. Linah stands transfixed, feeling the ground around her quiver. From the balcony, she can see hooks of smoke begin to rise between the buildings, from the south. After fifteen, twenty minutes, the balcony door slides open.

"Finally," Zain says.

Linah sighs. "Found me."

Zain looks confused. "Were you hiding?" He slides the door closed and sits opposite from her, his bare feet dirty. "They bombed another building. The newscaster said so. Everyone's freaking out upstairs."

"Do you think we're going to die?"

"Don't be stupid," Zain says but his voice trembles. In the moonlight, his eyes are huge and shiny.

They watch the lights arch across the land, like fireworks in reverse. From here, the entire skyline is lit up, smoke billowing, covering buildings and sea, as though the earth has been replaced with fire and smoke. Are the woman's children waiting for her call? Linah wonders. What does she do in that large apartment once the sun sets—for Linah imagines a marbled, stuffily decorated apartment, old Beirut style, sprawled with uncomfortable, gilded furniture, a *guest living room*, large bay windows—now that she is no longer waiting?

"We'll take Tika with us if we leave," Zain says. This is how they are sometimes, intuiting each other's thoughts.

They are silent for a moment, thinking of the woman.

"I wish Teta were here," Linah says suddenly. She pictures her grandmother sweeping through the apartments, snapping at the adults to buy something other than stale chicken, complaining about the heat. Her prickliness would be a tonic. There were certain things her *teta* understood wordlessly, like the Eid she told Budur to let Linah wear jeans for dinner if she wanted. Linah wants to tell her grandmother about the woman at Abu Rafi's, to hear her say something smart and sharp and perfect.

Zain tosses something at her, and she catches it instinctively. A matchbox. He grins. "Bad-word club." He holds his palm out, the cigarette pack slightly bent. "I found them in your shorts. On the bathroom floor."

"What about the ash?"

"Fuck the ash."

Zain lights an unbent cigarette for Linah. She holds it, smoke trailing the tip, with a sort of wonder. She remembers the girls on the railing, how they held the cigarettes with their two fingers sticking pertly up. Linah mimics the gesture and takes a drag. The smoke scorches and she coughs. Zain does the same.

"It burns." He gasps.

"But it gets smoother." Three, four, five drags, and the smoke goes down more easily. She parts her lips and watches it drift from her mouth. Zain clears his throat. "I think Jiddo wrote the letters. He was writing to someone named Mustafa. Do you know who that is?"

Linah scans her memory. The name is dimly familiar, but she can't place it. She shakes her head.

"Well, he was someone in Palestine. Jiddo sent him the letters. I started reading one of them. He wrote something about a house." Zain unfolds a paper from his pocket and reads, stumbling over the Arabic. "*There are rooms for each of us here, and even more. It reminds me of your mother's house, how you always said it felt too big after she left.*"

"If he sent them, why were they in the storage room?"

Zain shrugs. "I don't know." He seems uninterested and Linah understands why. The letters suddenly seem far away, something that happened years ago. They aren't *now*, like the bombings or the woman's voice breaking in the store.

"Abu Rafi is a motherfucker." Linah says the word slowly, cautiously. It is the first time she has fastened any of the bad words onto a person.

"Look," Zain whispers, gesturing at the scene in front of them. Even with the explosions and ambulance sirens wailing in the distance, the air so thick with smoke it tickles her throat, it is somehow enchanting. The missiles roar white and dazzling, like comet tails.

The colors, the brilliant light. It reminds Linah of when she was younger, years ago in Boston, one summer night when their families went to a carnival. It had rained earlier and the air was sweet and damp, the grass still dewed with water. Her sandals made a squelching sound, and, later, when her father washed her feet in the bathtub, streaks of grass and soil circled the drain.

There had been a Ferris wheel and they all rode it together. While they inched toward the top, fireworks exploded above them, marbling the sky with color, aglitter like rock candy. *Look at that sky*, she heard her mother call to her father. *You could just eat it up.*

Watching the water burn, Linah remembers her mother's voice, the way her hair had whipped around, dark, beautiful, a memory she'd entirely forgotten. She remembers how Elie bought them all ice cream, her fingers sticky afterward, remembers Souad kissing his neck. Linah thinks of how she misses him, how he is halfway across the world, and she feels sad for Zain and even Manar. The memories fill her with longing, the way memories of her childhood leave her wistful. Make her feel as though she is spinning, bursting out of her skin, the world around her lunatic and whirling, the world *hers*—even the burning buildings, even the bombs, even the sounds of people crying on the street—but it is moving fast, so fast, her childhood receding while she is still trying to catch her breath.

"Khalto Riham was saying the Israelis won't stop bombing for weeks." Zain's voice startles her. Linah tries to shrug, though Zain is looking away. The smoke is hurting her lungs less and less. She attempts to make a smoke ring, but it comes out wobbly.

"It's sweet," Zain says.

"Menthol."

"My dad hit my mom once." Zain speaks musingly. The words hang between them. Linah wants to say something, something about adults being flawed, or how they break things without meaning to, but then she changes her mind. Suddenly, all she wants to do is see Zain smile. She jumps to her feet in one swift motion, holding out the cigarette to him.

"Hey!" Zain's face is startled as he takes the cigarette.

Linah steps back and shuts her eyes. She counts to three and flings her body forward, her hands obediently catching her, hoisting her into a handstand. She can hear the smile in Zain's voice when he speaks.

"Wow," she hears him say, "how do you *do* that?"

Linah keeps her eyes shut, her body vertical. In a moment, her arms will begin to ache. But for now, she feels light as air. She wants to do cartwheels. She wants to find the wiry-haired maid and ask her to move in. She wants to hug Zain, to show him how her heart pounds out of her skin sometimes. She wants to run inside, throw her arms around her father, and kiss his cheek. Whisper into his ear, *There's a lovely lady here for you, Karam.*

"Amazing," Zain says.

Linah opens her eyes, keeping her body straight as an arrow, her breath coming fast, not wanting to speak and spoil things, the world upside down. For a moment the tiles of the balcony are her roof and the stars wheel past her feet like some mossy, glittering carpet.

ATEF

AMMAN
June 2011

It began with her forgetting the word *pomegranate.* "Hand me a—" Alia said one evening last year. The most peculiar expression spread across her face, like she was a sleepwalker awoken too soon. She blinked.

Atef waited. "What?"

"One of the, ah . . ." She began to look afraid. "The red one," she'd finally muttered, pointing at the fruit. Small incidents followed: her wandering around the neighborhood, the misremembering of Atef's birthday.

"Something's not right," Riham finally said weeks ago as the two of them sat in the garden. "This thing with Mama. Something's wrong."

Atef averted his eyes. "She just gets that way, Riham."

"She's getting—" Riham hesitated. "Worse. More confused. Mixing things up."

Atef thought of his wife, her tea with two and a half sugar cubes every morning, the little rituals of her life. "I'm sure it's nothing. Getting older. Happening to all of us. Just yesterday it took me twenty minutes to find my keys." His chatter is telling. Over the last few years, Alia's eccentricities had flared up—how she puzzled over directions, her confusion with names—but they were always cloaked in general cantankerousness.

"Baba." Riham took a long breath. "Yesterday, when she came over for dinner, I left her for a minute because I got a phone call. It took me an hour to find her afterward."

Atef's heart stilled. "Where was she?"

"On the balcony."

"Oh." Relief emptied his lungs. "She's always liked the view."

"No." The faintest impatience rose in Riham's voice, so rare it silenced Atef. "You know those aluminum latches, the ones we used to lock when the children were babies? Well, they were open. She was trying to climb down."

"What?" He thought, uselessly, of the pale windflowers in the garden, an argument he'd had with Alia months ago, when she'd called his love of flowers hopeless. "Why would she do that?"

Riham sighed, and it was in that small exhale that Atef understood he'd been protected, that Riham had been shielding him as much as she could.

"She says it's the war. That Saddam is coming and she has to escape."

THAT EVENING, he had watched Alia as she ate dinner, washed her face, got into bed. And suddenly he saw. Like the optical illusions his grandchildren loved, once the image emerged, he couldn't return to not seeing it. There was his wife, her skin ashy, her hair frizzed and white.

"That girl," she pronounced before bed, "is stealing my lipstick." Atef didn't ask which girl.

Smoothing her hair back from her face, Atef's hand slid over her thin, mottled scalp, the delicate bone of her skull.

"She won't let us dye it," Riham told him later. "She thinks the hairdresser is trying to poison her."

He realized that, for once, he was seeing Alia as she was. That, for the past decade, he'd seen his wife made up, never without perfect hair and manicured fingernails, layers of foundation powdered across her skin, the lips outlined and filled in with her coral lipstick. That beneath it, all along, was this frailty.

From the kitchen there is the sound of female laughter. *Souad*, Atef thinks. But when he walks in, Linah and Manar are sitting at the table sprinkling zaatar on pita bread spread thick with strawberry jam. They are both wearing gypsylike dresses of gauzy fabric. Linah has woven sea-colored glass beads through her hair, which is gathered atop her head; the beads scatter in every direction like fireworks. Their chatter stops at the sight of him.

"Hi, Jiddo," Manar says, her voice bright.

"Is Teta ready for the doctor?"

Atef hesitates. "We're working on it. Riham and Umm Najwa are talking to her now."

"She'll go," Linah says softly, and Atef knows someone has already told them about Alia's outburst this morning, how she refused to get dressed, yelling at him that she didn't need to see a doctor.

"Seen your father?" he asks Linah.

Linah shrugs. "Maybe outside."

"How is it possible," Manar begins, "in this day and age, that everyone is always looking for someone in this family? Everyone has a cell phone." She turns to Atef. "Mama was just asking about you."

"It's a post-tech metaphor," Linah quips, "for how alone we all are."

"Please. It's textbook narcissism. Assuming people need to appear at our whim." Manar snaps her fingers. A speck of zaatar dots her chin. Atef is enjoying listening. He likes the girls, their wit, their deadpan.

"True," Linah says thoughtfully, waving a piece of bread around like a wand. "Look at how Mama panics when one of us doesn't answer the phone, like, *immediately*." She still has the choppily cut hair, the lip and nose piercings, from her early adolescence. There were rumors, last year, of drugs. He overheard a conversation she and

Riham had once, a reference to an arrest, some boy she ran away with for a few weeks.

He is touched that they've all come. The grandchildren, especially. He expected excuses, begging off. Souad still in Beirut; Karam and Budur in Boston; the grandchildren all over. For the past few years, they've visited less and less, and Alia is too unwell to fly herself.

But there had been a cascade of phone calls all day—Zain, Linah, Souad. They called with their flight information, times of arrival, soft words of concern.

The grandchildren spoke in faltering Arabic when they arrived, leaving their lives—Abdullah from university in London, Manar from an internship in Manhattan, Linah and Zain's summer camp in Vermont. It didn't matter what they were doing. They came.

RIHAM STRIDES INTO the kitchen, her face tired. "She's coming. Umm Najwa's getting her dressed. Morning, girls." Umm Najwa has been Alia's nurse ever since she broke her hip years ago.

"Morning," they return.

"Baba, you should get the files ready." The pile of medical records, from doctor visits in Beirut and Kuwait, that he keeps locked in his study alongside passports, his diploma, the children's birth certificates. *My husband, the hoarder*, Alia used to say. *It's come to good use*, he returns silently now. *I've kept your whole history.* As Atef leaves the study with the stuffed manila envelope, he finds Abdullah in the hallway, looking hesitant.

"Jiddo," he begins. "I wanted to see how you were doing."

Atef feels a startling lump in his throat. "I'm—" There doesn't seem to be a word convincing enough. "I'm just waiting on your grandmother."

"It'll be good to know," Abdullah says softly. "Whatever it is." His grandson's starting to get wrinkles around his eyes, his hairline receding. He resembles his father more and more. For a long time, they worried about Abdullah, with his piousness and rigidity, the afternoons he spent yelling about politics with older men from the neighborhood. Atef tried to talk with him, but the boy remained unreadable as stone. Then the towers fell in America, and the war started in Iraq. Suddenly, something within Abdullah eased, seemed to snap awake.

Now he pulls his grandfather to him, abruptly, surprisingly—the boy is usually more restrained—muffling the word as Atef says it.

"*Inshallah.*"

Everyone is in the kitchen when Atef returns, Karam and Souad standing around the girls at the table. Riham is adjusting Alia's blouse, pulling a loose thread from the fabric. Zain is stirring his coffee, raising his eyebrows at Manar while Souad speaks.

"We don't know how long we'll be gone," she is saying. "Make sure you baste the chicken, do *not* forget to take it out at seven . . . Zain, are you listening? Manar, make sure to take it out at—"

"Mama, *okay!*"

"We're not six," Zain says.

"The chicken needs to be basted in lemon juice," Souad continues, undaunted, "and then put some salt—"

"Oh my *God.*"

Karam tugs at Souad's sleeve. "Come on."

"*Yes*, Jesus, please. Get her out of here."

"Manar, hush."

"Okay, time to go," Riham says soothingly.

Alia makes a sudden, violent sound and they all turn to her. She is standing by the doorway, her head ducked forward. Atef can see pink scalp beneath her thinning hair. When she lifts her head, there is a flash of teeth. She is laughing.

"Mama," Karam says. She turns to him, smiling girlishly.

"I hated the movie," she says brightly in Arabic. "It was *outrageously* dull."

"Let's go," Atef says.

• • •

In the car Atef sits up front with Karam, Alia and their daughters in the back. Atef fiddles with the car radio, finds a station with Ziad Rahbani singing. Static crackles every few seconds. Atef can feel Karam steal glances at him as they drive, Riham's voice audible as she speaks with Alia.

They pass the storefronts on Mecca Street, street vendors shaking bags of dates at cars, a boutique bikini shop with mannequins wearing ocean-colored spandex. Atef doesn't look out of the windows, not at the restaurants or pretty coeds walking on the street, the girls who get younger and younger every year. Atef looks straight in front of him, at the windshield, staring at everything and nothing at once.

Beside him, Karam opens his mouth, then shuts it. Atef knows the boy wants to say the right thing. *There is no right thing.* Atef wants to tell his children that they don't understand, that their view from the sidelines is incomplete, that somehow in the murky cave of his marriage—not exactly happy but not unhappy either, given to strain, months at a time when Alia retreats into her fury and Atef into himself—is a miraculous conch of love, something unpolished but alive, pulsing.

The specialty clinic is attractively built, spare and white and sunny. They register in the atrium and Atef thinks about the people who come to these offices and hear horrible news, of brain tumors and cancer, then have to walk back out into the atrium. The beauty of the space, he thinks, must be devastating. As for the rest of the patients—merely brushing a close call, nothing but migraines, clean blood tests—they must be dazed with relief, suddenly grateful for every dust mote.

Please, Allah, let us be among the dazed.

The prayer is shoddy and shameful. Atef is a man of makeshift faith, at best, lacking his own mother's quiet belief or Riham's tenacity. He wants a God who coolly pats his hand, a God who has better things to do. Riham and Souad talk to the receptionist behind the desk, Riham carrying the photocopied pages of her mother's medical file. *Bless her*, Atef thinks. The women in his life are more efficient than the men. Atef thinks of Manar and Linah. In a hospital, they would take brisk charge.

"I'm going to be late for Sima's."

"Alia, Sima will wait."

"How do you know? I said I'd be there at six." Sima had been a neighbor of theirs in Kuwait.

"I already called her, said we'd be a little late. She said not to worry, that you should see the doctor first."

"You did?"

"Yes." Atef tries to make his voice reassuring. He talks to Alia with the tone he used when the children were young, a voice that reemerged when his grandchildren were born.

"Mama, this is Dr. Munla." A short, balding man in khakis. He smiles and shakes Alia's hand.

"Madame Yacoub, it's a pleasure."

"I'm late for Sima," Alia informs him.

The doctor is unruffled. "Then we'll make this as quick as possible." He turns to the others. "We can go to my office."

"I hate seeing her like this," Atef hears Souad whisper to Riham. "It's like watching a lion caged."

They follow the doctor down a hallway decorated with landscape paintings. His office is painted a bright robin's-egg blue, diagrams of brain anatomy covering the walls. There is a plastic model of a brain on the doctor's desk, different sections in pastel colors. They sit around the room, Souad perching on the exam chair. The doctor sits at his desk and lifts his arms, as though performing for them.

"We're going to do several tests today," he begins. He speaks for some time about machinery, the validity of MRI imaging, measuring brain fluid, testing reflexes, cognitive assessment—vague, ominous-sounding tasks that they don't understand.

"For brain imaging?" Riham asks.

"My brain is fine," Alia says.

"I'm sure it is, madame," the doctor says. "It's just routine."

Atef desperately likes him, in that way one likes people who carry tremendous power to bring bad news. He can envision the doctor after work, sitting on some balcony somewhere as he pours a glass of arak, touching his wife's hair, telling her of the terrible ways the human body can betray.

"I'll take you in now," he says to Alia. "We'll start with some basic tests."

"I'm late for Sima," she says once more. She chews her lower lip and looks adrift.

"We'll be done before you know it," the doctor says.

The four of them return to the waiting room. Half an hour passes by; an hour. There is a television mounted on the wall and they obediently watch what's playing, a movie that's halfway through.

"Is that woman his wife?" Karam asks.

"I think she's a police officer," Riham says.

Souad leaves twice to smoke. She barely glances at the television, instead texting on her cell phone. Every now and then, the corners of her lips twitch up. There is a man, Atef intuits, has been for some time. But in this way his youngest is oddly private. She hasn't mentioned anyone since Elie.

When he and Alia go to Beirut, they stay with their daughter. After the war, she redecorated the apartment, painted over the walls. Souad filled it with black and white—black couches and tables, white walls and rugs. Even the curtains were black, lacy like a widow's veil.

Atef couldn't imagine living with all that monochrome, but Souad always seems happy when he visits—this, too, hints at a romance—mocking him, morbidly funny. She shows him around Hamra, pointing out places that have changed, taking him to the small boutique shop she and her friend opened a couple years ago.

"It's the most impractical thing to do in this economy," she said cheerfully, walking around the closet-size space, one wall made entirely of glass and overlooking a busy street where college students scurry by. Unusual, pretty things fill the store, mirrors and coral necklaces and leather-bound notebooks.

But she must be onto something, because people want beautiful things even in hard times—perhaps especially in hard times—and the store keeps her afloat. Atef ends each trip feeling wistful, watching his daughter living the life she has foraged, like an island survivor in a palace of shells.

The movie ends and another begins, a thriller with an elaborate car chase in the first five minutes. "It's taking long," Atef finally says.

Riham checks her watch. "We want him to be thorough, Baba."

"She's going to be frantic."

"The doctor's great with her."

"I bet it's a good sign." Souad looks up from her phone. "If they'd found something, he'd be hollering at us to come in." She pronounces *hollering* incorrectly, her Arabic dwindled after so many years abroad. *Your daughter, the Amrikiyeh*, Alia scoffs.

The thought of his wife, hawkish and strident, hurts and Atef stands. "I'll get us something to drink. Coffee? Juice? There's a *dikaneh* across the street."

"I'll go, Baba," Karam says, but Atef waves him off.

"The walk will do me good."

"Coffee," Karam says. "Sugarless for me."

Atef turns to his daughters. "And you?"

"Sprite."

"Orange juice."

Leaving the hospital is a relief, the sun lovely upon his face. He walks rapidly, as though shedding the place, tall buildings on either side, hospitals and businesses and banks. Atef turns past an outdoor café where a group of young women sit, smoking cigarettes and chatting. One of the women wears a sleeveless dress, showing arms covered in intricate, colorful tattoos. This is the Amman that is coming, the future—inked women, beautiful gay boys, youth and subversion. Atef is strangely cheered by the thought.

On his way back, as he approaches the clinic entrance, he sees someone waving her arms. Souad.

"Baba! We've been looking for you," she cries. "The doctor's finished."

The office seems starker, the doctor grim behind his desk. A nurse has taken Alia to another room and Atef wishes he could go to her.

"Many of the tests won't be back for a few days. But I'd like to talk about preliminary impressions."

Madame Yacoub, the doctor says, is changing. Atef notices for the first time the diplomas hanging in their gilded frames, the calligraphy elegant and precise. They look imperial.

"It's not good news," the doctor says matter-of-factly.

They listen. The doctor's words fall, oil drops in water, beads, sliding over Atef. He watches his daughters' faces, his son's. The words float in and out, as though Atef is submerged, lifting his head above water every few minutes.

"In terms of cure . . . what will happen . . . to prepare yourself . . . research is showing . . ." Atef feels drunk watching the man's mouth move. Suddenly, everyone is rising, Karam shaking hands with the doctor.

"I'll see you next week," Munla says. "I'll have more information then." He shakes Atef's hand, and Atef doesn't want to let his hand go.

They find Alia in the waiting room. Outside, they stand dully in the atrium. Atef crosses and then uncrosses his arms. "I guess we go home now."

Souad sniffles. She embraces her mother.

Alia frowns and leans back, eyes her daughter sharply. "What have you done?"

And in spite of themselves, even as Souad cries, they all laugh.

The traffic is bad and by the time they reach the house—a silent car ride, even the radio crackling in protest—the sun has already set. Umm Najwa is standing outside the house, smoking. She drops the cigarette as they climb out of the car. She scans their faces hard, then nods. "Well."

In the foyer of the house, a metallic scent greets them. Souad drops her purse, sniffs.

"God*damn* it. I told them to turn the oven off." Her voice rises as she stalks off. "Did I or did I not tell you idiots—"

"I'm tired," Alia grumbles.

"I'll take you to bed," Atef says.

"No." Umm Najwa puts a gentle, firm hand on his arm. "I'll do it."

"It should be me," he says. His mouth is terribly dry. He tries to remember the last time he drank water. Hours ago. Before the hospital.

"You go sit. *Yalla*," Umm Najwa says to Alia. "Let's get you in bed."

"We should wait for him," she says brightly.

They watch her warily. Finally, Atef speaks. "Who?"

Alia tilts her head, looks at Atef as though he is the one who is confused. "Mustafa." Atef feels an invisible fist inside his stomach clench.

"He'll come later," Umm Najwa tells her soothingly. "Now we'll go and take a nice bath."

For moments after they disappear down the hallway, none of them, not Atef nor Karam nor Riham, say anything.

"It's always going to be like this," Karam says, the realization in his voice.

Riham shakes her head. "No." She begins to unwind her veil. "It's going to get worse." She speaks plainly, which is, Atef thinks, the most Riham of responses. To accept, to welcome the bad news.

He follows them into the living room, where Abdullah, Zain, and the girls sit. Souad stands in front of them, blocking the television. Everyone looks tense.

"It was one thing," Souad is saying. "One goddamn thing." The children are defiantly silent.

"What happened?" Karam asks.

"The chicken is burned. All of it." Souad glares; the children avoid her eyes. "I swear to God, I could entrust toddlers with more—"

"Mama, we get it," Zain snaps. Souad looks taken aback, then continues.

"Oh, you get it? Really? Then tell me why we're having *fries* for dinner."

"We can order in," Abdullah says.

"Souad," Riham murmurs. From the foyer, the sound of a door opening and shutting.

"What's that smell?" Budur walks in, carrying grocery bags. She had told Karam to go to the hospital with his family, respectfully busying herself for the day.

"They burned the chicken!"

"It's just a little crisp," Abdullah offers.

Linah and Manar whisper something and giggle. Across the sofa Abdullah lets out a snort of laughter.

"Shut up," Souad barks. "It's one thing to be useless, it's another to be insolent."

"We can order in?" Budur says innocently. Karam shakes his head at her.

"You're all spoiled!" Souad rants.

"Jesus Christ, no one wanted chicken anyway," Linah mutters.

"Linah!" Budur drops the bags. The anger is contagious, rushing like wildfire between them.

"Guys, guys." Karam holds his hands out. "Let's all take a breath, okay? We're tired, it's been a long day." He turns to the children beseechingly. "The doctor did some tests. It's not good."

The four faces transform.

"What happened?" Zain's brow furrows.

"Did you tell him about the memory thing?" Abdullah asks.

"It's Alzheimer's," Souad spits out. Atef wants to hit her. He watches the children—what children?—grow dismayed. Budur gasps. Zain blinks and ducks his head, and Atef wants to hug him, the boy always first to tears.

"Souad!" Riham admonishes.

"Are they sure?" Manar looks stunned. She turns to Karam. "What does that mean?"

Karam opens his mouth but Souad rushes on, furious. "It means she needs help and she's going to keep forgetting things and what she needs is good grandchildren, not idiots who sit around watching this *shit* and not following directions—"

"*Souad.*"

"—so instead of false shocked sympathy, maybe you could help out, all of you, instead of tramping around at night and drinking and smoking weed and—"

As she speaks, something happens to the four children, a hardening, their faces bricking over. Atef can see it coming. "Enough," he implores.

Too late. Manar hisses: "Oh, as if you even love Teta in the first place."

For a moment, there is a sensation of suspension. Free fall.

"Manar, *habibti*," Riham begins.

"No, no, let her talk. She hates me."

"I don't *hate* you—what are you, five?"

"She doesn't mean—"

"Zain, stay out of it."

The voices rise. The children sit up and suddenly they are divided. Alliances between the children—*what children?*—and the adults. Atef realizes he has been lumped together with the adults and wants to argue the injustice of that. Budur takes a step forward, distraught.

"Everyone's upset," she calls over the bickering. "And saying unnecessary things. Unkind things. We just need to—"

"This has nothing to *do* with you," Linah says acidly to her mother. "Why are you always involving yourself in everything?"

"This isn't helping anyone," Budur says.

A low, sarcastic snort. "Oh, give me a fucking break."

"Linah!" Karam yells.

"*What?*" Linah hurls back.

"We're sitting here," Manar says, "worried about Teta, trying to distract ourselves, then you guys come home and start screaming hysterically about chicken."

"Like they're going to understand," Linah tells her.

"Wasted breath."

"Goddamn it, Linah," Karam begins, but there is no time, because the others are already speaking, louder, louder, their voices a cacophony.

"You guys are always making a big deal out of nothing! This is just like last summer."

"Leave her alone!"

These are mine, Atef thinks. *These children.*

"*Kis ikhtkom*," Souad hisses in Arabic. "You barbarians."

"Oh God, here we go."

Atef feels the sound gathering before he makes it, a squall between his ribs.

"*Enough!*" he roars.

Everyone falls silent, staring at him—gentle Jiddo who rarely speaks, quiet with his peppermint candies, who sits in armchairs and watches television—with newfound amazement.

He finds Souad and Karam sitting on the veranda, swaying back and forth on the swing. The sky has darkened and stars are visible. They look chastised, a duo of misbehaving children. He thinks of what Linah said, all the things he doesn't know of their lives.

"Baba," Souad begins. "That was . . ." Her voice trails off. Finally, she pats the swing next to her. "Sit."

There is a pack of cigarettes on her lap and she taps one out; Karam takes another.

"Don't smoke," she tells him, exhaling a milky stream.

"Okay," Karam says, touching the cigarette tip to a flame.

"Insubordinate." Souad turns to Atef. "I tried."

Atef stretches his legs out, his left loafer falling onto the floor. He inhales greedily, wants one himself, but it always hurts his throat.

"Look at that," Souad says. Atef thinks she is referring to the smoke, but when he turns to her, she is gazing at the sky, the yellowish stars.

"Which one's the North Star?" he asks. "I can never tell."

"You find the Dipper." Holding the cigarette steady between her teeth, Souad extends her arm. "And then you trace the line. Follow the pointer stars. There." Atef follows his daughter's finger and suddenly he sees it, bright, higher in the sky than the others.

Atef lets himself picture the courtyard of the nearby mosque, the rustle of olive trees, the blank stone of the graves. Death in rows. His son once told him about a cemetery plot in Boston where seven, eight generations of a family were buried. Karam marveled at the concept, full centuries of family buried in the same dirt. Here, there was only Salma and Widad, the aunts that moved here from Nablus. No one knows where Mustafa was buried. Atef, when his time comes, will be buried here as well. What about his children, he thinks, would they be buried in America? Beirut? What about the grandchildren? The thought of their death startles him and he twists his mouth, admonishes himself with a silent *God forbid.*

His daughter's laughter is the balloon string tugging him earthward. It pulls him back into himself. He and Karam turn to her, curious.

"Remember that black dress? That time at Khalto Widad's house for dinner? How she stood up to leave and when we asked her why, she said—"

"'I hate this collar,'" Karam supplies. "'A hundred dinars to itch like hell.'"

The bubble of laughter between them grows into a hysterical giggle. Souad is the first to pop it, her gasp of laughter suddenly turning into a sob. Atef feels the weight of his daughter droop against him. She puts an arm around his shoulder, tucks her chin on it. He remembers her monkeyish limbs as a child, the way she would stick her tongue out at passersby on the street. "Baba," she whispers. He waits but there is nothing else.

The veranda door slides open; Riham steps out in front of the swing. She stares at them for a second.

"Not now, Riham." Souad ashes the cigarette. "No lectures on smoking."

Riham holds her arm out, wiggles her fingers.

"Gimme." The three of them gape at her.

"Have you lost your mind?"

Riham waits, her arm extended. Souad glances at Karam, then erupts into laughter. She hands over the cigarette, looking at her sister, astonished.

"Is this happening? Am I hallucinating?"

Riham puts the cigarette between her lips; they watch her take a long, solid drag, like an inmate on furlough. Tilting her head back, she holds the smoke for a second before blowing it all out in one exhale.

"Mother," Souad says, her voice stunned, "of God. Who the fuck *are* you?"

"Souad," Atef says automatically.

"Sorry, Baba."

"What?" Riham asks innocently. She flicks the cigarette; the four of them watch it arch over the veranda railing. There is laughter in her voice, a girlish joy at surprising them. "It's been a long day."

ATEF REMAINS OUTSIDE after his children leave. Alia, Karam, the grandchildren. His mind darts and then skips. What is there left to think about? So the children know. The grandchildren know. Weariness settles over him and he repeats it: *They know, they know.* It relieves him of a certain weight. So they've seen their parents up close, as one does with statues in Florence. The cracked toes and chalky masonry.

Suddenly he is asleep. He accepts this fact, understands it as he understands that where he is now—standing on a sunlit street corner, cars honking around him—is a perfectly reasonable place to be.

Of course he is here. He looks down and sees his hands are unlined. The hands of a young man.

"Atef." The voice is low and soft and laughing. It is Alia. She is impossibly young. She looks almost like a child, wearing a long swirling skirt, her black hair cut close to her chin. *This is my life*, he thinks, *this street corner.* He remembers the skirt. He recalls his wife walking toward him, smiling, music drifting from the open window of a car. Looking around, he sees the grocery store, the familiar lot. Kuwait.

"Out of oranges again." That voice once more, almost seductive. "I'll bring you some back from Amman." She takes his hand in her own.

The oranges. Atef remembers abruptly, violently. He hasn't thought of them, he knows, since that day. He remembers the glowing spheres, Alia pulling them out of her suitcase after a summer with her mother, packed between socks and bras, but he knows, even as he clasps her hand, that the memory is false. A lie. She never brought any back. But he remembers the promise, his heart light to hear her laughter, even as he dreaded her trip. All this time, a part of him was waiting for the gift.

"You're going to forget." He hears himself speak. Immediately her hand goes slack and Alia stops. Her expression is a mixture of admiration and pity. She places a hand on his cheek and he is overpowered by nostalgia. For this. For this moment—for those years, his young wife's hand. For Kuwait. For everything as it used to be. Because he knows that the dream is about to end, that it will all be over in a minute.

She keeps her hand against his cheek. *Speak*, he wants to scream, *quickly, there is no time left.*

"*Habibi*," she says. Dark hair perfectly coiffed, plum lipstick, those beautiful legs. "I can't stay."

Atef wakes with a jolt, like someone being shaken, but when he looks around, there is nothing of the dream. Everything unaltered.

Just him on the swing, the swish of traffic from the distance, the stars threaded between telephone poles. The road, the honking, Alia—he can still feel the heat of the Kuwaiti sun. He touches his face and it is wet. It feels like he has been crying for days. He rubs at his eyes, embarrassed.

He expects to find Souad and Riham in the living room. But there is no one there. *Bedrooms*, he thinks. He wonders where the grandchildren have gone.

The house, slapped silent after the earlier fight. From the hallway Atef can hear muffled tones and the sound of the mournful, folksy music Manar prefers. He moves in that direction.

"*Allah*." The word pops out of his mouth.

Alia. Slumped on the armchair. She must have come back out by herself. There is a dusting of egg yolk on her chin. Only the lamp is on, grotesquely shadowing her face. For a moment he is still, cannot bear to touch her. He moves slowly toward her. She is dead, he realizes.

Suddenly there is a rustling sound; it takes a few seconds for him to understand it is coming from his wife's throat. Not dead. Asleep. Her chest is moving, he sees. As if to punctuate her aliveness, she lets out a long snore.

Atef feels oddly let down. He had prepared for an epiphany. He reaches down and strokes her hair, but the gesture is forced. He knows if she wakes, she will snap at him.

The only light comes from the kitchen. From that room he can hear voices calling out. Laughter. He walks toward the noise hungrily. At the edge of the hallway, he stands still, peering through the door. The door is slightly ajar and the voices of the grandchildren are audible.

". . . so fucked."

"She called me Yasmin this morning. I don't even know who that is."

"It's probably a dead friend of hers. So fucking morbid."

"Remember how she used to scold us? Earlier I set a mug down and jumped, thinking she'd come out."

"'Don't they use coasters in Amrika?'" Their laughter is kind.

"God." Manar's voice sobers. "This house feels like a mausoleum. I told Gabe last night, if he got sick I'd burn the house down. It's just too sad. It's like she's this living ghost, moving from room to room. I don't know how he stands it."

They are talking about him, Atef realizes.

"He loves her," Abdullah's voice reproaches.

Manar falls silent with the rest. Atef can hear them thinking about his love.

"But doesn't it feel"—here a long pause—"so small?"

Atef hears the tremor in Manar's voice. He remembers an argument years ago, between her and Abdullah, when she'd stood up during dinner and yelled at him, *Even a saint can be a dick.* Alia had told the story over and over, laughing.

"Maybe it's not about being small or big." Linah takes a breath, then exhales; Atef can smell a cigarette. "Maybe it's like becoming part of someone. Like there's no you that exists without them."

"She's right." Zain pauses. "It's what he always wrote about."

Atef shoots upright, his ears burning. He cranes forward to hear his grandson's sentence.

". . . He has to remember for the both of them now."

HE FLEES TO the garden, the familiar maze of shrubs and trees, stumbles in the dark for the familiar dip of land that leads to the fig tree, where he sits.

Of course he'd known about the letters. After the boxes went to Beirut, he'd realized too late the letters were in them. He'd stopped writing them years before, but the proximity was comforting, finding the brown spine of that book every now and then, knowing the life housed within.

He kept reminding himself to check the boxes when they visited

Beirut, but the summers were always whirlwinds, a hurricane of arguments and children running around, protests and roadblocks in the city. He'd remember on the plane home, vow to check the next time.

Years after the war, he finally did, quietly sneaking into the blue apartment's storage room while everyone went to the beach, going through every single box. It took hours, the air filled with dust and mold. He eventually found *A Lifecycle of Plants*, but it lay limply in his hands, flat. Just a regular book. The letters were gone.

His mind spun through possibilities. Alia? *Oh God. Oh God, please.* But no, she would've said something, would have thrown every single page in his face. His own children were unlikely culprits: Souad too uninterested, Riham too deferential, Karam too respectful.

The grandchildren, then.

He was stunned to find himself smiling. Slowly, then laughing, harder and harder, alone in the small room. It was the oddest thing: he didn't mind. It was like dropping the weight of a planet. Like finally stepping back.

What had they thought reading them? He will never know. To ask would be to spoil the whole thing, he thinks now. Better to give the world over intact, let them speculate. They know him. Yes. He is glad.

A FAINT GLOW from the veranda reaches the garden, outlining the rows he planted in the summer. He can see the silhouette of windflowers, their leaves spiky in the dusk light. *Your ridiculous flowers.*

She is leaving him. She has already left him. The rage is like a Roman candle lit from both ends. His mouth is dry. She is leaving him, just as her brother did. His fingers sink into the soil around him and he thinks of Nablus.

THAT DAY, half a century ago, the sun rose onto a cool and pink morning. Israel had invaded Gaza and the Sinai. There was fighting near the old city. Atef's skin prickled with anticipation. *It's happening,* he thought. *It's happening.* The air seemed tinted, hills vibrant in the light.

When he arrived at Salma's old house, Mustafa was sitting on the front stairs. His legs were tucked at an odd angle, to the side. The cigarette between his fingers was nearly out. Even when Atef bounded up the stairs, Mustafa kept his eyes on the ground.

"What are you doing out here?"

"Atef." The entreaty in Mustafa's voice wasn't unfamiliar. It flickered now and then, the oil-like insecurity beneath the veneer of all that was Mustafa—handsome, magnetic, loved. Atef felt a deep irritation. *Now of all times?*

"What are you doing out here?" he repeated. Mustafa flung the cigarette, his voice sinking soft as a boy's.

"I think we should leave."

Atef blinked. "Leave." He felt the word in his mouth, a flat stone.

"Go to Kuwait. Or Amman. We can drive into Jordan. The troops are falling back. Nablus is going to fall. We can be in Amman by dinnertime." He shifted his legs and Atef understood the awkward pose—at Mustafa's side was a small dark suitcase.

He was leaving. The imam flashed in Atef's mind, the men in the mosque, the blue and white flags everywhere. The flyers, posters that screamed *Arabs are animals, barbarians.* Leaving. He thought of the house behind Mustafa, Khalto Salma's house, of Alia, who would have given anything to be left behind. Who would have smashed the windows and salted the earth before leaving it. Mustafa's scared face.

Atef sought the thing that would hurt the most.

"You coward. You fucking *coward.*" Atef's voice shook and he heard every word crack, its own gunshot, watched the invisible trail of smoke, but it was too late. He was like a man possessed. *I need him, I need him, I need him,* his mind panted. "How long have you been planning this? You want to run to your sisters? Hide behind your mother's skirts?"

Mustafa froze. His eyes found Atef's in disbelief. Every muscle on his beautiful face tensed, the two men facing each other for a taut, arrested moment. Atef prepared himself for a punch. He urged himself for the final, horrible insult.

"You want to leave, leave. The men will stay."

Mustafa flinched; it was an unnecessary blow, like shooting a corpse one last time. His face opened like a window, saying everything, all that would come later: The soldiers would come to arrest them in three mornings, the men that would ravage Salma's house. The cells they would sleep and wake in for weeks. The electricity, Atef's flesh thrumming until he sang out Mustafa's name, tossed his name to the torturers, said his name to every question they asked.

How the last time Atef would see Mustafa alive, he would be kicking, kicking at a soldier, and Atef's stomach would turn, remembering how he'd called him a coward.

None of this had happened yet. In that moment, the bombs were falling elsewhere, Nablus was still quiet. It was morning and the world was changing. Mustafa finally moved; lifting an eyebrow, he rose, bowed his head sardonically to Atef, then turned and opened the front door. He swept inside, marking his choice. He dropped the bag in the foyer.

ATEF SHAKES WITH the desire to rewrite everything that happened. For years, that was his fiction. *Here is Palestine,* he would think. *Here are the streets we'd walk in Nablus, the neighborhood we grew up in. Here is everything we loved.*

With a mental brushstroke he re-creates it, everything, the voices of men hawking *bateekh, bateekh* on the roads, the marketplace cramped with sweating bodies. Mountains scooped out like melons, crags left bare, smoothed from centuries of wind and rain. Miles of land unspool, whole villages, houses as old as the earth itself.

Then he re-creates Mustafa. Every eyelash. His peppery smell. The spark of the cigarette landing in soil. The blue of Khalto Salma's front door, the way the frame was splintered.

Punch me, he wants to yell at Mustafa. *Tell me to fuck off, hit me in the face. Pick up that goddamn suitcase, walk down the driveway. I would've followed you. I would've followed you. Take me with you. You can save yourself. We can both live.*

But instead, Mustafa lifts his eyebrow and opens that door, and they both walk through it.

Atef can see his family move around in the house, their shadows flitting in the golden windows. Someone turns on the front porch light. It is cool outside, bracing, Atef's shirt too thin. His legs hurt from sitting too long. Above, the night sky is stippled as a speckled egg. In the breeze, the dying petals of windflowers rustle against one another like skirts. He always loved their yellow.

He moves like a fever, his body its own engine, flinging toward the flowers, hands blind in the dark, fumbling until he finds the spindly stems, their hopeful little throats. He pulls one out, then another. The stems are small in his fingers. A rock pricks his fingertip, the pain heady and welcome.

I'd burn the house down. Yes. Right down over your own head. He rips one windflower after the other out. His fingers begin to bleed.

"Jiddo."

He turns, panting. The four grandchildren stand in a row, watching him.

"Jiddo." Abdullah swallows. He is choosing his words delicately. "Mama and the rest are asking about you. They wanted us to bring you in."

"I had to pull them out." Atef gestures at the limp flowers. Abdullah looks alarmed. They move closer to the tree.

"She hates them," he manages. The grandchildren glance at one another. Linah moves first, the beads in her hair clanking together as she kneels in the dark. First Zain, then Abdullah follows, tugging at the flowers with her.

Atef watches them. He remembers the children years ago, putting on plays, organizing birthday songs. For one birthday they'd baked him a cake. A disaster. He'd eavesdropped outside as they'd fretted over the mess they'd made, worrying about the cracked eggs. He could have gone in and cleaned, or scolded them, but he was frozen, motionless in face of their beauty.

Zain and Linah set the flowers in a pile. He tries to imagine being their age. Sixteen. The impossibility of that youth. Manar walks over to Atef, kneels.

"Your grandmother used to live in a house with a garden. In Palestine. With her brother." Atef feels his breath catch. "I used to go there a lot."

He has to remember for the both of them. Yes. Atef continues talking. "A good house. There was a table under the trees. In the summer, we'd sit out there for hours."

Manar pulls her knees up, resting her chin on her hands. "Which house was this?"

"Your great-grandmother's. Khalto Salma." Atef can remember the sound the wind made as it rustled in the doorway, the magnificent rise of the house.

That house. The ones that came after. He thinks of them, instinctively touching the soil again. All the houses they have lived in, the *ibriks* and rugs and curtains they have bought; how many windows should any person own? The houses float up to his mind's eye like jinn, past lovers. The sloping roof of his mother's hut, the marbled tiles in Salma's kitchen, the small house he shared with Alia in Nablus. The Kuwait home. The Beirut apartments. This house, here in Amman. For Alia, some old, vanished house in Jaffa. They glitter whitely in his mind, like structures made of salt, before a tidal wave comes and sweeps them away.

"I thought I had more time—" Manar stops, embarrassed. Atef waits. "To ask her things."

"About what?"

His granddaughter shrugs. "Her life."

He can feel their eyes upon him. *Poor innocent things*, he thinks. What is a life? A series of yeses and noes, photographs you shove in a drawer somewhere, loves you think will save you but that cannot. Continuing to move, enduring, not stopping even when there is pain. *That's all life is*, he wants to tell her. *It's continuing.*

He thinks of his beautiful wife, that afternoon in her mother's garden, the mosque light he saw when he met her. Nablus, filled with flowers. How in love he was, with Mustafa, with his defiant sister, their house, their wealth. *I wanted all of it*, he wrote once. It was true.

"*Ya* Alia," he says aloud before stopping. He wants to tell her everything. "My poor girl." He has been crying without realizing it. His grandchildren are staring at him, Atef understanding that he is changing their lives, these children who will take this moment and make something of it, turn it into their own lives, remember on their deathbeds the cool air, the stars, their grandfather weeping under a fig tree.

"Jiddo," Manar says timidly. Atef sighs, turns to her.

"What?" He waits for the platitudes, comfort. But there is only silence. The four children facing him like an army. The girl takes a long breath.

"Stay out here," she tells him. Her voice is strong. "We'll tell them to leave you alone." Around them, the night pulses with wind and insects. "Stay out here a little longer."

The girl presses a gentle hand on his shoulder, and Atef does.

MANAR

JAFFA
September 2014

Madame, madame, you come here, we make best fish for you!"

"Fresh watermelon and cream!"

"You like lamb, madame? You like kibbeh?"

"*Shaar el banat!*"

The eager voices of waiters carry along the Jaffa port. They stand outside the restaurants, sweating in their suits. It is early evening, the sun nearly set, though the air is still hot and humid, thick with the saltiness that reminds Manar of Beirut. Her thighs are sticky beneath the long skirt. The morning sickness of the day—lasting well into the afternoon—has passed and she is hungry. The men smile as she walks by, shake tasseled menus in her direction. When she first arrived in Jerusalem, the chattiness of vendors had thrown her off and she'd respond automatically, more than once allowing herself to be shepherded into a café or a store.

But weeks have passed now, and Manar sees such banter as endearing, harmless. Especially because her time is nearly up; in less than a week she'll board a plane, spend endless hours over the Atlantic, and then be, unceremoniously, back in Manhattan.

She pauses in front of a restaurant. There is an ornate menu propped up and she scans the items—kibbeh, *samak harra, warak anab*. A small bald man appears at her side, speaking in Arabic.

"We have a back area with a wonderful view. We'll get you a table next to the water, you'll be able to feel the spray on your face!"

She smiles inwardly. She is used to such theatrics.

"Do you have *muhammara?*"

"Ah, Lebanese?" The man's smile widens. "Yes, yes, we'll make it. Special just for you!"

Manar lets herself be ushered through the restaurant, a gold tapestry spelling *Allah* spanning one side of the wall, and onto the veranda, where several small tables are, indeed, overlooking the Mediterranean. The view is astounding. Instinctively, as has become her habit in certain moments, her fingers clutch her purse, which houses—past the bottle of prenatal vitamins, her passport—the soft, frayed pages of the letters. Her rabbit's foot.

"Be good to her," the man says to a young waiter. "She's a Lebanese sister."

Manar resists the impulse to correct him. It is exasperating how easily her accent gives her away. It is like a fingerprint, something branding her, exposing her upbringing—Lebanese father, Palestinian mother, Paris, America. A mutt, Seham, her best friend, calls her.

Back in Manhattan, she and Seham meet for drinks after work, sometimes with the other girls they know from school, girls drawn to one another like magnets, commiserating over shared upbringings. They are all young and smart, most of them Palestinian by origin but raised in Denmark, Australia, Seattle, with neutral names like Maya and Dana.

"No wonder you're messed up. You've been emotionally code-switching all your life," Seham likes to say, and while Manar used to protest, lately she has been accepting it, reveling in the notion that her problems, the disarray of her life, all spring from her heritage.

The flight to Tel Aviv had been long and uncomfortable, the rows of seats filled with Hasidic men and exhausted parents with toddlers. Manar surprised herself by falling asleep for several hours, but somewhere over Portugal, the plane began to rock and she shot upright. Her stomach turned. She barely made it to the cramped toilet before vomiting heartily.

Afterward, she exhaled and spat into the sink. Washing her hands, she avoided her reflection but caught a sidelong blur nonetheless—tangled hair, pale face.

"Christ, Bleecker much?" she mumbled to herself. It was an old joke between her and her cousin Linah, a nod to the sloppy NYU girls spilling out of bars in Manhattan.

Back in her seat, Manar leaned her forehead against the icy window, shut her eyes. She felt a sharp homesickness for Manhattan, though she had been gone for only half a day. The tree-lined streets of Greenpoint, their apartment perpetually smelling of dim sum.

And Gabriel. Sweet, lovely Gabe. His thinning hair, his ex-wife and alimony. His bewildered face when she told him about the trip.

"You want to go *now?*"

"There isn't going to be a better time," she had said.

"There lit-*e*-rally"—his fingers tapped the syllables in the air; the man could veer toward the pedantic when frazzled—"couldn't be a worse time."

Five weeks earlier, he had filled their apartment with lilies and popped a champagne cork, though they filled her glass with Sprite. He got down on one knee and cried a little, held out a hand for hers. She said yes, but he made her repeat it two, three times, until they were both laughing.

"I want to see it," she said.

"But it's not going anywhere," he countered. "What's the urgency?"

But that was precisely it—the urgency was there was *no urgency.* There never would be. For years she watched news reports of the settlements, the phosphorus dropped over Gaza, camps swelling with eyeless children. Anger held her up with burning little hands, assembled itself into chants of *Free Palestine, free, free Palestine* with the rest of the Justice for Palestine group during Apartheid Week at Columbia. For years she kept a poster taped above her desk of a young man mid-hurl, a stone flying in the air. Along the border were sentences calligraphed in Arabic. His arm arched like an arrow, his face hidden beneath a scarf. The stone had just left his fingertips. A part of her knew such posters were romanticism, envy at best. Still, she hoped he hit what he was aiming for.

The sun dips into the sea. From Manar's table, she can make out a fisherman on a distant rock. At the table next to hers, a brunette in an expensive-looking dress sits with two men, laughing and talking. There are two bottles of arak on the table, the plates littered with fish bones and napkins. The men are handsome, fair-skinned. The bearded one looks over at Manar several times and smiles.

Manar busies herself with the menu, aware of how sensual the air feels, the beauty of the seascape around her. Throughout her time here, the awful facts—checkpoints, soldiers, camps—are often softened by captivating landscapes.

"Yes, madame? Are you ready?" An older waiter appears at her side. Something about the flower he has tucked into his lapel, jaunty and red, reminds Manar of her father.

She smiles up at him. "*Muhammara.* And whatever else you recommend."

"Ah, what a responsibility." The man pretends to study the sea, then snaps his fingers. Even his profile has something of Elie in it, the lifted chin, the hawkish nose. "*Hammour*, grilled, with green beans and potatoes, hummus on the side."

"Perfect."

"And anything to drink? We have wine, arak . . ."

"Just water, please."

"Water," the waiter repeats. He approves.

Wherever she goes, she keeps the letters in her purse, wrapped in tissue paper and bound with twine.

Zain gave them to her the last time he visited from Boston. "Take these with you," he said, holding out the parcel, and she blinked back tears. They were his prized possession, *prized* being the operative word, as he had stolen—*borrowed,* he insisted—the letters years ago and never returned them.

"Zuzu," she began, but he held a hand up.

"You should have them out there. You can try to find things in the letters, maybe even the house."

She had felt the urge then to tell him everything, about the baby, about Gabe's proposal, confessing—*Yes, he was married, but it wasn't working anyway, she went back to Iowa with her family, I wasn't sure if I wanted to keep the baby but I can't seem to get rid of it, I love him but he's so American, sometimes I feel suffocated by everything I have to explain to him*—all the things she will have to tell the family. But she simply held her hand out, took the bundle.

"Thanks."

The letters have stayed with Zain all these years. During the summers he brings them to Beirut, where the family gathers for long weeks. The four of them—Linah, Zain, Manar, and Abdullah—sit out on the balcony, lighting cigarettes and discussing the letters. Abdullah helped translate the passages from Arabic, as the rest of them confused tenses and verbs. They talk about the letters like a book, their grandfather writing about the war in Nablus, his years in Kuwait. The people he refers to—a dead great-uncle, old friends, their own parents—seem as exotic as characters in a movie, and as unlikely.

She knows some of the passages by heart. *I worry about the children. Sometimes I wake up in this city, look out at the desert. I swear I can hear the* adan *in Nablus. I can hear Abu Nabil hawking his bread. Brother, I can smell your cigarette, hear you telling me to hurry.*

They come up with theories, what he has told their grandmother, what is secret. They're not supposed to have the letters, they know this much. The filching has made them precious.

• • •

Manar's status as the other woman was a technicality; Gabe's wife had already left when Manar met him. Manar loved his neuroses, his flaws, the smattering of hair on his shoulders and back that he hated, saying it made him feel beastlike. His tenderness. He wept openly during wedding speeches and made a point, every single night before bed, of cupping her face and saying *I love you.*

She told Gabriel everything. About her chaotic childhood, chubby daughter of bickering parents, dragged from Paris to Boston to Beirut. Half Palestinian, half Lebanese. How she would make herself ill on the first day of school—the other children always mocked her glasses, called her May-nard—once drinking curdled milk that had cramped her stomach for days. She told Gabe about her parents' divorce, her love for her father and her disdain for her mother.

After the divorce, she claimed her father for herself, but sometimes she is envious of Zain's resentment, the way he still calls him Elie instead of Baba or Dad. She wishes she could wash her hands of her father, fault him for everything. But that would be relinquishing a lovely, familiar topography. She told Gabe of the truce they'd called, she and her mother, though she still felt waves of rage toward her at times. Of how a fight over parking last year ended with Manar, twenty-four years old, screaming like a teenager, *We weren't your children, we were your audience.*

She told him about sitting in classrooms that smelled of chalk and sweat listening to teachers chatter about Salinger and decimal fractions and the ancient Romans, or listening to her friends during recess, all of whom were awfully in love with some boy or another, but how only half of Manar was there. How her history professor once said *Arabs* instead of *terrorists* while discussing 9/11, and everyone turned to stare at Manar, her skin burning like a flag.

She told him about how the only times in school that she'd felt crystallized into her whole self were when she walked down the silent hallways, stepped into the empty bathroom, and looked at herself multiplied in the small mirrors above the sinks, the smell around her bleach and piss.

"It's just three weeks," she'd told Gabe. "I'll be fine."

"Let me come with you."

"Gabe," she finally said. "Please."

He was silent for a while. She knew she was hurting him, that he wanted to be part of this. *You can't*, she didn't say. *You don't understand what it's like.* Darling Gabe, born and bred in white suburban America.

He spoke quietly. "This isn't the time to be wandering across the world alone."

Not alone enough.

Her truth shamed her; the decision came after she'd found out about the pregnancy.

Palestine was something raw in the family, a wound never completely scabbed over. Her grandparents rarely mentioned it. Manar's plan of visiting was always derailed by something: her grandmother's illness, meeting Gabe, Zain's graduation.

Only the children discuss it, during the Beirut summers. For years, Manar nursed an image of herself, dusty, solemn, walking onto Palestinian soil, squinting in the sun. So when she peed on that stick and a little blue cross appeared, marking her to this new, alien life, that image flashed before her. She couldn't explain it to Gabe. She had to go now; she is as alone as she'll ever be again.

When she told her grandfather about her trip, he said only that she should be careful.

"You don't know what can happen." Manar heard static for a second, the line faltering from Amman to Manhattan.

"Does Teta want anything?" Even asking the question made Manar flinch, thinking of her grandmother in her state: convinced the maids were spies, that Saddam was coming back.

"Alia," her grandfather called out. "Manar asks if you want anything from Falasteen." A mumble. "Falasteen." There was a long pause, then her grandmother's muffled voice, punctuated by a sharp, rare laugh from her grandfather.

"She says, whatever they ask you, give them hell."

In the late afternoons, Manar wanders through the Old City, finds cramped teashops to sit in, listens to voices haggling over the price of sandals and soap.

Every weekend she packs her worn backpack, walks east to the bus station near Damascus Gate, boards one of the buses to a different city. Tel Aviv, Haifa, Hebron. And the West Bank—that concrete wall a menace, always jolting her freshly when it appears—Bethlehem, Ramallah, Nablus.

These places she has read about, circles on a map, suddenly emerge, smelling of fruit and car exhaust. *I'm in Ramallah*, she marvels to herself. *This is Haifa.* Her pang for Palestine had always been an amorphous thing. It was a hat rack for all her discontent. But suddenly Palestine is real. It is filled with people who have her hair and voice; people *live* here, she realizes stupidly. They wake under this sun, celebrate anniversaries, march at funerals, watch settlements and checkpoints multiply. While she was busy sleeping with American boys and writing essays about the diaspora, there were people over here *being Palestinian.*

At checkpoints, she shows her passport, waits for the click of fanged metal doors; the Israeli soldiers always nod her through. She tries to keep her face impassive, to communicate scorn in her walk. *The passport is my key*, she writes Zain once.

It is difficult to capture this trip in her e-mails. Certain evenings she sits at the Internet café near the hotel, at a loss what to write to friends and family and Gabe. She uses words like *arresting* and *eye-opening*—how to explain the rows of teenagers in uniforms, the women sandwiched together in checkpoint lines, the confusion of being hit on by Israeli men, the way every Palestinian she has met has been kind but pitying, as though aware *She is not like us*—and clicks Send.

A part of her had fantasized that the trip would restore in her some faith, a land to which she'd feel unflinching attachment. She wanted to be shaken to the core. She'd envisioned reading Darwish in seaside cafés, kneeling to gather handfuls of soil into her pocket.

But from the beginning, nothing has felt as it *should.* When the plane intercom crackled on, a man's voice murmuring, *We are landing in Tel Aviv Ben Gurion International Airport*, everything seemed to accelerate. It all happened in minutes, the flight attendants plucking headphones, fastening overhead bins, the Hasidic man across the aisle rocking with prayer. Manar pressed her forehead against the window, craning to see the strips of ordinary land. From the air, it could be anywhere—grids of buildings, highways spidering like veins between the swaths of reddish earth, the slate blue of the Mediterranean flicking against the shoreline.

Her mind was strangely blank as she watched the landscape. She clasped her purse.

The passport control lines were long and slow. Manar watched American-looking families smile up at the officers in the glass booth, lugging their diaper bags and backpacks. A trio of tanned girls giggled at something a security guard said. Passports flitted between the officers' fingers like birds, the pages flipped through, stamps steady and final. *When it's your turn,* Seham had told her, *be polite. Avoid eye contact. Smile.*

When her moment came, Manar slid her passport under the glass and waited. Her officer was thick-browed, a younger Pacino.

"Manar," he mused. He rifled through it, the pastel, faded stamps on the pages, paused at a recent one. Even through the glass Manar recognized the Arabic lettering. Beirut. The man narrowed his eyes toward her.

"Arab?"

He directed her, in accented English, to a waiting room, a cordoned-off space with a mounted television, where a heavyset female officer took Manar's passport and told her to sit.

Several other people sat in plastic chairs lining the dirty windows. *They'll have you sit with the other Arabs.* Across from Manar, an older woman fanned herself with a newspaper, jiggling her leg and cursing quietly.

"Every time. Those dogs." When an officer appeared, asked her to follow him, the woman spoke to him in Hebrew, then, switching back to Arabic, muttered, "Of course, Your Majesty, of course."

The television played a news report in Hebrew, footage of a fire somewhere. Manar waited. Her legs were cramped from the long flight but she was afraid to stand and stretch, then ashamed of that fear.

After nearly three hours, a young officer appeared in the doorway and said her name. He looked twenty. She rose, her heart pounding, the leather purse strap sticky between her fingers. The man led her down a drab-looking corridor, several doors ajar.

"In here." The room was windowless, painted the shade of milk. There was a long table, a metal chair on either side. Manar sat, the man barely glancing up as he shuffled through a file of papers, her passport clipped to the top. "So." He looked up. "Why are you here?"

They want to make it hard, Seham had said. *That way, we don't want to come back.*

The questions were predictable, repetitive. He asked about her family, where she grew up, her life in New York. There was a smattering of acne around his mouth; she could tell from the way his fingers hovered over his jawbone he was self-conscious about it. In spite of herself, she felt a tug of sympathy.

"And your father?" he asked.

In Connecticut, writing bad novels, she wanted to say, but jokes seemed unwelcome. "In America as well."

Where had her mother been born? When had her grandfather left Nablus? Where did her mother live now? Why were there so many Lebanese stamps in her passport? Had her grandfather ever returned to Israel? What precisely did her grandfather do in Amman?

The interest in her grandfather was disorienting. Her tall and quiet *jiddo*, always clicking peppermint candies against his teeth when he sipped tea. During the summers, entire evenings could go by without him speaking.

When did her grandfather get a Jordanian passport? Who purchased the house in Amman? When had her grandmother left Nablus?

"I don't know," Manar said to the officer over and over.

He looked at her with disdain. "You don't know?"

He brought her water and crackers. He asked her to write down where each grandparent was born and she paused, uncertain. *Nablus*, she wrote for her mother's parents and, beside it, a question mark. Was it Nablus? That was where they left, she remembered. Had there been somewhere before that? She racked her memory. A faint nausea began to trickle over her like a raw egg.

Pick your battles, *Manar*, she could hear Seham saying.

But she was hot and tired and thirsty and was already speaking, her voice shrill and angry: "My grandfather's in his eighties. He hasn't been here"—she couldn't bring herself to say *Israel*—"in decades. What's the point of these questions?"

The young man looked up sharply, a frisson of something—contempt, distaste—rippling through his eyes.

"It's security, miss."

He left her for a while, twenty, thirty minutes. She could hear voices in the hallway, someone laughing. The floor was made of ugly diamond-shaped tiles. She began counting them, then gave up. Finally the door opened. The officer set her passport on the table.

"Your purse," he said. "I have to search it."

Everything was excruciatingly slow, her own fingers lifting the purse strap from her lap, his fingers opening the flap, pulling out lipstick, vitamins, several sticks of gum. She watched him rifle around, finding the zippered pocket. She could feel the jagged metal beneath her own fingertips. He pulled out the bundle of letters. For a moment, neither of them spoke.

"This?" He looked up at her sharply. He unwound the twine. "What are these?"

An image of Zain's face, trusting, floated up to her. The lines upon lines, an entire history in words. She imagined her grandfather's story in this man's hand, her *jiddo*'s tidy rows of writing. His life. They'd take the letters. Linah and Zain would kill her.

"Miss?"

Help me, she whispered silently and something stirred, miraculously, leaping through her esophagus, her stomach darting, splitting her until she bent over. Vomit streamed from her mouth like relief, hot and toxic, splattering the ugly tiles. She could feel the man's shocked eyes on her. Her breath was ragged.

"I'm pregnant," she said triumphantly.

The officer looked irritated, as though they were playing a game and she had cheated. *Bullshit*, he seemed to be thinking, but was too afraid to say it. She could see his mind whirring, imagining potential articles on the *Huffington Post*, lawsuits, miscarriages.

Not worth it, his shrug said. He dropped the letters back into her purse, pushed it toward her with the heel of his hand.

He stood, nodded behind her, toward the door, the long hallway, the passport lines, the rows of cabs, the land.

"Go," he said.

Nothing quite as dramatic happened after the airport, but the feeling of things being *off* has persisted. Everywhere she goes, she feels surplus, unnecessary. Her first time in the Old City, she was fascinated by the Wailing Wall. She froze, watching the throngs moving like water, toward the wall, away from the wall. A group of young people near the entrance wore uniforms. The female soldiers were unsettlingly beautiful.

In every guidebook she read, there was the same truism—the

magic of Jerusalem. How you would walk through it and breathe history. How you could feel it in the stones. Reading the books, Manar felt a rising excitement. Would she touch it then, finally? That parched, grasping part of herself, thirsty to feel something that would link her, in some ancestral way, to the world?

But Al-Aqsa had been a disappointment, the Holy Sepulcher as well. Though each marketplace was perfumed with spices, each mosque framed with beautiful calligraphy, she felt uninspired. Sometimes she felt a swell as the sun set over Jerusalem, the city alive with its low, intimate thrumming. But the moment was always interrupted by something, a motorcade whizzing by, a child's cry, her own phone ringing.

It reminded her of vacations as a child. She prepared for cities the way she prepared for exams, reading about them, researching history and sightseeing, and something in this erudite approach left her floundering when she actually got there. Before a trip to Quebec or the Grand Canyon or London, she'd take out books from her school library, devour images of mountains, skyscrapers, fill her mouth with borrowed adjectives (*stunning*, *colossal*, *breathtaking*, *otherworldly*) so that when she finally arrived, there was nothing left to see, nothing left for her—already prepared for the awe—to say.

Nablus was the biggest disappointment of all. She'd expected to feel kinship. Though her grandparents' stories were infrequent, this was where they grew up, where they had met and wed.

Manar had formed an image of Nablus: an expansive, generous land peppered with olive groves, valleys between yellow hills. In one of the photos, her younger grandparents grinning into the camera, she could see slivers of indigo sky, bunches of wildflowers.

But there were no wildflowers. The bus from Ramallah was musty, cramped with the sweating bodies of middle-aged men. Outside the window, swaths of land blurred by, blanched hills dotted with trees. *Biblical*, Manar thought, of the groves, the occasional cluster of goats or donkeys.

A prickle of claustrophobia as the bus drove into Nablus—those endless cliffs and hills, the vast rising at either side. It made her feel caved in. Landlocked.

She'd looked for her great-grandmother's house for hours, finally showing an old photograph of Alia's to marketplace vendors who shrugged and gave vague directions toward the cliffs. She walked and walked until she saw a pale minaret in the distance, remembered in a flash her grandfather mentioning a mosque, and headed for it; she eventually arrived at a row of houses and, suddenly, there it was: the pitched roof from the photographs, a hedge of jasmine bushes. A house unmistakably shaped like the one in the photograph, though different, the front yard smaller, the exterior repainted blue, the wire clothesline gone.

Manar stood there for a long time, holding the photograph in her hand, her grandmother and grandfather half a century younger, a bearded man next to them, his arm casually draped around Alia. Her great-uncle. Mustafa. He'd died a long time ago, before any of them had been born. Manar looked at the grainy photograph, then the real house, then back again. She bade herself to feel something, some internal tectonic shift. But she just felt like an interloper, trespassing on memories that had nothing to do with her.

This morning, Manar decided on a whim to visit Jaffa. The city has a pacifying effect on her, the shoreline jutting out to meet the sea. The city is worn, shabby but enchanting, the walls scribbled with graffiti. Up close, Jaffa shows its age.

Even here in the restaurant, the tables are cracked, the wood faded. The waiter brings Manar her fish decorated with lemon slices, a sprig of mint tucked at the corner of the plate. She is touched.

"Enjoy," he tells her.

Manar lemons and salts the fish. She chews slowly, the tastes a revelation—lemon peel, coriander, mint. She watches the coastline, the trio at the nearby table. The woman has twisted her dark hair into a bun and, in the dusk light, her profile is regal. She makes a dismissive gesture toward the men, frowns. The three of them speak in animated, accented English but the waves are loud, and Manar can hear only snippets of the conversation—something about a day trip, a lost suitcase, the woman's desire to go to Petra.

As the sky darkens, the waiters light lanterns. The effect is romantic. On the beach, some hundred yards away, a veiled woman sits with two small children on a bed sheet spread over a rock, all of them eating fruit.

The bearded man catches Manar looking and smiles at her. He lifts his glass, raises it in a gesture of salute. Manar does the same, then looks away, her cheeks hot.

THE FAMILY on the beach has finished eating. Manar watches the mother fold a shawl over one of the children's shoulders and brush her hair back. At the nearby table, the woman stretches and yawns.

"Ariana," the unbearded man says. The woman's brow furrowed.

"Don't start with me, Robert," she says, sipping at her lit cigarette. *Italian*, Manar thinks.

"It's just for a day. Two, max." The man is blond, generic, with a British accent. He looks like the men who flood the financial district in Manhattan, except that he is dressed like an expat—cotton pants, pale button-down shirt. He smiles at the woman even as she rolls her eyes and looks over the water.

The mother on the beach, Manar knows, is married, has a husband somewhere, a home where she folds blankets and sprinkles salt over pots of rice. She wouldn't have met her husband at a bar or on vacation but through her family, their fathers deeming the match suitable. Manar envisions a simple ceremony, matrons ululating as she entered the courtyard, her father taking the husband aside—a tall, nervous man—and whispering a few stern but kind words, telling him to take care of his daughter.

Unexpectedly, Manar's eyes well up, and her plate, the beach, blur into greens and yellows. She ducks her head, blinks.

She won't have that with Gabe. Her father, indistinguishable from most white men in Connecticut save for his trim mustache, is absent. Her mother will be confused but happy for her. Her grandfather will say nothing. Manar will never have, she knows, the stability of a preordained life. They have all forfeited that—her friends, Linah, even her own mother—most of all Manar herself. By saying she wanted a different life, by choosing the pubs, flirtations with strange men, and, yes, the sex. The night after night of dating, shaking the hands of men who would break her heart, wearing lipstick and straightening her back. A pregnancy out of wedlock. Yes, she thinks. Something has been lost.

"AMERICAN?"

Manar blinks. Over at the next table, the woman is staring directly at her. Her voice is throaty.

"Uh." Beautiful women make Manar anxious. "From all over. Partly from Palestine."

The woman's face breaks into a smile. The men are smoking, eyeing Manar with interest. "We work at an NGO here. I'm Ariana." Her accent is lilting. "What are you doing in Jaffa? Travels?" She pronounces it Yaffa, like an Arab.

Manar nods. "Just visiting."

The bearded man speaks, stubbing his cigarette out. "We're going to a festival near the water. Some friends put together a concert, like a fundraiser. It's not far from here."

Ariana props her elbow on the table, drops her chin into her hand. She smiles, alluringly.

"You should come."

THE WALK is short and pleasant, and though the sun has set, there is a lingering heat. The men and Ariana bicker. The bearded man is Jimmy, the blond Adam. They have known each other for years. The four of them walk in a row, taking up the entire width of the sidewalk. From the way Adam often glances at Ariana, Manar deduces a history, some unrequited love or a former fling. Jimmy, however, looks at Manar when he talks, his mouth frankly sensual. In her loose, flowing blouse, she isn't showing yet.

"When I first moved here, I gave myself one month, two, tops. All the shit here, those goddamn checkpoints—I figured I wouldn't be able to handle it."

"Then what happened?" Manar has heard a hundred versions of this story since her arrival.

Jimmy shrugs. His shoulders strain against the thin fabric of his shirt. "Fell in love. All of us did. It breaks your heart, but it's impossible to leave."

"Don't let him bullshit you," Ariana calls. "Jimmy's about as romantic as a steak knife."

"You the pot or the kettle, Annie?" His teeth gleam as he smiles.

"Don't call me that." The sulkiness in Ariana's voice betrays their dynamic. Adam in love with Ariana. Ariana secretly drawn to Jimmy. Jimmy a free agent.

Which makes me *what?* Though Manar knows the answer—random girl at the restaurant, tagging along for some music and company, then disappearing back into her life and out of theirs. Something about the simplicity of it is perversely appealing.

"There." Adam points. Manar can see a twinkle of lights up ahead. Music pulses from the distance, a mix of electronica and *dirbakeh*.

"Quick toke?" Jimmy fumbles in his pocket and they all stop obediently.

Jimmy lights a slim white joint, and the scent of hashish fills the air. They each take long, luxuriant tokes. When Adam hands it to Manar, she is reluctant but inhales deeply, overcompensating, and is rewarded by an instant rush. She silently apologizes to Gabe. *One toke*, she reasons. *It can't hurt.*

"Christ."

Jimmy laughs amiably. "Strong shit, eh?" When Manar hands him the joint this time, she returns his open stare, feels her entire being buzzing with this, all of it—the two men, beautiful Ariana, this night so far away from New York, Gabe, the life awaiting her there, even the stones, thousands of years old, surrounding them.

As good as any, she thinks.

THE MUSIC is surprisingly inviting, people dancing in groups on the sand. The singer is a homely woman, her voice hauntingly clear above the drums. Teenage boys move through the crowd surreptitiously, selling beer. When Jimmy buys her one, she lifts it to her closed lips and then tosses it discreetly on the sand. Ariana and Adam have vanished, dancing somewhere in the throngs of people.

"Give us a dance?"

She thinks of Gabe. Their closetful of his cable-knit sweaters. His earnest love. *It's just dancing*, she tells herself.

She lets Jimmy tug her into the crowd, the bodies moving to the beat, the music loud and feverish, lets him spin her over and over until she isn't thinking about Gabe anymore, or Manhattan, or anything.

"Where are you from?" Jimmy's breath is warm in her ear.

Manar considers. "We moved a lot. But my grandparents, well, my mother's parents, are from Nablus. They left during the '67 war."

"And before that?"

Manar cocks her head. "What do you mean?"

"A lot of people"—Jimmy twirls her around, slightly out of breath—"went to Nablus after '48. But they were originally from Jerusalem or Acre or Jaffa."

"I know that." The trace of petulance in her voice is telling. She *does* know that and yet had never applied that to her grandparents. She thinks of Teta, sitting in that armchair in her living room in Amman, blinking at the television, that perpetual expression of confusion on her face. *Where did you grow up?* Manar asks her silently. *What do you remember of it?*

Now Manar is in the center of the crowd, making serpentine circles with her hips, hair falling into her eyes. Jimmy dances nearby, singing along to the Arabic lyrics. She is pouring another beer into the sand, then lifting the empty bottle to her lips. She is kicking her shoes off.

It all reminds her of the celebrations she read about in history classes, the extravagant parties the ancient Greeks used to throw before battle. Naked women, orgies, wine by the barrel, and, everywhere, wild music. She thinks of the slaughters going on, the occupation surrounding them, all the revolutions that flicker and blaze and die. It would seem like such a monumental, brave, lovely act, all this revelry in the face of war, except that Manar knows it has always been like this.

It fascinates Manar—not just history in general, with its empires, collapses, and revivals, but also the faint, persistent echoes that seem to travel through the millennia. Land eaten and reshuffled, homes taken—daughters and sons speaking enemy languages, forgetting their own—the belief that we are owed something by the cosmos.

Then she is moving through the dancers, Jimmy's arm around her, the two of them walking in the sand—*Where are my shoes?*—up to a cluster of large rocks. Jimmy guides her between the rocks, out of sight of the revelers. The music is distant, drowned out by the waves.

"I'm glad you came out with us," he murmurs. "*Ya sitt* Nablus." Manar feels her heartbeat in her throat.

He's going to kiss her. She could let him. It could be a story she tells Linah and Zain, Seham back in Manhattan. *You'll never believe . . .*

Suddenly, an image of Gabe pouring Sprite into the champagne flute. Manar pulls back.

"My shoes." Manar faces him for a moment. In the moonlight he looks older. "Wait here."

His smile is slow, distracted. Manar walks rapidly, her bare feet sinking into the sand. She walks past the boulders, past some men smoking, past the crowd—where people are still dancing, perhaps kissing, perhaps loving one another. It is late, she thinks, so late it is nearly early and soon the sun will begin to rise. She walks until she reaches the cobblestone street, little pebbles piercing her feet. For ten, fifteen minutes, she keeps moving, until she cannot hear the music anymore, away from the beach, between houses, until she finds a secluded-looking archway between two trees and, finally, she sits.

Manar remains in the archway for a long, long time, as though in a trance, until the low thrum of the muezzin stirs her. Suddenly, she is aware of everything. The sky beginning to lighten, her filthy feet, the growl in her stomach. Even the contents of her purse are jumbled around; her phone has run out of battery. The fold of shekels that she'd tucked in her wallet is gone. But here, yes, here is the zippered pocket, the bundle of paper, and Manar pulls out the letters, opens them for the hundredth time, like an archaeologist afraid she missed something all along. She goes through the pages until she finds her favorite passage.

Last night, I dreamed of refugees stealing rubble—a woman's braceleted hand, someone's eyes, it begins. The word *eyes* is crossed out, then rewritten above.

> *I dreamed of the men in Zarqa, the camps, in army bases all over America. They met in secret rooms, unfolded maps, and pointed, grooming for war, woke and stamped outside in boots. Their rage woke them. It marched their legs up trails, snowdrifts, sand dunes, their breath precise and measured with each step. Onward, onward, the land urged them. They aimed their rifles at a target, imagined an enemy heart, and pulled the trigger.*

Impulsively, Manar begins to read aloud. Her voice is hoarse from the singing earlier. She thinks of the plays she used to do with Zain and Linah years ago, imagines an audience listening in the archway in front of her.

"But Mustafa, we still thirst for it. Our mutiny is our remembering."

She pauses for a second, the sound of a car in the distance, the purr of someone's engine. She returns to the page, transfixed.

"*Our remembering the hundred names of that land*," she continues. "*This is what it means to be alive.*"

FINALLY, MANAR PACKS the letters away and rises grimly, walks down the street until she finds an unopened store, and pauses, checking her reflection in the glass. It is disheartening—savage hair, drooped mascara. She scowls at her reflection.

"Idiot," she mutters. The precision of the word pleases her and, unbidden, she smiles. She trails her fingertips across her abdomen. Suddenly aching for the sea, she walks the narrow streets, past shuttered beauty salons and bakeries, until she makes a turn and there, pale in early light, the water waits.

Jaffa. There is that desire, the old wanting, to say something. For someone to bear witness as she speaks.

Bits of shells and pebbles pierce her feet along the sand, a cool relief as her toes touch water. She takes a breath.

"I've come here for no reason." The starkness of the words strikes her as hilarious. She begins to laugh. "No . . . reason . . . at . . . all." The laughter takes on an edge of hysteria and it occurs to her that she might cry. Sobering, she walks along the shoreline, the water icy against her ankles.

It is beautiful, all of it—the hastening of the waves, how the water gathers itself as though spilling white petals onto the sand. The sky has the colorlessness of moistened paper; it looks like it might tear. And the sunlight touches everything, spinning it into gold. Her tired mind alights on myths—Midas, Icarus, the stories she spent years memorizing. Everything she has forgotten.

She sits, the water lapping her skirt. A testimony, she decides. On the wet sand, she writes letters with her finger.

Alia, she traces. *Alia Yacoub*. She pauses, considering. *Atef Yacoub*. The sand is soft beneath her toes, ticklish. She draws a line between the two names and another one below. A family tree. *Riham*, *Karam*,

Souad, she traces. Next to her mother's name, Manar writes *Elie*. She draws an *X* between them. A handful of stars, like white freckles, are still visible in the sky. *Abdullah*, *Manar*, *Linah*, *Zain*.

Looking at the names, she speaks again. "We were all here." She speaks slowly. She holds her wet palm to her cheek, then runs it through her hair. She imagines her whole family standing on this shoreline, in a row. Oddly cheered by the image, she pulls her knees to her chin and muses to the waves, "Even you, Teta."

She draws a final line from her own name. *Gabriel*. Below, an arrow that leads to a small question mark. *Leah? June? Dara?* There is a human, she realizes, that she will have to name.

Shutting her eyes, Manar tips her face toward the sky. When she opens them, a man and his young boy are walking along the sand, watching her. The man has a fishing net hoisted around his shoulder, dirty, gray knots. He is frowning, a mixture of disapproval and concern on his face as they walk closer to her. The boy's face is beautiful, a fawnlike docility about his eyes. He stares at Manar, openly curious.

"*Yalla*." The father nudges his son. He eyes Manar warily.

Manar is shaken with the desire to protest, to speak with the man in Arabic. But she can see herself through the fisherman's eyes: drenched, squatting in seawater. Not a woman in the throes of revelation, but something peripheral, another unnecessary foreigner. *Ajnabiyeh*, she can hear him thinking.

This is what makes her drop her eyes. It is what pulls her up, rising unsteadily, the wet skirt clinging to her legs as she bows her head in apology. A large wave washes over the sand, the water eating her words, her family come and gone in this sea that belongs to none of them.

"I'm leaving," she says to the man in Arabic.

As she walks past them, she glances up only once. The man is still watching her, but his expression has changed. She nods, and the man nods back.

EPILOGUE

Beirut

The television is always on. Always there is the sound of war, elsewhere. In certain moments the sounds buzz together into incoherence, a language she neither recognizes nor trusts. At these times, Alia tries to keep her eyes on the long, Z-shaped scratch on the coffee table. Or a chip in her coral nail polish; the slight fray of the curtains. Whatever is undone. Alia finds the flaws when the blankness comes and she clutches them as though for life.

The comforting sound of the washing machine, Umm Najwa's feet pattering down the hallway, and Alia wakes. She likes this bedroom, the greens soothing, sunlight streaming through the thin curtains. Still, she misses her bedroom in Amman. The almond tree outside her window.

The pain is worst in the morning.

"Umm Najwa," she calls, and within seconds the woman appears at the door.

"Good morning." Umm Najwa has a coarse Palestinian accent. "Are we getting up?" Fists on her hips, she eyes Alia. "It's a special day," she continues cheerfully, "do you know why?"

Alia turns away from her. She breathes in the cotton of her pillow.

"Go away."

• • •

THERE IS A BABY in this house. Or perhaps it is the other house, loud with voices and slamming doors. The rooms seem interchangeable, everyone appearing and vanishing, and at the center is the baby. Everyone is smitten with her. Cooing and singing lullabies, applauding when she gurgles. Once Alia asked about the mother, and the girl with frizzy hair walked over and kissed her cheek. When the baby cries the girl bounces her on her hip. Sometimes the mother—the name, Manar, arrives simply, fluently, to Alia at times—gives the baby to Alia and she holds her.

In those moments Alia freezes. She smells the baby, her scent of milk and sugar. When she looks up, everyone is watching with shining eyes.

THEY ARE WRONG. She knows something is different. Amiss. When she remembers what it is, there is a sorrow that scalds her throat, as though she has eaten a handful of chili peppers and cannot remember to swallow. This is why—though how to put to words that silken rope of remembering, of weaving through days, then losing what is lost again—she answers with such gruffness when they ask questions. Faces lit with hope, their voices small as children's, even Atef's. *Alia, do you remember Zain? Mama, do you know where we are?*

"Yes, yes," she answers caustically at such times, transforming their expressions into hurt. "What do you think I am, an idiot?"

ONE OF THE KINDEST people in the house is a skinny girl. Young, eighteen or nineteen. Her body is girlish with sharp elbows and knees, but there is something womanly about her face, even aged. *Such sad eyes,* Alia thinks, wants to ask her what has broken her heart. She imagines some tragedy, perhaps a dead lover—*so young*—or illness.

But whenever the girl catches sight of Alia, her face turns luminous.

"How's the lovely?" she teases. "Shall we go see the plants?" And slowly the girl helps her up, taking most of Alia's weight. Despite her frame, the girl is strong. Alia suspects a sturdiness about her bones. The girl likes to take her to the balcony, a view of telephone wires and people and water.

Once outside, the girl pulls back leaves of tall, tangled plants, dozens of pots dotting the balcony, some with tomatoes on the vine, others sprouting flowers in shades of white and blue and purple. Alia likes to watch her pluck the dead, browned leaves, water the soil. They sit for what feels like hours, until the sun sets over the water. Aside from talking to the plants, the girl doesn't speak much. Sometimes Alia catches the girl lost in thought. The sadness seems pronounced then, etched into the downturned mouth, the long, dark eyelashes.

Once she asked her, "Do you want to go outside with me? We can find a nice café, get some tea."

For a moment, it seemed possible. Walking on the street, people and cars around her. She would go with her. This girl with sturdy bones. But then she was afraid again.

"I want to stay here," Alia said in a small voice. "I want to stay here."

"Okay," the girl—*Linah*—said, "okay. We'll stay here. Let's sit for a little longer. Look, this one's starting to bloom."

The girl pulled up a blossom, her hand spilling purple and gold.

EVEN WHEN she doesn't remember—and this is more difficult to put into words, those moments of inundation when she scrambles to piece herself together—she knows something is wrong. They are all faces to her, kind, alien mouths and eyes. They want to give her water, tea, bread. They bring her blankets and ask what she thinks of the weather. They want to know if she is hungry, if there is anything she wants.

THE TELEVISION is always on. Waking and sleeping and eating, Alia can hear its sounds. Occasionally they watch a movie or music video, bursts of color and girls dancing to the *thump-thump-thump* of a drumbeat. But usually it is the news channel, solemn newscasters speaking of solemn things. Even when the living room is empty, the newscasters continue to talk.

What they say never changes. There is a war, Alia knows. She understands this intuitively; in fact, it seems to her the only truth she holds immutable. There is a war. It is being fought and people are losing, though she is uncertain who exactly.

A young girl wears nothing but dirt. An explosion has dismantled a city. People gather the entrails of their families. A man sets himself on fire. A man burns a flag. A man holds a woman underwater. A man hangs from a tree. A man is eaten by flies.

They talk about it.

"I don't think she should be listening to this."

"What can we do? I need to know what's happening. Besides, she doesn't—"

"She shouldn't be seeing these things!"

The newscaster says *dictator* and there is a photograph of a man with pale skin and a mustache. Remembering flickers within Alia; she once found the man attractive. The man is sending wolves to eat his people, the newscaster says, and Alia pictures a snowy hillside atop which the man stands, his aquamarine eyes narrowed. He whistles and dozens of creatures snarl. Strike. Their gray bodies streak the hillside as they rush the villages, pounce on children and men. Instead of paw tracks, they trail bones.

"Turn it *off*."

"She's not even watching."

It isn't wolves. Alia knows that. It is men. Regular men, with their own mustaches and beards and slender wrists. They are taking these cities by fire, upending the houses and eating all the bread. They are lining children up and taking their dresses, shooting them in the mouths. A wolf can be killed. Trapped, skinned. But Alia knows that certain men—she remembers them, with their flags and their teeth—have skin like steel, are reborn into other men in the morning, grow more terrible, more powerful, with each sun.

"Look. She's sleeping."

THERE IS A KNOCK at the bedroom door. Alia keeps her face against the pillow.

"Mama." The door opens. "Mama, remember, we're going out today. Remember? What would you like to wear?"

Alia hates the shake in her voice when she says, "I'm tired."

"It's time to wake up." The voice is firmer now. Footsteps, a swishing sound. Sunlight fills the room. Alia scrunches her eyes shut. The woman sighs. "Mama, open your eyes."

A moment passes. Alia peeks. The woman stands above the bed. She wears a gauzy dress, her hair cropped short as a boy's. She looks anxious as she scans Alia's face.

"Atef . . ."

The woman's eyes light up. "Baba's in the living room. Come and see him."

Alia leans on her daughter's arm, padding heavily down the hall. Her hip is excruciating if she steps the wrong way. She fell in the bathroom months ago and something shattered. There was a hospital room for a long time after that, a television playing the same Turkish soap opera on repeat.

They reach the entryway and Alia pauses.

"It's okay, Mama. Baba's here."

Atef. Alia takes a step, and the room is full of people watching television and talking. There is a platter of *manakish* on the coffee table, mugs of tea. The baby is in her mother's arms, kicking her feet. Atef sits on the armchair. He smiles at the sight of Alia. They all speak at once.

"How's the pretty mama?"

"We're going out today, remember?"

"Teta, would you like some *manakish*?"

"Alia, sit." Atef's dark, serene eyes. Her daughter leads her to the sofa, and Alia smiles and nods as everyone speaks to her, talking of a seafood restaurant and music. Atef cuts a triangle of the *manakish* for her. The bread is thick and good. The baby begins to fuss, and the young man stands.

"Come here. Let's fly." He makes whirring sounds, the baby waving her fists and gurgling. Alia has heard talk of the baby, in hushed tones, away from the mother. They click their tongues. *I can't believe she married an American*, they say.

"Teta, you want some tea?"

"We'll have the cake afterward."

Alia watches the young man. "Zain." Her voice causes the others to still. The television blithely chatters on. They turn to her, smile.

"That's right, Teta." The man shifts the baby onto his hip. "I'm Zain."

The baby smacks her lips and laughs.

"Give Teta a kiss."

The child smiles flirtatiously at her. "Teta, up. Up!" Her pale eyes are dauntless. Her honeyed hair floats around her in a cloud, light but frizzy. Alia remembers a game she played with Riham and Souad and Karam, swooping their little bodies in a circle, making a whistling sound as she lands them on the floor.

She looks down at the bread. The cheer on their faces is tiring. How can she explain this fatigue to one not in her body? *Decades of tired*, her mother used to say.

"Mama, what would you like to wear for your special day? Umm Najwa said perhaps the gray dress."

"Umm Najwa said she'll do your hair, Mama. A nice braid."

"I'm going to wear a green skirt," the girl with kind eyes says. She sits on the arm of the couch, her shaggy hair disheveled. "Your favorite color."

Alia tries to smile, but her throat catches. She remembers green, a wisp of fabric floating on a clothesline, her mother's arm reaching for it. She starts to rise.

"Mama!" The tone is scolding. "You need to be careful, remember. You need to tell us when you want to get up."

"Take me to my room." Alia hears the tremor in her voice.

"Okay," the woman says. Her tone turns beseeching now. "We'll get you in a nice dress, yes? The brocade."

"She'll look so beautiful."

"Like a queen."

Behind her, the child calls out, "Up, *up!*"

In the bedroom Alia asks the woman to leave, and, reluctantly, she does. Being alone is intoxicating. Alia sits at the edge of the bed. There is no view of trees and flowers outside the window. Instead, there are more telephone wires, the balcony of another building. Someone has opened the window and a breeze ruffles the curtains, filling the room with salted air.

"*Ya* Allah," she says aloud. Her voice is glassy to her ears.

It is Nablus and she is eighteen. Outside the window, fig trees are beginning to sprout their olive-green leaves. The air is light and delicious. Beyond the window is the day, vast and unfolding, a banquet hall filled with people awaiting her. *I've asked for candles surrounded by flowers*, her mother has told her. *A dozen for each table. I want the air to be sweet as sugar.*

The anticipation is thrilling. Mustafa will walk her to the car, they will do a *zaffeh* and she will spin in her white dress. And Atef. He is waiting. She imagines him nervous, his habit of popping a peppermint candy into his mouth, and smiles.

She must do her hair. She squints in front of the mirror, her curls messy and frizzed. She should've listened to Salma and soaked them in olive oil, but it is too late. There is a brush on the armoire and she yanks it through her hair. She frowns at the creams and perfume atop the dresser. Where is the kohl, the vermilion lipstick? She finally finds a pot of rouge in one of the drawers and rubs it onto her lips, then her cheeks. There is a crumbling eyeliner pen and she makes circles around her eyes.

She is beautiful. The reflection brings tears to her eyes. She admonishes herself not to ruin the makeup.

You'll be bright as the moon tonight, her mother has told her. Suddenly she is filled with longing, missing her mother powerfully, though she is in the next room, dressing and picking out a veil. A thought nags at her, like a moving creature in her peripheral vision. But she shakes her head, returns to the reflection.

In the closet, dresses hang. The colors are polite and subdued. They have moved her clothes, she remembers, much of her things already in the small house two streets down. The house she will enter as Atef's wife.

She rummages in the closet until her fingertips dart against something satiny. She pulls it out, a dusky dress without sleeves. A different dress, she thinks, a new one.

It fits around her hips but catches halfway up and she tugs, finally fishing her breasts out, fitting them in the dress. She gives her hair a pat, sniffs at her armpits. There is the sound of footsteps in the hallway. Farida, Alia thinks, or her mother. A knock, then a male voice saying her name.

Atef!

Alia feels herself blush, her hands instinctively at her exposed collarbones. Before she can call out to him, the door opens. She turns slowly, exposing herself like a flower, her eyes shyly on the floor.

"You can't see the bride yet," she teases. "Mama will be furious."

There is silence. Alia hears it as awe. After a moment, she lifts her eyes to his. He is still. His face has changed, she sees. His hair is gray. Perhaps it is chalk or dust. He must bathe. She suddenly has the urge to lean in, though she has never kissed before, not with anyone. She steps toward him, stops only when he bows his head. When he lifts it, she is stunned to see tears mottling his cheeks.

"Alia," he says, and she hates her name, abruptly, for being able to carry such sorrow, such unbearable weight. "Alia."

She knows if she hears her name once more from this man—for she sees that he isn't Atef but a stranger—suddenly she knows that she will not wed, that Nablus and the party, the candles, the white dress, all of it will be ruined. She will be ill, will begin to shriek, will throw every last one of the beautiful perfume bottles against the wall. And so she turns and, ignoring the agony in her hip, rushes to the bathroom and locks the door. She stands for a moment, breathing heavily. Her reflection does the same. She sees and cannot remember and weeps.

It takes a long time for them to convince her to open the bathroom door. Even then she refuses to let in Umm Najwa or Atef. It is Linah who finally murmurs her way inside. She helps Alia change into a nightgown. Alia sits on the closed toilet seat while Linah wets a towel, wipes the makeup off her face. Linah rinses the towel in the sink; the water runs red and black.

"Close your eyes, lovely," Linah says, her breath warm against Alia's face. "Just a couple more swipes."

"You smell of cigarettes."

Linah looks startled. She winks at Alia. "Our little secret, then."

"Where's the baby?"

"June? Manar's with her. She's putting her down for a nap."

"I want to go home." Her eyes spring hot.

"Oh, Teta." Linah stops, the filthy towel dangling from her hand. She looks at her sadly. "I know."

Linah eases her onto the bed. The door shuts quietly behind her. The air in the room is heavy, the sound of traffic audible. Alia watches the sun make tribal patterns on the ceiling until she falls asleep.

In her dreams a man is pouring tea into glasses, then methodically pouring the tea out onto a beautiful Persian rug. The room is cavernous, white everywhere. Alia watches him with horror, the burgundy and cobalt rug soaked with tea.

You're ruining it, she tells him.

He looks at her with amused eyes, turns over another glass deliberately. The tea spills.

It's better than fire, he says.

Alia wakes breathless, her heart thumping. The room is dim and gray and for an awful moment she thinks she has lost her sight. But it is just the setting sun, the light being leeched. She has slept for hours.

Something about that spoiled rug makes her ache. She hates dreaming, hates the people that populate her dreams, arriving for brief slivers before vanishing, leaving her with bits and pieces out of which a whole can never be made.

ALIA WALKS CAREFULLY to the living room, leaning on the wood-tipped cane they brought her. It is a sign of acquiescence. At the doorway, she stands unseen for a moment before rapping the cane against the wall. She walks into the room.

Flowers. Dozens of them, clouds of purple and blue. Hibiscus and jasmine and several long stems of yellow roses. A bouquet of balloons is tied to the chair where Karam sits. They are all there, Manar and her baby, Zain and Linah and Abdullah on the sofa. The names come to her instinctively. Effortlessly. Riham is carrying a cake into the room; Souad and Atef talk to each other in lowered tones. Their voices are merry.

"There she is!"

"Lovely as the moon!"

"Oh, Mama, thank you for using the cane."

"Zain, help her sit."

"Teta, take my arm," Zain says. "We brought the party to you." He seats her next to Atef. "Since you weren't"—he clears his throat—"since you weren't feeling well, we wanted to celebrate here."

"Do you remember what today is, Mama?" Riham asks her.

"My birthday," Alia says.

The smiles are authentic now. There is a relief that ripples through the room, like a gust of wind. The voices relax.

"We got a cake with raspberry icing."

"And cherries!"

"And cherries. Coconut too, I think."

The cake is a spongy pink, strawberries and cherries arranged in a circle around the border. Her name is written in the center.

Karam flips the light switch off, plunging the room into darkness. Alia feels the same panic of waking. As though sensing this, Atef finds her hand and Alia squeezes. They sing and she watches the flames, mesmerizing licks of orange and red. First they sing in Arabic, then English, then Manar and Zain and Linah sing in French. The baby wriggles in Manar's arms as she sings. In the candlelight the grandchildren are beautiful, tanned and animated. Everyone applauds when they finish, even Alia.

"Happy birthday," they all cry out. When Souad leans down to kiss her cheek, she whispers something about love and her eyes glitter with tears. Her daughter. She once stayed out all night and Alia slapped her face. Alia remembers that like a dream, like a story that happened to a neighbor.

"Here's to a hundred years," Riham calls out as she and Umm Najwa cut the cake, an oozy pinkness appearing as they slice into it.

A hundred years. The baby would be an adult, perhaps wed. Alia finds the thought oppressive.

There is laughter and talking. The grandchildren tell stories and the adults act dismayed, shaking their heads. Zain and Linah sit cross-legged on the rug. Abdullah and Atef wave their hands around, amiably arguing about politics. Abdullah calls some politician a megalomaniac, and the other grandchildren agree. Everyone talks about how delicious the cake is. They agree to try the cheesecake next time. Alia smiles and opens a parade of beautifully wrapped gifts—scarves, jewelry, a photo album—and holds the baby when Manar hands her over.

"She loves her *teta*," Manar says, smiling.

Finally Karam catches her eye from across the room. "Mama, you're tired, right?" he asks softly and she nods. Her darling boy.

Umm Najwa stands above her bed with a glass of water, her palm cupping a rainbow of pills. She hands them to Alia one by one. When Alia has taken them all—blue, red, orange—Umm Najwa sets the cup down and turns the light off. There is a sliver of light from the streetlamps.

"Good night," Umm Najwa says. "Happy birthday."

Alia feels the familiar relief at being alone. Beneath it, throbbing; some discontent closer to grief than anger. She thinks of her mother—the wishing hollows her, for her mother to appear—what she might tell Alia if she were here. *Sleep now. The morning will heal.*

It's better than fire.

Her mother knew something on the eve of her wedding day. Alia remembers the tightening of her lips, the downward glance. But she, self-involved and joyful, had said nothing, making a note to ask later. But *later* was elusive; there was the dancing and lights, her wedding night, then the whirlwind years of being a wife, then the war, Kuwait, Mustafa—the thought of him empties her lungs of air, nearly fifty years later. Mustafa. She is decades older than he ever was. And life, life has swept her along like a tiny seashell onto sand, has washed over her and now, suddenly, she is old. Her mother is dead. There is no one to ask the questions she needs to ask.

Alia wakes to the sound of someone moving in the bedroom. Atef. She listens to him getting ready for bed, clothes folded and put away, the *dishdasha* he still wears to sleep. He goes to the bathroom, a strip of light visible below the door. She hears the sound of running water, the toilet flushing.

When he lies down next to her, he is careful, thinking her asleep. The delicacy of his movement is heartbreaking.

"Atef," she says.

He turns to her, his face barely visible in the dark. There is a honk outside, the city fitfully settling into sleep.

"Atef, I liked the flowers. The yellow ones."

She can see his teeth as he smiles. His hand travels the landscape of the blanket and finds hers. *He loves me*, she thinks. Atef in the garden, glancing up at her. It has been a lifetime. They are teenagers. Atef, always, loving her. She moves toward him, her body heavy and graceless. She puts her hand against the side of his face. She wants him with a ferocity. *I'm young*, she thinks, and she is. Their lives are beginning.

"Alia," he says, but she cannot bear his voice. She tells him to be quiet. She pulls him toward her, dreamlike, her lips finding his, the air sour between them—her breath? His? She is embarrassed by the stale odor of her body—as they kiss. Her hip cramps but she ignores it; she tugs and tugs until finally he yields, his weight atop her, his hands skimming her thighs and stomach. She gasps and touches her own breasts, so withered and papery, but she will not think of it now, will not think of anything.

"God." The word falls like water from his mouth.

She clasps between his legs until he grows hard and she pulls him into her, the sensation painful at first, bodies remembering their dance. They heave and arch until, finally, a wetness erupts inside her and Atef gasps like the wounded.

They lie silently afterward. Eventually, the silence gives way to the steady breathing of Atef's slumber. Alia turns to her side, feeling the wetness between her legs. She doesn't want to wash. She wants this fragment of Atef to remain.

Alia thinks of the cake, the voices singing for her. She half dreams of canvases, someone plucking her eyebrows bare. A boat capsizes and she imagines the sound of a baby crying, faraway. The sound is replaced by the whooshing of a car outside. Alia wakes and blinks. The baby cries again, louder this time, and Alia realizes the sound is real.

She rises from the bed. The baby is alone, she thinks. She will feed her.

She takes cautious steps, steadying herself on the hallway wall. The living room is dark, though the balcony door is open, and the light of streetlamps bathes the sofas and table, the television's blank screen. The crying is louder, coming from the balcony. Alia feels indignant—how could they have left the baby alone?

But when she steps onto the balcony, she sees the mother is out there, rocking back and forth on the swing. She whispers to the child cradled in her arms. The swing makes a creaking sound each time the mother pushes back. She is guiding the baby's mouth to her breast. Her dark hair has fallen, covering her face, and she doesn't see Alia. The mother's naked breast is visible and the sight of it, of the moist nipple, is startling. She steps back quickly into the living room.

She sits on the armchair near the balcony door, the nighttime air cool. She should bring the baby a blanket, sit with them outside, but suddenly she is too tired to move. There is a mewling sound and then silence, and Alia knows the baby has latched onto the breast, feels the phantom sensation in her own nipples, remembers strikingly that relief.

The woman begins to sing, her voice husky.

"Yalla tnam, yalla tnam."

The words are familiar as water, as Alia's own hands, which lift now to her face, against her cheeks.

"Yalla tnam, yalla tnam."

The song alights within Alia, a remembering akin to joy. Her mother's garden, a courtyard somewhere in Kuwait, as she sang to a baby at her own breast. She sits in the dark, listening to the ancient, salvaged music.

Acknowledgments

To my first reader and editor, Gina Heiserman, who shared her time and love and expertise with incomparable generosity and in return asked only that I keep writing; I will always be grateful. I am enormously indebted to Michelle Tessler, my wonderful and dauntless agent, who took a chance on a sprawling beast of a manuscript. A huge thank you to my editor Lauren Wein for her alert, thoughtful dedication and for continually assuring me that this was a story worth telling. Thank you to Pilar Garcia-Brown, Hannah Harlow, Taryn Roeder, Ayesha Mirza, Tracy Roe, Lisa Glover, Lori Glazer, and all the incredible, welcoming people at Houghton Mifflin Harcourt for being such a pleasure to work with. I'm grateful to Victoria Hobbs at AM Heath for finding the book a home across the ocean, and to the lovely Jocasta Hamilton and the team at Hutchinson.

Thank you to Madeline Stevens, for being kind enough not to say *I told you so* when her editing advice was echoed by literally everyone. I am hugely grateful to the poetry community, from my attentive editors and publishers to the incredible people I've encountered at open mics around the world. Without the poetry I would never have found the prose. Thank you to my brilliant and darling friends, scattered across the globe; you know who you are and why I love you. Thank you to Lisa and Kip, and the delightful Heiserman and Perkins clan. I couldn't have finished this book without the support and sarcasm of Atheer Yacoub and Michael Page. Thank you to Dalea, Kiki, Sarah,